To our families and friends,
who patiently supported and encouraged us
with their prayers and love
during the writing of this story,
this book is lovingly dedicated.
May the Lord richly bless them all.

The authors gratefully acknowledge the generous assistance provided by:

Philip Bergen, Librarian
The Boston Historical Society
Boston, Massachusetts

Joan Diana, Head Librarian
Pennsylvania State University, Wilkes-Barre Campus
Lehman, Pennsylvania

Vivian Price and Ruth Knox
The Jefferson Madison Regional Library
Staunton, Virginia

Melinda Frierson
The Historical Society for Albermarle County
Virginia

These individuals helped us gather necessary period data and maps, shared their extensive knowledge of various settings, and forwarded biographical information on prominent figures who played a part in colonial America's fascinating history.

Also to:

Starling and Ruth Bartlett

For the books and magazines they so graciously sent us concerning Big Bend, Virginia.

Special thanks to fellow writers and friends:

Sue Rich
Jo Frazier

$$1$$

December 16, 1773

The rain-slicked streets of Boston lay ominously quiet. To Susannah Haynes, waiting in her two-story clapboard home on Milk Street, the heavy silence seemed louder than a death knell, louder even than the tolling that had summoned the townsmen to Old South Meeting House every day that week.

She clutched a knitted shawl close over her homespun nightdress and stared out from the upstairs bedroom window. Moving closer, Susannah pressed an ear to the cold pane and strained to hear any sound that might announce the return of her husband, Daniel. But aside from an occasional distant shout drifting her way from the center of town, there was only stillness. "Oh, Dan," she breathed.

Then another distressful thought pressed down on her. Dan's headstrong sister Jane had also dashed off into the volatile night and had yet to return. And it had been too long, much too long.

With a sigh Susannah opened the window and leaned out into the December cold, peering toward Griffin's wharf, where three East India Tea Company ships had been docked for some time. Mere hours ago the harbor had been illuminated to near daylight by the glow of hundreds of torches. But now it lay in darkness, even the lingering scent of smoke washed away by the drizzle of the night.

What reckless action had the townspeople taken? The mob had dispersed so swiftly. And what about the British soldiers, forever anxious to put a stop to the people's rebelliousness?

A drop of rain plopped down from the eaves onto Susannah's cheek, dampening a strand of loose tawny hair. She brushed it aside and gave one last lingering look up and down the deserted street.

Suddenly the distant sound of hoofbeats echoed on the night air, growing steadily louder, until the rhythmic galloping stopped at the gate.

Jane! It had to be. Susannah slammed the window shut and rushed down the staircase and to the back door. She opened it a crack and peeked out, but she saw no sign of a rider.

A loud pounding shook the front door.

Her hand flew to her throat as she hastened up the hallway. Thank heaven the bolt was securely in place. "W-who's there?" she managed, then held her breath.

No one answered.

She hesitated. It could be news of Dan or Jane. Taking a deep breath, she undid the lock, raised the latch, and leaned out. A lone horse stood at the hitching ring, its reins thrown carelessly through the iron circle. But the walk was empty.

"Who's there?" she called into the darkness. Running footsteps sounded alongside the house. In seconds the pounding resumed, this time from the back door.

Susannah turned inside and hurried up the hall to the kitchen.

She had barely lifted the latch when the door burst open. Lt. Alex Fontaine, her brother's former friend—and Jane's betrothed—pushed past her, a wild, angry glint in his steel gray eyes.

"Alex!" she said. "What is it? Where's Jane?"

The officer of the Crown ignored her questions as he charged from one room to the next. Then he took the stairs two at a time, clomping over the floorboards in a frenzy as he checked every bedchamber.

She chased after him. "Stop! You'll wake my baby! I insist that you leave my home at once."

Alex peered down his long nose at Susannah in passing as he descended no less noisily. She followed close behind, getting angrier by the second at his high-handedness. When he reached the landing, he turned and grabbed her shoulders. "Where are they?"

"You're hurting me!" She tried to wrench out of his grip.

"Answer me."

"Who? Dan? Jane?"

"Jane. *And* that traitor-brother of yours." His fingers dug deeply, painfully, into her flesh. "Where are you hiding them?"

Susannah had never seen Alex so livid. She had to force herself to remain calm. "What are you talking about?"

"Don't play the innocent with me, *Mistress Haynes,*" he grated, shaking her shoulders. "I'm sure you know perfectly well about that little incident your husband's sister caused at the shipyard, aiding and abetting a smuggler, then escaping with that turncoat brother of yours. But I'll not rest until I've captured them, you can be certain of that."

"Jane? But I thought—," Susannah began. "You must be mad! She wouldn't do such a thing. You've been misinformed."

"Oh, there's no misinformation here, I assure you. I was there and witnessed the entire thing myself."

"Witnessed what?"

Alex's cold eyes narrowed, turning his elongated face into one of villainous disdain. He released Susannah so abruptly she almost lost her balance. "Yes, of course, the wench would lie to you about this—just as she has about everything else since the day I met her. But your sister-in-law just put a noose around your brother's neck. One that will hang her and Ted both!"

She struggled to comprehend this tirade. "Alex," she said, attempting a placating tone, "it's obvious that you're upset.

Once you've calmed down, I'm sure you'll see things in a more rational light."

"You're quite right," he almost spat. "I'll see that smuggling scurvy rat Yancy Curtis hanging right alongside of them. Yes, and another officer will confirm everything just as it happened. Both of us heard Jane pleading with Ted—a uniformed officer of the Crown—to let Curtis go free, when the pirate had been caught in the very act of smuggling. She even gave him her horse before making good her own escape with Ted. What an utter fool Ted was to let her bewitch him again. And what a fool I was! But no more."

Hope rose in Susannah. If Jane was with Ted, perhaps she had finally come to her senses, after all.

"Where is your husband?" Alex demanded. "Speak up!"

Susannah turned away, unwilling to meet his gaze. "Why, I'm afraid I do not know. Dan had business—"

"The business of helping a traitor to abscond with *my fiancée,* no doubt. "

She swung to face him. "How dare you imply such a thing!" She clenched her fists. "Whatever happened in that shipyard, my husband was not a party to it. Now, I'll thank you to leave my home at once." She folded her arms with finality.

The lieutenant lifted his nose and glared down at her.

For a second she feared he might strike her. But he did as bidden and stalked toward the front door, where he stopped and turned, a sneer twisting the edge of his mouth. "You were fools, the lot of you, for making an enemy of me. I shall have soldiers posted outside to keep watch for them. They will pay for their treason . . . with their necks."

His fingers brushing the hilt of his saber, Alex turned stiffly and strode out, leaving the door standing wide open.

Susannah slammed it after him and rammed the bolt into place. Her breath came in heaving gasps as she leaned her forehead against the doorjamb and listened for him to ride off. Alex was truly angry. But even more, he was hurt. Jane had both betrayed and shamed him, and he was out for revenge.

Susannah was really fearful now. Where were they? What would become of them? She drew an unsteady breath.

A floorboard creaked behind her. She started and whirled around.

An Indian!

"Forgive me, sweetheart. It's me." Dan, wearing war paint, caught her as her sagging knees gave way, and he pulled her into his arms. "I saw Alex's horse outside and thought I'd better not show my face until I wash up. I sneaked in the back way. Was he here visiting Jane . . . or did he come about the little tea party down at the *Dartmouth?*"

In the comfort of his embrace, Susannah struggled to compose herself. She tipped back her head and looked up at him. His wavy chestnut hair was tied back beneath a bright bandana headband. With his dark sable eyes and his skin smeared with bootblack, he might truly have passed for a red man—at least to a casual observer. But then his mouth tweaked into an easy smile and completely erased the momentary illusion.

She felt the heaviness of reality return. "In the mood the lieutenant is in right now, you'd most likely have been arrested regardless of whether or not your face was painted. Oh, Dan . . . I've never been so frightened. Or worried."

"Shh. I know, love." Tightening his hug, he rocked her tenderly. "But I'm all right. Oddly enough, there were no authorities at all on the wharf. Not civil, not military. It was as if they'd been ordered to stay away! And now you're saying that Alex came to arrest me? It doesn't make sense."

Susannah eased away and looked at him. They needed to get that paint off Dan's face before anyone else happened by to see him. She took his hand and tugged him toward the kitchen. "You New Englanders do insist on keeping things stirred up, don't you?"

"Well, my lovely British lass, this time we stirred ourselves up one huge batch of saltwater tea."

"I beg your pardon?"

He gave her a crooked grin. "We dumped every single chest

of East India tea leaves from the *Dartmouth* overboard. It was great fun. Great fun."

Unable to resist the mischief dancing in his eyes, she smiled, then sobered. "Well, Lieutenant Fontaine didn't come about that. I'm afraid he was here about a far more serious matter."

"You think my arrest for vandalism would not be serious?" he asked lightly.

She didn't smile this time. "Ted has deserted, and Jane is with him. Alex is determined to find them both. He's out for blood."

Dan blanched beneath the war paint. "I thought Jane was here. With you."

Susannah slowly shook her head. "She was, for a while. But shortly after you left, she took her horse and rode away as if she were fleeing from the devil himself. It seems she had informed on Yancy. Somehow she found out he was smuggling tea on the north end and told Alex."

"*She did what?* How dare she carry information from our house—"

"Please, sweetheart, let me finish. She was feeling so guilty about what she'd done that she went to warn Yancy. And you know my brother patrols the north end. Alex has been looking for any excuse to discredit Ted before their superiors and must have set a trap. He caught Ted and Jane helping Yancy escape."

"Ted—*a British lieutenant*—helped Yancy? The redcoats will hang him for that." He paused and shook his head. "You realize what this means, don't you? At the risk of his own life, your brother has chosen the righteous cause of the Colonies over the Crown's tyranny, at last. For that I'm truly thankful."

Susannah nodded her agreement, then motioned for Dan to sit at the table while she poured a basin of water. "Apparently, Jane has repented of her willful ways."

"What makes you say that?" He lifted his face as she returned and began sponging away the paint with a cloth. "Jane has always been concerned only about her own happiness, or the next party frock."

Susannah stopped her ministrations momentarily and met his eyes. "She's had a change of heart, Dan. Truly she has. If you'd been here and seen for yourself the pain in her face as she confessed some of the dreadful wrongs she's done to people she loved most, if you'd heard her voice, you'd not question her sincerity for a second."

"Well then, God does answer prayer—sometimes in the most unlikely ways. And you're right about something else, too. Alex will return."

"He's already accused you of helping Jane and Ted escape. We'd best get the rest of this bootblack off before he has your real crime to add to the list." She rinsed out the cloth and scrubbed harder, while he, with surprising levity, feigned howls of pain.

When at last all traces of the evidence had been erased, Susannah relaxed, thankful that for this moment, at least, he was home. And he was safe. She stood back and drank in the way his cheeks glowed.

A light tapping sounded at the back door.

Dan shot to his feet.

Susannah grabbed him. "Oh no. Not already."

Dan hugged her tight. "Almighty God," he whispered, "we plead for your protection."

2

The knock at the kitchen door came again. Feeling condemned, Dan held Susannah tighter for a precious moment. What had he gotten himself into? And what about his wife and son? If the hours he'd spent locked in a British shed one wintry day three years ago had taught him anything, he would have listened to Susannah and kept his promise to her to concentrate on his ministry. The townsmen had had more than enough help at their little "tea party."

He exhaled slowly, then released her and started toward the door. He felt her spring to his side, and as he put an arm around her, he could feel the throbbing of her heart. Ignoring his own fear, he gave her an encouraging hug. "Well, let's find out who it is."

He lifted the latch and let out a breath of relief when he recognized a familiar face. "Mr. Powers!"

"Evening, Reverend Haynes."

"Please, come in." Dan turned to Susannah as he closed the door after the visitor. "Sweetheart, this is Stanley Powers, one of the men I met recently at the town meetings." He turned back to the man. "What brings you by?"

"Mistress Haynes." The barrel-chested tradesman whipped off his hat and gripped it between both hands, turning it around and around in his beefy fingers. He switched his attention to Dan. "Your sister and her military friend are at

Clark Bender's house. They're on the run as traitors, hidin' from the lobsterbacks."

Dan tightened his mouth into a grim line. "I heard. Lieutenant Fontaine has already barged in here and questioned my wife. They're at Mr. Bender's, you say?"

Powers nodded his balding head. "The young lady said you're not to worry, she and her gentleman are fine."

"Fine?" Dan asked incredulously. "You must be joking!"

"No, not a'tall. We have their escape all planned out. We should have the two of them off the peninsula within the hour."

"Not past the guards at the Neck, I'll wager. Ted Harrington is far too familiar to his men for any sort of disguise. And my sister is no less recognizable, considering the time she's spent in the company of Lieutenant Fontaine this past year."

"Aye. And by now the lobsterbacks will be on the Neck thicker than fleas on a dog. We'll be rowing the youngsters across the bay."

"Which way are you taking them?"

"Cambridge. But they plan to go on from there to Worcester, to your other sister's place."

Dan drew in a quick breath, and Susannah clutched his arm. "No. That's not wise. Lieutenant Fontaine already knows where Caroline lives. He'd hightail it there in an instant, if he hasn't already left."

"What should they do, Dan?" Susannah asked as she looked with concern into her husband's face.

Dan stroked her soft cheek and drank in the sight of her, memorizing her delicate features, her gray-blue eyes, the tiny cleft in her chin. He would have to call the picture to mind in the dark days ahead. "There's no other recourse, love, than for me to spirit them somewhere into the backcountry. I know a number of Sons of Liberty from my postriding days. They'll help me get them to a spot where they'll be safe."

Her eyes clouded with anxiety. "But, Dan, you have duties here. What about the congregation? They're your sole responsibility since Reverend Moorhead has taken so ill."

The sight of his wife's distress wrenched Dan's heart, but he could not allow himself to waver. "At times like these, the elders of the church must step into the breach. But as for my sister and your brother, this is one responsibility I cannot ask another to take."

"You mean one danger you can't ask another to risk," she answered in a flat tone, her features pinched with dread.

"I suppose that is what I mean, yes. Please, understand that I must do this."

She was silent for a moment, then sighed in defeat. "I suppose God's hand must be in all of it."

Dan grabbed her in a hug, vastly relieved—until he remembered that she'd be left here alone again to make excuses when the redcoats came back. It was an awful burden to place on her slender shoulders, yet there was no other choice. "I have no idea how long I'll be gone, sweetheart. I'll send word as soon as possible and let you know where I am. Take care. And don't let Alex Fontaine bully you."

A longing gaze from her shimmering eyes sent an ache to his heart. "God be with you, my love."

Powers shifted his weight to his other foot. "Let's be off."

Dan removed his greatcoat from the peg near the door and drew it on, then started outside with the stocky man. Midway across the threshold, he turned for a last look at his wife, then went to her. He had to embrace her once more. Given the circumstances, he had no way of knowing when he'd have her in his arms again . . . if ever. He lowered his mouth to hers for a last kiss.

She clung desperately to him.

"I'm . . . sorry, my love." How he ever forced himself to walk away, he could not have explained. Especially when he heard her voice follow him.

"I love you, Daniel Haynes. No matter what happens, I've no regrets. None whatsoever."

He swallowed down the great lump in his throat as he strode after Stanley Powers.

Susannah somehow managed to maintain her control and lift a hand to wave when Dan glanced back as he and the other man cut across the neighbor's backyard. Moments later, the sight of him was lost in a haze of tears. His good-bye had sounded so *final.* The touch of his kiss still lingered, as did the intensity of his embrace

She mopped her tears with her handkerchief, then returned it to the pocket of her nightdress. Yet she couldn't stop trembling from the knowledge that three of the people dearest to her were being hunted by the British—her own former countrymen.

The night chill still hovered in the dim hallway, where each step and sound was magnified in the oppressive stillness. Susannah pulled her shawl tighter against the dampness and started up the stairs. But unable to bear the thought of going to her own darkened bedchamber, she went instead to the nursery. She set her lamp on the small table, then crossed to the crib and picked up her year-old baby . . . the son with the tawny hair like hers and the big brown eyes like his father's. She hugged his sleeping form to herself and bowed her head. "Heavenly Father," she whispered on a ragged breath, "please keep us all safely tucked within the palm of your hand."

On the lookout for any red-uniformed patrols, Dan followed closely behind Stanley Powers as they neared Union Street. Then, avoiding the light of the streetlamps, they turned up a narrow side street and went around to the back of an unassuming brick house. Powers rapped twice on the kitchen door.

As Dan followed him inside the dwelling, he spied his brother-in-law.

Ted, no longer in uniform but dressed in serviceable civilian clothes, got up from the table with a doubtful expression on his face.

An older man also rose, whom Dan recognized from the

town meetings. He'd seen that gap-toothed grin dozens of times but had never learned the fellow's name. And beside him, a plump, aproned woman stood, folding and stacking blankets on a large piece of oilcloth alongside cheese and bread and other foodstuffs.

"Clark," said Stanley Powers, "this is Reverend Haynes, our young waif's brother."

"How do, Reverend," he said, extending a big, work-worn hand. "Bender's the name. Clark Bender. Glad you could come."

"Sir." Dan nodded and shook his hand, then took a step toward Susannah's waiting brother and grabbed him in a bear hug. "What's this I hear about you, Ted?" he said as they drew apart.

Ted's usually hard-set jaw slackened as his mouth curved into a sheepish grin. "I—"

"Is that Dan's voice?" Jane said from the next room. Just inside the door she hesitated for a breathless instant, glancing first at Ted, then at Dan. A mysterious smile lit her dark eyes as she nibbled her lip.

Dan couldn't decide if his sister's grin showed guilt or shyness as she stood there in a soggy dress, her normally neat auburn hair all askew and tumbling in damp disarray about her shoulders. Ted moved to her side and put his arm around her, looking nervous.

For the first time Dan could remember, Jane's expression dissolved into one completely devoid of guile, and he realized that Susannah's evaluation of the girl's change of heart had to be true. She had apparently come to her senses—not just about her loyalties, but about her feelings for Ted. The two seemed genuinely in love.

His chest swelled with indescribable joy at the marvelous and unfathomable workings of God. All the same . . .

"I already had one sister run off with a wanted man," he said sternly. "I'm not about to be a party to such a thing a second time. . . ."

Ted and Jane exchanged an expression of despair.

"Without the benefit of marriage, that is," Dan finished.

Jane's mouth gaped open. Ted looked from her to Dan in disbelief.

"Ahem." The lady of the house moved into view, her hands firmly planted on her wide hips. "What about the banns, the proper papers, an' all?"

"We shall take care of the vows before God and witnesses now, Mistress Bender. The rest can be arranged in due course . . . that is," he added, eyeing his normally vain sister, "if Jane is willing to be wed in her present attire."

As the older woman shrugged and returned to her task appeased, Jane surveyed her wrinkled, rain-spotted dress in mock horror, then burst out laughing.

Obviously misreading her feigned dismay, Ted took her hands. "Don't fret, my love. I've yet to see a more fetching or beautiful bride."

Dan had to admit he was beginning to see some real beauty emerging in the face of this once-proud and haughty sister who had provoked him to no end of prayer. A new softness filled her countenance, and a radiance shone in her eyes. He turned toward the hearth, where the two tradesmen stood smirking over coffee as they witnessed the display in undisguised enjoyment. "Excuse me, Mr. Bender. Would you happen to have a Bible I might borrow?"

"Surely do, Preacher." He started for the hall.

Two rapid knocks rattled the kitchen door, and a wiry little man poked his head inside. "We'd best be on our way now. Another patrol just passed by. That makes three. But the rain's started up again. It'll make good cover."

"Thanks, friend," Dan said, "but I've got a wedding to perform first."

"What? The lot of you must have gone mad. Lobsterbacks are everywhere. They're searchin' every nook and cranny for that young deserter," the stranger said, poking a finger at Ted. "Between him and all the face they lost havin' to stand aside while the tea got dumped off the *Dartmouth,* they're angry enough to hang each other!"

"You know, son," Stanley Powers said, clamping a hand on Dan's shoulder, "Crocker's right. I'd scoot outta here, right quick."

Dan glanced at Jane and Ted, who appeared utterly crestfallen. He truly hated to disappoint them, but . . .

"Perhaps you're right. There's no reason to cause you good folks any more risk. You've already done so much."

Mrs. Bender let out an audible sigh and shoved the oilcloth packet into Jane's arms while Clark Bender grabbed his coat.

Dan raised a staying hand. "Wait. No need for any of you to come. Tell me where the rowboat is, and Ted and I can handle the oars ourselves."

The man's countenance relaxed. "You sure?"

"Completely. I have friends who will help in Cambridge. We'll leave the boat hidden in the marsh."

"Well, least I can do is wish you Godspeed." He turned to the latest arrival. "Crocker, tell the reverend where you tied your boat."

"The *Little Amy* is the smallest sloop at the end of the short pier next to the mill pond. The rowboat's tied to her. And be careful. Them soldiers could be back anytime." The lean fellow moved from the doorway to let them pass.

Dan shot a look at his brother-in-law and noted some new worry lines. He felt the same himself and wondered if it was apparent.

But Jane breezed out the door with a bright smile. "We'd better hurry. And don't worry, Dan. God will protect us. Isn't that what you're always saying?"

3

An icy drizzle added to the bitterness of the December night as Dan hastened with Jane and Ted toward the pier. Despite the lateness of the hour, Dan noticed lights burning in most of the homes along the way. Clusters of local men hovered about in the glow of the streetlamps, and an air of uneasiness pervaded the town. No doubt, details of the tea escapade at the harbor were common knowledge by now, and everyone waited for Governor Hutchinson's retaliation, whatever form it might take.

As the dampness seeped steadily into his heavy coat, Dan turned up his collar. He knew Jane and Ted must be equally uncomfortable. Their cloaks had barely begun to dry in the shelter of the Bender home and now clung heavily to their bodies.

Coming to the end of a darkened alley near the short row of west-facing docks, Dan motioned for the others to stay in the shadows while he checked to be certain no one else was around. He barely had time to cross the road before the unmistakable clatter of approaching horses carried to his ears. He dashed to the nearest warehouse and flattened himself against the side.

Three mounted soldiers held burning torches high as they reined in. "One way to find out," he heard a voice say.

Dan's heart thundered in his ears. They had surely seen him running. He did not move and hardly dared breathe. But as his glance followed their movements, he saw them veer toward the men at the corner. Relief flowed through him.

"You, there," a gruff voice demanded. "We are on the king's business, in search of a deserter and a woman. They're riding double on a military horse. Have you seen them?"

Dan saw several surprised glances being passed among the group as they shifted their footing.

"What's that?" someone asked.

"I'm quite certain you heard me," the soldier announced gruffly, "but I'll say it again. Did any of you see an officer of the king's army riding double with a woman this eve? I demand a reply."

"'Fraid not," another answered, while his companions shook their heads as if to verify the statement. The cockiness in their demeanors led Dan to surmise that the group had expected the question to be about the tea dumping.

The patrol hesitated. The officers peered steadily at the townsmen as if waiting for someone to give a conflicting response. But when none came, they abruptly reined their mounts to the side and rode away.

"Must be a whole lot more going on tonight than we thought," one of the men under the lamplight remarked.

While the men were busy staring after the departing soldiers, Dan exhaled slowly and motioned for Jane and Ted to join him. They didn't waste a second as they hurried across the dark road.

"Are we anywhere near the boat yet?" Jane asked softly.

Dan nodded. "Just beyond the end of this warehouse is the last pier before the water mill." When they reached it, he led the way out over the inky water.

After some difficulty reading the words in the darkness, Dan spied the *Little Amy*. Locating the tiny craft alongside, he crept up the plank and jumped into it, with Jane and Ted close behind.

Hoofbeats echoed from the direction of Prince Street.

Dan reached up for his sister. "Hurry!"

She complied at once, followed by Ted. The freezing rainwater that had collected in the bottom sloshed about their feet, adding to the cold as they huddled down, still as death.

Dan watched helplessly as waves caused by their sudden weight in the boat rippled across the surface of the water and moved outward from their position. He prayed that the soldiers wouldn't notice.

The patrol veered onto the pier. The hooves of the horses made hollow reports on the wooden slats, then halted as eerie shadow patterns from the torches flitted among the secured boats.

"They'll not get far," a voice said with conviction. "Sooner or later we'll catch them if we must search every stable, house, and vessel in this rebellious town."

The horses started up again, coming closer as the patrol stopped at each slip.

Dan worked his gloves off his numb, stiff fingers. While he feverishly struggled to untie the knot in the sodden rope that lashed the boat to the sloop, Ted deftly picked up the oars from the bottom of the craft and slid the paddle ends soundlessly into the water one at a time.

The patrol now searched a cod boat a mere two slips away.

A glint from the erratic torch flames reflected against the whiteness of Jane's fear-widened eyes as she flipped her hood over her head and ducked lower into the boat.

The stubborn knot finally gave way, and Dan pushed off.

Crouching low, they floated toward the open water of the Charles River while Dan carefully took one oar from Ted. Then they started rowing soundlessly, barely breaking the surface of the water, sliding into the cover of darkness.

Before they had gained a dozen yards, the gold-orange glow from a torch spread toward them across the shining ripples. Dan flattened down into the craft and held his breath.

Endless seconds passed before the light veered away, casting them again in the blessed blackness, and Dan heard Ted let out a breath. He peered over the side and saw that the soldiers had moved on.

Nudging Ted, Dan gripped his oar and checked over his

shoulder at the pinpoints of Cambridge light, a good five miles away on the north bank of the Charles. The two of them began rowing in earnest.

Jane regained her seat and huddled into her soggy cloak, her teeth chattering as the night wind bristled across the water. She hugged her knees and buried her nose.

When at last the boat reached the marshy outskirts of Cambridge, Dan and Ted worked their way slowly up narrow reed-filled channels toward drier ground. He regretted that they had no torch of their own to help them get their bearings and choose the best route to safety, especially with Jane to consider. His sister's fortitude and determination had astounded him, and he wanted to see her safely stowed away where she'd be free of the threat of harm—and pneumonia, from the sound of her.

As if she had picked up on his fears, she spoke. "I doubt anyone will be able to follow us now. Not in this maze."

"You could be right," Dan replied, wondering where they could best beach the rowboat. "But it truly astounds me that the redcoats are more interested in capturing one deserter than they are in finding the perpetrators of the tea party."

Ted exhaled in disgust. "Don't forget, *my old friend* Alex is leading the pack. I doubt he'll stop searching even if he's given a direct order to withdraw."

"I'm sorry, darling." Jane reached over and clasped his hand. "That's all the more reason for Dan to finish our wedding ceremony now. We've wasted far too much time already."

Ted paused with his oar in midstroke and lifted her hand to his lips. "A year, my Jane. You were lost to me a whole year."

Dan couldn't help but recognize the lovesick tone in their voices as the unguided boat veered clumsily into a thick patch of tall grass. "It may sound quite simple to you two," he rasped as he dug hard into the mud with his oar to free them, "but there is a little matter you haven't considered. Witnesses. Remember?"

"Well then," Jane said on a sigh, "get us out of here, and let's find some. I've been an old maid far too long already."

He chuckled as his brother-in-law broke into action and started rowing again with a new spurt of energy.

After a few more minutes they could burrow through the reeds no farther. Dan lifted his oar into the craft. "This is as good a spot as any to leave Mr. Crocker's boat. We'll have to wade to dry ground from here. With a little searching in the daylight I'm sure he'll be able to locate it easily enough."

"Finally!" Jane stood up and gathered her cloak, and the rowboat wobbled.

"Wait, love," Ted warned. "I shall get out first and carry you. You'll never manage in those skirts." He took Jane's hand and stood with her. "Er, just where *are* we going?" he asked Dan.

"To the wheelwright who hid Emily and Rob. It's not too far from here, if I gauged our course correctly."

After a few minutes of slogging through ice-edged puddles and stiff muddy sections, they emerged at last on dry earth. Ted lowered Jane to the ground but hugged her shivering body close to his side as they trudged down a back street in their wet boots.

Dan checked the landmarks illuminated by a town streetlamp. "It's just over this way another block. I surely wish it weren't so late, but there's nothing to be done about that. Come on."

At last they reached the modest two-story structure that housed Sean Burns's thriving wheelwright business on its lower floor. Dan mounted the back stairs to the dwelling above, with Jane and Ted a step behind. He rapped sharply on the door, waited a moment, then knocked again.

A lamp went on inside, casting an oblique moving circle of gold as someone carrying the light approached and pushed the curtain aside. Then the door opened, and a stocky man in nightclothes leaned out. "Daniel? Daniel Haynes?" A woman in a ruffled nightcap moved to his side.

"Forgive me for disturbing you and your good wife at such an unearthly hour of night, Mr. Burns. I'm afraid I'm at your door begging for help again. We need a few hours rest and a place to dry off."

Sean Burns peered beyond Dan to the bedraggled pair behind him. His questioning eyes returned to Dan.

Dan offered an apologetic grin. "This is another sister of mine on the run, with yet another fugitive . . . a former officer of the Crown. I had to get them out of Boston in a hurry."

"Surely ye're not meanin' sister Jane that wee Emily spoke so often aboot," Mistress Burns said, her Scottish brogue drawing out the *r*s.

Jane pushed back her drenched hood, revealing her matted, equally wet hair, and curtsied. "It does appear to run in the family, doesn't it?" she giggled. Then her teeth began to chatter again.

"Well, don't keep standin' out in the cold rain. Come in. Come in. Warm yourselves at the hearth. Sean, stir up the coals, and I'll put on the kettle." They stepped away, allowing room for the threesome to wipe their boots and enter.

Mr. Burns chuckled. He went to the hearth and grabbed a poker while Dan and the lovers gravitated to the warmth. As the crackling blaze came to life, they held their hands out to the flames.

Jane sneezed.

"Ah, now, just look at the lot of ye," Mistress Burns said, clucking like a mother hen as she regarded the sorry-looking group. "Drippin' wet and freezin' and bound to catch your death. What is there aboot young people nowadays that they can't keep themselves safe and warm and dry? Stay there right close to the fire, and I'll go round up some blankets so ye can all get oot of those wet clothes."

"That's most kind of you, Mistress Burns." Dan shook his head as he watched her amble off in her plaid housecoat. Then he turned to the woman's husband. "I can't begin to tell you how much I appreciate your willingness to help. And your dear wife as well."

The wheelwright swung the kettle over the center of the heat with his work-hardened fingers. "I've no doobt there be few of the likes of me Maggie around. 'Twas a lucky enough day when I managed to persuade her father I'd spend me life seein' to her happiness. And not bein' blessed with our own wee bairns, she finds joy in motherin' other folks whenever she can. Should I see to your horses, lad?"

"We're afoot. We had to row across the river. We escaped only by the grace of God." Dan's gaze wandered over the interior of the cozy dwelling, with its handmade furniture built to last generations and the woman's colorful touches such as braided rugs and crisp curtains. He had yet to drop by unannounced without finding the same loving hospitality that had been extended to them this eve. Sean Burns was highly regarded among the patriots as an honest and loyal friend.

"This might be enough," Mistress Burns said, coming back with an armful of wool and flannel blankets and articles of dry clothing. She set all but one down on a kitchen chair, then shook it out.

"Where ye headin', lad, after ye leave us?" her husband asked Dan.

"Thought maybe it would be safest to take my sister and Ted inland, maybe as far as the Green Mountain country. From what I've heard, Ethan Allen and his men are quite handy at keeping what's theirs safe from . . . intruders."

A low laugh rumbled out of the wheelwright's chest. It was common knowledge that the "Green Mountain Boys" had quite handily kept the New Yorkers from forcibly claiming that territory for their own. "Well, with the Christmas season nigh upon us, ye might be able to hitch a ride with one of the families headin' inland to celebrate with relatives. I'll ask around tomorrow and see what I can find oot for ye. But ye need to be gettin' to bed. This night's all but gone."

"No!" Jane said, going rigid. "We can't go to bed yet." She swept a coaxing glance in Ted's direction. "Not until we've finished with today's business."

"Today's gone, miss," Sean Burns said, looking from her to Dan and back.

Ted straightened his stance and wrapped her small hand in both of his. "She means, sir, we were in the middle of our wedding just a short while ago. We'd like to see it through."

"Now?" the older man asked in disbelief.

"Now." Jane and Ted, having spoken in unison, laughed and leaned into each other.

Mistress Burns's cheeks rounded with her smile, and her eyes twinkled. "Ah, well. I see. We'll carry on, then . . . on one condition." She eyed each of them. "That ye all get oot of them wet clothes first."

※ ※

Stripped and wrapped in a dry blanket, Dan stood in a bucket of warm water, holding an open Bible.

In a second slightly larger tub, and also wearing nothing but thick, warm blankets, Jane and Ted stood side by side, facing him. Ted pulled one arm free and wrapped it around Jane's waist to steady her as they struggled in vain to contain their obvious mirth.

This was his socially correct, always proper sister? And Ted—who had never sported so much as a smudge on his immaculately pressed uniform? Dan's glance went to the two witnesses attired in bedclothes . . . and among the four of them, he saw not one solemn expression. He shook his head. "I'm fully aware this is not exactly normal for such an auspicious occasion. But I would think that at least you, Jane and Ted, would make some effort to be serious. This is, after all, a lifetime vow you'll be taking."

Ted's face fell for one brief instant, and Jane feigned a grave look. But they both sputtered into a laugh as they all but collapsed against one another and howled.

Dan rolled his eyes heavenward and breathed a prayer for patience—and perhaps forgiveness. He had some difficulty trying to maintain his own solemnity.

Ted's laughter quickly subsided, and his expression sobered as he waited for Jane to quiet also. He stroked her cheek lovingly with the backs of his fingers and took a deep

breath. "He's quite right, you know. I can't ask you to do this
. . . marry me without so much as a bouquet of flowers or a
bridal veil. Truly, I would understand if you wanted to wait till
another time."

She gazed up at him, and the radiance of her smile was
mirrored in her eyes. "And miss telling our grandchildren
about this? Never."

4

Susannah looked out at the overcast sky and sighed. Surely Dan could have found some way to contact her in the two days since he had left. It sounded so easy to entrust them to God's care, but her mind would not rest. She wanted to help them herself or, at the very least, hear from someone who had. Not knowing where they all were—whether they were even safe— was taking its toll on her sleep.

But not a soul had come to the door with word. Soldiers kept watch at the front gate, and Susannah was hesitant to go out alone. In a frenzy to stay occupied, she had already scrubbed and polished all the floors and every piece of furniture in the entire house. But nothing had kept her mind from wandering to Dan and praying unceasingly for his safety.

With baby Miles asleep in her arms, she ascended the stairs to the nursery and laid him gently in the crib. How at peace he looked, with a chubby thumb in his mouth, as if nothing at all were amiss! She tucked a blanket securely around him and closed the door behind her as she left the room.

From outside a stern voice carried above the workday bustle on the busy street. "Halt!"

Hurrying down to the front door, Susannah drew back the bolt and inched it open a crack. All she could see was another soldier approaching the one who had been posted just beyond the wrought-iron gate all morning. Her spirit plummeted. The king's men might have run off someone trying to come with news of Dan. Dejected, she smoothed her indigo linen dress as she went to make a cup of tea.

Just as she entered the tidy kitchen, someone knocked on the back door. "Ben!" She flung herself into her brother-in-law's arms, barely noticing the cold breath of winter that clung to his coat. "Dan and Ted, have you seen them?"

The lanky young man, a courier now for the patriots, gave her a comforting hug, then held her at arm's length. "I'm sorry. I only just learned of their escape a short while ago when I stopped in at the Green Dragon on my return from Salem and Newburyport. Thank heaven that's as far as Sam Adams sent me. Paul Revere wanted to go to Philadelphia himself with news of the tea party. He's hoping to exert the necessary influence there and in New York. All could be lost if they give in and allow British tea ships to unload in their ports."

"Ben, please." Susannah grabbed his arms. "Have you no news of Dan? Has no one heard anything?"

He gave a helpless shrug, his face serious. "All I heard was that they went up the Charles in a rowboat that belonged to one of the local men. The owner brought it back yesterday. I just came from his place, as a matter of fact."

"And?"

"And he still had Jane's horse, so I rode it back and put it in the stable. Yancy Curtis had left the pacer down in the vicinity of Long Wharf with another of the Sons of Liberty while he made his own escape. They're also keeping Ted's mount well hidden."

"Then Yancy is safe, at least?" A tiny ray of hope flickered within her. At least Dan's friend Yancy had managed to elude the authorities, despite his near capture two nights ago. Surely the Almighty would also protect Dan and the others.

Ben began unbuttoning his heavy coat. "Yancy caught a pilot boat just as it heaved off to guide a ship out of the harbor. No telling where that rascal will wind up."

The glimmer of optimism inside Susannah vanished as another thought made its way into her consciousness. Dan,

Ted, and Jane had to be out there someplace—on foot. And if so, they were all the more vulnerable to capture.

Ben draped his coat over the back of one of the dark, wooden kitchen chairs. "I'm sure they're fine."

Susannah found the trite comment more irritating than comforting. She folded her arms and turned away.

"Whoa!" he said teasingly as he gave her shoulder a light squeeze. "Where's all that faith you and my big brother are always hiding behind?"

She turned her head and met his gaze with a look of chagrin. How could her faith have slipped to such a low level in so short a time? "You're quite right. Surely our heavenly Father has the matter well in hand . . . I pray," she added on a doubtful sigh.

Ben's grin softened the contours of his square jawline, and his light brown eyes twinkled. "Think about it this way. If the lobsterbacks are keeping such a close watch on this place, Dan hasn't been apprehended. So he and Ted and Jane must still be safe. There are patriots aplenty who'd be glad to take them under their wing."

"Yes." She returned his warm smile. "And you're right about the guards. Besides, if Lieutenant Fontaine had caught them, I'm certain he'd be out on my front stoop gloating, enumerating all the charges he plans to heap on their heads."

With a nod, Ben strode to the hearth and moved the kettle over the heat. "How about some of that contraband tea I brought you last week?"

Susannah felt her cheeks flame. "Oh! Forgive me, Ben. I've not been a proper hostess at all—and with you having to brave both the soldiers and the cold to come here." She snatched his coat from the chair and rushed to hang it.

Suddenly a knock reverberated from the front door.

Her breath caught. She turned and sought Ben's face.

"Stay here. I'll take care of it."

"No." She raised her chin and moved to his side as he got up. "We shall both go. After all, it could easily be someone with news for us." Nervously, she patted her chignon into place and accompanied her brother-in-law up the hallway. Ben motioned her behind him as he unbolted the door and opened it.

"Excuse me, but may I speak to Mistress Haynes?"

Recognizing the voice of one of Dan's church members, Susannah stepped forward, ignoring the menacing stares from the uniformed figures at the edge of the yard. "Oh, Mr. Pringle. Do come in."

He nodded and complied as Ben secured the door behind him.

"I'm afraid I haven't kept the parlor fire going, but you're more than welcome to join us in the kitchen for tea. You've met Dan's brother, Ben, have you not?"

"Seen him a time or two, as I recall," the tradesman answered with a jovial smile that seemed to emphasize his large ears. "Good to see you again, lad."

She fought to restrain herself from blurting out the questions uppermost in her mind as she hung his cloak on a peg and the two men shook hands. But as they all started toward the kitchen, she could hold back no longer. "Do you have news?"

"That I do."

Ben gave him an exuberant clap on the back. "That's what we were hoping. Come have a seat right here," he said, sliding out a chair while Susannah quickly measured tea into the teapot and filled it with steaming water.

"You know," the man began, "I started to come last eve, after the wheelwright from Cambridge dropped by my cobbler shop on the pretext of having a pair of boots resoled. But when those uppity lobsterbacks glared at me as if they dared anyone to come near your house, I walked on by. Of course, once I heard Ben here had gotten through—"

"Mr. Pringle. Please," Susannah interrupted. "What have you come to tell us?"

"Oh, forgive me. The wife says I talk too much. But what with all this tea-dumping business and that coward, Governor

Hutchinson, planning to resign—first intelligent thing he's done in years, if you ask me—it's hard to keep up with all the goings-on."

She resisted the temptation to stomp her foot. "Yes, I understand. But about Dan. Is there a message?"

"Why, yes. Yes, there is."

As she stood at the pine sideboard, Susannah felt a lessening of the weight that had been pressing on her heart. She set a cup before each of the men and then at her own spot before sinking gratefully to her chair and clasping her hands together while she waited for him to elaborate.

His chest puffed out slightly. "The wheelwright says I'm to instruct you to pack your things. Your husband wants you to go to his family in Rhode Island and stay there where it's safe. Till after Christmas, at least."

Speechless, Susannah felt her mouth gape as the man turned to Ben with barely a pause in his words.

"Just wait'll Reverend Haynes returns and discovers the damage that's been done to Long Lane Church."

"What did you say?"

"Some no-account soldier dogs ransacked the whole place, saying they were searching for the reverend and your brother, Mistress Haynes. They busted up all the pews, broke out windows—" He wagged his head. "Terrible. Terrible. It'll be weeks, maybe months, before we can hold services there again."

"So I heard," Ben answered grimly, avoiding Susannah's astonished gaze. "The soldiers are straining at their leashes. They can hardly stand the fact that they haven't been allowed to do anything to make us pay for the tea party. The Presbyterian church was the only place they've been loosed to vent their wrath, since the general has gone to England for Christmas and the governor refused to let them make any arrests. Of course, he knows if he did, he'd never be able to stop the riot that would follow." A cocky grin widened his mouth. "Even if he had every soldier that's posted in the

Colonies at his disposal, it wouldn't be enough to hold us back. And he knows it."

Susannah suppressed her irritation at their having changed the subject so casually. She'd had no idea that the church on Long Lane had been entered and damaged. The news was both alarming and dire. When Dan found out about it, he would be furious.

Her gaze fell upon the china pot and brought her back to the task at hand. The tea must have finished brewing. She rose and filled the cups.

Mr. Pringle, obviously in cheerful agreement with Ben's last statement, chuckled, barely taking time to nod his thanks to her. "And when word gets back to England that Hutchinson has done absolutely nothing, his letter of resignation won't be nearly enough to satisfy Parliament. I'll surely love seeing that old thief caught up on the fence with wolves snapping at his heels from both sides."

"Well, that'll take a spyglass," Ben said with a laugh. "He's packing to leave for the holidays, and rumor has it the Hutchinsons are taking a whole lot more than their party clothes."

Susannah plunked down her cup in frustration, the china clinking loudly. "Mr. Pringle. Surely there must have been more to my husband's message than you've told me. Where have they gone? Are they safe?"

The tradesman shrugged a beefy shoulder. "I can't rightly say, Mistress Haynes. According to the wheelwright, the reverend thought it best to keep his destination secret until things settle down a wee bit. That's all I know." Lifting his cup to his mouth, he slurped his tea noisily.

Susannah stared pointedly, willing him to continue. That could not be all, not when she so desperately needed to know so much more.

"Oh. Come to think of it, there was one other thing."

She brightened.

"Your husband said to tell you he loves you."

It was such a simple statement, yet it filled her with warmth. She took a deep breath and relaxed against the chair back.

"This will be the first Christmas Eve we've spent apart since he asked me to marry him three years ago." The words saddened her spirit again, and she sighed.

"That right?"

She nodded. "He promised me at the time that he'd give up his rebellious ways for the ministry. Now, here it is, a scant three years later, and he's defying the Crown again."

"Defying them for *your brother,*" Ben reminded her none too gently. "And it's high time Dan quit hiding behind that pulpit, if you ask me. The die is cast. Once Britain hears about the tea party, they won't let it pass. Not those arrogant long-noses. They're still berating themselves for not doing more about the burning of the *Gaspee* the summer before last. They'll blockade the harbor at the very least. Or try, anyway. But the north-end boys won't stand for it. And neither will anyone else, for that matter."

Ben's voice rose with excitement, and Susannah found his confidence quite unsettling. She diverted her attention to Mr. Pringle, who appeared to have more sense about the matter.

He stood and, taking a last gulp, set down his empty cup. "Well, guess I'd best be going. No sense having the soldiers thinking this was any more than a neighborly call."

Ben got up as well. "Be sure to bid any of the congregation you might come across farewell for Susannah. I'm going to hire a wagon and have her and the baby out of here before General Gage returns from holiday, because mark my words, he'll unleash his soldiers." He grimaced. "He's not the coward old Hutchinson is."

As the visitor agreed, the baby let out a cry upstairs.

Susannah rose. "I do thank you, Mr. Pringle, for risking the soldiers' wrath to pass on Daniel's message. Now, if you'll excuse me, gentlemen, I must see to my son."

She heard the creak of the back door as she headed for the stairs, and then Mr. Pringle as he spoke again. Something about the way he lowered his voice made her stop and listen.

"But just how do you plan to get your sister-in-law past those guards outside, if you don't mind my asking?"

"Oh, don't worry," Ben announced cheerily. "They're not posted to keep her in, but to catch Dan and her brother."

"Well, now, I wouldn't be too sure of that if I was you, lad."

5

Cold and miserable, with winter's bitter breath raking across the snowy landscape, Dan hunched deeper into the turned-up collar of his greatcoat. He shifted his position in the deep wooden bed as the group of farm wagons fitted with skids slid over the uneven, snow-packed roads. Only three days before Christmas, and he was nowhere near home. Instead, along with Ted and Jane, he accompanied a family heading for Bennington, a town that lay on the far side of New Hampshire in the Green Mountains. Two of the other wagons would turn east and continue on to Brattleboro.

Susannah and baby Miles weighed heavily on his mind. How were they faring? And what in the name of all that was good was he doing traveling farther and farther away from everything he held dear? Once again he called himself a fool for ever having insisted upon taking part in the harbor incident a week ago. He should have remembered his real calling and remained at home, *where he belonged*. If he had been there when Alex came with his questions, Dan knew he would have been above suspicion and perhaps might even have calmed the officer.

As he stared forlornly at Jane and Ted, Dan did his best to ignore the incessant giggles and chattering of the youthful Warren offspring also bouncing along in the family wagon. The newlyweds sat across from him on the hay amid crates piled with gaily wrapped gifts. Oblivious to the cold and dampness of the December day, they smiled and whispered as they huddled together under a thick wool blanket. Their inaudible phrases were punctuated by Jane's soft laughs as she gazed into Ted Harrington's blue eyes. Ted's eyes were so much like Susannah's that Dan couldn't look at him without growing more lonely.

"Oh, come on, Noah," twelve-year-old Rebecca Warren said teasingly with a jab of her elbow. "Try and knock down a pinecone, if you're that good. I dare you." She flicked one of her long brown braids behind her shoulder and tipped her head in challenge.

Her older brother's freckled face dimpled with a mischievous grin. Inserting another smooth stone into the leather thong of his slingshot, the sixteen-year-old drew back, taking careful aim as the wagon rolled along the icy, rutted road. Then he released the rock. It ricocheted off the bark of a winter-bare birch.

"Nice try," Rebecca singsonged, her expression gloating.

"Aw, that was just practice." Noah removed another stone from the pocket of his warm coat. His second found its mark, scattering shards of the pine cone in all directions. Grinning, he straightened his shoulders with manly pride.

"Bet you're not that good with Pa's gun," Rebecca teased.

"Shows what *you* know about things," he retorted. "Just last week I—"

"You *children* are so annoying." Leah, the oldest daughter, deliberately turned her head toward the bench seat up front where their parents and youngest brother sat. "Mama, make them settle down." Easily a year younger than Noah, she folded her plump arms and pouted in superior fashion.

Eliza Warren turned partway around and sighed, her placid face lined from years of hard work and sacrifice. "Rebecca. Noah. We've miles and miles to go. Let's please try to get along. Why don't we sing some nice Christmas carols?" As if to coax them into the proper frame of mind, she began to sing, her bright soprano voice echoing over the frozen ground:

All my heart this night rejoices,
As I hear,
Far and near,
Sweetest angel voices. . . .

Jane and Ted chimed in, along with folks in the other wagons:

"Christ is born," their choirs are singing,
Till the air
Everywhere
Now with joy is ringing.

After a few moments of making faces at each other, the young people also took up the melody:

Come and banish all your sadness,
One and all,
Great and small,
Come with songs of gladness;
Love Him who with love is yearning;
Hail the star
That from afar
Bright with hope is burning.

Convinced his own sadness was too hard to banish, Dan didn't force himself to sing along. He did manage to give the others the semblance of a smile before looking off into the distance, recalling the last time he'd heard that song—at the church on Long Lane. His thoughts drifted to the elderly Reverend Moorhead, who had been so ill over the past few weeks that he hadn't appeared at several of the services, and Dan had preached in his absence. The last time Dan had visited him, the man appeared near death. Feeling a renewed weight of guilt, Dan wondered if there would be a Christmas Eve service at all, now that he himself was not around.

The wagons of carolers—these families who had so graciously given them haven—broke into "Hark, the Herald Angels Sing" with enthusiasm. Blessedly retrieved from his remorseful musings, Dan let happy memories of Susannah wash over him. The thought of her warmed him despite the chill temperature that caused everyone's breath to vaporize and rise in frosty mist.

But too soon his longings made him all the more despondent. He slid a gaze toward his sister, who was reveling in her newlywed bliss. She appeared far younger than her twenty-one years. Ted, too, seemed unconcerned, as if it mattered not that he was a hunted man. Fighting back pangs of jealousy, Dan shot an irritated glare at Ted. It was one thing to trust almighty God, but quite another to have no more concern about present circumstances than a newborn babe.

As if someone had read his thoughts, a woman in one of the other wagons broke into "Away in a Manger," and the group all joined in.

Jane snuggled closer to Ted and gave herself to the sweet melody, and Dan found himself unable to drag his gaze from the innocence that now dominated her. He let out a breath, feeling guilty for his attitudes. He had prayed long and hard for his headstrong sister. If the Almighty chose to answer those petitions in these present strange circumstances, then whatever sacrifice Dan was called upon to make—missing Christmas at home with Susannah, becoming a fugitive himself—was a small price indeed. *All things work together for good,* he reminded himself.

A wondrous peace filled Dan, and he added his voice to the others on the second verse.

"Soldiers!" someone hissed from the wagon beside them.

Dan quickly leaned over the side rail and looked down the road.

Astride glistening, long-legged horses, a mounted detachment galloped toward them.

He stretched his foot across and nudged his brother-in-law's leg with the toe of his boot, motioning toward the redcoats with his head.

Ted's eyes grew wide, and he stiffened.

Jane peered around him toward the thundering horses and gave a small cry. She and Ted began burrowing into the hay they had been sitting on.

"Sing out, Noah!" Dan rasped, noticing that the others had fallen silent while seeking the source of alarm. "Put some life into it!"

Beside Dan, the lad puffed out his chest and straightened to his full height. "Hark, the herald *soldiers* come . . . ," he sang out, falling immediately into the proper lyrics as the others caught on and hastily entered in.

Without missing a word of the carol, Rebecca and Leah inched over Jane and Ted, arranging their full skirts to hide the pair.

Dan pulled his hat lower. With a week's growth of beard, he felt fairly certain he would not be recognized unless Alex Fontaine happened to be among them. He took a deep breath and belted forth the refrain, his baritone voice nearly drowning out all the others until he reminded himself not to draw undue attention.

The patrol, consisting of two sergeants and two corporals, reined their mounts to a trot. Staring with haughty malice from one wagon to the next, they rode by without stopping.

Thank Providence for small favors! Relieved, Dan began to breathe a little easier.

Suddenly John Warren, the driver, drew hard on the reins and stopped.

Dan peered past the man. The patrol had blocked the road ahead of the first wagon. As the singing dwindled away and ceased, he flicked a glance toward the spot where Jane and Ted lay hidden to assure himself that nothing appeared out of place.

Rebecca, trembling with fright, tugged the ribbon from one of her braids and started unplaiting her hair.

Dan gave a wink of encouragement.

Taking the cue, Noah retrieved a knife and a chunk of wood from his pocket and bent to whittle.

"Where are you from?" the officer in charge snapped at the driver of the lead wagon.

"Lexington."

"Your destination?"

"Connecticut Valley. My brother's place, for Christmas holidays."

"Your brother's name?"

"Landers. Carl Landers. Has a farm north of Brattleboro."

The officer unsheathed his sword. "So you say." He paused in ominous silence. "Search the wagons."

Leah let out an audible gasp. Rebecca and Noah froze at their tasks. Then the lad bravely set to his work again, with his sister following his lead.

At the sound of scraping metal, Dan knew the soldiers were employing their bayonet-tipped muskets. Stretching up to look beyond the Warrens on the driver's seat, he saw that the redcoats had not dismounted. They had positioned themselves one on each side of the first two rigs. From their smug expressions, it was obvious they thoroughly relished their duty as they used their weapons to raise blankets and stab between boxes and trunks.

Catching a movement from the corner of his eye, Dan noticed Noah shoving at something with his foot. Looking closer, he recognized it with alarm: the hem of Jane's skirt. Even as Leah fluffed hers over the incriminating cloth, Dan had a sinking feeling that within moments they'd all be caught. Not just him and Jane and Ted, but all these good people.

He saw John place a comforting hand over his wife's and give it a pat as the two of them made an effort to relax and smile at young Jamie on the seat between them.

Finished rifling through the other two wagons, all four soldiers approached the Warrens'.

In desperation Dan stood and jumped out even as the soldiers approached. He cleared his throat and slid a hand casually into his coat pocket. "Hear there's been some big trouble down in Boston Town. The patrol that searched us yesterday said folks dumped a whole shipload of tea into the bay. That must have been a sight to see. You looking for the men who did it?"

"No," a corporal said. "We're—"

"What—or whom—we're looking for," the sergeant next to him interrupted as he edged his mount nearer, "is none of your concern." His menacing eyes hardened into dark slits. "Get back in your wagon."

"Just asking," Dan said as he complied. "Heard they did it no more than a stone's throw from navy headquarters."

With his saber, the officer slashed out, stopping abruptly just inches shy of Dan's throat. "A loose tongue is a simple thing to remedy."

Dan stared back, not daring so much as a blink.

Just as suddenly the officer swung the sword away and pointed in the direction the patrol had been heading before the encounter. "Forward!" Jabbing his horse's flanks with the heels of his jackboots, he galloped away, his men following close behind.

Once they were out of sight beyond the next rise, all the others began chattering nervously and laughing among themselves. In seconds Mr. Warren flicked the reins and started the horses again.

Giggling, Leah and Rebecca moved aside and helped Jane and Ted brush off the piles of straw that clung to them.

"Whew!" Ted looked across to Dan, the fear in his eyes still apparent. "I thought for a moment we'd met our doom."

Unruffled, Jane smiled as she picked stubble out of her hair. "I wasn't worried in the least. Dan always knows just what to do. And if he doesn't, God tells him."

Dan felt his mouth drop open. Was this his sister talking?

A hearty laugh burst from John Warren's sparse frame. "'Out of the mouths of babes,' as they say." He squeezed his wife's shoulder playfully, then his deep voice boomed out in a joyful song. "Praise to the Lord, the Almighty, the King of creation! O my soul, praise Him, for He is thy health and salvation!"

The others joined in on the next line, and the hymn rang through the winter-barren glen as the horses plodded steadily along the road.

Ted, who hadn't resumed singing as yet, exchanged a concerned look with Dan. From his brother-in-law's meaningful glance, Dan determined that they alone understood the grim severity of the situation. None of the families with whom they were traveling resided in Boston, where animosity between the townsmen and the soldiers was on the verge of exploding into violence. And Jane, poor dear, was obviously adrift on the sea of romance and not about to spoil her fantasies with anything as depressing as reality.

Well, Dan thought, settling back against the side of the wagon, *at least Susannah and Miles should now be safely on their way to Rhode Island.* On his parents' horse farm, they'd be amply cared for.

Or would they? Dan shifted on the hard surface of a trunk. The last time Susannah had been at the farm, his mother had blamed her for everything that went wrong—things Susannah didn't even know were happening. "Bad luck," Mother had called her. But Susannah had nothing to do with his baby sister, Emily, helping Robert MacKinnon escape from the authorities and becoming a fugitive with him. In fact, only weeks ago Mother had finally come to her senses and written, making peace with Susannah. He prayed fervently that when his wife passed on the news that Jane, too, was now wanted by the Crown, Mother would not revoke Susannah's welcome.

Had Mother's change of heart been as complete as Jane's? He prayed so. Dan closed his eyes, envisioning his mother taking Susannah in and smothering her and little Miles with all the love and affection she possessed. He smiled to himself.

Susannah put a wrapped bundle of table linens in the wagon Ben had hired and turned back toward the kitchen for the pile of blankets. Ben and Mr. Harris, the jovial man from next door, came out toting a chest of dishes. Thoughts of Dan still pressed agonizingly on her heart. Despite her conviction that God would take care of him, she ached to feel his embrace and know he was near. Safe.

Veering to the corner of the house, she cast a wary glance toward the front, where a red-uniformed man stood at the front gate. The moment Ben had driven the rig up to the back door, barely an hour ago, the second guard had hurried away and had yet to return. Had he reported her imminent departure?

Entering the house again, Susannah went down the hall to the front window and peered between the lace panels as she had done a dozen times already.

This time, to her dismay, Alex Fontaine strode purposefully up the walk. He yanked off his gloves and slapped them against his leg as he neared.

Susannah's heart plummeted. Breathlessly she waited for his knock. And even though she'd expected it, his determined pounding unnerved her. With a fortifying breath, she patted her hair into place in a calming pause. She shot the bolt back and unlatched the door. "Good day, Lieutenant."

He did not return her strained smile. "Madam."

"Won't you come in?" Knowing he would anyway, Susannah stepped aside.

Surprisingly, he remained where he was. "No. That will not be necessary." He cast a confident glance toward the sentries, where the second had come back and resumed his post.

The back door closed just then, and Susannah heard Ben and Mr. Harris as they walked through the kitchen and into the hall. She drew what little strength she could from having them there. It wilted as Alex's feral smile curved a corner of his mouth.

"Ah, yes. Young Master Haynes. Or perhaps I should say young *Rebel* Haynes. From now on I'll be making a point of keeping a special eye on you, too, Mr. Postrider—who never seems to have the same route twice. Because of your sister, I've been lax with you. But no more."

Ben moved next to Susannah and put an arm around her

waist. "You needn't trouble yourself on my account. I've been transferred south. And I'll be escorting my sister-in-law as far as my parents' home."

"I think not," Alex stated flatly. "I would be most lonesome." He peered down his long straight nose at Susannah. "Most lonesome, indeed, if the mistress of this house were to leave me here alone in this hostile hovel of a town. She and I, you see, are going to become good friends. Quite good friends."

Ben tensed, and Susannah felt the hand at her waist bunch into a fist as he opened his mouth.

Fearing the hotheaded young man would infuriate Alex even more, she sought his boot with her foot and ground her heel into his toe.

With a sharp intake of breath, he held himself in check.

The lieutenant swung his glare back to Ben. "So it would behoove you to empty that wagon and depart. Mistress Haynes will not be going anywhere."

As Alex turned and marched out to the street, Ben slammed the door with resounding force, then turned back to Susannah.

She clutched his coat sleeves with both hands and searched his face. "I'm to be kept prisoner? Here in Boston? Dan won't be able to come to me. I won't be able to go to him. This cannot be. It cannot."

Ben drew her close and wrapped his arms around her as he let out a frustrated breath. "Oh, don't you worry. I'll find a way to get you out of here somehow, even if I have to sneak you out in the middle of the night." He tightened the hug briefly, then released her.

"But Alex is eagerly waiting for any wrong move from you."

Mr. Harris stepped forward and shook his head ominously, his amiable face manifesting strain. "Son, it would be one thing if she was alone. But there's a wee babe to consider. We'd be putting the little tyke at risk, too."

"He's right," Susannah whispered. A cloud passed in front of the sun, darkening the thin sunlight and draining every last ray of hope from her.

Ben punched a fist into the doorjamb. "I hate this! I'd like to smear that highborn nose of his all over his face."

"I know you would," Susannah said soothingly as she took his hand and rubbed his purpling knuckles. "But that wouldn't change a thing except land you in jail. And I need you to be strong for me now . . . strong enough not to rashly lose your temper."

Ben sighed and gripped her hand between his two larger ones. "You're right. I guess the best thing for me to do is track Dan down and see what he wants done about this."

"Yes," she cried, grasping the tiny flicker of hope she saw in his light brown eyes. "Dan will know what to do. And you can find out if he's safe. I need to know that. But do be very careful. Alex is quite bitter over Jane. Quite vengeful. Heaven only knows what he might try."

Ben nodded and gave her another hug. Then stepping back, he flashed her a mischievous grin. "Tell you what. I'll do that if *you* post a letter to Mother telling her about all of this. I don't want to be within ten miles of her when she finds out that another of her daughters is on the run. I'd sooner face a whole regiment!"

6

Splitting off from the other families along the way, the War-ren wagon traveled on, across the gently rounded Green Mountains, then north to the small wilderness settlement of Bennington and the farm belonging to their oldest son, Charles.

As they approached, Dan studied the exterior of the small, two-story house of milled lumber and stone. He had seen nothing but log cabins for many miles. Unobtrusive, yet appealing and well kept, this dwelling had the appearance of having been built with great pride and care. Tidy shutters painted a rich dark green and a generous front porch reminded him of his parents' home. At the thought, he realized Susannah would soon be arriving at Haynes farm, if she hadn't already.

"Wonder if Charles will hear us comin'," John Warren mused aloud as he guided the rig toward the front yard.

The words had hardly left his mouth when the door burst open. "Pa! Ma!"

The younger Warrens gave a cry of excitement and sprang to their feet as their older brother leaped over the shallow porch steps in his shirtsleeves and charged toward them, his obviously expectant wife waddling more cautiously in his wake.

Dan watched all the Warren family scramble down from the

conveyance to a bevy of hugs and kisses and exuberant claps on the back, and then John Warren walked his way.

"We brought a few extras with us. Come and meet 'em, Charlie. You, too, Beth."

Dan and Ted hopped out, then Ted reached up for Jane and swung her down as the Warrens closed around them.

Mr. Warren gestured toward the threesome. "This here's Reverend Daniel Haynes, and with him are the newlyweds, Ted and Jane Harrington."

Charles, thin as a rake like his father and with the same prominent nose, grinned and stuck out a hand. "How do. This here's my wife, Beth," he added, wrapping a lanky arm proudly about her. "We're right glad to meet you. And glad you all made it through the mountains, from the look of that sky."

"Just what your ma and me was thinkin' the whole way," his father said. "Most likely the reverend's prayers held off all but a few flurries."

"You must be cold and hungry," Beth said shyly, a rosy glow on her cheeks as she tugged her shawl tighter around her ungainly body. "We'd best be gettin' in the house."

In the parlor end of an open common room, Dan relaxed in an upholstered chair near the fireplace, absorbing as much warmth as possible. Ted had volunteered to tend the horses, and Jane had accompanied him. Remembering the first sweet days of his and Susannah's life together, Dan knew it would take more than biting cold weather and leaden skies to dissuade the lovebirds from snatching time alone. His reflections were interrupted as the conversation between Mr. Warren and his eldest son drifted to his ears.

"Yep," the older man was saying, "even from as far up as Maine they went, just to gather in Boston. If it wasn't that I was so busy tryin' to get ahead of my barrel orders to come here for Christmas, I'd have gone myself. Nobody was about to sit back and let Britain force a tea monopoly on us, not after all them other fast tricks she's pulled already."

Noah sat forward on a straight-backed chair, his youthful face alight, eager. "I hear tell upwards of a thousand men got together ever'day, demandin' that the king's lackey, Hutchinson, send them tea ships packin'." His smirk revealed his delight at being able to relate something significant to his older brother.

"So what happened, Pa?" Charles prompted, his gaze as intent as his posture. He didn't appear even to breathe while he waited in earnest to hear everything they had to say.

Dan had heard the story over and over already as the older man had related it to folks all along the way. He shifted his attention to the toasty warm farmhouse, fragrant with the scent of the Yule log. Everywhere colorful feminine touches made the plain dwelling homey and welcoming. And made him lonely.

A nagging question assaulted him again. Could these present circumstances be a result of his wanting to assert his own will over that of the Almighty? Hoping with all his heart that it was not so, he cast a prayer heavenward for forgiveness.

The back door opened, and Jane and Ted came inside on a blast of winter air. "Oh, it is heavenly warm in here," Jane said as they hung up their cloaks. She turned as two of the Warren girls carried in a plate of sliced bread and a bowl of pickles to the table. "May I help?"

"Always glad for another pair of hands," one of them said, motioning with an elbow toward the kitchen.

Jane's nose and cheeks glowed from the cold, making her appear not much older than Rebecca, Dan thought. And the tender glances Ted cast after her made him recall the anxiety in Susannah's eyes when he'd left.

"Say, Ted," Charles called out. "No need to get in the way of the gals. Come over and join us. I wanted to ask you somethin' anyways."

With a nod, Ted strode to the last available chair and sat

down, casting a glance toward the door that now cut him off from Jane. "And what is that, pray tell?"

"Well, it's like this. Since Pa says you was once in on all the British doings, I figure you oughta know what the Crown might do to us all, after that tea dumpin'."

Ted cocked his head thoughtfully toward the other young man. "I'm afraid I wasn't informed of all the latest plans, but I'm quite aware that both the king and Parliament have grown increasingly impatient since the burning of the *Gaspee*. Efforts to find and arrest the perpetrators of the incident have been thwarted at every turn."

"Have they ever!" Noah piped in exuberantly with a grin at his brother. "And we're gonna keep right on thwartin' 'em, too. Right, Charlie?"

Charles shot a playful frown at the kitchen door. "Keep it down. You know that kind of talk sets Ma to worryin'." He switched his attention back to Ted. "So you don't have any idea what may happen?"

Ted's eyes followed Jane as she brought something to the table. He shrugged. "I would say, given the added embarrassment of the event at Griffin's Wharf, the port will suffer a blockade. The Crown will try to starve Boston into submission. At the very least."

"That's what I figured." Charles' mouth tightened, and he whacked his knee with a work-roughened hand. "Too bad folks along the seaboard have gotten so soft with their easy livin'."

"Here in the Green Mountains," Noah boasted, "they don't show their backsides to nobody, eh, Charlie?"

"That's right," Charles admitted with a determined grin. "We sure did get our point across to them judges from New York when they tried to come in here and get us to pay for our own land all over again or get out. Just because some bigwig from London decides the New Hampshire grants aren't valid no more and that this land belongs to New York now, don't make it so. We're the ones who paid for it. Broke our backs clearin' it. It's ours, and none of them simperin' Yorker settlers is comin' in here wavin' a piece of paper sayin' any different."

"Now, Charlie," his mother said, leaning her head in from the kitchen. "From what I hear about that hothead, Ethan Allen, he just might get all you Green Mountain Boys arrested. New York has a price on that one's head."

Noah puffed out his chest. "It'll take a far sight more 'n anything they've done yet to put a ring in Ethan's nose, Ma."

She cleared her throat with a significant stare at Dan. "Maybe the good reverend should explain to you boys how folks should respect authority. There are peaceable ways to do things, too, remember." Smiling, she disappeared back into the kitchen.

Charles sent a wry glance to the others. "And wouldn't we all relish using peaceable means if they accomplished anything."

John Warren chuckled. "Always spoke her mind, that one. Guess there's no stoppin' it now."

"Aw, Pa," Noah moaned. "You'd think she'd be on our side."

"'Specially since John Junior died helpin' me clear this place," Charles added. "If my own brother gave his life for this land, how can I do less?"

The younger lad grimaced. "Ma thinks it's God's will when a tree falls on somebody and kills him. But she says runnin' off the Yorkers is baitin' the law on purpose, and that's temptin' the Lord. Don't that beat all?" He grinned at his father. "Pa, can I stay here an' help out? I've been practicin' loadin' and firin' your old Dutch musket, and I'm gettin' better every day."

Carrying a bowl of steaming potatoes to the table, Beth aimed a reprimanding look at Charles.

Guilt flamed his face.

Dan felt heat rise upward from his own neckband and knew he should say something to lessen the youth's passion. "You, er, could strive to find some amiable way to resolve the differences which now exist between you and New York. The constant use of force surely causes more harm than good in the end."

Charles set his jaw and looked from Dan to Beth. "Took me near two years of breakin' my back to make this a fit place to bring a wife. I'm not about to give up the future I carved outta this land for us and our child soon to be born, just because some uppity official across the ocean made a stroke of the quill on some fool paper. But that don't mean I plan to involve any of my other brothers in my own fight." Watching his wife retreat in apparent satisfaction, he went on. "No more than a handful of them bigwigs has even set foot on this land. No new line that Parliament draws on a map means spit to me or any of the rest of us. Fact is, we're thinkin' of declarin' this territory here its own colony. How does *Vermont* sound? Means green mountain in French, so I'm told."

"Gentlemen." Placing a platter of meat on the table, Eliza Warren rested a hand on her wide hip and glared at the lot of them, her husband in particular. "On Christmas Eve, our thoughts should be on the wonderful gift our heavenly Father sent us. Don't you agree, Pastor Haynes?" She shifted her gaze to him as if he should have redirected the conversation long ago. "We are truly pleased to have you under our roof in this wilderness where there's no church within easy distance for Christmas vespers. I'm lookin' forward to some appropriate words on this season of peace once dinner is over. But for now, we'd be honored if you'd bless this special meal. Girls. Come in here for grace."

Dan rose with the others in the parlor and walked toward the small table.

As the girls came in from the kitchen, Jane linked her arm in Ted's.

"Almighty God," Dan began, "we thank thee so much for this gracious family and the home that has been opened to us. We humbly ask thy blessing upon all who dwell here. I ask also for thy protection on those loved ones who cannot be with us. May Susannah and our son be even now enjoying a feast as bountiful as the one provided here on this Christmas Eve.

Look after my friend Yancy Curtis, and show all of us some peaceful way to solve the growing dilemma that surrounds us. We ask this in the name of thy Son. Amen."

Dan saw Noah nudge Charles and make a snide face. *Peaceful way,* he mouthed.

As the men stepped to the table, Eliza Warren put an arm around her daughter-in-law. "This poor table weren't made for such a descendin' horde. Us womenfolk will eat in the kitchen. If you need somethin', give a holler."

Ted gave Jane a reluctant kiss on the cheek and kept his eyes fastened on her until she was out of sight.

"Sit down, Ted." Dan pulled out a chair and sank onto it, wondering if he had looked that lovesick in his early days with Susannah. Then, recalling the perpetual sappy grin on the face of that crochety old innkeeper, Jasper Lyons, he decided it must be a universal symptom. Dan quickly added a silent prayer of blessing for the Lyons, as well as his youngest sister, Emily, her husband, Robert, and their baby daughter, who now resided with them in faraway Princeton, safe from the wrath of the British navy.

"Fine, lofty-soundin' prayer," John Warren said. "But it appears to me those scoundrels in London have far more on their minds than any peaceful dealin's with us. You know as well as the rest of us that they don't listen to one thing we colonists have to say. Never have, never will."

"John," Eliza called impatiently from the next room.

He shifted on the hard chair.

"Do be sure the *reverend* samples some of my special Christmas bread," she added in a more pleasant tone.

The man rolled his eyes but complied by passing the plate of golden brown bread Dan's way.

Braided so perfectly, the holiday bread resembled one Susannah might bake. The memory made Dan's throat tighten.

A knock sounded on the door.

"Who could that be on Christmas Eve?" Charles put his napkin aside and rose.

Dan and Ted exchanged nervous glances, then Dan looked beyond their host to a figure in the shadows. For an instant the lanky caller in the tricornered hat resembled his brother, Ben. Dan dismissed the notion as quickly as it came.

But the voice that spoke was unmistakably Ben's. "Is this the house of Charles Warren?"

Dan jumped up and rushed to the door with Ted at his heels. "How on earth did you get here?" Dan asked.

"Let me in, and I'll tell you!"

Even before his brother finished stomping the freshly fallen snow off his boots, Dan grabbed him in a bear hug. When they drew apart, Ted did the same.

"Who is at the door, dear?" Beth Warren asked from the kitchen portal.

Jane let out a squeal and, pushing past the others, ran straight for her brother.

Square-faced, his cheeks red from the cold, he grinned and grabbed her in a powerful embrace, then held her at arm's length. "What's this I hear about you? Sean Burns in Cambridge says you finally managed to snag Ted. What took you so long?"

Jane jammed her hands on her hips. "Finally?"

Reaching around her, Ben gave Ted's hand a hearty shake. "Congratulations . . . or should I offer my condolences?"

Anxious to know why his brother had come, Dan interrupted. "Time for all this later. Tell us how you found out where we were."

"From Clark Bender. He came by with your message."

"Oh, good. Then you got it." Relieved, Dan ran a hand through his hair. "But you should have accompanied Susannah and the baby to Rhode Island before traipsing after us."

Eliza stepped forward. "Let the poor dear man warm up before you question him to death. An' from the look of you," she said, switching her attention to the gangly newcomer, "you could use this feast more than the rest of us."

Ben flashed a disarmingly charming grin while Dan struggled to keep the still-unasked questions about his family at bay.

"Leah, dear," Mrs. Warren called out, "set another place. Rebecca, fetch him a chair. Noah, see to his horse. Looks like it started snowing out."

Flexing and unflexing his hands, Dan began pacing while Ben was seated and served. By the time his younger brother had taken his second bite, Dan was ready to explode. He stopped and faced his brother. "Ben. Why didn't you go with Susannah?"

He took a sip of hot cider, then set down the cup. "She didn't go. Couldn't. Lieutenant Fontaine wouldn't allow it."

"What?" The word came out as a near croak. Dan felt as though someone had punched him in the gut.

Ted jumped to his feet. "How dare he interfere!"

At last finding his voice, Dan slammed a fist into his open palm as fury raged through him. "I can't believe this." Stalking halfway to the fireplace, he swung back around and rubbed a hand over his face. "So help me, if that cur so much as laid one finger on her, I'll—"

"Calm down," Ben said. "She's unharmed."

Dan took a huge gulp of air, then released it. Then he looked desperately at Ben. "I want to know exactly what Fontaine said. Every word."

"Just that she's not to leave the city. He's using her for bait. He's positive you'll return sooner or later, so he has guards posted day and night to catch you."

Anger charged Dan's blood with molten heat. "And you left her there to fend for herself? How could you do such a thing?"

"I left her in the care of your congregation," Ben said evenly, his dark brows elevated.

"I am to blame for this," Ted said, reaching out to Dan. "I've brought this trouble down on you and Sue. I shall go back at once and turn myself in. I'll inform them that neither of you had anything whatsoever to do with my desertion."

"No." Dan shook his head. "What's done is done. We cannot undo it. And Ben is right. The good people of Long Lane

Church will be more than happy to look after Susannah until we get you and Jane out of harm's way. And, God willing, Fontaine will allow Susannah to leave soon."

"I'm not so sure of that," Ted admitted. "Alex can be quite relentless when he feels he's been wronged."

"I agree with Ted," Ben said. "I never saw that redcoat so livid. He was arrogant, downright vengeful. I say we raise an army of our own and storm the Neck. Rescue Susannah, just like we took care of that devil tea ship."

Noah, just back from taking care of Ben's pacer, swaggered confidently toward the table. "We'll get the Green Mountain Boys and the Sons of Liberty to join us. We'll show those lobsterbacks."

"Splendid! And don't forget the boys down on the rope walks," Ben added with an enthusiastic grin. "I'm sure they'd be more than happy to bust a few heads."

"Wait one minute." Dan raised a calming hand. "My first concern is the safety of my wife and child. I would not put them in the middle of a violent brawl, which is what this sort of thing could quickly turn into. Now that I've had a moment to regain myself, I'm positive this is not the time to do something rash. First and foremost, we must pray for the Lord's leading. He knows far better than we the wisest recourse for us all to take."

"Pray?" Ben asked, astonished. "That's all? Pray and wait?" He let out a disgusted huff. "It's time you started acting like a man again, big brother. Because I'm going back for her . . . with or without you."

The dismal hue of the heavy clouds matched Susannah's mood as she stared out through the parted kitchen curtains. Would there never be sunshine again? Or a clear blue sky—even today, Christmas Eve? Eight endless days of threatening storms, of sleet and cold, were wearing on a body, and she longed to see an end to them—however temporary the respite might be.

The draft from the unheated front rooms and hallway stirred the blanket Susannah had tacked up to keep the kitchen warmth in place. She gazed despairingly at the dwindling wood supply out in the woodshed. It could not last much longer, nor could it be replaced without a man in the house. That thought made her even gloomier. For a fleeting second she considered taking the axe out to one of the guards and suggesting he make himself useful, but she knew that wouldn't do. She wondered how much effort it would take to try the task herself.

Miles babbled away as he sat on a quilt, playing with some toys Dan had carved for his son's first Christmas a year ago. Susannah remembered how lovingly her husband had toiled to fashion and paint each one just so and how proud he'd been of his efforts. The memory brought a wistful smile to Susannah's lips.

Crossing to the hutch, she took down a china cup and saucer and its matching floral teapot. She could still envision the way Dan's sable eyes had danced as she had removed the Christmas wrapping and discovered the exquisite tea set—the very one she had admired one day when they had been passing a shop window. "You'll soon be the wife of an ordained minister," he had said. "You'll be called upon now and then to serve generous portions of tea as well as sympathy in the parlor of our parish house." She had laughed even while fighting back the tears the lovely gift had stirred.

Susannah sighed and measured tea into the pot, then added boiling water from the kettle. Cooking a big meal for the holiday seemed so pointless without Dan that she hadn't bothered to make the effort. Instead she sliced some bread for herself and spread it with butter and jam. "I'm the one who could use a generous portion of sympathy at the moment," she muttered as she sank onto a chair and took a bite.

"Mama?" The baby looked up as if she'd spoken to him. Clutching a toy cart in his chubby hand, he slowly got to his feet and toddled over to her. He held the plaything out.

"Why, thank you, sweetheart," she crooned with forced enthusiasm. "What a lovely gift." Laying aside her bread, she drew him into her arms and got up. "I have something for you, too." From a pottery jar on a shelf near the window she took a cookie and handed it to him. She couldn't bear the thought of giving him his actual Christmas gifts without Dan there to share the joy of watching him open them.

Outside, the first feathery snowflakes of a new storm fluttered to earth.

She pushed the curtain aside and pointed at them. "Look, sweetheart, God has given us a gift, too. Wasn't that lovely of him?"

The child's eyes lit up, flooding Susannah with inspiration. She grabbed his warm coat and cap from where they hung and bundled him up, then threw her own cloak around herself and took him out the back door.

Miles gasped at the first bite of winter's blast, then laughed.

Susannah giggled. "We can taste the snow, sweetheart.

Watch." Raising her head, she stuck out her tongue and caught a fat flake. "Mm. Cold. You try it."

A snowflake landed on his moist, pink tongue. The sugar cookie was forgotten as it dropped from his grasp. "Mm," he mimicked.

The oppressive cares lifted momentarily from her heart as Susannah laughed and danced with her son in the falling snow. He laughed, too, harder than ever before as she whirled him through the sparkling flakes.

"There you are," said a man coming around the corner of the house.

Startled into silence, Susannah stopped. Her heart throbbed against her chest as she turned, expecting to see a red uniform. But a friendly smile met her gaze. "M-Mr. Calloway," she said, flustered at having a church elder catch her acting in such foolishness.

He smiled as if nothing at all were amiss, snowflakes speckling his curly brown beard. "We knocked, but you didn't answer the door. Then we heard you back here."

"We?" How many others had heard her childish display?

He nodded. "Since it's Christmas Eve and all, some of us thought you might want a little company. Hope you don't mind that we just popped in on you."

Susannah cast a despairing look down over her dull olive housedress and smudged apron, both of which she'd worn yesterday as well. She was also more than aware that Miles had tugged some strands of her hair free and could only imagine how disheveled her chignon must be. Instinctively she reached up to explore it with her fingers. Then, taking in Mr. Calloway's Sunday suit and impeccable appearance, she self-consciously brushed snowflakes from the baby's knit cap. At her feet lay the half-eaten cookie, which brought the grim realization that she had almost no food in the house. "Um, just how many people have come with you?"

"Most everybody from church, is all," he said cheerfully. "Why don't we go inside?"

❦ ❦

Susannah sat with the baby on the floor of the parlor, basking in the warmth of the crackling fire and the wonderful fellowship while her son was engrossed in one of several new playthings. Not only had the thoughtful elders brought a cartload of wood along with them, but also the good women of the church had come bearing an abundance of baked goods, dried nuts, and smoked meats. They'd also brought fresh-cut holly, braided with bright red ribbons, to decorate the mantel and staircase railing. Platters of holiday treats and goodies were now sitting here and there, still only half empty after everyone had eaten his fill.

The world didn't seem such a lonely, empty place after all when so many dear people truly cared about her. She gazed around at the three dozen or more smiling faces of parishioners occupying every chair in the house or standing in clusters wherever an empty space still remained in the crowded room. Even the presence of the king's men at the end of her walk no longer seemed so threatening. In fact, it would all be so perfect, if only Dan were there with her.

As Elder Calloway rose to his feet, she tossed off the sad thought and gave him her full attention.

"I think another carol would be in order," he quipped. "And to finish the evening, Mistress Shaw has graciously offered to give a dramatic reading of the Christmas story." He paused, then broke into the opening words of "Hark, the Herald Angels Sing."

Everyone joined in, including Miles, whose off-key babble continued even after the conclusion of the last verse. The sweet sounds sent the group into peals of good-natured laughter.

As the precious story of God's gift to the world was recounted by the older woman, Susannah's heart swelled. Had it been only a few short years since the wonders of salvation had finally dawned within her during a message preached by the late evangelist George Whitefield? She still remembered that mercurial day, the incredible peace and joy that burst forth in her when she truly understood that Jesus was God's precious gift to her, given freely, generously. No longer was she shackled and burdened by her misconception that she must earn his favor by performing an endless string of good deeds. She was simply called to repent and accept him.

As the reader's voice died away, Susannah rose and looked at the dear faces all about her. "I cannot begin to tell you all how much your coming here has meant to us. I thought Christmas was going to be quite cold and empty this year, but you've made this a wonderful family time, my sweet church family. I thank you from the depths of my heart for the food, the wood, the toys for the baby. But most of all for your love and kindness. I shall never forget this night. Daniel would be so pleased." Her throat tightened, and she swallowed. "May God bless you all."

Mistress Brown, the midwife who had attended Susannah during Miles' birth, stood, her plump face beaming. "The good Lord knows what he's doin', missy. He's never one to desert one of his own."

Susannah blinked back threatening tears. "I keep reminding myself of that, especially with the soldiers hovering about day and night as a constant reminder of Dan's present danger."

"Oh, I wouldn't be worryin' about them," Mr. Calloway said encouragingly as he stroked his dark curly beard. "Long as the people of Massachusetts Colony stick together, there's not too awfully much those lobsterbacks can enforce." He started to turn away, then swung back. "Oh, I nearly forgot. Mr. Green has had word of Seaman Curtis." He nodded toward Elder Green, a baker from down at the wharves, where ships secured their bread before setting sail.

"Truly?" Susannah's spirits rose at the mention of Dan's dear friend. Yancy Curtis, the sailor and sometime smuggler, whom many considered quite rough around the edges, had been the first person to welcome her to the Colonies upon her arrival from England. And after Jane and Ted had helped him to escape capture, he had sailed off into the dark night on a pilot boat, and there had been no further word of him.

The baker stepped to the window and moved a heavy drape aside, then faced Susannah. "One of the harbor pilots came by my shop and told me he took a very out-of-breath Yancy aboard the night of the Tea Party. Got him on the coastal packet he was guiding out to sea. It was headed south, making stops all the way to Georgia. No tellin' where our young smuggler will hop ship. My guess would be Philadelphia or someplace south of there. From what I hear, that curly red mop of his is gettin' too well-known betwixt here and there."

"That's for certain," another elder chimed in with a chuckle. "Always been too free in his ways for his own good, that one."

"I happened across a warrant for Seaman Curtis's arrest," a third gentleman said, "nailed to the front of the Customs House for every ship's captain to see. There's a twenty-pound reward, no less."

The initial joy Susannah had felt upon hearing of Yancy's escape now dimmed. Because cash money was hard to come by in the Colonies, twenty pounds would be a very tempting sum to many. "Perhaps you might lead us in a prayer, Elder Calloway, for Mr. Curtis's safety."

"And don't stop there," Midwife Brown added. "He needs more than his salvation in *this* life. That boy needs to do some serious considerin' about the afterlife, too. The way he carries on in the taverns. Such sinfulness. Such sinfulness." She wagged her head.

The other ladies, their expressions solemn, nodded in agreement.

8

Jostling along in an open oxcart, his legs dangling from the back, Yancy watched the rolling, snow-patched Virginia farmscape pass by. Some scraggly cornstalks were still standing here and there, stiff and dead, their dried and curled leaves rattling with every gust of wind. The tobacco crops had mostly been plowed under, but occasionally along the edge of a field, evidence of the major cash crop still lingered, with clumps of the brownish red leaves rotting in soggy masses amid mounds of snow.

"Whereabouts did you say you were from, lad?"

Yancy swiveled toward the front, where Mr. Downs, a stocky farmer in heavy woolen clothes, sat beside his slave. They had picked Yancy up some hours ago along the Three Notched Road that ran north from Richmond all the way to the Shenandoah Valley. "I move around."

"Oh. Reckoned you weren't from these parts, or you'd be sportin' better boots than you got on," he said. "We get lots of wet and cold weather here."

Ignoring the chuckle that rumbled out as the man turned and faced forward, Yancy glared. He hadn't exactly expected to end up in the hills of Virginia, of all places, but the home port of the packet he'd grabbed in Boston turned out to be Yorktown, and with Christmas so near, it had sailed straight through so the crew could spend the holidays with their families.

By chance, Yancy had come across Dr. Corbin Griffin in one of the Yorktown mughouses, a kindly medical man who had an office on Main Street. Yancy had taken an instant liking to the good doctor when he had been so vocal about what would befall any tea ship that dared try to unload in Virginia. He said he personally would see to it that the cargo was dumped overboard.

The man generously took Yancy in on Christmas, providing the sailor with a temporary haven from the authorities. An ardent patriot, Dr. Griffin had visited with several other local sympathizers on Christmas Day until he managed to find one who had family visitors traveling inland to Richmond the following morning. Hearing that Yancy was a friend of Boston's Sam Adams, many of whose fiery letters had been published in their paper, they were more than willing to take him along.

So the day after Christmas, Yancy had coasted along for a few days in a fine coach with a benevolent family by the name of Hazelton, who not only gave him transport but also supplied him with an extra set of warm clothes and a few other necessities. Yancy just wished someone in the family had had larger feet and could have given him a pair of more suitable boots as well. Already his light, loose-topped seafaring boots were much the worse for wear after all he'd been through.

As they came to a fork in the road, the cart veered off onto a narrow track.

"Guess you'd better hop off here, young man," the farmer said. "Charlottesville's just up ahead. No more than five or six miles." He nodded, and his dark-skinned Negro slave, Jonas, halted the oxen.

Yancy gathered the bundle of his new possessions and jumped down. "Thank ye kindly. Happy New Year to ye both."

The cart rolled away, leaving only the sound of the wind whistling over stone walls and through the winter-stripped trees along the road.

Yancy drew a deep breath and exhaled. Glancing into the distance, he beheld what the farmer had called the Blue

Ridge Mountains. Quite a contrast from the flat coastal plains he was accustomed to. Many miles now stretched between him and the sea, and this depressing reality settled over him with finality. He only hoped it wouldn't be long before he could safely return and seek another berth aboard ship. It would take some time to become accustomed to being a landlubber.

Still, Yancy couldn't help but admire the setting. Farms large and small spread out in the valley behind him on the gently rolling land. He could imagine what it must look like in summer, planted with corn and barley, rye and tobacco. Shoving his hands into the pockets of his coat, he started trudging toward the next rise on Three Notched Road.

Ahead, he saw two Negroes herding some milk cows back to the barn. Black faces were a common sight here in the South, where, according to what he'd heard, the population numbered more slaves than freemen. Not wanting to be caught staring, he continued on his way.

The road curved as Yancy crested the small hill, but to his dismay the contour of the land barely leveled out before sloping upward again. He rolled his eyes and looked back over his shoulder, hoping for the welcome sight of another wagon, but the road was empty.

Coming at last to the top, he spotted a canvas-topped wagon in a dip in the road below. An older man of medium height and build was staring hopelessly at a broken wheel that jutted out at a rakish angle from the rig. A few feet from him, her fists planted on her hips, stood a comely dark-haired wench. Her irritated voice echoed off every tree and boulder in the hollow.

A slow smile tugged at Yancy's mouth. *Ah,* he thought, *who could resist such a fiery spirit?* He'd offer assistance, then gratefully accept a ride . . . and if he were very lucky, perhaps he'd be seated next to the beauty, who even from a distance made a glorious splash of color against the gray wintry landscape.

"Ahoy, down there!" he called with a jaunty wave. "Could ye use a helpin' hand?"

❦ ❦

Balancing a spare wheel upright, the older man turned his head in Yancy's direction, and a wave of elation softened his roundish face. "The Lord be praised! I'd be most grateful, young man."

The fetching lass did not seem at all ashamed of having had a stranger overhear her disrespectful tone of voice. Taking a step backward, she raised her chin and boldly met Yancy's gaze as he neared the wagon and the team of draft horses.

In that second, he noted that she seemed smaller up close, a full head shorter than he, with an oval face, dark brown eyes, and full, pouty lips. Within the shelter of her fur-lined hood, a strand of rich brown hair that had worked its way loose tossed back a spark of the bright sunlight. She folded her arms.

"You're a true answer to prayer, lad," the gentleman said as he rested the new wheel against the off-kilter wagon. He wiped his hands on a kerchief from the pocket of his fine wool frock coat, then clasped Yancy's hand in warm welcome. "Blair's the name. Marcus Blair. And this is my daughter, Felicia. You couldn't have happened by at a more opportune time, I must say." His generous mouth spread into a wide smile, adding laugh lines to the other creases in his face. Scraggly graying brows winged upward above his faded blue eyes.

Flicking a glance toward the lass, Yancy masked the delight coursing through him that she was not the old man's wife. *That might have tangled things up,* he thought as he took Blair's proffered hand. Yancy couldn't help but notice how soft and uncalloused the older man's palm felt in his own firm grip. *Obviously not one accustomed to physical toil,* he decided. And fairly confident he was far enough inland to be honest, he saw no need for pretense. "Glad to meet ye both, Mr. Blair. Miss. Me name's Curtis. Yancy Curtis."

She gave him a curt nod but didn't speak, and her posture remained rigid.

Ah, a cool one, he told himself and purposely flashed his most charming and irresistible smile. When it was met with pursed lips and a look of disdain, he knew he had his work cut out for him. He cleared his throat and diverted his attention to her father. "What might I do to help ye?"

Mr. Blair sheepishly shifted his stance. "I hate to admit it, actually, but you see . . . I, er, haven't as yet had many occasions to gain experience in replacing wheels."

"He means he's had none," Felicia retorted in a flat tone.

Her father nodded. "We're city folk, you see. Or, I should say, were. Until recently."

"And shall be again," she said with steely determination.

From the way the older man exhaled wearily, Yancy surmised the reason for the heated disagreement he'd stumbled upon. But then, one never knew exactly how little details like this might turn in his favor. He removed his newly acquired three-cornered hat and raked his fingers through his hair before blotting his forehead against his sleeve and replacing the hat. Cool temperature or not, there was enough heat in the tension between Mr. Blair and his spirited Felicia to cause a quick thaw.

Spirited Felicia . . . Yancy liked the sound of that. "Can't say as I've had much practice fixin' wagons either, seein's how the sea's been me life up till now. But I'd heard enough yarns about the mountains, how they were even wilder and more beautiful than the ocean." He slid his gaze to the lass. "I decided to come see for meself."

The sound that issued from Felicia was tinged with incredulity.

Yancy chose to translate it into a simple clearing of the throat and paid it no mind even as she turned away and shook her head. "Have ye a jack handy?" he asked her father.

The man reddened. "Sorry to say, it appears that one was not included when I purchased the wagon."

"Nor was any good sense," Felicia muttered.

This lass was a gale in the making, blowing herself up to a full nor'easter. As Yancy shot a glance her way, he was amazed that her dark tresses weren't billowing wildly about her, nor the ground beneath them rocking like a stormy sea. He reined in his thoughts. "Ah, well. 'Tis lucky for you, Mr. Blair, that I'd set a westerly course. I'll put me back to it and be your jack." Checking the interior of the rig, he discovered that besides a rather elegant bedstead stacked against one side— which Little Miss Priss would truly grace most enchantingly— it contained only trunks, foodstuffs, and basic necessities. It wouldn't be so heavy that they would have to unload everything. He put his shoulder to the side and began leaning into it as Mr. Blair retrieved a large wrench from a toolbox beneath the seat. "Have ye not loosened the lug yet?"

"Why, no. The thought hadn't occurred to me. I suppose I should do that first, shouldn't I?"

"Makes it easier. Here, let me." Taking the tool, Yancy relished the opportunity to show off his muscles. Though the wheel nut was quite tightly in place, he swiftly wrenched it loose and unscrewed the grimy part. For only the briefest second did he feel tempted to toss it to Felicia, but he knew it wouldn't further his cause if he messed up her expensive kid gloves . . . even if it would take her down a peg. He dropped the thing onto a snow-covered grassy mound, then positioned himself under the wagon again. "Soon as I have the wheel off the ground, sir, pull it off and shove the spare one onto the axle."

One of the horses nickered and took a step or two, dragging the crippled rig along.

Yancy jumped out of the way just in time. "I see ye haven't set the brake yet, either."

"Do forgive me, young man." Mr. Blair scrambled to pull the brake on. "I'm terribly sorry. I thought it couldn't go anywhere with the wheel broken and all."

Felicia tapped the toe of her suede boot in exasperation. "Fuss and bother! Do you see now, Papa? We've no more business riding off into the frontier than—than—" She released a pent-up breath at Yancy. "Nothing I've said for the past month has made the slightest difference. It'll take him getting somebody killed before he regains his senses. I just know it."

"Now, Leece," Mr. Blair said soothingly as he went back to his task, "I know you're more than upset that we left behind the life we knew in Williamsburg. But in time you'll come to view this as the great adventure I do. Ready, Mr. Curtis?"

Yancy filled his lungs and put his back into lifting the wagon. As it cut into his shoulder, he realized it was far heavier than it appeared. Straining against the weight, he squinted up at Felicia Blair as she rolled the spare wheel toward them— one, Yancy noticed, that had several missing spokes.

Putting that thought aside, he let himself drink in the grace of her movements. With her chin at that haughty angle, she put him in mind of Jane Haynes, whose spirit he had truly enjoyed challenging. Such a pity that things hadn't worked out with that little spitfire. But maybe he'd fare better with this one.

Whatever small discomfort this hard task caused him, it would be worth all of it and more if the distressed lass would, in turn, seek solace in his arms. He'd make it his quest to lure her there. "Mr. Blair? I'd be much obliged if ye'd let me ride along with you a ways. Seems we're both headin' in the same direction . . . toward a great adventure."

Dusk tinted the sky with the first streaks of mauve and violet as Yancy guided the double team the few remaining miles to the village of Charlottesville. It had been more than obvious that Mr. Blair was used to having slaves do all his driving for him, since he had proven himself less than adept at it. As Yancy offered to take over, he could understand some of Felicia's anger. She did have cause to feel more than a little insecure traveling with her father. An ill-equipped wagon, no servants to take up the slack. It all seemed quite odd, yet very fortuitous for him. And despite the fact that the bulk of his own life had been spent at sea, he'd done some pretty fancy teamstering during his smuggling days.

The wagon hit a rut, bumping Felicia into Yancy before it lurched back onto better ground.

He smiled to himself that she couldn't inch any farther away on the crowded seat. He knew she was aware of him as well. She expended a great deal of effort to remain aloof and to keep her legs angled toward her father as she sat ramrod straight and stared directly ahead. To keep himself from laughing aloud, he began whistling under his breath.

A few moments later he raked his glance ever so casually past her to her father, who was absorbed in reading a big black Bible. "If ye don't mind me interruptin', Mr. Blair, ye said ye hailed from Williamsburg. What sort of business are ye in?"

Light blue eyes peered over the gold reading glasses perched on his nose. "I was a druggist for many, many years. But now I've had a higher calling."

Felicia closed her eyes and expelled a harsh breath.

Blast. He'd touched on another sore subject. But it was too late now. He might as well learn all he could. "By higher calling, do ye mean an exploration of the mountains?" he asked, waiting for the next storm that would flash in Felicia's dark eyes.

The older man gazed off to the snow-covered Blue Ridge range. "Why, I hadn't considered that added blessing! Now that you mention it, they are most wonderful to feast one's vision upon, are they not? But to answer your question, lad, my calling is to the souls who have ventured into that heathen wilderness before me. Souls teetering on the very brink of hell's fire for a lack of the Word of God. Satan is waiting to snatch them at every turn. If the settlers survive the chills and fevers, then a felled tree or a rattlesnake could be waiting—if an Indian doesn't scalp them first. I feel a tremendous urgency to go to them, to bring them salvation, before it's too late."

"Oh, I see. You're a minister. I have a friend, Daniel Haynes, who—"

"He most certainly is not a minister!" Felicia announced tacitly.

Yancy raised his brows at her haughtiness. Perhaps he'd been too optimistic about the wench. Her voice alone could turn these snow-packed hills to glaciers, trees and all.

"In one respect," Mr. Blair continued with overstated patience, "my daughter is correct. I have no papers of ordination. But if a sinner comes to believe in Jesus as Savior because of my humble words, that makes him no less cleansed, no less a miraculously changed child of God. Don't you agree, Mr. Curtis?"

Felicia's dark brown eyes shot icy shards his way, daring him, making him bolder. "I'm sure ye're right, sir. The summer before last, at the burnin' of the *Gaspee*—"

"*You* were at the burning of the *Gaspee?*" Her tone reeked of accusation.

Wanting to kick himself for that slip of the tongue, Yancy shifted on the seat and slapped the reins across the back of a lagging horse. "Well, maybe that isn't a good example. I've a better one that's more to the point. Two weeks ago, I witnessed an unbelievable miracle. A young lady of long acquaintance, by the name of Miss Jane Haynes, had strived her whole life for no greater purpose than to elevate her standin' in society. She was so determined in her goal that she refused the affections of any deserving colonist, preferrin' instead some vain aristocrat of a lobsterback." He slanted a knowing glance at Felicia.

She stiffened and elevated her chin as he continued.

"Nothin' I or anyone else in her family said to her made any impression whatsoever. She'd even gone so far as to betray her own sister, just to gain favor with the king's puppets—and also to betray me. I had washed me hands of her already, mind ye. But suddenly one night, out of a drizzlin' cold rain, she rode right into the teeth of the lion to save me. Said she'd repented of her *wicked ways*—" He cocked a vicious smile at the lass. "And now, hopefully, she's safe again in the bosom of her family."

"And exactly what crime had you committed, dare I ask,"

Felicia quipped, undaunted, "to send her to the authorities in the first place? The torching of the *Gaspee,* mayhap?"

The girl was like an English bulldog, Yancy thought. Once she got a hold of something, she never let go. Yet there did seem to be a vulnerable uncertainty behind her haughty airs. And awhile back, when she hadn't been aware of his perusal, he'd noticed that the corners of her lips curved upward when her mouth was relaxed, not down as they would if she were naturally mean-spirited. He'd find a way to sort her out.

"Sweetheart," her father said in a placating tone. "I do believe you've missed the lesson in Mr. Curtis's story. Redemption is waiting for everyone. And it can come to us from the least-expected quarter—even an itinerant preacher. Isn't that so, lad?"

The remark caught Yancy off balance. He'd only been trying to put the snooty young wench in her place. He hadn't realized the double meaning his words had taken. But who was he to argue? It might be to his advantage for the old gentleman to consider him above being the carouser his daughter suspected. Besides, he really had seen his share of miracles this past couple of years, hanging around the Haynes family. "Absolutely, sir."

Felicia perked up and pointed ahead of them. "Thank heavens. A town, at last. A warm fire." Removing a fold of her cloak that had fallen across Yancy's knee, she aimed a menacing glare up at him. "Perhaps even a hot bath. I feel particularly in need of one this day."

Seeing that her father's attention was centered forward, Yancy gave the wench a bawdy wink. Aye, but he did love a spirited filly!

As Yancy maneuvered the team along the main street of Charlottesville, a village nestled at the foot of the mountains, the rays of the setting sun silhouetted the contours of the range against a brilliant purple-and-rose sky. He watched in amusement as a handful of boisterous men carelessly crossed the thoroughfare. As if oblivious to the wintry cold, others stood on the boardwalks outside the ordinaries, tankards in hand. Obviously this was a town where the celebrations to welcome in the new year began early.

Beside him, Felicia clucked her tongue in disapproval. When a gangly youth walking alongside the wagon gawked openly at her, she tugged the hood of her cloak more snugly over her head so that it shielded her face.

"Excuse me, lad," Yancy said at the boy's crestfallen expression. "Might ye tell us where to find a coachin' inn?"

He tipped his hat and gestured farther down the street with his pewter mug. "Turn right at the end of the boardwalk. When you come to the courthouse square, Swan's Tavern is right there. Oh, an' tell them Billy Baker sent you. Ma'am, gentlemen." His stare did not waver until Felicia looked his way.

Marcus Blair gave a grateful nod. "Well, thank you, young man. May the Almighty's hand of blessing be upon you in the coming year, making it a prosperous and *sober* one."

Yancy caught the young fellow's smirk as his hazel eyes

rolled skyward, and he knew the words most likely carried no more weight with the lad than they would have with the other merrymakers. It was, after all, New Year's Eve. Surely the old man believed in welcoming it with enthusiasm.

When they reached the inn, Yancy noted that the sizable establishment allowed barely enough room for passengers to unload in front. He veered onto the shallow drive. "I'll let ye both off right at the door, then stable the team out back for ye."

Mr. Blair smiled approval as a young Negro boy hastened around the building. The wagon came to a stop, and the old man tossed two carpetbags out, then jumped down and helped his daughter.

Flicking the reins over the horses' backs, Yancy didn't miss the pointed stare the lass directed at him and took it as her warning not to make off with the rig and leave them stranded. As if he wanted to be tied down to an outfit, he thought, when it was so much simpler to be footloose and able to go wherever he fancied. After all, it wasn't as if he were a pauper. He had worked all his life and had his share of coin tucked here and there on his person.

After he'd tended the animals and gone inside the noisy common room, Yancy searched through the smoky haze for his two new companions. He caught the barest glimpse of Felicia's skirts as she headed up the stairs.

"Ah, there you are, Mr. Curtis," came her father's voice at his elbow. "My daughter and I will be taking supper in our rooms. You're welcome, of course, to join us if you wish and to share my bed. It's the least I can do to repay you for your assistance today."

Thinking of the promise of lively festivities downstairs, Yancy blurted the first thing that came to mind. "Thank ye, but another driver I met out in the stable is anxious to hear the latest about the tea business in Boston. Says he'll buy me supper in exchange."

"Oh, I see. Of course. By all means you must relate what you know of it. If you would like to continue on with us on the morn, we'll be leaving at first light."

"Much obliged." Watching the kindly gentleman turn for the stairs, a prick of guilt niggled the sailor for having lied to him. But this was one night of the year he looked forward to celebrating, and there was a crowd already gathering. Were he to be caught going to bed before midnight in one of the seaports, he'd be laughed off every wharf up and down the coast. Besides, he rationalized, it wasn't that much of a lie. Once he started entertaining folks here with tales of the Boston escapade, he wouldn't likely have to pay for food or drink the whole night long.

The touch of soft lips on his face drew Yancy out of his deep slumber. Ah, there was nothing as sweet as a woman's kiss, he assured himself groggily as the fuzzy image of dark-haired Felicia Blair taunted him. He grinned and reached out to gather her into his arms.

A large sloppy tongue licked his hand.

Yancy's eyes sprang open. In the dim predawn light filtering into the drafty stable, he made out a huge shaggy dog crouched beside him. He bolted upright, slamming his head into a crooked board that jutted out above him. With a groan, Yancy rubbed the sore spot, then his throbbing temples as the stable smells assaulted him with nauseating reality. He ran a hand down over his whole face and squinted, trying to clear his vision. Taking stock of the haphazard bed of blankets he'd strewn about the hay not so very long ago, the events of the night all came back to him. The Blairs! They'd be leaving first thing!

Staggering to his feet, he held his head in both hands and stumbled toward the door to check the sun's position. Why, oh, why, had he drunk so much rum?

The mangy canine nearly upset his precarious balance as it pushed past his legs and bounded outside.

Suddenly aware of loud snoring in the far corner, Yancy

glanced back at the driver he had met last night—the driver who could sleep all day if he wanted to. The stage wasn't scheduled for a run to the coast until tomorrow. He tossed the fellow a grudging look and stepped out into the blinding sunshine. No one should have to get up on New Year's Day.

At the well, he broke the skim of ice formed inside the bucket and dipped his hands into the frigid water, then splashed his face and dried off on his kerchief. He did what he could with his hair by raking his fingers through the wild strands, rinsed out his mouth, and picked all the straw within reach off his rumpled clothes.

Yancy tried to ignore the throbbing in his temples. He only hoped his eyes weren't as bloodshot as usual after a night of reckless imbibing. But being fair skinned, and a redhead besides, he knew he probably looked worse than anyone else in the whole sorry lot of merrymakers. Oh well, there was nothing that could be done about it now. He paused a moment at the inn door and filled his lungs with a restoring breath of crisp January air.

Yancy found Mr. Blair and Felicia having coffee alone in the otherwise empty common room. An encompassing glance around the place indicated that some of the dark trestle tables still had not been cleared of last night's celebration. A chair or two still lay askew. Yancy crossed the room toward the Blairs' table near the fireplace.

Felicia gave a curt nod, as if she were royalty reluctantly giving audience to a town peasant.

Mr. Blair only managed a tired smile. "Good morning, lad. I would suggest you go tell the cook in the kitchen what you'd like before you join us. She was the only person we were able to rouse from bed this morn."

"Well, it is a holiday," Yancy reminded him.

"Of sorts," he conceded, his tone rife with irritation. "But most certainly not a holy day."

Retreating to the kitchen, Yancy couldn't help comparing the older man's manner this day with his gentle demeanor of yesterday. Maybe the pair had been kept awake till the wee

hours with all the loud singing and celebrating. He himself
had done more than his fair share of keeping the patrons
entertained with a colorful recounting of Boston's latest adventure.

In the kitchen a stout Negress was frying ham, and the
pungent aroma assaulted Yancy's queasy stomach as he
walked toward her. When her surly black eyes met his, he had
no doubt she was as unhappy about being up this morning as
he was. But despite his headache, Yancy knew he really should
try to eat something. Heaven only knew when they'd have
another meal. He gave the cook an apologetic shrug. "Sorry
we had to disturb ye so early, considerin' last eve. But I'm the
driver for the couple out there. If 'tisn't too much trouble for
ye, might I have the same as them? And is that coffee I smell?"

"Sho 'nuf." Her generous lips spread into the beginnings
of a knowing smile. She sliced another slab of meat and
plopped it into the pan.

Yancy helped himself to the steaming coffee and took a
swallow, feeling the heat of it course through him. "Mm. You
make it good and strong, just like I need about now. Could be
I'll survive last night after all."

The slave gave a chuckle as she kept on with her task.

Returning to the Blairs, Yancy pulled out a chair, but ad-
justed it so that it was partially turned, facing the hearth and
away from their inquisition. No sense in broadcasting the fact
he was so bleary-eyed. He held his hands out to the warmth.

"Last night, Mr. Curtis," the older man began, "did I happen to hear you mention that you had personal knowledge of
that affair in Boston some weeks past?"

Without thinking, Yancy flicked a glance toward the daughter. If she already considered him suspect for taking part in
the burning of the *Gaspee,* perhaps she had now decided he
should carry the full blame for the Tea Party as well. But
surprisingly, she only appeared curious. The realization bol-
stered him as he returned his gaze to the safety of the hearth.
"I'm afraid I don't know much about it. I was set to sail that
night on a coastal packet. But the whole wharf was alive with

the news. Far as I know, at least up until I left, no authorities tried to stop the people or make any arrests."

Mr. Blair clucked his tongue. "I fear for the town of Boston. As a druggist in Williamsburg, I was privy to most of the port gossip. People were always coming to my shop with news of the latest happenings. I couldn't help but note that the Crown is becoming very impatient with the northern colonies."

"No more impatient than we are with Britain always meddlin' in our affairs," Yancy said with a righteous huff. "If they had their way, they'd take away all the rights in our charter, the way they've been attemptin' to do for the past few years. We can't even elect our own governor in Massachusetts anymore." He swung around to face his companions. "That may not seem like much to you Virginians, being from a royal colony, but to us who have had such freedoms for more than a hundred years, it's a fightin' matter."

The older man laid a calming hand on Yancy's arm. "Dear friend, I do understand your cause. Truly. Of late I've begun to appreciate how precious freedom can be. Especially in this past year. The Spirit of God has been sweeping across Virginia in a mighty way—a glorious awakening. And many of us have become so filled by the love of this heavenly Comforter that we can do no less than encourage all our neighbors and acquaintances to receive this wondrous outpouring as well. To awaken hearts to the freedom which can be found only in Christ. To read the Holy Scriptures for themselves—each man praying for his own wisdom to understand God's Word, having his own communion with the Almighty. There's nothing in this world that compares with that." He punctuated the sentence by slapping his palm on the table. "Each of us should be free to walk where the love of God leads us, to say what is on our hearts—whether or not we have a piece of paper from the Church of England granting us the right to do so."

Yancy knew the old fellow was working himself up to what could turn into a fiery sermon . . . but he drew solace from the fact that at least the man would be too occupied to take much notice of Yancy's rum-ravaged face. But out of the corner of his eye, he observed one of Felicia's long, graceful fingers tapping absently against the bare pine tabletop as she gazed off into the distance.

"Why, only last month," her father continued, "two of my brothers in Christ were arrested for doing just that. Taking the message to the lost."

"One more reason—," she cut in.

He touched a silencing finger to her lips, his expression pleading. "Hush, Daughter. Not this morning. Not today."

The hardness in her stubborn gaze gradually softened, until for the first time Yancy saw genuine love for her father in the girl's eyes. She took hold of his hand and gave it a squeeze. "Very well, Papa," she murmured. "Not today."

It was also the first time Yancy had ever seen her smile. Its tenderness tugged at his heart in a way that surprised him.

The cook brought them their food just then and set a heaping plate before each of them. Yancy's stomach gave a lurch. He grabbed his mug and took a quick gulp of coffee. Suddenly he noticed that the Blairs had bowed their heads, and he was extremely glad he hadn't dived right in out of habit. He bowed his head also.

"Almighty God our Father," Mr. Blair began, "we thank thee most humbly for this bountiful food thou hast provided us this day. We ask thee to bless it to our bodies, and bless also the hands that prepared it. Now we bring before thee the hearts of all those souls abiding in the rooms upstairs, who wasted so many hours of the night past in noisy debauchery. May they see the error of their ways and repent. We ask this in the name of thy dear Son. Amen."

"Amen," Felicia whispered.

Yancy wondered exactly how much of that censure had been directed at himself, and he began to have second thoughts about continuing to travel with the overly religious man across from him. But when he straightened up, his gaze came to rest on the lass whose smile had stirred a new chord in his heart, and he settled back in his chair. Listening to a few sermons now and again would be a small price to pay for the chance of having Felicia Blair look upon *him* as tenderly. As he raised his coffee cup again to his mouth, he peered at her over the rim. Her hair was loose and unbound, save for a satin ribbon behind her small ears. Waves of shining mink brown hair rippled over her shoulders, where it curled against the violet frock she wore. *Aye,* he assured himself. *Worth that price and more.* Forgetting his reluctant appetite, he forked some ham into his mouth.

By the time Yancy finished the meat, a plan had formed in his mind. What he needed more than anything about now was a chance to sleep off some of the exhaustion that was draining him. If he played his cards right . . .

"Er, Mr. Blair? I've been thinkin'. It wouldn't be wise for us to leave civilization and head up into the mountains before we see to that broken wheel, ye know. Could be we'll be needin' another spare somewhere along the way."

The older man's faded eyes grew thoughtful. "You're quite right, Mr. Curtis. It would be most foolhardy to go ill-prepared for the journey."

After a last quick swallow of coffee, Yancy rose. "Don't bother yourself about it, then. I'll go out and cart the wheel to a wheelwright. For a wee bit extra, there must be one around willin' to work on a holiday."

"Wait, lad." Mr. Blair drew out his purse. "You'll need money to cover the expense of the repairs."

"There's plenty of time for that. We can settle up later. I'll probably only be gone two or three hours at the most." Then, before the man had time to raise another objection, Yancy grabbed his coat and dashed out.

Yancy felt someone shaking his arm. The rough motion caused his sore head to bump uncomfortably against the worn saddle he was using as a pillow. Remembering that he had stretched out in a corner of the wheelwright's, he worked his eyes open.

Felicia! Yancy groaned. Just what he needed, to be caught like this when all he had done was trade the broken wheel, plus some cash, for a good one. What would her father think of him?

"Come! Please!"

But the lass obviously had more on her mind than a wagon wheel, and Yancy lumbered to his feet.

She grabbed his arm and started tugging at him urgently. "Hurry! You must help me. It's the sheriff. He just came and took Papa away!"

10

"Jail?" Yancy took Felicia's shoulders and swung her around to face him. "Did ye say the law took your father to jail?"

"Unhand me!" Dark brown eyes flashing, the lass wrenched from his grasp. "I'm not one of your tavern doxies. But yes, the potbellied, ill-mannered oaf of a sheriff hauled my poor, foolish father off to the courthouse by the back of his collar— as if he were no more than some troublesome yowling hound. You must help him."

His brain still muddled by the effects of the hangover and insufficient sleep, Yancy squeezed his gritty eyelids closed, then reopened them. She was still there. And still staring at him impatiently, hands on her hips.

"Well? Aren't you coming?" She clutched his arm and began pulling him toward the shop doors.

"But, the wheel." He grabbed his coat and threw a fleeting glance over his shoulder at the one he'd purchased earlier after tracking down the wheelwright.

"There's no time to think about that now."

Mildly relieved that at least she hadn't noticed that no one was in there working on the broken one, which was suppos- edly in the midst of being repaired, Yancy stopped resisting.

As they turned into the glare of the sun, he cringed. Where were clouds when a body needed them?

The main street, Three Notched Road, took them to the turnoff to Court Square. Still befuddled by this odd slant of events, he was no less concerned about his own imminent fate. "Your father seems such an honest sort. What did he do that would bring the authorities down on him?"

Felicia kept up her swift pace. "My Papa is now—and always was—completely above reproach in all his business dealings. He's been arrested for preaching without a license."

"He needs a license just to preach?"

She raked him with a withering glare.

"But preaching . . . to whom? I left ye both in an empty room."

"*Two hours* ago! Oh, what's the difference? I did try to stop him, but he wouldn't listen. You do believe me, don't you?"

"Aye." Yancy was hard pressed to keep from grinning. Never had he seen such an unstoppable mouth as this lass possessed. But still, if she was so capable of speaking her mind, why did she need him? "Miss, why are we in such a hurry? What exactly do ye want from me?"

Felicia stopped and turned. The expression in her wide eyes told him she considered that question one of the stupidest ever asked since the dawn of time. "Why, to speak to the sheriff, of course. Make him release Papa. The dunderhead refused to listen to a word I had to say. In fact, he threatened to lock me up as well, if I didn't stop 'wagging my flapping tongue.'" She mimicked the last phrase with profuse exaggeration.

Yancy couldn't restrain his grin this time. Yet he was more than grateful that she missed seeing it as she stalked off again. How he would have loved to have seen her face when the official said that to her! But his smile dissolved when he realized that she wanted him to show his own face and very red hair to the sheriff. After all, if a description of his likeness was being circulated throughout the Colonies, the sheriff would most likely remember and report it at the very least. "Look, lass. I think you're makin' far too much of this. Surely your pa will only be jailed overnight. He wouldn't be required to appear before a judge for merely talkin' about the Almighty."

Felicia's maroon cloak swirled about her as she swung to face him. "You think not? I can tell you haven't been to Virginia for some time. Now, I want you to go into the sheriff's office and tell him whatever it takes to get my father out." A regal grimace ruled her features. "You and that other coarse man should get along just fine."

She sure knew how to sweet-talk a fellow. Still, he couldn't go in there. He had his own hide to consider.

"Come along!" Felicia turned and started on her way again.

"Nay, I can't. Er, I mean, the sheriff isn't gonna pay any heed to what someone who only met your pa yesterday has to say."

Turning around very slowly, the girl put her fists on her hips and glared. "He doesn't have to know that. Tell him you're our driver. That you've been with us for years."

That would help a lot, he rationalized. Especially if she were to verify that he isn't Yancy Curtis, the sailor . . . but wait a minute. Miss Priss, here, was expecting him to lie for her uppity self. "So now you're expectin' me to be puttin' me own principles aside an' start tellin' falsehoods for ye. Seems a lot to be askin' of a stranger ye barely know." He added an insinuating smile.

Felicia stiffened. "It's not for me. Surely you can manage a white lie or two for the good man who picked you off the road."

She might act feisty and downright spoiled at times, but a favor *would* put her in his debt, especially if he actually managed to gain Mr. Blair's release. He rubbed his jaw and met her desperate gaze. "If I'm to do this, I'll not use me own name, since I'm widely known along the coast. I'll take a more common one. Brown. Aye, that's it, John Brown."

She tossed her head, her momentary relief freezing solid again as she swung away and began walking. "Very well. But do stop dawdling. I don't want Papa to be confined any longer than necessary. He's really such a gentle man—rather fragile, particularly since Mama passed on."

Reaching the two-story wooden courthouse, they went in

the main entrance and down the wide hall, their footsteps echoing their presence against the walls and polished surfaces. Yancy stopped a foot or two behind Felicia at a door with a sign above that announced the sheriff's office. He struggled to keep his heart from pounding clear out of his chest as he pulled his hat farther down over his unruly curls.

"No!" Felicia scolded. "Take it off."

Swallowing down the lump in his throat, he complied. After all, he was a fearless smuggler, was he not? Used to facing danger in all manner of tense situations. It was merely this particular risk that concerned him now, and for two people he scarcely knew. He forced himself to reach for the handle, then paused.

"Come on!" Felicia whispered as she opened the door and swept right past him.

He straightened to his full height and strode manfully after her. Right off, he spied the potbellied official, sitting across the room with his feet propped on the hearth. A young deputy lounged in a similar pose, neither of them looking any better for last night's celebrating than Yancy felt. He was grateful that at least they'd done their merrymaking at some other ordinary, or both of them would have remembered he'd just arrived from Boston.

Felicia paused at the cluttered counter. "Sheriff?"

He groaned and looked her way, then lumbered to his feet, his waistcoat buttons straining over his protruding belly.

Aware that the lass would be more detriment than help in the cause, Yancy grabbed her hand. "Er, wait outside, miss."

"No. I have something I—"

"Outside," he ordered. "Now. There's a good girl."

"But—"

"*Out.*"

Her lips pressed into a thin line, she gave a huff, then, thankfully, whirled about and stalked out the door.

Knowing he'd likely have a fit of her temper to deal with later, Yancy directed his attention toward the sheriff, whose satisfied smirk matched that on the boyish face of the buck-toothed deputy.

"How do ye do, sir," Yancy began. "Name's Brown. John Brown. I've been the Blairs' driver for some years now, and—"

"Amazing," the balding sheriff cut in. "I'm surprised anyone could put up with that one's mouth for so long." He chuckled, and the deputy gave a snort.

Despite his initial nervousness, Yancy grinned. "She can be a handful if she isn't put sternly in her place, that's a fact. But she's not why I'm here. I understand you've arrested her poor, demented father. The fellow took a fall last winter and hit his head. Hasn't been right since. That's why we were travelin', ye see. I'm takin' him to stay with his sister over in the Shenandoah Valley." He snickered significantly and gestured with his head toward the closed door behind him. "If ye think the young lass has a sharp tongue, ye should meet the aunt! And I don't mind tellin' ye, if I don't get old Mr. Blair there in short order, I'll be in one peck of trouble."

The official raised his sparse brows. "Addlepated or not, the man was causing a considerable disturbance. Folks around here would think I was shirking my duty if I let him simply walk out of here without just punishment."

"But, sir, I left him alone barely long enough to see about getting a replacement wheel for the wagon. How much trouble could he have caused? When I went out, he and his daughter were sitting by themselves in the ordinary . . . and he was quite calm at the time. Not the least agitated."

"Humph! That's not what I found! I was dragged out of my warm bed on a holiday by the boy from Swan Tavern. Your employer was lambasting some hapless wayfarers who'd ventured down for what they thought would be a quiet breakfast, proclaiming rather loudly their sin of drunkenness."

"And lucky for him," the deputy piped in, his voice squeaking on the last word, "that we came when we did. The customers looked ready to tar and feather the old fool."

Yancy nodded with immense relief. "I thank ye, then, for

savin' him. I wouldn't want to be explainin' how he'd come to harm . . . me bein' responsible for him, an' all."

The sheriff drummed his fingertips thoughtfully against the top of the counter as he faced Yancy. He tipped his head as if reluctant. "Well, you certainly have your work cut out for you, with him *and* that impudent girl of his."

"Isn't that the truth!" Yancy said with a loud guffaw.

"Tell you what," the official began. "I'll keep Blair here just for tonight—that ought to satisfy the folks at the tavern. Won't do the old man any harm, either. Even folks who've had their brains jarred loose need to know they have to mind their manners."

Yancy reached out a hand and gave the sheriff's a warm shake. "I appreciate your wisdom, sir. And your mercy. Truth is, I could use a day off from havin' to watch his every move. First thing tomorrow, I'll be back to fetch him."

"Tomorrow." The stout man gave a nod.

Exiting the office, Yancy wasn't the least surprised to find Felicia right outside the door. And the furious expression on her face indicated she'd been eavesdropping.

"How dare you imply that Papa is *addlepated?*"

"Hush up."

"Don't you hush me!" she hissed.

Grabbing her elbow, Yancy steered her none too gently down the hall and out of the sheriff's hearing, with her dragging her feet every step.

"I told you to get Papa out of there. Now. Today."

"Ye should be glad he's gonna be released tomorrow, after the hullabaloo he caused."

"And I thought that was *your* forte," she retorted. "You and all those boisterous ruffians with whom you spent the night drinking."

Coming to a halt just inside the front entrance, Yancy jerked her around to face him.

Just as he opened his mouth to speak, someone came racing into the building and slammed into him. Hardly bothering to give more than a nod of apology, the freckle-faced man dashed to the sheriff's office and yanked the door open. "Sheriff! He's at it again! That man you arrested is preaching out the basement window. And he's starting to draw a crowd."

"What?" The sheriff came wheeling out of the room and charged down the stairs at the far end of the hall.

Yancy bolted after him with Felicia on his heels. They caught up just as the man was unlocking a heavy wooden door. Mr. Blair's raspy voice poured forth into the basement hall.

"As the great psalmist penned it, 'The Lord upholdeth all that fall, and raiseth up all those that be bowed down. . . . The Lord is righteous in all his ways, and holy in all his works. The Lord is nigh unto all them that call upon him, to all that call upon him in truth.'"

Looking over the sheriff's shoulder, Yancy saw Mr. Blair standing on his cot, preaching out the partially opened but barred window. And at least three women stood listening to his fervent words.

Mr. Blair turned from the window with an almost childlike smile. "'And, behold, the angel of the Lord came upon him, and a light shined in the prison.' . . . And here, I see, is the good sheriff. Have you come as *my* angel of mercy?"

11

Yancy gawked at Mr. Blair. If he had asked the old druggist to playact being demented, the man couldn't have been more convincing—standing on his bed, his arms spread wide, a joyous zeal emanating from his eyes.

Near Yancy, the sheriff stood openmouthed for several seconds before he regained his blustery bravado. "Get down from that cot!" he bellowed. "And shut your trap."

One of the women outside, round and plump, in layers of woolen skirts, moved closer and bent low as she rapped against the windowpane, hugging her heavy cloak against herself. "Sheriff Benning!" Muffled only slightly by the glass barrier, her shrill tone more than revealed her displeasure as she wagged her head. "I insist that you cease speaking so roughly to that poor man whom you've unjustly locked away." She pursed her mouth into a tight circle.

"I'll thank you to tend to your own affairs," he yelled back.

Her eyebrows arched high in offense. "I most certainly will not! Why, when I heard you had imprisoned this dear soul for doing nothing more than what was righteous and good, my friends and I had to rush down here at once and see for ourselves if it was true."

The law official grimaced as the woman's tirade continued.

"If anyone should be locked up, it should be all the drunken sots who kept the whole town awake last night.

Where were you when those guns were being fired, I ask? Have you arrested *those* troublemakers?"

A sheepish red crept over the sheriff's whole face. "Those fellows were just ringing in the new year. A perfectly natural thing for a man to do."

"Only a *drunken* man," she retorted. "And I must say, I am most displeased with the rude manner in which you spoke to me. I've a good mind to tell my husband about it—and I needn't remind you what fast friends he and the judge happen to be."

The sheriff raised a calming hand. "Now, now, Mistress Davis. I spoke in haste, in the heat of the moment."

"Just as you acted hastily when you arrested this nice man. Perhaps, Sheriff Benning, in deference to the start of a new year, we should both show a little mercy to our fellowman."

Her two companions, one thin with a beaklike nose, the other elderly and frail, also leaned forward and peered inside the low window with more than casual interest.

Sheriff Benning clenched his hands into fists.

Yancy was amazed to feel Felicia's cool fingers slip inside his and hold tight as they waited for some response from the man.

With a gesture of defeat, the sheriff shook his head and sighed. "Perhaps you good ladies are right," he mumbled.

"What's that you say?" Mistress Davis's high voice shrilled.

"I said," he repeated more forcefully, "you're right. All of you."

A satisfied smile unfurled from the woman's tight-lipped stubbornness. "Then we'll bid you good day." Mistress Davis shifted her attention to Mr. Blair and patted the window. "And Godspeed to you, dear man. Godspeed to you."

Yancy chuckled, and as if suddenly brought back to the reality of her present state, Felicia grew rigid and tugged her hand free . . . but not without difficulty. Ah, but it had been an entertaining few minutes, he assured himself with a grin. Entertaining and enlightening.

❦ ❦

As Charlottesville receded behind them, the reins grew slack in Yancy's grip while he leaned around for a last look at the small town, its town square and courthouse jutting out from its northeast corner. He chuckled to himself and breathed deeply of the fresh and *free* pine-scented air. A slow-thinking gent was at more than a little disadvantage when faced with a nimble-tongued woman. And from his experience with the ones he'd come across since first setting foot in Virginia, the place must be chock-full of them! He sputtered into a full-bellied laugh that bounced back from the thick woods crowding Three Notched Road.

Felicia, perched next to him, doggedly retained her starched posture, refusing to see the slightest humor in either her father's release or their hasty departure. But the mere sight of her rigid demeanor made him laugh all the harder until tears blurred his vision. Shifting the double traces to one hand, he used the other to wipe away the dampness.

As his mirth subsided, he looked beyond the lass to Mr. Blair, whose eyes were closed, his head leaning against one of the bowed hickory limbs that supported the canvas top, a smile on his lips.

The sight warmed Yancy. He returned his attention to the road, guiding the horses to the outer edge, away from the deep ruts that would disturb the kindly old man's rest.

Coming to a steep incline, he snapped the reins, urging the animals to a faster pace. He hoped they'd lean hard into their halters the whole distance. But partway up they slowed, straining under the weight of the wagon. Mr. Blair jerked awake, and Yancy handed the reins across to him. "If you'll keep the horses moving, sir, your daughter an' me'll get down to lighten the load."

Felicia stared at Yancy incredulously. "You expect me to jump down from a moving wagon?"

"Don't worry," he said as he leaped over the rolling wheel to the ground. "I've had me fair share of practice unloadin' valuables in a hurry." A half-smile tipped one side of his mouth as he reached for her.

She sought her father's face as if hoping he'd take her side in the matter. "Papa."

"We must think of the well-being of the beasts God has entrusted to our care, Leece."

"And what about the daughter he entrusted to you?"

"I'm positive Mr. Curtis is more than able to see you safely to earth," he said gently but firmly.

She gritted her teeth and eyed the rolling barrier she was required to avoid.

"Scared?" Yancy mocked, keeping pace with the wagon.

She cocked a fine brow, ebony eyes flashing. "No more than you were to go into the sheriff's office."

Her tongue hadn't lost its sharp edge, Yancy noted. "Then jump, will ye?" he ordered impatiently.

He immediately regretted revealing that she'd hit a sore spot. The corners of her lips curled triumphantly, and she threw herself at him with far more force than necessary.

Yancy nearly toppled over backward when she slammed into his arms. He staggered to regain his balance.

"I thought you said you wouldn't have any trouble catching me," she crooned smugly as he lowered her to her feet. Turning her back, she strode up the hill, her velvet cape swaying with her movements.

Yancy glowered at her haughty departure, envisioning what good use he could make of a hickory switch on the wench's backside. Releasing a disgusted breath, he hastened after the wagon, pushing it from behind with all his might.

When the hill leveled out, the older man halted the team. "Climb aboard, you two."

Felicia wasted no time in hurrying over to the rig. But upon reaching it, she hesitated, as if only now realizing how incredibly high the thing was and that in her skirts she would require assistance. She cast Yancy a wary glance.

Mustering the most wicked smile he could, he walked up to her.

She gazed up to the sky, pretending supreme aloofness.

Yancy placed his hands on either side of her waist. She had tossed off her hood during her climb up the hill, and the sight of her bountiful hair tumbling free was far too much to resist. He blew on her neck—even though he knew it would infuriate the little spitfire. It was one thing she would find hard to complain to her father about, he thought with a chuckle.

She bucked her head back in retaliation, barely missing his forehead.

Yancy kept himself in check. Grasping her tightly, he lifted her into her father's waiting hands. Then he heaved himself up and collected the reins.

Within seconds after he'd started the horses forward again, Felicia took out her kerchief and swiped furiously at her hands. "Papa, would you tell this—this *man* to turn the wagon around and take us home? Surely after today's mortifying incident you can see what folly it is for us to continue on in this silly quest of yours."

The old gentleman seemed taken by surprise. He turned a painful look toward the lass. "Leece."

"Mercy sakes!" she said with a huff as she twisted and untwisted the handkerchief in her fingers. "What possible future can there be for us? More embarrassing incidents wherever we go? Papa, you were thrown in jail. And we were told never to tarry again in Charlottesville—as if we were diseased or dangerous! Thank heaven no one in that place knew us, or word could have gotten back to Williamsburg."

"My dear." He stilled her agitated hands with one of his own. "Did you not see, as did Mr. Curtis and I, the wondrous miracle that took place this morn? The champion that God sent to rescue me?" He looked beyond her to Yancy with a smile. "Wasn't Mistress Davis marvelous?"

The remark caught Yancy off-kilter. That harpy? A miracle? But then on the other hand, the old bat had, quite handily, blackmailed the sheriff into releasing Mr. Blair. If he wanted to believe she'd been sent by the Almighty, what harm was there in that? He grinned and returned his attention to the road. "Well, she did seem capable of blowing up a mighty storm. To be sure, I had no idea this colony bred such a lot of high-spirited females."

The lass ignored Yancy, swung back round to her father, and clutched his arm. "Papa, I beg you. Be sensible. We might not be able to free you from the next jail. Please, let's go back home. You can open another shop just as successful as the one you sold. I know your customers would be happy to have you return. You were a wonderful druggist, and everyone loved you. *That's* your calling."

With a sigh, Mr. Blair patted her hands again as they gripped his arm.

"Then if you won't do it for yourself, do it for me," she pleaded with fervency. "For me, Papa. I've never asked you for anything this important in my whole life. I want to go home. I had some fine young gentleman callers, remember? At least until you started preaching at them. If we went back, I could become betrothed to one of them instead of riding away from civilization and any worthy man who might ask for my hand. Do you want your only daughter to end up a spinster?"

"Leece," he answered, his placid tone a marked contrast to her near hysteria, "those young men were anything but interested in spiritual matters. I want better for you."

"Better? Their fathers are both prosperous merchants. And how can you say they have no inclination toward godly matters? Their families fill their pews at church every Sunday."

"Ah, yes. But do they fill their hearts with God's goodness and love? I want far more for you, my dear, than some crass match of advantage. I want you to know love. The kind of lasting love your mother and I shared, may God rest her soul. I want you to love your husband that way."

From her sudden silence, Yancy knew Felicia had been shocked speechless. But it lasted only a moment.

"Well, that's fine. I, too, think it would be more . . . pleasant . . . to wed someone I truly cared for. But, Papa, how do you propose I'll find love way out here, in the wilds, with nothing save unwashed, uncouth, uneducated woodsmen?"

Her father smiled gently and opened the Bible that lay in his lap. "My dear daughter, it would seem that our heavenly Father has rescued us both. And considering those misguided notions of yours, he did it none too soon. Pray that he will fill you with the same Christian joy and purpose that I have found. Embrace God, my child, and the blessings he will heap upon you will be boundless. You'll see."

"B-but, Papa—"

He raised a hand, effectively silencing her. "Please, Leece. Let us enjoy the peace of this lovely winter day he has given us—the blue sky, the sun warming our faces."

Felicia released her breath in a whoosh of defeat, clamped her arms over her bosom, and stared straight ahead.

Yancy rubbed a hand unobtrusively across the bridge of his nose to hide his wonder. The old man had had the final word after all! Regardless of how the lass challenged his decisions and tried to thwart each one, she still gave in. Perhaps the shrew could be tamed after all, by the right husband. Of course, she considered herself far above the likes of him, sitting on that high horse of hers, and all.

What was he thinking? Yancy lost his grip; just as the reins slipped away, he grabbed them. Him? Wed? Set anchor in some port with this wench? Not as long as the sea winds still blew over the salty brine!

Squaring his shoulders, Yancy tried to steer his wild imaginings onto some safer course. With a sidelong glance toward the pair occupying the rest of the wagon seat, he made up his mind. The minute he could round up someone to take over as driver for the Blairs and look after the sweet old fellow, he'd heave off. After all, they needed someone who knew these mountains. Someone who could shoot some fresh game now and then, too, he thought as a rabbit dashed across the road and back into the forest. Yancy followed it with his gaze until it disappeared.

Another question popped into his mind. What if that had been a pack of wolves? or a catamount, pouncing down on them from some outcropping of rock? or Indians? And hadn't he heard tales of no-account thieves waiting to rob unsuspecting travelers? He cleared his throat uneasily and looked over the top of Felicia's dark head to her father. "Excuse me, Mr. Blair. What sort of firearms have ye brought along?"

The older man glanced up from his Bible without the slightest concern. "There's no need for any, lad. The good Lord will see to our protection."

12

"We're glad you know where to steer this rig," Dan said to Charles Warren as the young farmer maneuvered the wagon rigged with skids beside Flower Brook and toward a clearing just beyond. "Last night's snowfall all but hid the ruts in the road."

"A body gets used to knowin' where he is after travelin' the area enough."

"I know exactly what you mean," Ben said, plodding alongside on his pacer. "Covering the post roads so often, I know every hole and rock before I ever get to them." His mount blew a frosty cloud out of its nostrils and gave a toss of its head.

"Is that our destination ahead?" Ted asked, emerging from a pile of quilts he shared with Jane. Grasping the back of the driver's seat, he steadied himself as the wagon lurched across a dip.

"Yep. This area is called the grants, and that's Pastor Griffith's place."

Dan focused his gaze upon the unpretentious log house and several outbuildings in the distance. Snowcapped stumps dotted the section of open land. "Charles, are you certain that Pastor Griffith and his good wife weren't too hasty in agreeing to take in my sister and Ted? If they have much of a family themselves, I can't see how there'd be one spare inch left over in that tiny dwelling."

Jane stood and moved into the crook of Ted's arm. Dan

knew her attention was fixed on the little place up the road, but she didn't say a word.

"Don't be frettin'," Charles said in an offhanded way. "All the Griffith children are grown now. And if the truth be told, the old couple's gettin' on in years and could use a helpin' hand now an' again. The missus says her joints get all stiff and achy in the winter."

"That must be the reason your pastor hasn't joined up with you Green Mountain Boys," Ben piped in. "At first I thought he must be one of those ministers who thinks he can *preach* trouble away. You know, send those Yorkers packing with some well-chosen prayers."

Dan didn't miss the insinuating glance his younger brother aimed right at him. But it would take more than a wise speech to penetrate Ben's overzealous hard head, so he held his peace.

"Well, I can't help hoping the minister has a substantial library, myself," Ted said as Jane settled back down in her warm spot among the blankets and pillows, and covered her legs. "I'd deem it a rare privilege, indeed, if I were able to do some studying while we're living here."

Charles gave an indifferent shrug. "S'pose he just might. But gettin' back to the pastor, Ben, he can belt out a mighty powerful sermon condemning strife and lawlessness. Shake a man right down to his boots, he can. But to be fair, he's been a mite lenient with us in regards to the Yorker business. After all, we did try to settle things in court first."

A few yards ahead, a pair of deer bolted and vanished into the forested seclusion.

"Beautiful, aren't they?" Charles mused. "I do love this wild mountain country. Anyway," he continued, "it stands to reason a New York judge will rule in New York's favor. Otherwise he'd be out of a job."

"More than likely," Ben affirmed.

Charles chuckled and went on. "Well, since New York tried makin' us pay again for land we already bought from New Hampshire, Reverend Griffith is right with us on this. Fact is,

I heard him say that name, Vermont, sounded pretty nice to him for our own colony. Only thing he's stone stubborn against is killin'. Won't allow none of that. And so far we haven't. Though we come a mite close once or twice. But—" He stopped abruptly and waved as a thin older man emerged from the house. "Howdy, Pastor," he called out.

The man turned and gave an answering wave.

Dan swiveled on the seat to say something to Ted, but his brother-in-law was otherwise occupied—kissing his new wife.

"Can't you two do something besides smooch all the time?" Ben asked in an exasperated tone.

Jane's dreamy expression hardened as she stuck out her tongue at him.

"What a face to fall in love with," he retorted with a shake of his head.

"Quite true." Ted cupped her chin in his gloved hand and kissed her again.

Dan laughed. "Don't worry, Ben. As they say, this, too, shall pass."

"That *is* a relief," he answered. "It would be a sorry shame to see a fine-honed soldier like Ted expire from lovesickness."

"You know," Charles remarked thoughtfully over his shoulder, "a fellow with a knowledge of military tactics would be real handy to folks up here in the grants. Once you and the little missus are settled in, we'll have us a talk."

"And soon as you lovebirds are settled in," Ben added with some exaggeration, "Dan and I are heading back to Massachusetts to practice some military tactics of our own. Right, big brother?"

❦ ❦

Yancy looked uneasily into the swiftly growing darkness of Virginia's Blue Ridge Mountains. Now that the sun had disappeared behind the hills, its comforting warmth had vanished as well. Cold drifted upward from the patchy snow, and a brisk wind added another kind of misery. Not a single holiday traveler had passed them in either direction on the rutted road. But even more ominous, the last dwelling of any kind they had passed was more than an hour behind them. Yancy had serious doubts that they'd happen upon an inn before nightfall.

He looked over at Mr. Blair, who seemed always to wear a childlike smile on his face, and decided not to mention the hopeless predicament no matter how dire it seemed. Or how near.

"Ah, 'tis a wondrous evening, indeed," the old preacher marveled, his voice crackly in the crisp air. "The Almighty's hand has been at work everywhere around us. There's a most intricate, gnarled oak just over there . . . do you see it? And look! A wild hare hastening back to his hole."

Yancy made an effort to appear properly enthusiastic while Felicia wilted into her annoying perpetual pout. Just as well. Not much had come out of that snippy little mouth yet that was worth hearing. She was a lot like Jane Haynes had been—before her change of heart. He couldn't help but wonder what had become of the auburn-haired beauty after she'd helped him escape. Or Ted or Dan, for that matter. Were his friends safe and well back in Boston?

"And there it is!" the older man said, pointing toward a cabin tucked snugly into the woods. "The haven our heavenly Father has provided for us this eve."

Awash with relief, Yancy was astounded. The preacher *had* planned ahead after all! "Who lives there?"

Mr. Blair's grin widened. "I have no idea whatsoever, lad. But won't it be a delight to find out?"

If he hadn't been holding the reins, Yancy would have thrown up his hands in disgust. The lass was right. The old man was daft. He hadn't had the foggiest notion where—or if—they'd find somewhere to set anchor before morning. And him with a daughter to look after.

As if reading Yancy's mind, Felicia turned to him with brows high in their I-told-you-so position, then averted her gaze straight ahead.

"There's the road just ahead," Mr. Blair said with unconcealed excitement.

Dutifully, Yancy steered the horses onto it.

But as they drew nearer the place, he noticed there wasn't a single footprint marring the smooth blanket of snow. Nor was there smoke coming from the chimney—or livestock in the pens, let alone farm implements or a wagon.

"Hmm," the druggist reflected. "I would say this must be an old hunter's cabin. Only the most necessary land around it has been cleared. Well, let's go have a look."

Felicia deliberately scooted to her father's side for help this time. A comical picture of her hurling herself at the old man and ending up in a heap flashed into Yancy's mind, and he grinned. He climbed down and followed them. No one could ever accuse Felicia Blair of lacking spunk.

Mr. Blair lifted the latch and pushed on the weathered door.

As it creaked open in protest, Felicia took one step over the threshold and stopped, gingerly brushing a cobweb off her face as she peered into the dim interior. "This is positively ghastly! We simply can't stay in this hovel, Papa. We must go on."

Her father gave her shoulder an encouraging squeeze, nudged her inside, and went in himself. "I'm afraid that is not possible, my dear. We left Charlottesville quite late and have run out of daylight. And the Lord has graciously provided us with this shelter."

"Which we wouldn't need if it hadn't been for your arrest," she added.

In the waning light coming through two small windows and the open door, Yancy could make out some beds against one end, a passable fireplace, and a makeshift table of sorts with kegs for sitting. He had seen worse.

The older man turned toward him. "If you would be so kind as to see to the horses, Mr. Curtis, I'll help my daughter set the place to rights."

"Aye. Glad to."

"But Papa!" The girl's hands flew to her hips. "Where would we even start?" Wrinkling her nose, she sent out a scathing glance that contained heat enough to set kindling ablaze.

Even as Yancy thanked providence for that perfect excuse to get out of there, he noticed a corncob broom leaning against the wall beside the door. He grabbed the handle and shoved it at the shrew on his way out, delighted at the few sweet seconds of speechless shock that crowned the moment.

Despite the cold, he took his time seeing to the animals, until nothing remained to keep him occupied. Then he returned with some reluctance to the tiny abode. A warm yellow glow poured out into the night through the windows flanking the door. The one nearest the hearth was propped open a little, more than likely to emit smoke, since the fireplace had obviously been out of use for some time. It allowed Felicia's words to escape as well.

"It's still far from fit, Papa. We should have gone on to the next town and secured decent lodging."

"What we needed, Leece," came her father's steady voice, "was a roof over our heads. This is all of that and more. See how much better it looks since you've swept it clean and we put pillows on the kegs and covered the table with a cloth. And the Almighty even provided the exact number of cots. Not one too many, nor one too few. Just what we needed."

"You expect that—that uncouth ruffian to sleep in here? With us?" Her pitch rose higher than ever.

Her harsh words set Yancy's teeth on edge, but he continued to eavesdrop.

"Of course. We cannot expect the good man to stay out in the cold with the animals. He's been kind enough to help us, my dear, and without asking anything in return. We're fortunate to have him."

"That's impossible." Yancy could picture her drooping mouth, her crossed arms, her flashing eyes. "How will I prepare for bed? Would you have me parade before some stranger in naught but my night shift?"

"Easily solved, my dear. Mr. Curtis and I will wait outside until you're safely tucked in."

"Hmph! And we'll likely find our throats slit before the dawn, too."

"Felicia," her father said sternly. "I shall hear no more about it. We are all in God's hands. It's time you start trusting your care to him."

To Yancy's utter amazement, she did not respond. He hesitated another full minute, then filled his lungs, steeling himself for a miserable evening, and went inside.

In the lantern light and crackling fire's glow, the cabin seemed amazingly presentable. The table cover, the pillows, even the dusted and shored-up cots all blended together in a cozy illusion of permanence—the complete opposite of the initial impression they'd all had. And the place was chinked sufficiently to prevent even the most persistent drafts. They'd fare quite well after all.

"Horses settled in now?" Mr. Blair asked, looking up from stoking the flames.

"Aye. Fed, watered, and out of the night wind."

"Good. Then the next order of business will be our meal." He glanced toward his daughter. "What would you like us to fetch from the supplies?"

She blinked. "So now I'm expected to be the cook as well as the servant, is that it?" She gestured with disgust toward the rustic hearth. "Not even Tisha could prepare a proper meal in that!"

Mr. Blair's unlimited patience astounded Yancy. The man took all her disrespect and selfishness in stride. And even now he gazed upon the mouthy lass with deepest love. "I know you miss Tisha and Seth, child. So do I. But we must try to make do without them now. I'm sure if we all pitch in, we'll become accustomed to doing for ourselves. It can't be too difficult." He switched his attention to Yancy. "Would you mind helping me bring in the foodstuffs and pots?"

Once the crates had been brought in and opened, Yancy surveyed the bounty in astonishment.

"I had our cook help pack what she thought we'd need," Mr. Blair explained.

With a resigned smirk, Felicia began rummaging through. Shortly she pulled out a sausage, then found potatoes and other vegetables in one of the gunny sacks. "If someone manages to unearth a knife, I suppose I can start peeling these. And I guess I'll need a pot of water. I didn't notice a well outside."

"There's a creek out back," Yancy said.

"Fine." She thrust a bucket at him. "You can get the water."

"Please," her father prompted.

She shot Yancy a glare. "Please," she repeated with syrupy sweetness. But the glint of hostility still shone in her ebony eyes.

Snatching the pail, he strode away. For a brief moment he'd almost thought the wench was mellowing. He should have known better.

13

Yancy returned to the cabin to find the older man, shirtsleeves rolled up, awkwardly peeling potatoes.

Felicia, a sack of flour in one hand and a crock of lard in the other, had her back turned. She let out a huff. "How am I supposed to know what in the world Tisha mixed together to make biscuits? I didn't sit in the kitchen all day."

"Oh," her father said, "I'm sure it can't be too difficult to stir a few things together and have them come out right."

She swung around on her heel, not even acknowledging Yancy's presence as he strode across the room and set the bucket of water on the floor beside her. "And is that how you mixed your prescriptions, Papa? A little pinch of this, a dollop of that?"

Yancy heaved a sigh and took the crock none too gently from her grasp. "I've done me time in a ship's galley. Just let me get some water boilin' for the vegetables, and I'll make some pancakes."

A look of near relief appeared for an instant, then the girl sauntered over to where her father diligently worked. She settled herself on another keg and took up a knife and a turnip.

Choosing the likeliest looking pot out of the assortment, Yancy filled it with water and suspended the cauldron from the lug pole above the flames. Then he found a bowl and scooped in a healthy chunk of lard and some flour and began mixing.

"I'm thankful that at least one of us is competent around foodstuffs," Mr. Blair commented as Yancy stirred in some water. "I wasn't altogether certain how to fasten the cooking pot properly. I have, however, been at enough fine tables that I should be adequate at setting one myself."

Somehow Yancy kept himself from asking how the old gentleman had managed to live so long without ever having learned anything about life's basic chores. But then, it would have been just as ludicrous to envision himself being waited on hand and foot by servants.

Watching the others hacking clumsily at the vegetables, he eyed their clothing, which, along with everything else about this pair, spoke of prosperity. Mr. Blair's frock coat and breeches were of the finest worsted wool, and though his buckled shoes were beginning to show signs of ill weather and hard travel, it was easy to see they were of excellent quality. And from the number of clothing trunks aboard the wagon, the lass obviously had no lack of fashionable frocks and lace petticoats. Even crumpled from their long ride, the violet gown she wore went especially well with her dark eyes.

Reining in his thoughts again, Yancy stooped down and leveled some coals with the poker, then tugged a crude trivet into place. "Er, this is just a suggestion, mind ye," he said reaching for a frying pan. "Ye might toss a chunk of salt pork in with the potatoes and things. For flavor, I mean."

"Say," the older man remarked. "That would be tasty."

"Anything *else?*" Felicia challenged as her fingers closed around the handle of a butcher knife.

"Nay. That'll do well enough." He felt her presence as she rose and brought over the bacon. He also figured she was irked that he, a mere seaman, was more adept at cooking than she. So as she dropped the meat pointedly into the boiling water, he quickly leaned aside, avoiding the splash.

"Ouch!" She snatched her hand to her mouth and backed away.

Served the shrew right, Yancy thought with satisfaction.

"What's amiss?" Mr. Blair asked. He gave Yancy the diced vegetables for the stew and peeked over his daughter's shoulder.

Felicia dragged her gaze from the red mark on her hand. "I told you I couldn't cook in these primitive conditions."

Yancy had had enough of the girl's mouth. He yanked the frying pan off the coals and stood. Dragging her to the nearest keg, he shoved her down. "Sit! And not another word!" He dipped his fingers into the crock of lard, then took her hand and slathered on the fat.

Mr. Blair hovered over them for an instant. "I see you have the matter under control. I believe I'll go out and gather up our bedding."

As Yancy witnessed the venomous look Felicia hurled after her father, he recalled that the sleeping arrangements were but one more bone of contention between father and daughter.

He returned to the fireplace and set the skillet back over the heat, then scraped the vegetables into the stew pot. Behind him, the wench was making not the slightest sound, and with his back to her, he couldn't help but feel edgy. While spooning pancake batter into the pan, he tried to imagine what the lass might have up her sleeve. He wheeled on his haunches. And wished he hadn't.

Felicia, her rigid posture forgotten, was now slumped in her seat, silent tears streaming down her face as she blew on her burned hand.

Yancy's insides knotted. There needed to be a law against women crying. The things it did to a man were unspeakable. Swallowing, he cleared his throat, then made his way to the table, wondering how Dan or Ted would handle this sort of thing. "Say, lass," he said, sitting down across from her. "If you'll just relax and try to look on all this as an adventure, as your father suggested, could be you'd start enjoyin' some of it."

She swiped angrily at her cheeks. "How would you know?

You may be experienced with tavern hussies around the wharves, but *I* was raised to be a lady, the wife of a proper gentleman. I was taught how to manage a household of servants, not to be one myself."

She sniffed, then gestured helplessly into the air. "I haven't the slightest idea how to cook or clean a house, wash clothes, iron. Yet my *father,* who *raised me this way,* has given all our people their freedom on this whim of craziness he considers a 'calling.' Slaves that were with us my whole life. Tisha. Seth. They were like family. And now—"

Her voice cracked as a new wave of tears broke forth. She pursed her lips for an instant, then spoke more forcefully. "And now Papa's dragging me off into this wilderness—and he's no more prepared for it than I am. He'd never so much as hitched a team before we left Williamsburg."

Yancy tipped his head slightly and tried not to notice her reddened nose, her crumpled features that somehow now appeared quite childlike. Even her voice had softened. "If ye were so close to your servants, ye shoulda asked them to hire on and go with ye."

"Papa tried," she admitted miserably. "Tisha was set against it. She said she wouldn't lift a finger to aid him in his foolishness and that we were like lambs being led to the slaughter. At the mercy of wild Indians, uncivilized trappers, fugitives, and heaven knows what else."

She wasn't far off the mark, Yancy knew, but he still felt the need to console her. "Ah, well. Your Tisha's imagination got the best of her. Womenfolk always tend to make more of things than they should."

Felicia's chin shot upward, and she branded him with a fiery glower. "Not only women. You should have seen your own face when Papa said he hadn't brought a single rifle along. You were scared. Just plain scared." One side of her mouth curled upward in derision.

Her nasty habit of implying he was a coward was beginning to wear thin. He purposely let some of his irritation creep back into his own voice. "Nay. I could never find meself as scared as *you* are."

"Scared? Me? I beg to disagree."

He gave her a snide smile. "Ah, but ye are. Of anythin' that isn't wrapped up nice and neat in that Williamsburg box of yours. But life's more like a jack-in-the-box. Jumps out at ye when ye least expect. So quit whinin' and get ready for it."

Her eyes darkened dangerously. "What a clever saying. But forgive me if I don't consider a father who's been bewitched by some itinerant Baptist pulpit thumper just one more pop from a box." She folded her arms across her bosom and averted her gaze.

Yancy stared at her defiant pose. "I think you're bein' just a wee bit hard on your pa. I've spent many a time in Rhode Island—which is a Baptist colony, by the way—and ye won't find a better bunch of decent, honest folk anywhere."

"So honest, I've been told, that their main occupation is smuggling . . . that is, when they're not out burning one or another of the Royal Navy ships."

He groaned inwardly at her single-minded memory. "I'm talkin' about the people and their loyalty to each other. For them their faith's for every day, not just for *filling some pew in church on Sundays.*"

The sudden arch of Felicia's brow told him that his comment had made its point. Ah, but she was a worthy adversary. Nothing got by her.

"Your pancakes are burning," she said ever so sweetly.

Yancy lurched up and dashed to the smoking skillet as the acrid odor began wafting through the cabin. Seeing the charred cakes were beyond help, he scraped them out of the pan and started over, continuing the conversation while he worked. "Your pa may be a little too enthusiastic for the time being. I've seen that happen quite a lot—especially back when Reverend Whitefield was makin' his preachin' tours up and down the Colonies. He'd get folks so enthralled you'd think them and Jesus were sweethearts. They couldn't talk about him enough, do enough for him. . . . But after a while, things would settle down to a more ordinary relationship. If you'll quit fightin' your pa every step of the way, let him enjoy his honeymoon with the Lord, soon enough it'll—"

"My honeymoon with the Lord?" Mr. Blair's bemused voice carried from the doorway as he came in, his arms full of blankets and feather pillows.

Yancy jerked around in surprise, wondering exactly how much of that little speech the man had overheard. Meeting his pleased demeanor, he figured it must have been only the last phrase or two.

"I had no idea, Mr. Curtis, that you, too, had experienced those first blessed rays of discovery. But I should have known." He shook his graying head as he toted the bundle of bedding to the cots at the other end of the room. "How faithless of me not to realize my Father would send me another of his most blessed followers."

Holding forth the pancake turner, Yancy came to his feet to set the old preacher straight. He sucked in a breath of air in preparation. But Felicia's smug expression made its way into his consciousness. Not about to give the little shrew the satisfaction of finding out he was no farther along on the heavenly road than she, he clamped his lips shut.

Dan strolled about the property with Pastor Griffith. Thin rays of morning light crowned the treetops of the surrounding hills as their breath vaporized in the crisp, cold air. The minister's walking stick dug into the uneven snow at regular intervals, poking a line of holes beside his footprints.

"I hope by next spring, Lord willing," the gray-haired man said, pointing his stick, "to have that whole rise behind the house cleared. The missus hankers for fresh fruit. Thought I'd set out an orchard. Apples, pears, perhaps even peaches."

Well aware of the hard work involved, Dan nodded thoughtfully. Leafless trees and evergreens liberally speckled the entire hill. "You've picked a fine spot, I'd say. Saplings should fare well enough there." His gaze remained fastened on the site.

"You didn't simply wish to be shown the farm, though, did you?" the older man asked.

Drawing himself up, Dan glanced into the perceptive hazel eyes with a sheepish grin. "No, not entirely. I wanted some time to talk with you alone."

"I sensed that, son. The moment I first saw you, I felt you were a kindred spirit. I'm grateful we could find some time apart from the others."

Dan smiled, wondering where to begin as they rounded the tidy barn and angled toward the far edge of cleared land. He finally chose to start simply. "Charles Warren said you're a Congregationalist."

"That's a fact. And according to your brother-in-law, you graduated from Princeton and are ordained with the Presbyterian Church. Were you born in the Middle Colonies?" He stopped and leaned on the handle of his walking stick as he perused Dan.

"No. My family has a horse farm in Rhode Island."

"Baptist country."

"Yes, but my mother is from Philadelphia."

"So she influenced you, then."

Dan grinned. "Sorry, but you're wrong again. She's an Anglican."

A frown furrowed the creases on the pastor's forehead as he chuckled. "I see. Or perhaps I don't. A son of Rhode Island preaching Presbyterianism in Puritan Boston. You must have found a lonely calling."

Dan couldn't help but laugh. "Not quite. You see, in my youth I was fortunate enough to hear George Whitefield preach during one of his evangelistic tours. And like so many others, I found his message of love and brotherhood very inspiring. Especially that which transcends denomination, skin color, and—dare I whisper it—even colony boundaries. And the College of New Jersey came closest to embracing those concepts."

The minister dipped his head in agreement. "Not always quite so simple for the folks living here in the grants in these trying times, I'm afraid." The wiry man turned and began walking again.

Falling into step beside the minister, Dan mulled over his next words. "I realize that subject is uppermost in everyone's mind in this area, Pastor, but I have a personal matter pressing."

"And what might that be?"

"It concerns my brother-in-law. Right now, Ted is at that wonderful time in his faith when he's eager to learn and absorb all of God's truths. He's been studying with me for over a year now."

"How marvelous. A joyous time for us as ministers, also."

Dan nodded. "And it is my deep desire for Ted not only to study the Word of God, but to be a part of its glory. To have a close relationship with the Lord—"

"I couldn't agree more."

Steeling himself for the older pastor's reaction, Dan continued, "A relationship that will keep him from getting bogged down with strangling church rules and regulations."

Reverend Griffith's smile seemed to freeze in place. "I see."

But Dan was sure the man didn't. "Trying to keep every jot and tittle of the law didn't seem to work very well for the Israelites, and we don't seem to be any more clever. Do you know what I'm saying?"

"Exactly." He turned to Dan. "And I can see you definitely are one of Whitefield's *new lights*—may God rest his soul. However, there is, I fear, a great chasm between the ideal and reality. We Congregationalists may no longer be quite the strict Puritans our forefathers were, but without some rules and boundaries even the simplest game will turn to chaos."

"I agree." A sudden gust caught Dan's scarf and tossed an end over his nose. He brushed it away as he kept slow pace with the older man, determined for Ted's sake. "In my opinion, sir, the rules are the basic truths, such as Jesus being the way, the truth, and the life. But as in a footrace, there's a starting line and a finishing line. And while a man runs the race, whether he tucks his chin or tilts his face upward into the wind, that should be between him and the Lord."

"Ah yes." Reverend Griffith chuckled and draped his free arm across Dan's shoulders. "To be blessed with the clarity of youth. Sometimes we older folk find ourselves in the dubious position of having to look 'through the glass darkly.' But I wouldn't fear for young Ted. I vow to do my utmost to teach and guide him without dimming his spirit."

"Thank you, sir. I believe you will. But . . . that still isn't quite all I wanted to discuss. I need your guidance myself, some of that wisdom you've gleaned in your lifelong walk with the Lord. I find myself caught in a quandary at the moment, and perhaps it might be best to tell you how a minister of God managed to become a fugitive."

The older man removed his arm from Dan. "By all means, lad, unburden yourself. But let's head on over this way for a while. . . ."

"So you see," Dan said after relating the circumstances of his and Ted's escape from Boston, "I fear that my younger brother's scheme to go dashing back there to carry out some daring rescue of Susannah and our son is a plot conceived in haste. I don't feel the slightest peace about putting them at risk. And then there's my sister and Ted. I also feel responsible for them."

"You can rest assured that they are most welcome here. And so are you, for as long as you need to be."

"That's very kind of you. My every instinct as Susannah's husband tells me to forget all but her plight. But if I refuse to go with Ben, he's at such a faithless state of mind, I'm afraid he'll do something rash on his own. I'm completely mired in confusion."

The minister smiled gently. "Looks as if your own glass, at the moment, is not only dark, but also beset by fog." He took a deep breath and released it slowly. "Let me mull this over for the rest of the day. This evening, after the others have retired, you and I will get together for some serious prayer."

"Thank you, sir. I appreciate it."

As they turned back in the direction of the cabin, Dan caught sight of Ted and Ben coming toward them.

"We're supposed to fetch you two for the noon meal," Ben announced when they drew within earshot.

Ted grinned. "And Jane and I would like you to know we've settled on our new names . . . until it's safe to assume our own once again."

"Oh? What might they be?" Dan asked as he and Pastor Griffith fell into step with the others.

"Paul and Ruth Goforth." Ted beamed with satisfaction. "Paul because he was a persecutor who saw the light and joined the persecuted, and Ruth for her vow 'whither thou goest.' Goforth just seemed to fit in with the rest."

Ben flashed a wry grin. "I'll be doing some going forth soon. Tomorrow at first light—with or without you, Dan—I'm off. If you're coming, you'll have to buy a horse. I'd imagine the good reverend could help you with that."

Ted stopped abruptly. "Someone's riding this way."

"Looks like Ethan Allen." Pastor Griffith picked up the pace. "He never comes without good reason."

14

"Ethan!" Pastor Griffith called out. "You're just in time for dinner!"

The colonel of the renegade militia waved before dismounting and tying his mount at the hitching post.

Strikingly tall, the man's height exceeded the sixty-nine-inch length of his flintlock rifle by almost a foot. A casual stance only emphasized his muscular build and commanding presence.

"Good day, Reverend," Allen boomed good-naturedly. His broad grin revealed a line of strong white teeth. He reached out a big hand and grasped the minister's warmly. "Did I hear you mention dinner?"

"Absolutely."

A twinkle flashed in Allen's eyes, and his wild, flaring brows arched upward. He gave his trim belly a couple of playful pats. "Sure there'll be enough?"

"I daresay not even the fatted calf would be enough for you, Ethan," the reverend said evenly, the spark in his own eyes belying his straight face. "But such as we have, you're most welcome to share with us."

The man laughed and thumped the pastor on the back. As he did, Dan felt Allen's gaze of assessment rove over him before flicking to Ben and Ted, then back to Pastor Griffith. "Heard you were entertaining some interesting guests, Parson. Thought I'd drop by and check them out for myself."

They entered the house and disposed of their heavy coats. It took a moment for Dan's eyes to adjust to the somewhat dimmer interior of the unassuming dwelling. But at the sideboard in the kitchen end of the rectangular common room, Mrs. Griffith beamed an encompassing smile as she sliced bread for Jane to stack on a plate.

"Good day, missus." Ethan removed his wide-brimmed hat and plunked it atop the peg holding his coat. "I'm afraid your good husband has invited me and my appetite to noon with you all."

One frail hand flew to her throat, and the other grabbed Jane's arm. "Quick, girl! Go nail the door to the smokehouse shut!"

Jane's mouth gaped as the huge man sputtered into laughter and was joined by the others.

"Don't fret, my dear," the older woman said as their mirth subsided. "I was jesting. Ethan, here, is one of our dear friends." She switched her attention to him. "I don't believe you've met Ruth Goforth, young Paul's wife."

Dan watched a curious glance pass between Jane and Ted, as if it would take them a little while to get used to their new identities. Then Jane curtsied. "How nice to meet you, Mr. Allen. We've heard naught but good about you."

He gave a nod. "Mistress."

As the man's gaze lingered on her a few seconds, Dan noticed how the glow of love and her new inner peace enhanced his auburn-haired sister, adding a beauty from within to her delicate, expressive features. Her wide brown eyes bore a softness he hadn't seen in many a year. And he realized, suddenly, that he was more than glad they were part of the same family.

"Soon as everyone finds a seat," the pastor's wife said, "I'll bring over an extra place setting."

Five chairs scraped the floor as the men chose spots around a large pine table whose size dwarfed the cramped room.

In the chair directly across from Ted, Ethan rested his

elbows on the tablecloth and turned a cocky smile on him. "*Goforth,* I believe you said?"

Ted fingered the neckband of his linsey-woolsey shirt. "Yessir, that's right."

"Strange. That's not what I heard." His untamed brows dipped in mocking challenge. "Word has it that the one with the pretty little wife was someone who'd taken a sudden dislike to the color red. Officer by the name of Harrington, if I'm not mistaken. Showed a clean pair of heels to Boston in the middle of the night."

Dan saw color tinge Ted's face and ears.

Allen scooted his chair back a few inches and relaxed his oversized frame into a more comfortable sprawl, the fringe of his buckskin hunting shirt swaying with each movement. "You and your wife have nothing to fear up here, lad. As long as you steer clear of Fort Ticonderoga, across the Hudson, you'll find yourself among friends."

Ted let out an audible breath of relief and exchanged a tender glance with Jane as she brought bread and butter and a pitcher of cream and set them on the table.

Blue enamel coffeepot in hand, Mistress Griffith made her way around the group, pouring fresh coffee into the cups.

The big man smiled his thanks. He then switched his attention to Dan, who was next to Ted, and Ben, on his own right. "And which one of you is the postriding Son of Liberty?"

Obviously in awe of Allen, Ben straightened his shoulders and met his gaze head-on. "Proud to say that's me, sir."

Ethan nodded slowly as he rubbed his jaw in thought. "Good for you. And then, I heard, some upstart Presbyterian minister came with the three of you." His eyes settled on Dan. "Some mob of stiff-necked Boston Puritans run you out of town?"

Dan grinned. "Not at all. Seems they've got as much as they can handle right now with those of the Anglican persuasion."

A burst of laughter rumbled out of the man's massive chest. He was obviously aware that most British were Anglican.

"From what I heard about your little tea party, it sounds like you can expect a sight more trouble."

"Pshaw!" Mistress Griffith said, bringing over a platter of sliced pork. "Enough of this talk until after dinner." She nodded her ruffled cap in her husband's direction.

"Shall we bow our heads?" Pastor Griffith said, following her lead.

After the hearty meal, the men pulled their chairs into a semicircle around the fireplace at the parlor end of the open room. Dan sat and watched as bright flames licked the fragrant logs.

Ethan Allen flung a cursory glance toward the kitchen, where Mistress Griffith and Jane were up to their elbows in dishes. "Looks like a good enough time for us to do some talking." He cocked his head in Ted's direction. "Since patriots along the way opened their homes to you, I'm assuming you're sympathetic to the colonial cause. Am I right?"

Ted shifted in his seat and met Dan's gaze before answering. "I do not approve of tyranny, no matter who perpetrates it."

"So you merely disapprove then? Or would you go so far as to say you're willing to oppose it?"

Hands on his knees, Ben leaned forward. "Ted's a soldier—a man of action. Of course he'd stand against the British! He's with us now, isn't he?" He nodded at Ted as if seeking affirmation.

Dan knew Allen was putting Ted in a tight spot, and Ted's searching look confirmed that, though he may have deserted, he hadn't considered coming to actual blows with his own countrymen. Hoping to appease the mountain man, Dan took it upon himself to answer. "My brother-in-law has been led of the Lord to seek his freedom through our blessed Savior."

"I can understand that," Allen answered. "But isn't the rallying cry among you Sons of Liberty, 'No king but King Jesus'?" A few seconds of silence followed the question, and then he looked once more at Ted. "If necessary, are you willing to go against the British and fight them?"

Dan couldn't help wondering if Ted's faith was rooted deeply enough to enable him to stand up against such a dynamic leader of men.

Ted stretched out his legs, and both his posture and his expression relaxed. "I try not to make any decisions without first consulting the Lord," he answered evenly. "Only with his guidance and blessing do I attempt to go anywhere or do anything. As you said, Mr. Allen, I'll have no other king but King Jesus."

"I see."

Although Ethan Allen's tight-lipped grimace revealed his disappointment, Dan was extremely proud of his brother-in-law. He breathed a quick prayer of thankfulness for Ted's demonstration of spiritual maturity.

"Well, then. Ben." The mountain man centered an intent gaze on him. "It appears you're the only one in the lot who's on fire for the cause . . . and we are in real need of a trusted postrider. If, of course, you've a mind to take a route up this way."

Ben's youthful face colored slightly, emphasizing the scattering of freckles across his nose. "Sorry, sir, but I'm not a postrider, exactly. I'm more of a courier for the North End Caucus. I take their messages and letters wherever they need to go."

"North End Caucus," Allen said, his expression brightening. "Sam Adams is one of them, right?"

Ben nodded.

"Well, son, I need you to take a message to them, from Colonel Ethan Allen of the Green Mountain Boys. Tell them we have a company of brave, freedom-loving men who have proven themselves here. And once the city folks down along the bay get tired of being bullied and cheated by those high-handed legislators across the water, we'd be more than happy to traipse on over to Fort Ticonderoga and take it away

from those lobsterbacks. Think you can tell them that for
me?"

Ben's pearly teeth flashed in an enthusiastic grin. "Yes, sir!
Mr. Adams will be mighty glad to know that. He surely will."

"And one more thing." Ethan tapped a finger absently on
his knee. "Tell your Mr. Adams that we'd take it as a real
kindness if he'd make it a point to keep us informed of events
as they transpire."

"You can rest assured of it. Once I give him your message,
he'll never forget you're up here again."

"Good!" Allen whacked Ben on the back, nearly unseating
him.

Dan snickered and shot his brother a teasing smirk.

Chuckling himself, Ethan turned his head toward Ted, who
was engrossed in watching Jane dry pots at the other end of
the room. Following his gaze, the man flicked an amused
glance at Dan and Pastor Griffith and shook his head. He
nudged Ted with his arm. "Since you and your wife will be
staying here for some time, you might find out you like it
enough to settle. In which case I have some parcels of land
you might find of interest."

"Thank you. We'll keep that in mind," Ted answered gratefully.

"And in the meantime," Allen went on, "folks will take to
you a lot sooner—and be more apt to keep the lobsterbacks
at the fort from ever discovering you're among us—if you'd
help out some."

"You're speaking of your Green Mountain Boys?"

"Ethan," the pastor reminded him, "the lad has already said
he won't be doing any such thing unless he's led of the Lord
to do so."

"Hmph. I'm not asking him to go out and shoot somebody.
But my men could use some pointers on soldiering from a
professional. In fact, I'd like to sit down with him myself for
an evening and talk tactics and strategy. What about it, Ted?"

"Sure he can," Ben supplied forcefully.

Ted cocked his head. "I don't suppose it could hurt. But I'd better pray about it first."

"You do that, boy," Ethan said. "And then a week from Saturday go on down to the Catamount Tavern in Bennington. They'll be meeting then, unless there's a blizzard. Wish I could be there, too, but I must get back to my family. I haven't moved them from Connecticut yet. Oh, and speaking of family—" he nodded to the pastor—"I just remembered that Frank Darling, downstream, gave me a message for you when I passed his place. Said his youngest had taken a turn for the worst. He'd like you to take a run over there, if you're not too busy."

"You don't say." The minister rose. "He's not the sort to ask lightly. It must be serious. I'd better go at once." Immediately starting toward the kitchen, he stopped and swung back to look at Dan. "I doubt I'll be back tonight. I'm afraid we'll have to save our talk for later."

"Whatever you say." Dan forced a smile. With Ben intent on leaving at first light, any decision regarding Susannah would probably have to be made without the older man's advice. And whatever Dan decided, it had to be of God. He could never bring himself to trust his wife's safety to anything less. One thing was for certain . . . it would take a considerable amount of prayer. He stood and offered his hand to Ethan Allen. "It was a real pleasure to meet you, sir. I'll be keeping you and your men in my prayers. Now, if you'll excuse me, there's something I need to do." With a nod toward Ben and Ted, he strode across the room toward his coat.

15

When Dan stretched and swung his legs over the side of the cot, the morning sun had already risen and added its warmth to the air drifting upward from the main floor of the cabin. His head still throbbing with weariness and indecision, he dressed, then climbed down the ladder from the loft toward the welcome aroma of brewed coffee.

The hours of prayer throughout his sleepless night had not helped him resolve his dilemma. His only answer had been the occasional howl of a wolf. Ben would consider him a coward if he remained to see Ted and Jane safely settled . . . especially with Susannah and Miles alone in Boston. Yet if he returned home now, he would most certainly be arrested, which would do them no good. And besides that, an attempt to spirit his wife and child out of Boston could fail and put them in even greater peril. His own need to be with his little family seemed inadequate reason to turn them into fugitives as well.

Then there was his hotheaded brother to consider. Reaching the main floor, Dan rubbed his tired face and straightened his shoulders. He noted absently that the place had been swept clean and the clutter from the day before had been tidied and put back to normal. He headed toward the kitchen.

"I used to feel that way about God, too," he heard Jane say.

Not wanting to interrupt so crucial a topic, he paused before moving into view.

"No one knows better than you how stubborn and willful I used to be. But once I realized how utterly empty and selfish my life had always been—and how truly unhappy I was making myself and everyone I loved—I had to turn back to God."

"As long as you're getting what you want, anyway."

Dan could just picture the toss of the head that had surely accompanied his brother's response. Ben was always in too much of a hurry to waste time seeking the will of the Lord— and that tendency didn't seem to be improving any as time went on.

"You can mock me if you want," his sister went on with barely a hesitation, "but I wouldn't trade the incredible peace I've found for all the tea that got dumped into Boston Harbor. Even while Ted and I were on the run from the British, I always felt as if we were in the palm of God's hand. The way the Lord protected us time and again was no less than miraculous. Even now he's brought us to stay with this loving couple, who will provide us not only with clothing and food, but spiritual nurturing as well. And Colonel Allen is looking into helping Ted find us a place of our own, and work besides. What more could we ask?"

"Well, that may be all plum pudding and cream for the two of you," Ben scoffed in irritation, "but what about the mess you left in your wake—Susannah having to deal with Fontaine's wrath all by herself, and Yancy! Only the Lord himself knows whatever became of him!"

Dan began to step forward, prepared to come to his sister's defense, but stopped at her reply.

"Oh, you needn't fret about either of them," Jane said cheerfully, as if their present circumstances were commonplace. "God knows what he's doing. Absolutely everything will be set to rights according to his plan. Meanwhile he's seeing to their safety and their other needs as well, just as he's promised to do for all those who put their trust in him."

Dan smiled at his sister's childlike faith. Simplistic as they were, her words came as a comforting message from God. A wonderful peace washed through him.

But Ben gave a scornful laugh. "You may feel that way about it now, while everything's all roses in this newfound faith of yours. But if I were you, I'd keep in mind that God didn't bother to come to the aid of Stephen when he was martyred at the Lion's Gate in Jerusalem, nor the countless other Christians down through the centuries. And I'm sure they had the same trust in divine deliverance that you have."

"Yes, they probably did. But who's to say that their very deaths were not their crowning moment—that they were *rewarded* by stepping that very instant into the holy presence of almighty God, whom they served in faith and love?"

The absolute trust conveyed in her answer made Dan smile again. Yet with Ben's mention of martyrs, he couldn't forestall the return of his fear for his little family. He had shared Jane's trust up until a few short weeks ago, back before things in Boston had reached the boiling point. Now he just felt tired. Very tired. He took a deep breath and strode to the table.

Ben looked up as he approached. "Might have figured you put her up to it." He tugged on the cuff of his light brown shirt.

"To what?" Dan asked innocently, though he was more than aware what his brother meant. He shifted his glance to Jane, busy at the hearth. She wore a faded but serviceable dark blue work dress and a bibbed apron, neither of which he had ever seen before. Her auburn hair was neatly tied back at the nape of her neck with a black ribbon.

"Never mind." Gulping the last mouthfuls of coffee, Ben plunked his mug onto the table. "About time you got up. My horse and the one Ethan Allen borrowed for you are both saddled and ready to go. And Jane is just about finished packing some food for us to take. Let's go." His chair scraped back as he started to rise.

Dan motioned for him to sit back down. "Give a person a chance to have some coffee, at least, would you?"

"You'll have more than that," Jane said, bringing him a cup of the steaming brew. "There's a big pot of porridge on the hearth, and you need a good bellyful to fortify yourself for the journey." Returning to the sideboard, she took out a wooden bowl and ladled in some mush, then brought it to him.

Ben leaned across the table as Dan took his first swallow of coffee. "You *are* coming with me, right?" His serious expression left no room for discussion.

Dan tried to formulate a reply.

"Well?" Ben demanded.

There was a hasty knock on the door.

Grateful, Dan sprang up. "I'll answer it."

The door burst open before he even got there.

"Mistress Griffith?" A small man, wearing a worn coat over his lean, sparse frame, rushed inside and hurried into the common room.

"I beg your pardon," Jane said, a mere step behind Dan. "The pastor's wife isn't here at the moment. She's out in the barn showing my husband the animals that need tending."

Worry creased his thin face as he turned. "Thank you, mistress. I must see her at once."

Footsteps sounded outside on the steps, and the door flew open again, this time to admit the pastor's wife and Ted. "Why, Mr. Darling," the woman said, removing her scarf and draping it over a peg while Ted hung his outerwear. "You look out of sorts. Is something amiss?"

He crossed to her and clutched his broad-brimmed hat tightly in his grip. "I'm afraid I have some bad news."

Mistress Griffith paused in undoing the closures of her coat, and her face paled.

"Your husband took a fall last night. Slipped on the ice just as he was leavin' to come home."

"Is he terribly hurt?" she whispered.

"Twisted his leg somethin' awful, so he spent the night with us. It's all swelled up this morn, purple as dusk. I can't seem to feel a break, but I'm sure there's one. Or at least a crack."

"Oh, my. I'd best hitch up the wagon and fetch him home, where I can take care of him."

He patted her arm. "Don't mind my buttin' in, ma'am, but myself, I think 'twould be best not to move him just yet. Let him mend where he is for a couple of days. The wife and me, we'll look after him proper."

Her fingertips pressed against her mouth, Mistress Griffith considered his suggestion. "That's quite neighborly of you, Mr. Darling, but I thought you already had your hands full with an ailing child."

He shrugged. "Least I could do, him ridin' over in the mud and snow to see my Belinda."

"How is the dear child?"

His bone-lean face lit up with a grin. "Worst was over before your man got there. He says, of course, 'twas his prayin' on the way over that did it. But leastwise the young'un has nary a rattle left in her chest."

"I'm so pleased to hear that." She smiled and turned to the others, then started, as if suddenly remembering her manners. "Oh! I should introduce you to our guests."

"Rightly so. Fact is, Pastor Griffith sent me to get one of them—if he isn't already gone, of course."

"He asked for one of us?" Dan asked, moving closer.

"Yep. The one that's the minister." Switching his attention to the pastor's wife, he continued. "Your man is supposed to preach a funeral over to the James place today. Old Mother James passed on, you know."

"That's right," she said with an anxious nod. "Mistress James. I'd forgotten."

"Well, your man says maybe that Presbyterian fellow could take on the duty for him."

"That's me," Dan said. "I'm Reverend Dan Haynes, and I'd be most pleased to repay the kind pastor's hospitality any way I can."

Ben's eyes flared, then narrowed to an angry glower, but

Dan felt nothing but relief. He had no doubt that God had delivered him from making an unwise decision.

Mr. Darling's close-set eyes studied Dan warily. "We'll be expectin' a proper service, you know. A Congregational one. No more, no less."

Dan smiled. "I understand, my friend. And that you shall have."

"Just let me get my husband's Bible and a few things together, Mr. Darling," Mistress Griffith said, taking the worn black book from the table. "Come into the other room with me while I fetch the rest of his necessities. You can tell me a little more about his condition."

Watching after them as they left the parlor, Dan turned and met his brother's ire.

"We don't have time for this delay, you know." He drummed his fingers on the golden pine tabletop impatiently.

"Ben," Dan said with a weary sigh, "I prayed the night through and still had no idea whether I should go with you or not this morn. But now, it seems, I've been given my answer. I'll be staying here . . . for a little while, at least."

His brother's mouth flattened into a thin line. "But what about your wife? You plan to leave her to the mercy of that lobsterback, Fontaine?"

Coming to the table with a cup of coffee, Ted took a seat. "Alex wouldn't harm her. No matter what his own personal concerns may be, he must know that half of Boston would be up in arms were he to lift a finger against Susannah. But he does derive a perverse sort of pleasure in taunting and making threats." He reached out and gripped Dan's forearm nearby. "Jane and I shall be praying day and night for Sue *and* Alex."

Ben snorted in derision and shook his head. "Well, you *old ladies* be sure to have a nice cozy winter, now. I guess it's up to me to go take care of what needs doing." He swung to leave, muttering under his breath.

Dan grabbed his shoulder, stopping him. "I'll not have you

do one thing to jeopardize the welfare of my wife. The Lord wants us to wait, and I'll not brook you taking matters into your own hands. You will not remove my family from God's will. Is that clear?"

Ben stared long and hard, then jerked free. He stalked toward the bundle of food Jane had prepared and yanked it up.

Dan stepped to the door ahead of him and blocked it. "I'll have your word on this, Ben."

His younger brother's eyes flashed as a muscle worked in his hard-set jaw.

"Well?"

"Have it your way," he grated between clenched teeth. "As long as she isn't in any real danger. The North End Caucus is sure to have an answer for me to bring back to Ethan Allen after what the colonel proposed. We'll talk again. Fair enough?"

Dan released a pent-up breath and relaxed his stance. "Fair enough. But do me a favor, would you? Don't leave just yet. I'd like to send Susannah a letter explaining."

"Say," Ted piped in, "that's a splendid idea. I shall pen a few lines myself."

"Me, too," Jane said. "I'm sure she'll want to know how the Lord has been watching over us. And I want to thank her for all her prayers and let her know she's in ours as well."

Ben shot a glance of disbelief from one to the other. Then he made a hopeless gesture as he brought his palm up. "*Now* you decide it would be nice to write her? Will you moonstruck fools never let me leave this asylum?"

Still astounded that God had provided his answer just at the exact moment he needed it, Dan chuckled and put his arm around Ben's shoulders. "Come over here and sit down, runt. Relax. Have some more coffee. We'll get right to the task." Depositing the younger man in a chair at the table, he walked to Pastor Griffith's desk in search of some paper.

Glancing over his shoulder at Ben, Dan hoped his eager, impetuous brother would not rashly interpret Susannah's situation in Boston as one of danger. After all, as Jane had said, God was in control. Susannah was safely tucked under his wing. Dan had to believe that.

16

Late afternoon sunshine slanted between the clouds, melting the snow on the roof of the wayside trading post. Water dripped from the jagged icicles that hung from the eaves.

Inside the building, Felicia watched for a moment as the glistening drops plummeted to the ground. Then she returned her attention to the tear in the hem of yesterday's dress. She put in the final stitch, then bit off the thread. She looked up from her chair near the stone hearth to see her father seated on a stack of meal sacks along the opposite wall. He was taking advantage of the last bit of daylight from the window. The smile on his face as he read his Bible made her all the more depressed.

Setting aside her mending, she picked up her suede traveling boots from the earthen floor near her feet. It was hard to believe that when she and Papa had left Williamsburg, a mere week or so ago, these exquisitely styled high-top boots had been newly made. Now, days of slogging through mud and slush and scraping against icy ridges in the rutted mountain roads had been their ruination. The once-lovely pearl gray brushed leather was now a matted charcoal, shiny and smooth in spots, with mud stains and water marks marring their fashionable lines.

Her efforts would be of little use, but nevertheless Felicia took a damp rag and began scrubbing gently at the worst spots . . . which were minor compared to the ones on the hems of her dresses and velvet cloak.

A gust of wind rattled the door of the rustic establishment, and the old broom leaning next to it fell with a bang.

Felicia shivered and tried to get comfortable on the hard chair. She couldn't decide which was the greater torment—her backside, tender from bumping along on the wagon seat, or her feet, sore from climbing so many hills. She'd have given her dowry for a decent night's sleep in a proper bed—back home, she added inwardly.

She gazed at her father again.

His own boots were also dull and worn looking, but he had simply stomped off the worst of the mud before coming inside. As he had said, there was not much point worrying about tracking dirt in on a packed-earth floor. He turned a page and immersed himself in the words, as if oblivious to the clutter of the disorderly trading post.

How typical, of late, she thought bitterly. He no longer regarded anything but religious matters to be of the slightest importance. She heaved a sigh just as Yancy and the gimp-legged old trader came in from the kitchen lean-to that was tucked against the back of the cabin.

She saw her father glance up momentarily before returning to his reading.

"Couldn't have found better if I ordered them special, mate," the seaman was saying. Stocking footed, carrying a pair of sturdy, almost-new boots in one hand, he brushed the other hand down the front of the fringed leather hunting shirt he wore.

The heavyset storekeeper clamped a beefy hand on Yancy's shoulder and grinned, plumping out his fleshy jowls. "Yep, knew the minute I laid eyes on you that you and that nephew of mine had to be the same size, that's a fact. Too bad luck didn't hold out for Cauley. Bad enough he come down with the fever, leavin' me to run the place by myself. But to get snake bit to boot. That finished him." He rubbed his double chin and shook his head. "I tole him to keep watch for them nasty critters in the woodpile."

Felicia cringed and peered warily beneath her chair, then searched toward the corners of the rude room so deeply shadowed with crates and barrels and piles of goods. Seeing nothing moving, she composed herself and glanced up, relieved that the men hadn't caught her show of fear.

"Dire way to come by another man's outfit, to be sure," Yancy said with a shrug.

"Yep. Bad day for me, too. Ain't found nobody to take Cauley's place." His beady eyes narrowed as he sharpened his perusal of the seaman. "Don't s'pose you'd consider helpin' out an ailin' old man yourself, would you? I'd keep you fed an' dry, that's a fact . . . and the place would be yours when I'm gone, of course."

Felicia arched her brows facetiously. *Fed and dry!* How would that ruffian Curtis ever turn down so *generous* an offer!

The redhead appeared to give the matter a moment's consideration. "Well, now, that's mighty kind of ye, Mr. Potts, but I'm afraid I can't. I made a promise to these good folks to see them through to where they're goin'. But I do appreciate the outfit ye provided. 'Specially the fine Pennsylvania rifle."

The words jolted Felicia. He must be serious, then, about taking them deep into the wilderness on the other side of the Shenandoah Valley.

"Ah, well," the portly man groused good-naturedly. "Can't say as I blame you. Truth is, I wouldn't be stuck here myself, if'n I could still get around, that's a fact. And leastwise, you won't have to go places lookin' like such a greenhorn now."

"Ye say you've got some oil I can rub into the boots an' rifle?"

"Cost you extra, you know."

"Just add it to me bill."

The trader took a rag from his back pocket and handed it over, along with a tin from a nearby shelf. "Best I go get a fire goin' in the oven." He hobbled away.

Crossing to a table along one wall, Yancy tugged out a chair and eased his long-legged frame onto it, then set to his task.

As he worked, Felicia took uneasy stock of the rifle . . . and him. Though she would be loathe to admit it, her gaze had lingered overlong upon the seaman when he entered the room. He did look rather like an adventurous explorer in the fringed outfit whose lines emphasized not only his height, but also his trim, muscular build. And if upon occasion she'd found herself envisioning him scaling the rigging of a great ship, she would have been the last to confess it. Now she realized it was no more difficult to picture him carving out a trail through the thick woods, fighting off marauding renegade Indians. . . .

His eyes flicked her way and caught her staring. He winked and flashed a rakish grin.

How rude and uncouth! Felicia felt a maddening blush flame up her cheeks, and she averted her gaze. The lout must think anything in a skirt would swoon whenever he smiled! Well, perhaps some hapless females might find his face appealing, with its weathered skin, the long nose that probably had been broken more than once in a fistfight, the ever smiling mouth. But her own taste ran to the more cultured types who knew how to dress properly and act civilized . . . gentlemen who knew how to treat a lady.

Yancy started whistling "Barbara Allen" while he rubbed oil into the butt of the gun, as if he hadn't a care in the world.

Felicia grew even more aggravated as she mulled over how much he and Papa had in common. Neither one cared one whit about everyday worries—most especially her welfare or future. But why should she want Yancy to care, anyway? The life she planned for herself included far more than anything some roving sailor might have to offer.

Pressing her lips together, she sent a searching look toward her father. A pang of jealousy jabbed her heart. Did he have to spend every waking moment with his nose buried in that big black book? What had happened to the loving man who would come home from the shop every evening and relate interesting tales about his day, amusing tidbits about his customers? If only Mama were alive. She would have talked some sense into him, made him see that he'd lost all perspective. Papa would have listened to her.

With sudden clarity, Felicia understood how selfish she had been in discouraging her father from remarrying. But Widow Abernathy had eight children, for goodness sake. If Papa had married her, the house would have turned into chaos. And Spinster Hargraves had made it known that she was also available. But, heavens! The woman was so rigid she might have shattered her bones if she had so much as bent over. No, she would have been an impossible taskmaster.

Papa stretched and yawned. Then, removing his glasses, he closed the book and got up, setting both items on a nearby barrelhead. "I think I'll just go out back for a bit." With a smile, he left by way of the kitchen.

Oh, please, Felicia prayed in desperation, *make Papa come to his senses long enough to take me back home. If he will, I promise never to be selfish with his affections ever again. I'll do my best to find him a suitable wife . . . one with a gentle temperament and good standing in society. Just please let him take me back home.*

Yancy leaned the gleaming rifle against the wall and started oiling his new boots.

Curious, Felicia thought about how impoverished he had appeared when he'd first crossed their path. Yet he'd had funds enough to purchase some dead man's entire outfit. He did appear rather pleased with himself and his new possessions—and worse, happy about embarking on the *new adventure* with her and Papa. She perused the weapon. Had he, a seaman, ever owned a firearm before?

She cleared her throat and attempted her most authoritative tone. "Excuse me, Mr. Curtis."

He turned his head.

"I am well aware that you're on the run from the law . . . from that *Gaspee* business, and heaven knows what other such devilment."

His eyes grew hard but didn't waver.

"I intend to keep your secret, of course . . . *provided* you convince Papa to turn around and take me home."

"And if I don't?"

She tipped her head. "Then I'm afraid I shall have to speak with the authorities when we reach Staunton tomorrow."

For a fleeting second he actually appeared nervous. But then just as quickly he regained his bravado. "Graspin' at straws, are ye?"

Felicia shrugged. "Does it matter? They'll hold you until they find out the truth. You'll rot in some rat-infested jail cell for weeks. Perhaps months."

"Jail?" Papa said, returning to the room. "Did I hear you say Mr. Curtis will be put into jail, Leece?"

Never had Felicia seen a more angry expression than the one Yancy flung at her before he turned to her father. "I'll tell ye anything ye want to know. But only you. What's say the two of us take a walk up the hill and give this new Pennsylvania rifle a try?"

Mr. Blair smiled and walked over to the weapon. He picked it up gingerly and ran a hand down the stock with admiration. "Yes. Excellent idea. High time I learned how to operate one of these things. There won't be any butcher shops where we're heading."

With a sickeningly irritating grin in her direction, Yancy pulled on his boots, grabbed the powder horn and leather bullet bag from the table, and strode toward the door, with Mr. Blair right behind.

Felicia folded her arms. "Do try not to shoot yourselves."

More than a little disenchanted with the mouthy wench, Yancy had to remind himself to relax his jaw as he and Mr. Blair headed toward the woods behind the trading post. The smooth leather of his new clothing brushed against his skin as he walked, and with each step he took, he appreciated the comfort of the substantial boots, which he had polished to near-new brilliance. Having such adventurous attire did much to lessen his irritation with Felicia.

"To what was my daughter referring, lad, when she mentioned something concerning you and jail?" Mr. Blair asked when they had left the business establishment far behind.

Yancy filled his lungs and expelled the air all in one breath as he wondered where to start. "Has to do with smugglin' more than anything, really."

"You said something about the *Gaspee,* as I recall."

"Aye, that was somethin' I had me hand in, so to speak. But nothin' ever came of it. The local authorities didn't work very hard at ferreting out all us culprits, if you know what I mean," he said with a conspiratorial wink. "The only real trouble came when some of me friends harbored a young cabin boy from the vessel. But even that smoothed over eventually."

"Folks around Williamsburg couldn't believe that nothing more came of the incident." Removing a kerchief from his pocket, the older man wiped his nose, then tucked the cloth away as they walked on.

"Oh, the British huffed and puffed up a storm. But there's not much they can do when no one is willing to betray a neighbor. 'Twas when I took part in unloadin' some tea up on the north end of Boston durin' that other harbor mess that I got in a little deep. Seems someone had set me up, and the lobsterbacks were waitin' to catch us red-handed. Did, too. Still find it amazin' that I escaped in one piece. But 'twill be awhile before I can show me face around there again. That's why I'm headin' for the backcountry. That's the truth of it."

The old gentleman stopped to catch his breath. He searched Yancy's face, then smiled. "It's quite a marvel the way our heavenly Father works things out for his own. He's brought us together to help one another, each with separate needs."

Taking in the bleak remoteness of the mountain terrain, Yancy couldn't help but wonder if either of them would do the other much good in the event an actual need did arise, like Indians or thieves falling upon them. "Your daughter plans to turn me in, hoping you'll give up and return home."

Mr. Blair patted Yancy's back. "Don't fret, lad. I'll have a word with Felicia. She's always been a sensitive and thoughtful girl, actually. It's just that I plucked her so suddenly from her settled life and carted her out into the unknown wilderness. It's thrown her off balance. But once I reason with her, I'm certain she'll come around." He grinned and reached for the rifle crooked in Yancy's arm. "Hm. Let's see. Just how does one go about loading this thing?"

Yancy shook his head. He couldn't have heard right. Surely the old gentleman had shot a flintlock sometime in his long life.

The last rays of twilight were losing their rosy hue as Felicia glanced one more time out the window of the cabin. They had to come back soon. Darkness came swiftly in the winter wilderness. A faraway shot echoed every now and then, so she felt fairly safe in assuming that Papa and Yancy hadn't accidentally shot one another. Still, she had loved the expression on the sailor's cocky face when she'd intimated they were so inept they might do just that.

"Here you go, gal," Mr. Potts said, handing her some wooden bowls. "Spread these around proper, like you womenfolk know how to do. Sure hope you all like rabbit stew. Other game's too hard to come by now that my nephew's passed on, leavin' an old cripple to fend for himself."

The nephew probably died on purpose just to get some peace from Mr. Potts's constant complaining, Felicia thought as the trader's whine faded. But she took the dishes and did as asked.

"Pretty sure I mentioned that I charge extra for seconds, didn't I?" the man said. "Be sure to tell your pa and that other fellow."

The sound of horses' hooves on the packed snow drifted from outside.

Mr. Potts limped over to the door and peered out. "Good, good. I can use some extra business."

Leaning around the innkeeper's bulk, Felicia saw some mounted riders with a string of packhorses.

"Howdy, Jed," hollered one of the newcomers. Swinging down, he looped the reins around the hitching post. The two others with him, one of whom was a young lad, did the same.

"You'd best set three more places, gal," Potts said. "Appears the Thornton boys from over Cheat River way will be spendin' the night."

"Cheat River? That's an odd name."

"It's up in the wild country, other side of Shenandoah. The Cheat runs almost due north to the Monongahela. An' where that one joins the Allegheny, at Fort Pitt, they become the mighty Ohio. Real wild country, that is. Wild an' beautiful."

Despite the trader's wistful tone, Felicia didn't consider *wild* and *beautiful* compatible in the same breath. Now, on the other hand, *wild* and *Indian* fit together perfectly. "But Fort Pitt is safe and civilized by now, surely."

"Gettin' there, that's a fact. Must be upwards of a hundred settlers there now. Course, I won't never see it again." He ambled away in disgust.

A hundred did not seem a very impressive number to Felicia, but still, with soldiers for protection, the thought of a fort allayed some of her fears. *If* she and Papa actually did go that far into the wilderness. She cast another glance out into the inky darkness of the forested hillsides, then began setting the extra places.

Mr. Potts brought a huge cauldron of stew to the table, and Felicia put a pan of biscuits on either side of it.

Footsteps approached the cabin. The door opened, admitting three males, each dressed in the practical garb of wilderness settlers . . . and all of whom stopped in their tracks and gawked at Felicia.

The oldest of the lot, a thick-necked oaf in his midtwenties with sandy blonde hair and blue eyes, whipped off his broadbrimmed hat in a wide sweep. "Ma'am. We'd no idea a'tall we'd be findin' ourselves such a purty flower in the dead of winter." Without warning, he headed straight to her and took her hand, bowing over it with a grand kiss.

Speechless for an instant, she nearly yanked herself away from the unkempt but formidable young man. At the last minute she decided she was too outnumbered to make a scene.

"Skinner Thornton, ma'am, at your service."

"He's the son of Ike Thornton," Mr. Potts supplied. "They got a settlement store. Doin' real well, too, from what Skinner, here, says."

"And if my cousin'll step aside," said the wiry fellow next to him, whose oily brown hair curled boyishly around his ears as he tipped his head, "I'll tell the comely lady I'm Drew Nesbitt. My folks own a lowly gristmill, but it's the only one on the river."

The youngest one, a half-grown version of Skinner, smiled shyly, maneuvering around his older brother with some difficulty as Skinner tried to elbow him away.

The gesture was enough to give Felicia the impression that the older boy was a bully—especially when he took her hand again.

"We mustn't forget our young Matthew here," he said patronizingly. But he did not release his hold.

She tried to wriggle free.

Matthew quickly removed his hat and broadened his grin.

"We noticed a wagon outside," Skinner said. "Some greenhorn still attemptin' to use wheels in the mountains in January?"

"Belongs to the gal's pa," Potts answered. "He's off huntin' right now, but he ain't likely to git himself nothin'. Bookish sort. Glasses for readin' an' all."

"You don't say." Thornton slid his cousin a satisfied smirk.

"Enough yappin'," the old trader said. "Might's well eat while the stew's hot."

As they all headed toward the makeshift long table, Felicia struggled to free herself. Skinner tightened his hold. "But we ain't learned the young lady's name." He gazed at her with hungry eyes. "My heart's a'thunderin' with anticipation. Feel it?"

Felicia gasped as he pressed her fingers against his chest. Mortified, she tugged harder.

His gaze flitted to the table, then to Mr. Potts. "Still usin' those old bent spoons, I see."

"I don't have time nor money to spend on foolish trappin's, and you know it. Food gets to your mouth just as quick with these."

"Tsk, tsk." Skinner shook his head. "We can't have the fair damsel usin' nothin' but the best. Matt, take Mr. Potts out to the horses and let him pick out eight new ones."

The trader frowned. "I told you already, I ain't got no money for—"

"I'm givin' 'em to you, old man . . . for always takin' such good care of us when we pass through."

"That right?" Mr. Potts's face brightened. "Well, now. That's mighty kind of you. Any spoons I want, you say? Even silver?"

Thornton laughed. "If you find a silver one, you can have it."

No. Please don't leave me here alone! Felicia begged silently. But the trader snatched a lantern and limped quickly out the door.

Matthew lagged behind. "The spoons are all the way at the bottom of one of the packs, you know," he informed his brother.

"Yep." He flashed a grin at Felicia. "Now, do as I say, if you know what's good for you."

Mustering all her courage, Felicia gave a sharp jerk in a useless effort to gain her freedom. "I'll thank you to unhand me," she said in her haughtiest voice. "This instant."

The forceful young man exchanged a conspiratorial glance with his cousin, who smiled and stepped closer. "Not until you favor us with your sweet name."

"Very well, if that's what it will take."

Skinner let go but grabbed a handful of her chignon instead, loosening several locks of hair in the process. He pulled her near. "Whisper it in my ear."

"*Let me go!*" Felicia cried. She shoved at his chest and stomped on his foot as hard as she could.

"A spitfire," he crooned savagely, grabbing her other hand. "I love a spitfire. Makes me wanna give her a big kiss."

The door crashed open. Rifle in hand, Yancy filled the open doorframe. He leveled a menacing stare at Skinner Thornton. "I see you've met me wife."

17

Felicia was never more glad to see anyone in her whole life. She almost lost her balance when Skinner released her. With a breath of relief, she flew to the safe harbor of Yancy's and Papa's presence.

The seaman's eyes glittered like icy shards as he stood in the open doorway staring at Thornton. "Name's Curtis. Yancy Curtis. And the lady, here, is *Mistress* Curtis." He left a significant pause, as if allowing the statement to sink in.

Surely there was no need to continue the farce, Felicia decided. After all, Papa was stepping past Yancy now, and the wilderness settlers wouldn't likely bother her again. She opened her mouth to correct the untruth.

"And a mighty fine son-in-law he makes, I must say," her father injected. "We've been blest to have him."

Felicia swept a glance from one to the other. Papa, lying? How could that be, with all those hours he spent reading his Bible and praying? But she kept silent as he moved to her side and wrapped an arm snugly around her. A blast of January air ruffled her skirts.

Drew Nesbitt cleared his throat. "Say, we were just about to sit down and eat. Join us?"

It was an obvious ploy, Felicia knew, to ease the tension that his cousin had caused. She saw Yancy slide his gaze toward the curly haired youth whose gangly leanness was no match for his own muscled strength. But Skinner, his neck thick as a bull's, was another matter entirely.

"Before it gets cold," Drew added.

"Where's Trader Potts?" Papa asked.

The young man cocked his head. "Just out at the packhorses with Cousin Matt, gettin' some new spoons. They should be back any minute. He told us all to start without them."

Yancy assessed the utensils on the table and sneered at Skinner Thornton. "Made him a generous gift of 'em, eh?"

Astonished at the seaman's perception, Felicia watched Drew shift his weight nervously from one foot to the other before slanting a glance at Skinner.

"My cousins are the Thorntons, from up Cheat River way," he explained. "Their father is a storekeeper, and he sent us to Richmond for supplies. Potts has been asking us to get him some new spoons the last two or three times we came through." He nudged Skinner.

Thornton finally broke the stare and exhaled. He nodded. "The old man wanted 'em real bad."

As if certain their ridiculous story would find easy acceptance, both young men walked to the table and plopped down with nonchalance.

Mr. Blair took Felicia's elbow and ushered her over, then seated her and himself. "Smells delicious, Yancy. Close the door and join us, why don't you?"

The seaman gave the door a kick, slamming it shut, but still didn't relax his stance. Or his glower at Skinner Thornton.

His predatory attitude was beginning to frighten Felicia. She'd never been witness to an altercation before, especially one where, given enough provocation, someone could get shot.

"Think I'll just wait for Trader Potts," Yancy said evenly. "There's a couple of things I want to talk over with him."

Drew Nesbitt picked up the ladle and began filling his bowl, but Felicia caught the slight tremble in his movements.

"Father Blair always says a blessing before we eat," Yancy stated defiantly.

Drew dropped the ladle back into the cauldron. Instantly the two young men bowed their heads.

"Almighty God," Papa began, "we do thank thee for this warm shelter in the wilderness and the chance to partake of such wondrous fare. . . ."

Her own head bent, Felicia lifted her lashes and sneaked a peek at Yancy.

He was grinning from ear to ear.

She stifled a giggle of her own. Knowing how long-winded Papa's prayers had gotten lately, the two cousins would be squirming in their chairs by the time he finished.

". . . And we ask thy blessing on the kind trader who'll be providing our beds this eve. We ask that thou might touch his infirmed leg—"

The door squeaked as Mr. Potts and Matthew returned.

"Amen!" Skinner Thornton said at the interruption with unmasked relief. He grabbed a biscuit, and Drew snatched up the ladle again.

"Well, look who's back from huntin'," Mr. Potts said, a teasing glint in his beady eyes. "You two happen to shoot anything, by any chance?"

"We weren't huntin'," Yancy explained. "I was showing my *father-in-law* some of the finer points of the Pennsylvania rifle."

"Grand rifle it is, too," Mr. Blair added before the trader could respond. "In no time at all, the lad will make as good a marksman out of me as he is himself. Right, son? Now, come on over and get some supper."

The seaman leaned his weapon against the wall at last and headed toward the table. He pulled out the chair next to Felicia's and sat down.

"S'pose everybody's met, by now," Potts said. "'Cept mebbe for this towhead." He ruffled Matt's blonde hair. "This here's Ike Thornton's youngest, Matthew." Then as he and the boy took the last two places, he pulled some shiny spoons from the pocket of his soiled shirt and tossed them in a clanging heap across the tabletop.

Felicia gingerly picked one up, wishing there were some inconspicuous way to wipe it off before she used it.

The heavyset man gave her a nod. "Course, these ain't from Williamsburg or Philadelphia, miss, but I hope they'll do."

She nodded politely. "You needn't have gone out for them on my account." As a flash of warmth flooded her cheeks, Felicia wondered if Yancy thought she'd had anything to do with that absurd spoon business. From the corner of her eye, she saw his mouth twitch. If he chose this moment to laugh at her, someone could get hurt. She jabbed his leg with her knee.

"So. Mr. Thornton," Mr. Blair said to the young man across from him. "How far away would that trading post of your father's be? It's up on the Cheat, you say?"

Drew Nesbitt snickered. "We'll make it in seven or eight days. But with that rig of yours, you'll get bogged down and covered up by the next big snow before you're halfway outta the Shenandoah."

"If Injuns don't get you all first," Skinner added with a snarly smile at Yancy.

"Or a stray bullet from someone out on a turkey shoot," the redhead returned with equal smoothness.

"Oh, now, I wouldn't worry about either of those possibilities," Mr. Blair said with confidence. "The good Lord wouldn't have brought me this far if he didn't have a purpose in mind."

Yancy relaxed back in his chair and picked up one of the new spoons, examining it with feigned interest. "You're absolutely right, Father Blair. Absolutely right."

Matthew, the lad, looked across at Felicia with utmost sincerity. "It's been more'n two years since we had redskin trouble, ma'am. An' if somethin' did start up, my pa and some other men's built a stockade for folks to come to till we run the Injuns off. So I don't think you should worry overmuch."

She forced a sweet smile and turned to her father, working

up to her most syrupy tone. "Did you hear, Papa? They had to build a stockade to keep themselves safe from murdering Indians."

"Yessir," Yancy said with a chuckle. "God is good."

Yancy hated to see the meal come to an end. It had been the longest stretch that Miss Priss had ever kept herself under control, not reverting to her harpy manner. He gave an elaborate stretch and yawned as he rose. "Come on, woman. We need to go out to the wagon and bring in the beddin'. I'm worn out."

The lass sprang to her feet like a jack-in-the-box. "I beg your pardon?"

"Our beddin'," he said, sliding an arm around her. "Your papa's, too," he said, turning to wink at Mr. Blair before grabbing the lantern off the table.

"But—," she sputtered as he steered her toward the door.

He couldn't resist stretching out the charade. Plucking her cloak from the peg, he put it around her. "It's been a long day. I can hardly wait to lay me weary bones down. How about you?"

"Me, neither," Matthew piped in. He got up and ran out after them. "Skinner an' Drew kept me hoppin' all day."

Yancy nearly burst out laughing at the expression on Felicia's face. She must have been ready to give him a piece of her mind once they were outside alone. . . . But now with the boy tagging along, she could only stand there with her mouth gaping, her ebony eyes flashing sparks as she glared up at him. He could just imagine the tirade taking shape inside that enticing head of hers. He grinned and draped his arm across her shoulders.

"Get mine, too, Matt," his brother called from the door.

"See what I mean?" the lad grumbled. "Won't do nothin' for himself. Only reason he and Drew brung me along was just to have somebody to fetch an' carry."

"I know just what ye mean, lad," Yancy said, giving Felicia a squeeze. "Some folks act like they're livin' in some fine house with nothin' to do but bark orders to some poor slave."

The lass wrenched out of his grasp. "And some people are just . . . just . . . oh, never mind." Angrily she stalked ahead, crunching across the thin layer of snow toward the wagon, dark curls from her loosened chignon bouncing with each step.

How about that, Yancy thought as he grinned after her. *For once she couldn't think of a biting retort!* He let the astonishing fact roll around in his brain, until a more serious one took over. Some of the meanness must have been scared out of her when Thornton grabbed her. Yancy clenched his fists as rage began to stir within him. He didn't want to think what might have happened to her if he hadn't come back when he did.

The thought of a pretty woman in danger suddenly reminded him of Jane and Ted. At his last sight of them, they had been racing away, with that uppity cur Fontaine scrambling onto his horse and screeching threats in their wake. Yancy hoped his two friends had escaped.

Matt veered off toward the packhorses, and Yancy took some quick strides to reach Felicia at the wagon where, huffing and puffing, she was trying to hoist herself up. He handed her the lantern. "I'll get those. Hold the light high, so I can see." He hopped onto the wagon bed.

Gathering blankets and feather ticks into his arms, he saw the girl glance at Matthew in the distance. *"Mr. Curtis,"* she muttered between her clenched teeth, "my father may be going along with your underhanded game at the moment to keep peace. But don't you for one minute think he'll stand back while you and I do a little cozy *bundling.*"

"Oh, now, I wouldn't make such a hasty statement, *Mistress Curtis.* Your pa says I'm a fine son-in-law, remember? Me lawless past notwithstandin'."

With a gasp and a pout, the lass whirled around and left, taking the light with her.

Groping about for the pillows, Yancy whacked his shin sharply on one of the trunks . . . but it only made him laugh.

❦ ❧

Dim light glowed from the banked fire in the hearth. From the open door of the one lean-to bedroom of the trading post, Mr. Potts's snores rumbled through the night, while everyone else occupied the floor of the common room on bedrolls and sleeping mats.

As he lay on the floor, Yancy managed to keep his amusement in check. With the Thorntons still around, the only truly safe spot for Felicia was between him and her father. It had been one hilarious sight watching her stiff movements as she spread out their bedding and slid ever so cautiously into hers, where she now lay straight as a broomstick, hands crossed over her bosom, nose straight up.

"Ye forgot me kiss, sweetheart," he said just loudly enough so everyone heard.

She drew a sharp breath.

"Mine, too, Leece," Mr. Blair said.

Relenting, she turned, eyes flashing in the glow of embers, and bestowed a curt peck on Yancy's cheek, then gave her father one before resuming her earlier position.

Yancy was hard pressed to keep the chuckle rumbling in his chest from bursting forth. When the lass's breathing took on the deep regularity of sleep, he rubbed the spot where her lips had brushed his face. In truth, he'd never felt anything so soft in his life, like the petals of a summer rose. And her sweet flowery fragrance still lingered as he drew in a long, slow breath. But roses were fragile. They required lots of care and protection. He'd have to keep a closer watch over this one.

He rolled toward the smart-mouthed lads whose bedrolls were lined up on the other side of him . . . and in the dim glow of the fire, he made out Skinner Thornton sneaking noiselessly toward the door, boots in hand.

Yancy eased to his stockinged feet and reached for the rifle he'd leaned close by against the stone fireplace. Careful not to disturb anyone, he moved without sound to the window and gazed in the direction of the stable, where he was sure that pirate had some weapons of his own.

But Skinner had not headed there at all. He was even now opening the door of the outhouse.

Yancy shook his head with chagrin and relaxed, but not entirely. Stepping with care to his sleeping mat, he picked up his pillow and blanket, then went for a chair, which he set in the corner near Felicia and her father. He propped the rifle within easy reach and sat down facing the door, doing his best to get comfortable for a long night vigil.

18

Cold and shivering with only a feather tick between her and the earthen floor, Felicia awakened with the first pale light of dawn. An assortment of snoring patterns drifted from the bedrolls strewn around the room. Memories of the previous night came back with force—especially of that blackguard Skinner Thornton. She shivered at how close she had come to being mauled by him and his cousin. But it shouldn't have given that dastardly Yancy Curtis leave to wangle his way into sleeping next to her. Knowing that even at this moment he was at her back, she sneaked a glance over her shoulder.

He was gone!

Craning her neck, she scanned the other end of the room, but he was not at the table. Any relief she might have felt was quickly swallowed by growing irritation. To think that the lout had risen before she'd had the opportunity to set herself to rights without having strangers staring at her the way they had last eve. And worse, anyone with the slightest amount of concern for others would most certainly have stoked up the fire, at the very least. Only a scant glow still remained in the hulk of the back log. Most of the embers had long since turned to ashes.

Seething, she tossed off her covers and crawled up on her knees, trying not to awaken the others while she snatched the small chance for privacy.

As she rose to her feet, her gaze happened upon a figure in

a chair in the corner: the seaman, sound asleep. A blanket was bunched up about him, and he had propped a pillow between his head and the chinked log wall. The rifle lay across his lap.

Felicia started to turn away. But in the growing outside light, her eyes were drawn to his face . . . and they lingered.

He looked so different in slumber. Gone was the cocky smirking expression, the mischievous grin that so easily raised her temper. A silly little curl made a shadow on his high forehead, causing him to look more like a small boy than a rakish sailor. And his face bore a soft innocence, one that truly surprised her.

Staring at the sleeping man who had befriended her and her father when they'd been in dire need, Felicia felt a smile spread over her lips. He might love to tease and taunt a person, on occasion, but underneath all that swaggering devilment, he truly cared about *her* safety. Enough to stand up to that bully last eve and enough to sacrifice a night's sleep to ensure that the cur never tried to finish what he'd started.

An unexpected tenderness warmed her heart as she slipped into her shoes. She tiptoed over to Yancy and gingerly straightened the warm blanket over him, rifle and all.

After quietly stoking up the coals and adding a couple of logs, she picked up her carpetbag. Then with one last look at him, she slipped into the kitchen to start heating some water and repair herself for the day.

Yancy hadn't realized that he'd dozed off sometime during the night, but when Felicia arranged the coverlet over him, he'd awakened. Not wanting to spoil the first kind thing she had ever done for him, he feigned sleep and watched through slitted eyes as she'd glanced back at him with that same look of tenderness she'd given her father the other day. As she left the room, he felt a chord stir in his heart, delicate and subtle, whose notes had never played until that moment.

It hadn't exactly been part of the plan for her to catch him guarding her, but it was too late now. She probably realized he truly was concerned about her well-being. And to complicate matters, her thoughtful act gave him a brief glimpse of the girl her father knew, the one Yancy hadn't really believed existed. This little turn of events could prove very awkward . . . and, he thought as his smile broadened into a grin, more than a bit interesting as well.

One of the other young men moaned and rolled over, bringing back with sudden force the reason Yancy had stayed awake most of the night. He decided to speak to Mr. Blair as soon as the older man awakened. They needed to devise some plausible excuse for remaining at the wayside inn until long after the Thornton party left. By no means did Yancy want to travel in close proximity to the threesome and have to watch the sneaky older one's every move all the way until they reached Staunton.

Staunton. Leaning the rifle against the wall, Yancy stretched out his legs. Trader Potts said the town was nigh onto two hundred miles from the coast, a far piece from the high sea for a sailor.

And a long time coming for any news from Boston and the fate of the Hayneses.

On the road into Boston, Ben patted the bulging leather mail pouch with satisfaction as he approached the guards up ahead. Thank providence he'd had the foresight to collect letters from the towns along the Worcester road. He had cut across to it, taking on extra miles just so the nosy lobsterbacks—and Lieutenant Fontaine in particular—would think he'd been to Worcester, where his two married sisters lived. A good ploy to keep the lieutenant from suspecting he'd been to the New Hampshire grants.

An unfamiliar corporal stepped into the middle of the roadway. "Halt and state your business."

"Postrider, mail for Boston," Ben said in an elaborately bored voice. He tried to ride on through.

A musket hammer clicked.

Reining in, Ben saw a Brown Bess pointed straight at his heart, bayonet fixed.

"I have my orders, *boy*. All postriders are to be escorted to headquarters for questioning." He motioned with his weapon. "Dismount!"

Ben leveled his gaze at the soldier. "Sounds like martial law to me. Something happen while I was out of town?"

"All I know is I'm followin' orders. Now get down." Without taking his eyes off Ben, the redcoat shouted over his shoulder toward the guard shack. "Private Moore! I've another one for you to run into town."

By the time Ben had walked the three miles up to Fort Hill, his feet were stinging from blisters. But far worse was the humiliation he'd suffered having to march in front of his own pacer while the surly private, astride Rebel, had kept a bayonet pointed at his back. No telling how many townspeople had recognized him while he'd been marched through the streets as if he were some common criminal. The fury building inside of him had been almost uncontrollable.

Reaching the South Battery, an imposing fortress situated on the southern point of Boston Harbor, the private dismounted at the gate and gave the pacer's reins to one of several smirking soldiers. Then grabbing the mail pouch, he shoved Ben on through and followed close behind, his rifle at the ready.

As they approached, Ben cast a hateful glare at the British flag flying above headquarters.

The soldier pushed him toward the entrance.

"Another upstart postrider," he announced as they passed the guard at the door and went through to the anteroom. He tossed the pouch onto the front desk just as an older lobsterback emerged from the inner office. "Sergeant Collins, sir!" The private gave a smart salute. "Delivering a man for questioning, sir." Then, salute returned, he swiveled on his heel and left.

Collins' shrewd eyes raked Ben up and down with disdain. He gestured toward a chair against the wall. "Sit there. And don't move. I'll be back." He seized the mailbag and went through a door behind him.

Ben assessed the cold, gloomy official-looking room, with its portrait of King George, wall maps and charts, its cluttered tables and sheaves of papers. He released a tense breath and tapped his fingers against his knees as he sat woodenly on the hard seat. No sound came from the hallway. He gave fleeting thought to just walking out and riding away on Rebel . . . if the thieving pirates hadn't already stolen the pacer. The redcoats did, after all, seem more interested in the mail than in him. Hopefully, at any rate. He stood, intending to check out the window to see if his horse was handy.

The inner door swung wide, and there stood Lieutenant Fontaine, his expression swiftly changing from one of suspicion to a triumphant gloat. "Ah. Haynes." His face hardened. "In here."

Squaring his shoulders, Ben strode in past the exiting sergeant.

Already behind a nondescript desk, Fontaine struck a kingly pose and peered over his long nose at Ben. "I wondered when you'd decide to visit *our* fair city again." Slowly he tipped the pouch and let the contents slide out in front of him, appraising every piece. Then he dropped the leather bag onto the floor.

Ben was thankful that he'd had the foresight to leave the letters to Susannah with Sean Burns in Cambridge before he reached the Neck.

The lieutenant took a handful of letters and fanned them like playing cards in his hand as he fingered and investigated them singly. A sneer curled a corner of his thin mouth. "Interesting. All from along the Worcester road." Yanking open a desk drawer, he took out a sheet of paper and looked it over. "This list says that Carver Owens has that route." His gaze slid in Ben's direction.

Not about to let Alex best him, Ben kept his own eyes from wavering. "And when did they appoint you postmaster?"

"'Twould be in your best interest, Haynes," he said, casually sailing the list onto the pile of letters, "to tell me where they are. Your parents would be most distressed were we forced to try you, too, for treason. Precisely where have you been?"

"Where haven't I been might be a more apt question, since I've been delivering invitations to each and every house in the Colony. Invitations to our next *tea party.*" Ben sneered at Alex. "Rumor has it, the last one was more fun than catching lobsters."

Veins bulged in the lieutenant's temples. He crumpled the closest piece of mail and sprang to his feet, his eyes blazing. He glared back at Ben and lowered his voice to a venomous tone. "You Hayneses are a stupid lot. Well, we'll just see if we can't wise up at least one of you a bit."

The brisk ocean breeze cleared away the morning fog, allowing the first rays of sunshine in weeks to warm the chilled town. Susannah noticed an abundance of carts, wagons, and foot traffic on Milk Street—more activity than she had seen since the harbor incident. Perhaps it was a good sign that tensions were beginning to ease once again. She let the window curtain drop from her grasp. Perhaps there might even be news of Dan and the others. Her spirits lifted as she considered the possibility.

She turned to face the room. Why, it might be a fine day to gather up the parlor rugs and beat some of the foul-weather dirt out of them. She smiled, recalling that most of the mud had been tracked in on Christmas Eve, by her dear church family, come to cheer her up.

A knock rattled the door.

Startled, Susannah dropped the rugs and flew to answer before the baby's nap was disturbed. "Alex!" Automatically her gaze sought the guards at the end of the walk to see if they were still in place. Everything appeared as usual . . . and yet the lieutenant's curious expression made her uneasy. Surely he hadn't captured Dan.

Fontaine smiled pleasantly. Too pleasantly. "Might I come in for a moment? I've news that might interest you."

Susannah's insides began quivering as she allowed him entrance, then closed the door. She toyed nervously with a fold of her indigo skirt. *Please, heavenly Father, give me strength,* she prayed desperately, fearing the lieutenant's gaze would fall upon her trembling hand. She raised her chin and followed him into the parlor.

He stopped and knelt down, his saber banging ominously against the floor, and gave the discarded rug a few straightening tugs. He smiled slyly, obviously aware of her eagerness to find out who had been at the door. Undoubtedly the guards reported how often she came to the window to search for her loved ones.

She motioned to a chair. "Won't you sit down?"

Staring at her for a full minute, he finally relented.

Something about his countenance made Susannah anxious. She desperately wanted to know why he'd come, but she couldn't let him see that. Feigning nonchalance, she retrieved her needlework from a seat near his and moved to one farther away, then casually resumed stitching.

He chuckled, a low ominous sound that made her skin crawl. "You look quite fetching, Susannah. Even in this miserable Boston weather you seem to bloom."

Without responding, she glanced up from her work and held his gaze.

He propped an ankle across his knee and appeared to relax. "I wonder if Jane is looking as attractive," he mused. "She's not one to endure adversity very well. And she does have a penchant for fashionable clothes and baubles. Tsk, tsk. She must be in such a state by now." He wagged his head. "Yes, such a state. Can you not imagine that harping tongue of hers? Poor Ted must be beside himself, considering all his other worries."

Ignoring the officer's attempts to bait her, Susannah maintained a polite expression as she concentrated on her sewing, utterly grateful for the steadiness of her fingers. She only hoped it would continue.

"Another interesting bit of information has been reported to me by loyal subjects in the countryside." He paused significantly. "Your young brother-in-law was seen on the road to Lexington soon after we last spoke . . . and he was carrying no mail. Peculiar, wouldn't you say—a postrider with no letters?"

Susannah studied the butterfly she had nearly completed. She was glad she'd chosen the light yellow shade for the edges of its wings. So pretty.

"Yes. And I've hired some very reliable, very loyal civilians to trace his every step. So whether he talks or not, I'll still find my darling Jane and her traitorous lover."

She pointedly laid her needlework down in her lap. "Are you implying that you've seen Ben?" she asked. "I really would appreciate it, Lieutenant, if you would get to the reason for this visit. It's such a perfect day, you see, for sweeping out all manner of filth. It seems a shame to waste it."

"Sweeping. Yes. And airing out things." He raised a hand and perused his fingernails. "Benjamin and I were just talking about that this morning . . . or was it yesterday? I can't quite recall."

Susannah's heart stopped for a second. She steeled herself to remain composed as she looked at the officer. "Is that your clever manner of telling me Ben has returned, and that you've spoken with him?"

A taunting smile hardened Alex's eyes. "You might say that. But, alas, our young friend seems as hesitant to speak as you do, so I expect we'll be having quite a few more conversations in the days ahead. He's certain to become more talkative, eventually. After all," he crooned, "sitting alone all day with only the same four walls to look at does get frightfully tiresome, if you know what I mean." He cocked his head as if a wondrous thought had just occurred to him. "You know, it's entirely possible he just might appreciate some enlightenment from you. Some encouragement, perhaps. Do let me know when you'd like to come see him, when you'd like to persuade him that his cooperation would be in the best interests of all concerned. But make it soon. I trust he's becoming quite lonely for a pretty face."

Susannah rose stiffly to her feet, her indignation at the impudent officer barely contained. "I demand to know on what charge Ben has been arrested."

Alex raised his dark brows in mock innocence as he stood. "Arrested? Did I say he was arrested? Detained. I prefer to think of it as being detained." His mouth curled in a sneer. "Until he tells me what I want to know. Or until you do." Smiling again, he crossed the room to Susannah.

He snatched her chin in his gloved fingers, tightening his grip as she tried to squirm away. He bent to within inches of her face. "In fact, I realize now that I've been neglecting you. And, as you said, this day is far too lovely to—"

Footsteps carried from the stoop, followed by a few light taps and the opening of the door. "Comin' through," a voice called.

The lieutenant wheeled toward the hallway.

Masking her surprise at seeing two neighbor men from across the street carrying either end of a stack of boards, a toolbox riding atop them, Susannah picked up her cue. "I thought you said you'd be here first thing this morning."

Alex removed a glove and slapped it impatiently against the side of his leg.

"Beg pardon. Had to get my saw sharpened," one man said. "Where do you want us to set up?"

"The kitchen, please. I'll be right with you, soon as I see Lieutenant Fontaine out." Gliding past him, she held the door open. "So kind of you to stop by with news of Ben. But as for your offer of help, I'm afraid I couldn't think of burdening you."

A muscle twitched in Alex's jaw as he filled the exit and glared first toward the men and then at Susannah. "I'll call again soon. Perhaps by then you'll be more receptive."

"Oh, I rather doubt it," she said airily. "But I shall be praying for you in your time of sorrow." Although she had uttered the remark in retaliation, it struck her that in truth she actually should pity the man. She touched his arm. "I do mean that, Alex. Truly."

He jerked away, his face contorted with fury. "Save your prayers for yourself, for all the good it will do you." With that he stormed away.

Closing the door behind him, Susannah shot the bolt for good measure. Then, her knees not quite so steady as they'd been, she went to join the men in the kitchen.

"I don't know how ever to thank you," she said, gripping a chair back while she regained her balance. "You couldn't have come at a more opportune moment."

"Well, now, Missy Haynes," bearded Mr. Simms said, "as long as those soldiers are watching *you,* we'll be watching *them.* Old McKnight, here, and me already had it all planned out what we'd do if any of 'em started pesterin' you—especially that one. Had the lumber set out waitin'."

"Oh, I think you're both absolutely wonderful. So wonderful I insist you sit down and have some orange pudding with sweet sauce. I made it just this morning. And some nice smuggled Dutch tea."

"Sounds good," stoop-shouldered little Mr. McKnight said as he wiped his hands on his kerchief. "But I think it's you that should sit. You're lookin' a mite faint."

Susannah smiled and sank gratefully onto a chair. "The Lord gave me the strength I needed to stand up to the lieutenant, but I'm afraid that when he left, so did the strength in my legs."

"Well, now, you set there and let us serve up the tea," Mr. Simms said with a pat on her arm.

"And puddin'," Mr. McKnight added. "I'm a fair hand at servin' that up. Where's your biggest bowls?"

With a laugh, Susannah pointed to a curtained cupboard, and more quickly than she would have believed possible, the three of them were all settled down with the refreshments.

Mr. Simms rubbed his beard as he looked around. "I s'pose we really oughta build somethin'. Otherwise that lobsterback will know we was just interferin'. What might you be needin', Mistress Haynes?"

Susannah felt a blush. "What I need most of all, just now . . . is a cradle." Her face flamed even more. She tilted her head self-consciously and smiled. "I do have one upstairs, but with little Miles running around now, I'll surely need a second one down here so I can keep a closer watch on the new little one we'll be blessed with."

Once the words had been spoken, her eyes flooded with tears. She hadn't allowed herself until now to admit her condition, any more than she could imagine giving birth without the comfort of Dan's presence.

"Well, I'll be," Mr. McKnight said. "Does the reverend know?"

"No," she could only whisper. She swiped at a tear. "And even if I could get word to him, I'm not certain I'd want to add to his burden with this news."

Mr. Simms shook his head and put one of his work-roughened hands over hers. "Don't worry, missy. He'll be home soon."

"I wish I could believe that," she said sadly. "But Lieutenant Fontaine is more determined than ever to bring all of them back for trial. Oh, dear! I nearly forgot to tell you! He has my brother-in-law, Ben, locked up. He's not been charged with anything as yet, but Alex said he'll keep him until Ben informs on Dan and the others." She searched the men's faces. "Please, is there some way to force the army to release Ben?"

Mr. McKnight came to his feet. "Tell you one thing . . . I'm marchin' straight down to Faneuil Hall this minute to tell Sam Adams and whoever else is there that the lad's bein' held without charge. Mark my words, they'll not leave him there to rot."

19

Ben paced the close space of the cold, dank cell where he had spent the past six days and nights. He heard the large outer door of the stockade clang open, and he stopped.

Footsteps reverberated in the hall, heading toward him.

Were the soldiers coming for him—or some other soul facing yet another interrogation? He tugged his greatcoat more snugly about himself. A rough stubble of whiskers scratched against the heavy wool fabric. He sat down on the crude cot along one wall and shifted his weight on the seat, trying to stretch muscles that were stiff and sore from cramped discomfort and disuse. At least if he were taken up to face Fontaine again, he'd be in a warm room for a little while.

Fontaine. The name gnawed at his nerves like a toothache. The echo of the lieutenant's voice continually bombarded Ben, ranting and raving, threatening all manner of torture.

Ben would never forget the sneer that had twisted the lieutenant's mouth when Alex had resorted to bribery during the last inquisition. *Surely someone as disloyal to her kin as Jane, one who would stoop to betray her own sister—not once but twice—deserves no better in return. And you'd find yourself with a purse full of coin in the bargain.*

A purse I'll stuff down your gullet, Ben had flung in return.

Rigid, Fontaine had called in two of his lackeys to inflict another form of persuasion. Far be it from Alex to soil his own gloves or bruise his lily-white hands inflicting the blows himself. But he had relished watching it all. Ben smashed his manacled wrists against the heavy wood door in fury.

"Ye needn't break it down," a voice said from the other side as a key scraped in the lock. The door swung open. "Come along, there's a good fellow."

Ben stepped out into the hallway and swept a wary glance at the two uniformed men. Then, with one positioned on either side, a hand on each of his arms, he was piloted down the dimly lit hall. The chain connecting his wrists lashed across his legs with every step, and Ben took perverse satisfaction in envisioning it wrapped around Fontaine's scrawny neck. What a pleasure it would be to strangle the life out of that puppet. Who knows, it might even be worth the price. Since there was no hope of freedom until he talked, he'd be in here forever anyway. And with Fontaine dead, at least he'd be incarcerated for a truly worthwhile deed. Even hanging would be preferable to being ground under Alex's heel day in and day out. Casually he spread his hands, measuring the length of the chain he had to work with. A few more inches would have been perfect, but he'd make do.

Within a few moments they came to the anteroom of the lieutenant's office. One of the privates stepped into the open doorway. "Delivering the prisoner, sergeant," he said with a salute.

Collins returned it and nodded. "Dismissed."

Good, Ben thought. *The fewer lobsterbacks around, the better my chances.*

The sergeant jerked his jaw, motioning for Ben to come.

His pulse quickening with anticipation, Ben started around the officer's desk toward the inner-office door.

"Haynes," the sergeant snapped.

He stopped.

"Come here. Hold out your hands."

Puzzled, Ben did as ordered. He watched, astonished, as the officer took a key from his pocket and unlocked the manacles.

"You're free to go."

"What?"

"Be off with ye."

"Wait a minute." This had to be some new perverse game being played out at his expense. "You're releasing me?"

"Aye."

Ben looked past the sergeant to the closed door behind him, then out the windows, but the lieutenant wasn't leering at him from anywhere. "I need my mail pouch."

"We sent it on days ago."

Not yet ready to relinquish all his suspicions, Ben half expected Fontaine to be hiding just outside the door, ready to pounce. "What about my horse?"

"Tied up out front. Now get out of here before I change my mind!"

Hardly able to believe this was happening, Ben walked past the guards at the door and stepped outside. A weak winter sun glared against the morning fog. Out of habit, he reached up a hand to tip his hat down, then remembered he'd left it in the cell. He disregarded an impulse to go back and instead kept heading straight for the main gate. The uniformed men scattered around the grounds paid him no mind.

Just as Sergeant Collins had said, Rebel stood saddled and waiting.

Ben walked him to the gates, where he wasted no time mounting. But even as he nudged the animal on through, he kept one ear cocked behind, listening for a flurry of following hooves to chase after him . . . or the crack of a rifle shot.

A few yards down the hill, he swung around in the saddle and took a last look behind him, amazed and relieved to discover only the usual traffic. Who would believe it? He truly was free after all! He slowed Rebel to a walk past the wharf, then headed for Milk Street.

He had to make sure Susannah was unharmed. Fontaine had hinted that he'd been paying her frequent visits as well.

"I say. Haynes! Ben Haynes!"

Recognizing John Hancock's well-modulated voice hailing

him, Ben reined in his horse and reluctantly veered toward the fashionably turned out man. As he did so, his gaze fell upon his own filthy hands, and he sent a hopeless glance down over the rest of his disheveled clothes. What a time to meet up with the most richly dressed man in Boston! Even in his best attire, Ben's would come in a poor second against the everyday clothing of this wealthy patriot.

"Get down, young Haynes," Hancock said as Ben drew near. "Stroll with me down to the Bunch of Grapes." A slightly amused expression played over the dandified gentleman's face as he took in Ben's appearance with polite tolerance. "You look in dire need of a tankard of cider."

"Thank you, sir, but at the moment I—"

Hancock raised a manicured hand. "*And* we must talk. It's urgent."

Hand in hand with little Miles, Susannah exited elderly Mistress Smythe's dwelling. She had been delivering sweet cakes, and she was not in any hurry to get home. The toddler bent down and picked up a shiny stone, then gave it a clumsy toss. She giggled with him. Behind her by several yards, one of her redcoat guards chuckled also.

Coming within sight of the house, Susannah saw a civilian dismounting from a Narragansett Pacer. She looked closer. "Ben!" Swooping Miles up into her arms, she ran the rest of the way.

Her brother-in-law, sporting a week's growth of beard, grabbed the two of them in a fierce hug. "Thank heaven you're all right!"

"Thank heaven you've been released!" she said at the same time, and they both laughed. "I'm so glad you're free."

"Free, yes." He grinned. "But not unwatched. I've been noticing a man in black keeping pace a few blocks behind me." His palm stopped Susannah's cheek just as she tried to look over his shoulder. "Don't. I don't want him to be aware that I know he's there."

Susannah shrugged and tossed her head with a laugh. "*My constant companions aren't nearly so shy about being seen.*" She waved at the two lobsterbacks standing across the street.

The one who had been following her lifted his military hat, and the other quickly checked both ways first and then nodded.

"They're not altogether certain how to act, actually," Susannah said, sliding her hand through the crook of Ben's elbow and steering him through the gate and toward the house. "Once I learned you had been arrested, I started taking them coffee and sweets several times a day. I had a question or two of my own, you know."

He glanced back over his shoulder. "One of them is leaving."

"Of course. Alex must be kept informed, you see. Heaven forbid I should go to the privy without his finding out. I've gotten quite used to it."

Ben's jovial countenance hardened to granite, making him look much older than his twenty years.

Susannah wondered what unspeakable tortures Alex Fontaine had inflicted upon her brother-in-law during his confinement. Unable to dwell on it, she brushed the discomforting thought aside as they went up the steps. "Well, come on in. I do hate to say this, Ben, but you look a frightful sight. I shall put on some water for a bath and find some clothes of Dan's that might fit you."

Ben took Miles from her as she rummaged in her knitted bag for the key. "You have no idea how wonderful a bath sounds."

She let a teasing glance roam over him. "Oh, I think I might." After working the key into the lock, she opened the door and went in.

Ben gave the baby a playful toss up in the air, and Miles grabbed a handful of Ben's hair when he caught him again.

Susannah's heart wrenched as the two hugged and laughed. She watched her brother-in-law try to disentangle the baby's hands from light brown hair that now was matted and dull. "Miles has missed you. And Dan." Blinking back tears that seemed ever near the surface, she forced a smile as she pulled her wiggly son away. "But we shall talk of that after you've cleaned up. Dan's letter was smuggled to me, along with Ted's and Jane's as well . . . but I want to know more. So much, much more."

Susannah was coring apples for baking when Ben, smooth-shaven and clean as new, strode into the kitchen with Miles perched on his shoulder. The sight of Dan's cambric shirt on his younger brother brought a twinge of loneliness, but she managed a smile.

"I knew that somewhere under all that grime there had to be a familiar face," she said, taking the baby. Setting him on a pillowed kitchen chair, she secured him around his waist with a diaper, then pushed him closer to the table.

"Something sure smells good," Ben remarked as he took a seat.

"It's only potato soup, I'm afraid, but I promised the baby we'd have it. He was ever so good while we were visiting Widow Smythe. I've sliced some sausage to have with it, though, and some bread. I hope it'll do." She dished out a small portion for the toddler and set it to cool.

"Right about now, I'd eat the potatoes raw. I haven't seen anything but stale bread and water for days."

"How horrible!" To make up for Alex's cruelty, Susannah filled a much larger bowl with the steaming white broth and brought it to him. She pulled over the plate of sliced bread and the meat, then got some coffee.

Ben began eating ravenously. Susannah saw to the baby's needs, fighting to restrain the questions that threatened to tumble out of her.

After swallowing the last chunk of his bread, Ben finally pushed his bowl away and smiled. "Well. Looks like I'm destined to live after all."

Susannah wiped the baby's mouth, then released him and

set him down. He toddled off to the toy box in the corner. "Where's Dan, Ben?" she finally asked, twisting the edge of her apron.

"He's with Ted and Jane, deep in the wilderness."

"Where?"

"In the mountains at a preacher's farmstead," Ben finished. "But it's best you don't know where."

Susannah released a breath she hadn't realized she'd been holding. "Some of that he told me in the letter. I'm grateful they've at least found refuge in a godly house."

"Refuge. Yes." Ben rolled his eyes impatiently. "And your brother and Jane are all tucked in for the winter as if they haven't a care in the world."

"But aren't you glad for them? After all, they're newly married." She studied his face as he gazed off into the distance. "I read once in the Old Testament that when a man marries he's not to go out with the army for a whole year or be in charge of business. God must place quite an importance on marriage, the way he wants young people to become one in their love."

Toying with the spoon that was lying by his bowl, Ben turned it over absently in his fingers, then drummed the edge of it on the tabletop. "All the more reason Ted shouldn't have gotten married at such a critical time. Particularly since the leader of a militia up there has asked him to join them. They hate oppression as much as we do. But, of course," Ben said, giving a sarcastic smirk, "both he and Dan are reluctant for him to go. But, Sue, all you have to do is take a look out your own windows to see that something has got to be done about those lobsterbacks. Once and for all."

She placed one of her hands over his, spoon and all. "One of these days, if you're fortunate enough, some very special young woman will come along and steal your heart. And then you'll understand what draws two people together and makes them want to spend their lives together, regardless of what might be taking place around them."

"Is that what Dan and you are doing?" he rasped, withdrawing from her. "Disregarding the tyranny that's happening all around you?"

His words stung. Susannah averted her gaze, finding a measure of solace in the sight of her son happily pushing a toy wagon along the floor.

"I'm sorry." Ben smiled weakly and shrugged. "I didn't mean that. You know I didn't. It just galls me that my brother is off elsewhere, while you've been left to deal with that arrogant British dog, Fontaine."

Expelling a sigh, she tilted her head. "In my opinion, for right now at least, Daniel is most wise to stay away from Boston. Your mother sent a letter a few days ago saying that soldiers showed up quite unexpectedly at the farm—and searched it from top to bottom. And the same thing has happened at both your sisters' homes."

Ben tensed as wrath darkened his eyes. "But you could go to him. I could see that you're spirited out of this den of lobsterbacks and up to Dan."

With a sad smile, Susannah shook her head. "How could I risk the danger with little Miles to consider? Besides, Dan requested in his letter that all of us wait until God shows us his will for us. The Lord loves us incomparably, you know. He'll see us through even this."

"And in the meantime," Ben said, not bothering to mask his ire, "you're left at the mercy of Fontaine."

"Not entirely. My good Christian neighbors are watching over me. And many of the congregation have started gathering here for prayer every Sabbath. Please tell that to Dan, will you, when you see him. And," she added cheerily, "whenever you are in Boston, I also have you."

"Yes. Well, I won't be here all that often anymore. On my way over here, I spoke with Mr. Hancock and Lawyer John Adams, who secured my release. And after I relayed a message from Colonel Allen, who I met on my trip, they gave me one to take back. Then I was given new orders . . . to run all the latest news up to the patriot leaders in the outlying areas of New England. We must be prepared for Britain's retaliation.

Our actions against the tea ship were loud and clear, and I'm certain their response will be no less."

"Oh, Ben." She shot a beseeching look at him, then rose and got the coffeepot. "You make everything sound so precarious. Please, please, don't do anything rash that will cause you to be arrested again or hurt." She poured the coffee and sank to her chair.

"Don't worry," he said wryly. "Hancock seemed to think I wasn't useful all locked up. He told me to pick up my orders and messages in Cambridge from now on instead of venturing across the Neck—which is another reason I want you out of here. I won't *be able* to check on you as often as I'd like."

"It's useless to keep on with this, Ben. I shan't leave Boston. Not until the time is right. And that's that."

"Well, then, at least let me hire a woman to keep you company so you won't be alone all the time."

Susannah shook her head. "Thank you, but no. I've no idea how long I'll be able to stay in this house. It's been provided by the church, and I can't add another drain on what money I have. Not while I have no way of knowing how long I may be without Dan's salary."

"Look, Susannah," Ben said, getting up to reach into his own pocket. "If it's only a matter of money . . ." He tossed a few shillings on the table.

She pushed it back toward him. "You keep this. Your family has sent us sufficient funds for our immediate needs . . . and I wouldn't want to expose a servant to Alex's inquisitions as well. Surely you understand."

Ignoring the coins, he cast a glance at the wood box. "A couple would be better anyway. You need a strong man. A brave, strong man."

"Ben, really. I'm quite fine. Alex has been by only once since you were arrested."

"To gloat, no doubt." He started for the back door. "Well, I'll bring in a stack of logs before I leave, anyway."

She sprang after him. "You're leaving? Now? Today?"

"I have urgent messages to deliver, remember?" he said, turning. "I'm a week late as it is."

"But *Dan*. Will you be seeing Dan soon?"

He nodded. "But I can't risk trying to smuggle a letter out past the Neck. If you want to write to him, do it within the hour and take it to the cobbler. He'll pass it on to the wheel-wright in Cambridge. I'll wait there till dark, then I have to be off."

Sighing, Susannah watched her courageous brother in-law with profound sadness as he went out. He'd been just a young lad the first time she'd met him. Now that youthful spirit was dead, replaced by a bitter zeal against the Crown. Such a great loss.

When Ben returned a short time later with his arms full of chopped wood, he crashed it angrily into the box and wheeled around as if he'd been stabbed in the back. "You're with child again, aren't you?"

Susannah stared, dumbfounded.

"Don't bother to deny it. I saw the cradle being built out in the shed."

Coloring, she took hold of his hands. "Don't say a word of it to Dan. I don't want him to worry."

"Oh, he *needs* the worry, make no mistake about it. He needs to get off his behind. No self-respecting man would leave his wife alone when she's in the family way . . . and expect her to stand off the enemy for him!"

"Ben, please. You mustn't. Promise me you won't tell him."

Gently loosening her fingers, Ben seized one of Dan's hats from the wall peg and jammed it on his head. "No, Susannah. On this you will not have your way."

The door slammed shut behind him.

20

Descending the steep, rugged trail that led down into the Cheat River Valley, Yancy checked the landmarks against the map Trader Potts had drawn. Then, certain the course was true, he refolded the paper and tucked it into his pocket.

His gaze shifted from the rolling, snow-covered hills to an even more pleasant view . . . Felicia, riding sidesaddle just ahead of him. Her fur-lined cloak followed the contours of her slender shoulders, draping her enticing form in burgundy velvet. Now and then a tendril of dark brown hair escaped the confines of her hood as the wind blew across her face, and the sunlight glinted like gold against the shimmering curls.

The mellow, dapple gray mare Yancy and Mr. Blair had purchased for her in Staunton seemed more than able to keep pace with the draft horses he and her father rode. And surprisingly, for a city-bred lass, she had taken to the animal right off.

Yancy marveled as she patted its black mane and crooned softly into its ear. To think he had considered the girl a shrew who needed to be tamed, one he couldn't wait to shed. She was simply feisty. Beautiful and feisty. And she was turning out to be a tireless traveler whose one complaint when they'd had to leave the wagon behind in Staunton was having to abandon her dear mother's bed. The promise he'd lightly made to return for it in the spring had promptly ended her reluctance. She had taken his statement to heart and accepted it without question. Now, the more he thought about it, the more determined he became to keep his word.

His stomach growled just then, and he chuckled. Fair though the lass might be to look upon, he couldn't say much for her cooking. The biscuits she'd made early that morning had been hard as rocks, so he'd merely pretended to relish the one he'd taken, contenting himself with only coffee instead. Still, she did seem eager to learn, and there was no denying he truly enjoyed helping her out. In time she might prove quite handy in the kitchen.

Something rustled the brush along the sloping incline to one side of the mountain trail.

Instinctively, Yancy's hand flew to his flintlock, drawing it out of the buckskin scabbard. He reined in his horse, then took a bead on the spot where he'd heard the noise.

Russet tail feathers peeked from behind a boulder, and a plump bird emerged with a distinctive gobble.

He smiled as he took aim and squeezed the trigger.

Startled, Felicia turned in her saddle. "What was that?"

"Supper." Yancy swung down and started toward it.

"Excellent," Mr. Blair called from the front. He turned his horse and plodded back toward Yancy's.

All his practicing had paid off. Yancy assessed with approval his first kill, feeling more than ever like a fearless frontiersman in his fringed buckskin clothing. He looped some twine around the bird's feet and tied it upside down to his saddle. Then, recalling the trader's warning that an unloaded weapon was a useless one, he began by pouring a measure of gunpowder from his powder horn into its long barrel.

Mr. Blair started down the trail again as Yancy finished reloading and hooked the ramrod to the barrel again.

Felicia, however, waited for him to climb into the saddle and come alongside. She took in the bounty with her gaze.

He couldn't help noting the admiration in her eyes. His old tendency to think of a clever remark and set the lass off—or to give her a bold wink—was forgotten. Instead, he sat up taller in the saddle and smiled. Having seen firsthand exactly how vulnerable she was out here in the wilderness, it had occurred to him of late that she shouldn't be subjected to suggestive looks or actions from any man, least of all himself. These protective feelings were completely new to him, and he had no idea until now how strong they could be.

While pondering the change in himself, Yancy realized they had reached the valley floor, sliced down the middle by the ice-bordered Cheat River. Daylight sparkled over the rippling currents, mirroring blurry portraits of the surrounding hills and cloudless expanse overhead.

"Hm," Mr. Blair said. "I smell smoke. Must be a cabin up ahead."

"Who would want to settle way out here?" Felicia asked, glancing at the wooded and hilly terrain dwarfing them in every direction. "A person wouldn't even have neighbors."

"Solitude has some benefits of its own, I'm sure," her father replied.

Yancy glanced at the swiftly flowing water, lost momentarily in thoughts of the sea. When he blinked again, he noticed they were coming up on a small dwelling atop a slight mound.

A plume of smoke drifted upward from the chimney of a crude cabin, making a gray-white column against the sky. Shutters were closed over all the window openings, which, Yancy surmised, most likely contained no glass panes. A few haphazard outbuildings, constructed of canvas over frames of evergreen, stood within a stone's throw of the ramshackle abode, along with a bullock for plowing and a handful of pigs and chickens. No one appeared to be outside working, despite the fact that the mild day was only slightly more than half over.

"Can't see much sense in stoppin' here, Mr. Blair," Yancy said, convinced that the place seemed less than welcoming. "According to the map, Thornton's Fort can't be more than ten or twelve miles further."

The old gentleman brushed at a wrinkle in his black worsted coat. "All the more reason to introduce ourselves to our new neighbors. After all, we've greeted folks at all the other homesteads along the way. One never knows just which ones might be members of my wilderness parish." He guided his horse toward the cabin.

Felicia turned to Yancy and rolled her eyes.

He grinned and followed her father's lead.

"Halloo the house!" the older man called.

Yancy and Felicia pulled alongside his mount just as the door creaked open on leather hinges.

A man stepped outside. He appeared not more than thirty years of age, but his eyes had the haggard look of the aged about them as he shaded them with one hand and closed the door behind himself. "I can tell you folks are travelin' through, but I'm afraid we can't take you in. We've got the pox here."

"The pox?" Yancy repeated with alarm. He had been aboard one or two vessels not allowed to make port because crewmen had the dreaded disease, and he was all too familiar with it. Beside him, he saw Felicia's knuckles whiten on her horse's reins.

The man nodded. "My woman and one of the young'uns come down with it last week. Best you move on."

"Is there anything you'd like us to send back from the outpost?" Yancy asked. "Food? Medicine?"

"Naw. We'll make do with what we got."

From the look of the place, Yancy doubted they could afford much of anything anyway.

"But," the man added as he glanced back at the cabin, "tell old man Thornton to send one of his boys out to the Richards place if he don't see me inside a fortnight."

Trying not to show the pity he felt, Yancy gave a polite nod and turned his mount toward the river trace again. But hearing only the lass's horse following, he swiveled in the saddle and glanced back.

Mr. Blair had dismounted.

Yancy reined in his animal.

"Your eyes are looking quite red," the druggist told the settler. "Is your throat sore as well?"

"Some. Like I said, you'd best be on your way."

The old gentleman moved to one of his saddlebags. "Have you any ipecac, young man? Castor oil and mustard?"

"Mustard." The fellow's voice cracked with emotion. "We got some mustard."

Mr. Blair nodded. He glanced back at Felicia. "Sweetheart, I want you to go on with Yancy to Thornton's Fort. God willing, I'll be along in a couple of weeks."

"What?" The question came out a hoarse whisper. "Papa! You can't be thinking of staying here. You've never had the smallpox."

He fingered the wide brim of his black hat as he appeared to consider his daughter's comment, then turned to the settler. "I'll be along presently." He strode purposefully toward Felicia's horse and covered her gloved hand with his. "I must do this, my dear. If someone in this home should pass away without coming to know the Lord first, I could never forgive myself. Besides, I'm about the nearest thing to a physician these good folks might see while they're in such dire need."

The color had long since fled the lass's face as she gaped at her father. Taking in her stunned look, Yancy nudged his mount to the other side of hers. "It's hard to believe I'm sayin' this," he said to Felicia, "but I understand why your father must stay. Don't make it any harder for him than it already is."

An angry glint overpowered the tears beginning to shimmer in her eyes. She opened her mouth as if to protest, then clamped it shut at the beseeching expression on his face. Looking beyond him to the beleaguered man, she sighed. "Papa, I beg you. Isn't there some other way? Surely we could send someone back to help him."

He didn't respond.

Felicia's shoulders sagged, and a tear escaped the corner of her lashes. "Papa . . . I—"

"There's a good girl," he said gently, reaching up and patting her clenched hands.

Untying the turkey, Yancy handed it to Mr. Blair. "Might be these folks could use some broth and fresh meat."

He accepted it with a thankful nod, then met Felicia's gaze with an unwavering one. "Yancy will look after you until I can come."

It suddenly struck Yancy that the little man was entrusting his only daughter to his care for an indeterminate amount of time. He would be responsible for protecting the lass from all threats . . . including his own carnal desires. Filling his eyes with the sight of her, he tried to swallow down his panic as he swung down and went to Mr. Blair's side. "Excuse me, sir. I need to see ye in private."

Escorting the old gentleman to a gnarled oak tree several yards away, Yancy put a hand on Mr. Blair's shoulder, and they stopped behind the thick trunk. He struggled for some proper way to express his confused thoughts. "I'm sorry to tell ye this, sir," he finally blurted, "but you've got the wrong person in mind to be lookin' after the lass." He ran a hand through his hair. "'Tis only fair I admit to you that I've not always been a gentleman around damsels. I've taken liberties, wooed many a wench, without considering anyone but meself. An' where your daughter's concerned, I find meself thinking thoughts I've no right to be thinking. She's far too temptin' a lass to be left with the likes of me. And that's the truth of it." That said, he released a whoosh of breath.

Mr. Blair stared at him for a moment without responding. Then he removed a kerchief from the pocket of his fine black frock coat and wiped his nose. He gave a long, hard look at Yancy and put a frail hand on the sailor's arm. "I know very well, lad, about the temptations of the flesh. There's not a healthy man alive who doesn't fight a constant battle against thoughts that are . . . less than pure, shall we say. But if you'll just learn to place your faith in God, son, he'll give you the strength to overcome temptation."

"But ye don't understand," the seaman began desperately.

He hadn't originally planned on remaining with the Blairs this long, and he definitely hadn't considered admitting what he was about to. But there seemed no way around it. "I've only been *pretendin'* with ye. I'm no more a real Christian than the worst drunken sot along the whole coastline. I can't be askin' the Almighty for favors when he doesn't even know I exist."

Surprisingly, the older man didn't look all that shocked by his confession. He merely smiled gently. "Oh, but he does, lad. He knows all of us *by name* and even counts the very hairs of our heads. And from what you've told me about some of your recent experiences, I rather think the good Lord's been keeping his eye on you for some time. And I think you know it."

Yancy was at a loss for words.

"So you see, dear friend, there's no need for you to just pretend to be a Christian. Salvation is yours for the asking. It's as simple as that."

Gulping down a great lump in his throat, Yancy couldn't help but wonder what that experience would be like. He feared it might be akin to losing one's self. And what would his seafaring pals think of it? Likely they'd laugh him into becoming a landlubber for good. "I'll, er, have to give it some thought," he finally mumbled.

The kindly old man put a hand on Yancy's shoulder. "Just don't take overlong, lad." He paused, casting another glance back in the direction of Felicia. "And I'm still counting on you to take care of Leece. I'll be praying for both of you every day until I can be with you again. Now, go along. Mr. Richards is waiting."

As Yancy and Felicia emerged from the thick woods into the clearing dominated by Thornton's Fort, neither spoke. Of the three homesteads they had passed along the river since leaving Mr. Blair, one had been burned out. And the other two, though inhabited, hadn't appeared much more prosperous than the Richards place. Yancy could only imagine the distress his pampered lady must be feeling.

In the stillness of dusk, the palisade of the fort jutted up from a rise—a further reminder of the danger and hardship of life on the frontier. But its spiked-wood framework, outlined against the dim evening light, was nevertheless a welcome sight. Even knowing Skinner Thornton would most likely be among the folk occupying it.

They rode through the open double gate leading into a compound flanked by several log structures. Assessing them, Yancy surmised that the fort housed the typical necessities required to be self-sustaining. A main establishment that probably served as store, meetinghouse, drinking place, and message center faced them as they came forward. On one side stood two small cabins and, on the other, stables, a corral, and a smithy, where even now the sounds of steady pounding split the evening quiet. He and Felicia had already passed a gristmill a ways upriver.

"It almost looks like a town," the lass said.

"Or at least the closest thing to one we're goin' to find out here," Yancy added, noting the smoke rising from the chimneys. Veering over to the front of the store, Yancy swung down and tied his reins around the hitching post, then went to help Felicia.

As they walked inside, heat from a huge stone hearth warmed their chilled faces.

"Well, look who's come!" the lad, Matthew Thornton, said from across the rectangular room.

A middle-aged, massively built man who bore a close resemblance to Skinner came to his feet at a long trestle table near the fire, along with a second fellow who was in stained and weathered hunting attire.

The lad dropped the harness he'd been oiling and also jumped up to come greet them. "Did you manage to get all the way through with that wagon of yours, Yancy? Mistress Curtis?"

Felicia shot a startled glance Yancy's way. Apparently the

story they had told the Thorntons about being married was
destined to follow them.

"No," Yancy replied. "We took your advice and sold the
wagon. Came here on horseback."

"Thinking of settling in these parts?" the boy's father asked,
coming toward them, a big beefy hand outstretched. "Or just
passing through? The name's Ike Thornton. I own this
place."

"Yancy Curtis," he said, gripping the hand that attested to
the trader's strength. Then, glancing at Felicia, he saw her
look of concern. He wrapped an arm around her shoulders.

"Isn't Mr. Blair with you?" Matt asked.

"He started out with us, lad. But when we came upon a
homestead where there was sickness, he stayed to do what he
could. He'll catch up later. Family by the name of Richards.
Smallpox."

"I take it he's had the pox already, then," the hunter said
with some apprehension as he sauntered over to join them.

Felicia's breath caught.

Yancy hugged her tighter against himself. "Nay. But the
lass's father is a very brave man. Lovin' and kind."

"Or crazy," the tall, bone-lean hunter said wryly. He turned
to the trader. "Heard the Powells, over on the Greenbriar, are
down with it, too. Ain't they kin to the Richardses?"

"Yep. They all spent Christmas together."

"Don't sound good, does it." Returning to the table, he
picked up his knapsack and pulled it on over his beaver-fur
jacket, then took his flintlock rifle and hat. "Think I'll head
downriver, Fort Pitt way." Swinging a glance toward Yancy, he
gave a nod. "Mr. Curtis, was it? You can come along, if you've
a mind to, and wait for her father there."

"Absolutely not," Felicia said firmly. "We'll do no such
thing."

Wishing they could follow the fellow's good advice, Yancy
only grinned. "Seems we're no saner than her pa." He looked
at the trader as the hunter shook his head and strode out.
"Have ye rooms to let?"

The man rubbed his stubbly jaw. "Don't often get women-folk coming through here in the winter. Or even in summer, for that matter. Mostly just hunters and such, and they're used to sleeping under the nearest tree. I suppose I could let you two have the loft at my place, though. For a small price." He glanced at the boy. "Run over to the house and get yours and your brother's belongin's out of the loft. And tell your ma we're having extras for supper."

"But—" Wide-eyed, Felicia whirled to face Yancy. "You and me together?" she whispered in a high squeak. "In a loft?"

The door opened and Skinner Thornton walked in. His attention swung immediately to the lass, and a crooked smile tilted his cocky mouth. "Well, well. The Curtiscs made it through after all."

21

"Sure are lookin' forward to havin' you two for company," Skinner Thornton said with a self-assured smirk as he escorted Felicia and Yancy to the family cabin. Another of his bold glances roamed over her.

Fighting the impulse to shudder, Felicia inched nearer to Yancy and slipped her fingers inside the seaman's strong hand. The reassuring squeeze he gave imparted some comfort, and she drew from it as she kept pace with him. But from Yancy's granite expression, it was more than evident that his distrust of the trader's son was growing.

"Who'd be livin' in this other cabin?" Yancy asked as they approached the nearest of the two lodgings.

"The blacksmith and his family. Man's got a passel of kids. Bustin' out the seams of the place, they are."

Felicia flicked a look up at Yancy and saw his mouth tighten. Her heart sank. It would have been far less uncomfortable had they been able to stay the night with someone other than the Thorntons.

When they reached the humble dwelling occupied by the trader's family, Skinner gave a mock bow and waved them in.

The familiar smell of smoke filled the gloomy interior of the tiny house. Wishing the area had a good mason who could build a fireplace with a proper draft, Felicia took a few shallow breaths, trying to accustom herself to the odor as the men came in behind her.

"These here are the Curtises, Ma," Skinner announced.

A harried, middle-aged woman in drab homespun took a fleeting look at the newcomers and self-consciously brushed off her apron as she leaned a broom against one corner and came over to them. She tucked tiny loose hairs into the severe bun at the nape of her neck and dipped in a slight curtsy. "I'm Nellie Thornton."

Felicia returned the woman's weary smile and took one of her rough red hands. "We're happy to meet you. I'm Felicia, and this is . . . my husband, Yancy." She couldn't believe she had actually said it. She took a deep breath, trying to keep her voice from shaking. "We're very sorry to be imposing on you."

Mistress Thornton nodded. "Oh, don't bother me none, having folks come through now and again, long as they don't mind that the place ain't fancy. Hang up your coats and find yourselves a seat. Rest a spell. I'll put on some coffee."

"Thank you." Ignoring Skinner, who leaned against the wall gawking at her, Felicia put her cloak on an empty peg, and Yancy hung his over the top. Then they moved to the humble sitting area. She sank down onto a pillowed rocker while he sat rigidly on a straight-back chair against one wall.

Felicia couldn't help but notice the rough-hewn furniture in the house. The pillows they sat on had seen better days and so had the flour-sack curtains. A plain table set with benches along the sides and chairs similar to Yancy's at the ends took up most of the other end of the room.

Surprisingly, an almost new spinning wheel occupied one corner. Felicia could imagine the poor overworked woman sitting there at day's end, spinning the very thread that then had to be woven into material and sewn into clothing for her family. The thought of the primitive conditions in the wilderness, the unending chores that she herself was so ill-prepared to undertake, nearly overwhelmed her.

Just as she forced herself to settle back and relax, an armful of belongings came tumbling down from the loft above.

"Watch what you're doin', Matt," his brother yelled.

"Pa told me to get our stuff outta here," the boy shot back.

A second huge, furry bundle came over the rail. Hitting the floor, the bearskin sprang open, and assorted boyish treasures scattered.

Felicia managed not to smile at the sight of a rabbit's foot, tomahawk, pinecones, and odd articles of clothing.

"Well, be careful of the comp'ny," his mother said, glancing around from the pot she stirred at the hearth.

"Mistress Thornton," Felicia asked, "are you quite certain we won't be putting you out?"

"Not a 'tall. The boys are used to it. They always sleep by the fire whenever one of the girls comes home to visit."

"Anyway," Skinner drawled, "it's a pleasure just knowin' you'll be sleepin' in my bed."

Yancy bristled, mumbling something under his breath as his hands clenched into fists. He looked ready to spring to his feet.

Felicia reached out and touched the seaman's arm. "Perhaps you should go get our things and put the horses up for the night. I'll see if I can help Mistress Thornton." She swung to look at Skinner. "Would you mind going with my husband and showing him where we should stable our animals?"

"Right fine idea, Bartholomew," his mother agreed. "Be quick about it."

Skinner clamped his mouth tight, a scowl revealing his displeasure at her use of his proper name. Then his beefy shoulders sagged. "Yes, Ma."

Yancy didn't look any happier as he rose. "I won't be long." He gave Felicia's shoulder a squeeze as he walked by.

The animosity between the two was clearly evident. Felicia breathed a silent prayer that they'd both make it back in one piece. Then she followed the less than enticing cooking smells coming from the other end of the room. "Smells wonderful," she managed to say. "May I give you a hand?"

The older woman looked up from slicing bread at the worktable, a spark of envy in her gaze as she appraised Felicia. "Sit and keep me company, if you like. Wouldn't wanna see them fine clothes get all spattered with grease and the like."

Felicia smiled. "Oh, I wish I had something more practical to wear around the house than all these cumbersome skirts. But until I'm able to get something else, these will have to do. Are you sure there isn't something I can do?"

Mistress Thornton scrunched up her face, adding another bounty of wrinkles to the fine lines already there. "Well, if you're of a mind to help, I suppose you can set the table. Here, I'll get the dishes." Crossing to a large crate atop a barrel, she started taking out some wooden bowls and mugs and carried them to the table. "Matt, aren't you done up there yet?" she called, craning her neck toward the loft.

"Just about, Ma."

"Well, hurry up. Time to go get Pa for supper."

The lad thumped all the way down the ladder, then threw his coat on and went out.

Smiling after him as she set places at the table, Felicia turned to see his mother wrestling a large cauldron from the hearth. "Here, let me help." Grabbing a flour-sack dish towel, she took hold of the other side of the kettle. "This is the first time I've been out into the wilderness," she told the older woman as they lifted it off the fire hook. "It's amazing how hard life is out here. For a woman, I mean. So few comforts."

"I expect." Nellie Thornton blotted her cheek with the corner of her apron and shrugged. "But menfolk love the freedom, the adventure. Always wantin' to be goin' farther, too. To see what's over the next mountain, across the next river. Leastwise I have the smith's wife next door. That's more'n most of the women scattered through the hollows and down the valley have."

To Felicia, this was another disturbing thought put into words. "Of all the cabins we passed in the valley, I don't believe I saw any within a mile of the next. It must be awfully lonely."

"Oh, I don't know." The older woman began ladling stew into a pottery tureen. "There's somethin' to be said for walkin' out in the spring and knowin' that everywhere you set your foot, far as you can see, the land's yours."

Maybe life wasn't all hard work and deprivation, Felicia thought. It was possible that seeing everything for the first time in the dead of winter was giving her a false impression.

"Yours, less'n the Injuns take a notion to burn you out," the woman went on.

Felicia gasped. She was grateful that Yancy chose that moment to come back in. She certainly did not want to hear another word about Indians.

He wiped his feet on the doormat and hung up his coat, then picked up the bags he'd brought in with him.

Noticing he'd only gotten her necessities and his haversack, Felicia breathed a sigh of relief. Obviously he had no intention of making this arrangement permanent. And he appeared unscathed. For that she was also thankful.

"Oh, Mr. Curtis." Mistress Thornton came from the fireplace with a lighted candle. "Take this up to the loft with your truck, will you? I'll be along directly to make up the beds."

"Yes, ma'am."

As Yancy climbed the ladder, a strong urge to tell the woman the truth nagged Felicia. She opened her mouth to speak, but heard the stomping of boots outside.

Skinner came in and met Felicia's eyes with a bawdy smile.

"Um . . . I'll go and take care of making the beds," she blurted. Seizing the linens Nellie Thornton had just taken from another crate, she flew after Yancy.

Accustomed to broad staircases, Felicia found climbing up a rickety ladder with skirts and an armful of sheets a major undertaking. But aware of beady, leering eyes boring into her back, she managed. She wasn't about to ask for help.

Yancy, thankfully, reached down and took the linens as she neared the top, then offered a hand the rest of the way.

Stepping into the dimly lit loft, Felicia noticed how much safer she felt with Yancy around . . . and how strong and warm his fingers were as they lingered an extra second on her arm. She almost couldn't breathe with him towering over her, and she dared not look up at him.

He abruptly let go. "I'll make one," he said, nabbing a pair of sheets.

Trying to regain her composure, Felicia glanced around and noticed there were two narrow cots snugged beneath the steeply slanted sides of the roof, with a trunk at the foot of each one. A crude row of shelves separated the beds where they abutted the wall. Checking over her shoulder, she noticed that the seaman had already stripped his bed and was tucking the clean sheets and covers on it so quickly it looked as if he were in a race.

If he was in such a hurry, she decided, she should be also. And truly, the sooner they went downstairs again, the better. Quarters were becoming close up here. She tugged the old sheets off her cot and quickly finished the chore. Then swooping the discarded linens into her arms to take below, she swung toward the ladder . . . and into Yancy.

Both their bundles of sheets plunged to the floor as Felicia's eyes locked with his. She swallowed and looked away. Yes, the quarters were entirely *too* close. The place was so stifling she could scarcely breathe.

"I'll, er, give ye a hand," he whispered hoarsely, retrieving the sheets. "At the ladder." He blew out the candle.

It seemed even warmer in the dark, Felicia thought, and without the light, the sound of his breathing was magnified. As his big hand closed around her fingers, her heart pounded and her breath caught in her throat.

"Here ye are," he said. "Can ye manage?"

Felicia was surprised to find that he'd drawn her over to the ladder. She nodded, then grasping him tighter, eased a foot cautiously over the side to feel for the first rung. With a weak smile, she started down.

Skinner, she saw, stood directly below.

More than positive the ill-mannered oaf merely wanted a view of her ankles, Felicia bit her tongue rather than stir up Yancy's temper again.

"Bartholomew," his mother called, "I need you to bring in some water."

"Aw, can't Matt do it?"

"I said," she repeated with emphasis, "I need *you* to get it."

With a disgusted shake of the head, he tromped over to retrieve the bucket and stormed out the door.

"This is truly delicious," Felicia lied outright after she washed down a stringy chunk of rabbit with a gulp of bitter herb tea. She hoped fervently that Papa was faring better with the turkey Yancy had shot.

"Mmph." Trader Thornton barely nodded as he shoveled in another mouthful of stew, eating with relish.

On the far side of him, the boys also slurped their helpings enthusiastically.

Deciding the family must be more intent on eating than making conversation, Felicia chewed another piece slowly, then swallowed somehow. Perhaps there might be hope for her own cooking yet, she decided, washing down the barely edible food. After all, Yancy had been ever so patient in showing her what he knew about it. In time, maybe her efforts would pay off. She tried a little more broth. Anything was better than drawing attention . . . especially from the elder son, who kept trying to catch her eye.

Through her lashes she saw him flick a glance at his father and then at Yancy beside her before giving her one more snide smile. She concentrated more intently on her food.

Mr. Thornton tipped his bowl up to drink the last of his stew, then wiped his mouth on his sleeve. "Fetch my pipe, boy," he said to Matthew. "And a fire stick."

Yancy set down his cup of tea. "Trader Thornton, when we first arrived, ye mentioned the possibility of our comin' here to settle. Might ye hold the grant to this township?"

"What's a grant?" Matthew asked, lighting his father's pipe.

His older brother snickered. "Ain't no grants given out for land this side of the mountains. Any fool knows that."

Thornton silenced his son with a glare, then turned to Yancy. "What he's tryin' to say is that Parliament's proclamation forbids the givin' or sellin' of land grants on territories taken from the French. A few men have been allowed to buy a license to trade with the Indians, but ol' King George doesn't seem to want to share his new kingdom with the rest of us. But since he's not here to object—"

"And never will he," Skinner piped in, his lip curled in derision.

"Folks just find a spot that suits them and start clearin' it," his father continued. "Guess you noticed we all like plenty of elbow room. Most folks stake out a good-size piece."

Yancy frowned in amazement. "You mean without any paper sayin' you own it, you all just come out here an' start farmsteads?"

Skinner tossed his head. "What *I'd* like to know is why anybody'd strike out for the frontier without the slightest notion of what he's going to."

"Boy." Thornton cocked a graying brow. "That'll do."

"Your son does have a point," Yancy admitted. "But we didn't exactly come seeking land. Somethin' ye said, though, reminded me of a rumor I heard not long ago. . . . The London hoity-toities are puttin' together another one of their acts. Talkin' about addin' all the Ohio territories to Canada."

"Canada!" The trader's fist slammed onto the table, rattling the dishes. "No Frenchie's comin' down here to lord it over us."

"He'd get a musket ball in his britches, that's for sure," Skinner added.

Yancy shrugged. "Well, looks like you folks around here will be havin' your own trouble with the lobsterbacks before long."

"Indians, Frenchies, lobsterbacks . . . just as soon shoot one as the other," Thornton announced.

Felicia gasped at the furor of his words. She sought Mistress Thornton's face, but the woman had just gotten up and taken some dishes to the worktable.

Obviously having noticed Felicia's dismay, the trader

cleared his throat. "You folks never did say how you come to be travelin' the mountains in winter."

"Me wife's father is a preacher," Yancy answered evenly. "He had a call so strong he set his mind to come up here with or without us. We couldn't let him go alone."

"A church?" Mistress Thornton swung back to the supper table and sank to her seat. "Oh, my."

Her husband's lip curved upward at one edge. "No wonder he took the notion to stay at the Richards place. To snag hisself a couple of hapless souls."

"Ike Thornton!" his wife said in dismay.

Obviously shocked at her reprimand, he scowled at her.

The woman cowed for a brief instant, then raised her chin again. "You know, Pa, you might could ride over to the old Wilkins place tomorrow with Mr. Curtis." She turned to Yancy. "It's abandoned, and we have a real need for a preacher. Could be, if the house suits you, all of us neighbors could pitch in and help set the place to rights. Don't you think, Pa?"

"Too bad the Wilkins couple hightailed it back to Richmond so quick," Matt mumbled. "I kinda liked 'em."

"The guy was henpecked through and through," his brother said in a snide tone. "Led around like he had a ring in his nose."

"That's enough!" their mother said sternly. "Martha Wilkins was with child. And too scared of givin' birth by herself out here."

"I can certainly understand that," Felicia said too quickly.

Skinner caught her eye, his look full of meaning.

Felicia tugged at Yancy's sleeve. "Why don't we go see the place for ourselves?"

The seaman was glaring at Skinner. She nudged him harder. "Yancy."

"Huh?"

"I said, we should go and see the Wilkins farm for ourselves. What do you think?"

He nodded. "Aye. Might be a fair idea."

"Good. Well," she yawned elaborately, "if you don't mind,

then, I think I'll turn in." She put a hand on Yancy's shoulder, staying with some force his attempt to rise. "Oh, you needn't come just yet, dear. Stay and visit. I'm sure the Thorntons would be quite interested in hearing about that Boston trouble we heard about on our way through Charlottesville."

"What trouble's that?" the trader asked eagerly.

With a sigh of relief, Felicia hurried to the ladder. At least Yancy would be occupied . . . for the moment.

22

In the tiny loft, Felicia changed swiftly into her cotton night shift and climbed into the haven of sheets and quilts. *Please, heavenly Father, watch over Papa and keep him safe. Bring him back to us soon,* she prayed silently, then closed her eyes tight, hoping to be asleep before Yancy came up.

The voices downstairs carried easily to her ears as the conversation continued, and during the seaman's recanting of the Boston incident, the tone became even more animated. When at last they quieted and Felicia heard the men leaving one by one to take care of whatever needed attention before retiring, she couldn't have been more wide awake if it had been the middle of the day.

"You have yourself one fine night, now," she heard Skinner say suggestively just as Yancy started up the ladder.

Her heart pounding in her throat, Felicia rolled over to face the slanting roof, her covers enshrouding her as if she were a mummy. The candle she had brought up earlier had seemed pitifully inadequate at the time. But now it seemed to blaze forth like the summer sun at its zenith while she lay still as death, trying not to give the slightest sign she was awake.

Yancy walked between the two beds and blew out the flame, and darkness enveloped them. Then there came a rustle of clothes, followed by the squeak of the wood frame of his cot. He tugged off one boot with a grunt, then the other. But amazingly, there was no thunk as the boots hit the floor. It gave Felicia a warm feeling to realize he was considerate enough to try not to awaken her.

When he crawled into bed, she released the breath she had been holding. She had no way of knowing exactly what the sailor and her father might have discussed during their private little talk this afternoon. Considering the outrageous way the rascal had blatantly flirted with her since he had crossed her path, the chat must have made a strong impact on him. But then, she recalled, ever since he'd saved her from Skinner Thornton, he'd been treating her with the utmost respect and consideration. A smile moved over her lips, and she relaxed.

Yes, Yancy had actually become quite friendly and helpful. He still exuded a kind of interest in her, but he was no longer aggressive. What a pleasant surprise it had been to discover he was infinitely patient when it came to cooking demonstrations—especially when her clumsy attempts left much to be desired. He hadn't ridiculed her, though. If she didn't know better, she'd think that underneath that rough exterior was the heart of a true gentleman.

Thank you, dear Father, that he hasn't been so bold as to try to steal a kiss, she prayed. Then, realizing what a silly goose she was, she stifled a giggle and squeezed her eyes shut. She'd been wasting far too much time and energy on these girlish notions about Yancy Curtis when she could just as easily have been getting some much needed sleep.

But for one fleeting second she wondered what it would be like to feel his lips on hers.

His bed creaked, and she heard him get up. Then a floorboard protested under his weight.

Had he read her mind? Was he coming over to her? Felicia's heartbeat doubled its pace. Steeling herself to face the threat, she rolled toward him to do battle.

In the faint glow of the banked hearth below, she could barely make out his shadowy figure . . . kneeling beside his bed, head bowed as he mumbled almost inaudibly.

The man was praying!

❦ ❦

His nose aching from the frigid temperature, Ben shivered in his saddle and snuggled deeper into the scarf shrouding the collar of his greatcoat. The occasional tentative snowflakes that had drifted down in the last light of dusk had quickly turned into an all-out blizzard, hampering his progress. He was nowhere near the wayside inn at Millers Falls, where he'd planned to stay the night.

Rebel, struggling for footing in the blowing drifts, emitted a nervous whinny.

"Good fella," Ben crooned. He leaned closer to the animal's ear and gave his mount a comforting pat on the neck.

A blast of wind howled through the trees, catching the end of Ben's scarf. He caught it with a gloved hand and wrapped it more tightly about the lower half of his face, then checked for the dozenth time to see that his mail pouch was securely closed. He didn't want any harm to come to the letters Susannah had written to Dan, Ted, and Jane.

Ahead in the distance he thought he saw a brief flicker of light, but then the blowing snow completely eradicated it. No doubt he had been imagining things. Ben's spirit plummeted. If only it had been a farmhouse! Perhaps he could have imposed on the kind people there for shelter until morning. The road was all but impassable already, and the lantern he carried had blown out some time ago in the storm.

The light twinkled again.

Elated, Ben steered his mount in that direction.

As he approached a substantial two-story house, a welcome glow poured from an upstairs window. Ben could almost feel the warmth of the hearth already. He guided Rebel to the sheltered side of the building, then dismounted and stepped into the wind again, huddling into his coat as he went up the porch steps.

He rapped on the door and waited. He tried again. But he was competing with the howling wind and all the storm's racket. Finally he pounded as hard as he could with his painfully cold fist.

At last a light shone through the downstairs windows and grew stronger. The door creaked open, emitting a whispery breath of warmth.

A woman in a worn flannel wrapper filled the doorway. The ruffle on her sleep-wrinkled cap stuck out in assorted directions above close-set squinty eyes as she pointed the long barrel of a pistol at Ben's chest. Beside her, a younger version of herself in similar attire held a lamp high.

"What on earth is a body doin' out on a night like this!" the older one's gravelly voice boomed.

"Sorry to bother you, ma'am," Ben said, his teeth chattering. "I'm a postrider. Got caught in the storm. I was trying to make Millers Falls." Taking a closer look at the mistrust in their eyes, Ben had second thoughts about requesting shelter. "Would you mind if I put my horse in the barn and slept out there with him? I'd just need a quilt or two, if it isn't too much trouble."

Even as he shivered and chattered the words out, he'd noticed the younger one eyeing him from head to toe and back again with intense interest. "No. You should come in outta the cold." Reaching out, she gripped a coat sleeve and yanked him bodily into the house.

Now that he was inside, the heat from the fireplace felt almost stifling. Ben's cheeks and forehead burned from the sudden change. Still struggling to catch his breath, he realized suddenly that the daughter had put down the lamp and was unwinding his scarf with one hand while removing his hat with the other.

He grabbed both of them back. "Wait. I must take care of my horse."

"Aw, don't you worry none about that, son," the mother said with a delighted cackle. "We'll see to it. You're about froze."

The offer did sound quite tempting, Ben had to admit. After all, what was there to be suspicious about? This woman and her daughter seemed genuinely concerned. And it wasn't as if he'd had his choice in lodgings. He peeled off his soggy coat, then noticed great puddles were forming around his boots from melting snow. "Oh! Forgive me. I'd better take these off outside."

"Pshaw!" the mother said, flopping a calloused hand. "You just sit right down here in the hall and take 'em off. A little water won't hurt nothin'." The woman's voice had a grainy quality, as if she'd used it up long ago.

Ben sank down onto the nearest chair. The young one sprang over and, before he could stop her, straddled his leg and started tugging a boot for all she was worth.

Almost too shocked to move, Ben gaped at her.

"Now, Bertie," her mother scolded. "This nice young man's horse is still waitin' to be looked after."

"Please," Ben protested, getting up with one boot removed. "I couldn't expect a lass to go out in this storm to take care of my pacer."

"Horsefeathers!" The older woman shook her head, stirring frizzled stray hairs from the long gray braid down her back. "If me an' Bertha had to wait for a man to come do for us, nothin' would ever get done around here!" She motioned with her chin for her daughter to go.

The younger woman's coy smile looked somehow out of place on her long, plain face as she beamed at Ben. Reaching for some heavy work boots, she took the next chair and jammed her feet into them. "You get yourself all nice an' warmed up. I'll be back directly."

She pulled on a thick fur coat, which gave her a remarkable resemblance to a big black bear. Suddenly Ben realized that he was turning his duties over to a woman. "Wait. I should do it."

"Oh, no, you don't." The mother's sturdy hand clamped down on his shoulder, reversing his attempt to stand. "Be sure to tie the rope round yourself, Bertie," she said as her daughter left. "Don't want you should blow away in the storm."

Trying to visualize the gale that could sweep this substantial gal off her feet, Ben managed to maintain a straight face. Bertha tromped out the door, slamming it behind her.

The mother set the gun down on a lamp stand and picked up the light instead. She took Ben's arm. "Come on to the kitchen, son," she said, leading him along in his stockinged feet. "I'm Mabel Preston."

Ben nodded. "Glad to meet you, Mistress Preston."

"Ma," she corrected, steering him to a chair. "That's what most folks call me. So you're a postrider, huh? Used to traipsin' all over the countryside."

He gave another nod and took the seat indicated.

Mistress Preston went to stoke up the blaze in the huge stone hearth, then began brewing some tea with water already hot from the fire. That done, she crossed to the larder and took out some bread, cheese, and a sausage and began slicing them. "Where abouts ya from?"

Ben's gaze took in the functional cooking room with a larger-than-usual assortment of pots and kettles hanging on wall hooks, and bowls and cooking tins set out as if in readiness for morning. *This must be the most used room in the house*, he thought. "My family lives in Rhode Island."

Ma Preston poured a cup of tea and set it in front of Ben. "Some fine, stiff-necked folks down Rhode Island way, from what I hear. We're still laughin' hereabouts over them burnin' that navy ship." A twinkle shone in her eye as she broke into boisterous song:

> *That night about half after ten,*
> *Some Narragansett Indiamen,*
> *Bein' sixty-four, if I remember,*
> *Which made this stout coxcomb surrender;*
> *And what was best of all their tricks,*
> *They in his britch a ball did fix. . . .*

Her full-bellied laugh followed. "Yes, sir, hardy folks down Providence way."

Ben chuckled and took a sip of the hot brew. He felt an

immediate liking for the gruff but enthusiastic woman. "We try not to let opportunity pass us by."

With a loud guffaw, Ma gave him a stout whack on the back. "I knowed you'd be one of us. Old Ben Franklin wouldn't have no Tories riding the post roads for him."

Ben didn't bother to inform her that Mr. Franklin had been in England for some years trying to influence Parliament on the Colonies' behalf and hadn't personally sent him out. Yet he knew that every postrider he came across *was* sympathetic to the cause, whether or not he had joined the Sons of Liberty.

Ma plunked a plate under Ben's nose. "Lord, bless this food. Amen," she said, then opened her eyes again. "Now, eat up, son. It'll help warm ya up."

The abrupt grace caught Ben off balance, but he was quite hungry. He picked up the generous slab of buttered bread and bit into it.

After refilling his mug, the older woman poured a cup for herself and took the end chair. "Life's hard enough these days without havin' useless aristocrats expectin' to be carried on our backs. Me and Bertie run this farm ourselves, and we don't see no reason why them bigwigs across the sea can't sweat an' toil for their own fancy clothes and things."

Noticing the number of empty chairs around the big pine table, Ben concluded there must have been a large family here at one time. "You don't have any sons who could come help out?"

A wistful smile gentled Mistress Preston's round face as she looked away. "Had me seven girls, but just the one boy. Last winter he fell through the ice on the pond . . . him and our best horse. Left me to care for his frail little widow gal and their two babes."

"Oh, I'm sorry to hear that. And she's sickly, you say?"

"Naw. Just one of them spindly females that hardly makes a shadow in bright sun. Nothin' like my girls. They all got plenty of grit. Ever' one of 'em a fit match for anything a New England winter can throw at us. Not that we don't love our little Abigail, mind you. She's a sweet gal to have around, her and her young'uns. She can't help bein' puny."

The front door opened, then slammed shut. Heavy feet stomped snow off at the entrance.

Ma smiled proudly. "Bertie didn't waste no time takin' care of your horse."

Hearing the girl clomping toward the kitchen, Ben imagined a huge furry bear.

But Bertha came into the room without her warm coat. With a look of ecstasy on her face, she slid lightly into the chair beside his with a fluidity that seemed impossible for one with her sturdy build. He chuckled inwardly; she was still in nightdress and ruffled cap.

"Thank you for seeing to my mount," Ben said. "I shouldn't have imposed on you, though."

"Why not? Wouldn't you do the same for a body?"

"Yes. But I'm a man."

"A right fine man, too," she crooned. "Ain't he, Ma?"

She looked him over. "Needs fattenin' up."

Also sizing Ben up herself, Bertha looked at him with eager sympathy. "Prob'ly don't have much good home cookin', do ya?"

"No." He shifted uncomfortably on his chair. "A postrider spends most of the time on the road. I haven't been home for months."

"Tsk, tsk." She shook her head. "Must make your *wife* mighty sad."

"I don't have a wife." Instantly Ben regretted uttering the words as Bertha leaned closer, raking him once more with her gaze.

"A handsome, dashin' fellow like you? And hardy? Able to ride scores of miles in any kind of weather? Seems a pure waste, don't it, Ma?"

"Yep." The older woman settled her bulk into a chair across from them. "And he's one of our Sons of Liberty, too." She switched her attention to Ben. "Any more happenin's since that Boston trouble?"

He shook his head. "But both sides are watching each other closely while we all wait for the Crown to decide what to do. It'll be another two or three months, anyway."

"Could be they'll send a mess of extra soldiers again, like they did in '68."

"You're probably right." Ben inched away from Bertha slightly. "The regiments already there have taken over half the Common as well as the port battery. None of us is in any mood to be overrun by any more lobsterbacks, that's for sure."

Bertha closed the tiny gap he'd made and leaned to speak into his face. "Would ya like more cheese?" She fluttered her lashes.

"No. No, thanks." Ben cleared his throat, then peered around the girl toward her mother. "That was a delicious meal, Ma Preston. But—" with a mighty stretch, he yawned exaggeratedly—"I'm worn out after this long day. Where might I bed down for the night?"

"Right upstairs," Bertha breathed. "And I'll be in the very next room if you need anything." With an inviting smile, she stood and picked up the lamp.

"I, uh, wouldn't mind staying out in the barn with my horse."

Mistress Preston slapped a palm on the table. "We wouldn't think of it. Both of us'll take you up. And," she said, shooting her daughter a menacing glare, "if you need anything durin' the night, *I'm a real light sleeper.* I'll be right across the hall from you."

Her not-so-subtle comment had the earmarks of a warning, but Ben was more than grateful for it. At least he wouldn't feel quite so threatened by Bertha. Just in time, he stopped himself from bestowing a kiss on the older woman's cheek. It wouldn't do to have *two* formidable women getting wrong ideas into their heads.

In the netherland of half-sleep, Ben heard happy giggles and a small child's laughter and thought for an instant he was at Dan and Susannah's. Then reality brought him fully awake. Not only wasn't he at his brother's house, he wasn't even in Boston. In fact, it was a miracle he hadn't frozen to death, lost in the blizzard last night. He scratched the stubble on his jaw. How could there be little children here, when he was lodging with an old widow and her unmarried daughter? Oh yes. There had been mention of a sickly daughter-in-law. Of course, by Preston women standards, what ordinary woman wouldn't seem frail?

Swinging his legs over the side of the bed, he came to his feet and crossed to the window. Hopefully he could take swift departure from this place and the amorous Bertha.

A brilliant clear sky met his gaze. The morning sunshine had turned yesterday's terror into a magical fairyland of glistening white. In the warm rays, clumps of snow tumbled from tree branches and landed atop huge drifts below. Every fence post and stone wall and boulder wore a sparkling crown. Not even a breath of wind remained from last night's gale.

Ma Preston and Bertha were already hard at work, repairing the door that must have blown off the chicken coop during the storm. Ben tugged on his brown breeches and tan wool shirt. If his luck held, he could be out in the barn and ready to go before the women finished up. It would be much easier to render his thanks someplace where he could get away quickly.

He heard more childish laughter. He glanced around the room as he combed and tied back his hair, then remembered that his boots had been left by the front door, along with his hat and coat. In his stocking feet he padded out into the hall toward the staircase.

The giggles grew louder as Ben neared one of the other upstairs rooms, its door standing partially open. He saw a pair of little ones bouncing atop a double bed and hurling themselves with reckless abandon into their mother's arms. Unnoticed by them, he stopped to watch the enchanting scene.

One sweet little face belonged to a honey blonde angel around three and the other to an impish, towheaded boy who was probably not quite two. Both were alight with such innocent trust and love, he found it hard to tear his gaze away as they leaped again to their mother.

As they stepped out of her hug and ran around the foot of the bed to scramble up again, he caught a glimpse of the object of their affection. She appeared hardly more than a child herself sitting on her legs on the floor, her arms held up to them. Softly waving golden blonde hair crowned an oval face with huge bluish eyes. A captivating smile drew up both corners of her soft, expressive mouth. "Come, sweethearts," she said, clapping her hands.

The tots flung themselves at her once more, and she caught them one at a time in a lingering, laughing embrace. But this time as she let go, she noticed Ben. "Oh, faith!" she whispered, blushing delicately. "We didn't mean to disturb you." She set the little girl on her feet and stood, brushing a strand of hair away from her eyes as her daughter peeked from behind her mother's skirts.

"You didn't. I don't usually oversleep." Ben noticed that even standing up she looked like a child. With the same petite, fragile form as Emily, the girl couldn't be any older than his youngest sister. Nineteen, twenty at the most. "I'm Ben Haynes," he finally said.

"Abigail Preston," she answered with a shy smile. As her blue-green eyes lowered to the children, her face became more animated. "This big boy is Corbin," she said, bestowing a hug on him. "And this is Cassandra." She bent and gave the little girl a squeeze. "Your breakfast has been prepared, if you'll just follow us to the kitchen, Mr. Haynes."

Ben stepped aside as she swept past, the toddlers in tow.

Cassandra, clinging closely to her mama, barely looked back, but Corbin grinned over his shoulder in proud confidence.

A step behind them, Ben pulled out his folded pocketknife and dangled it by the leather thong.

As the lad hesitated and reached for it, his mother gave a gentle tug on his other hand. "You mustn't bother people."

Ben swooped him up. "Oh, don't worry. I have a nephew not much younger than Corbin. I'm used to it."

"You don't mind? Truly?" Something fragile in the timid smile Abigail flashed his way stirred Ben deeply, in a manner he'd never before experienced. He shook his head and ruffled Corbin's flaxen hair as they started down the steps.

Abigail stopped suddenly and turned. "Oh, I nearly forgot. Bertha wanted me to be sure to tell you she made your entire breakfast herself. It was very important to her that you know this."

"I thank you." Seeing that she had continued on again, Ben was assaulted by his recollections of the aggressive, man-hunting young woman he'd confronted last eve. More than likely she'd burst in on them any moment.

While Abigail Preston gathered together his rather lavish meal, Ben watched her. Both sides of the crisp apron she wore over her blue cotton dress overlapped at her spine, the ties trailing down from her tiny waist. She moved about the kitchen with graceful fluid motion. Suddenly he wished he had shaved before coming downstairs.

He sneaked repeated glances at her as he ate, watching her

clean up the huge stack of pans and dishes Bertha must have used. And even as her little ones vied for her attention, she smiled gently and spoke softly to them.

Corbin, with a touch of Preston rowdiness, galloped around the table, the closed pocketknife clutched in his fist.

Little Cassandra peeked around her mother at Ben again as she had been doing every little while, and he made a comical face. Although slow in making an appearance, a sweet smile finally curved her lips, and he felt he'd been given a gift.

When footsteps sounded outside, Ben remembered too late that he had intended to make a speedy escape. Even as the front door slammed, he thought he might still make a dash out the back. He sprang up and took his dishes to Abigail. "Thank you so much for the delicious meal—"

"Glad ya liked it," Bertha said exuberantly as she came into the room. "*I* cooked it all special, just for you." She flicked an irritated glance from him to Abigail and back as she unfastened her coat.

"Yes," Ben said with a nod. "And it'll keep me satisfied all day, I'm sure." He stooped to retrieve his knife from Corbin as the boy made another circuit around the table.

He ducked and eluded Ben's grasp.

"Let me," Abigail said, wiping her hands as she bolted after her son. "Corbin," she coaxed. "You know nice Mr. Haynes only let you hold his pocketknife for a while. It's time to give it back."

"No," the boy whined. He lunged under the table.

Abigail pushed the chairs in one by one until Corbin's only route was straight out to the end, where she flew to nab him just as Ben swooped him up. Their shoulders brushed.

Ben's heart lurched.

Coloring slightly, Abigail lowered her lashes and took her son. "Sorry," she whispered. "He usually minds me." Setting the boy down, she knelt and took him by the shoulders, looking him in the eye. "Corbin, what do we do when we have something that belongs to someone else?"

"Give back," he said almost inaudibly.

"And then what do you get?" she said, her voice light and teasing.

"Kiss."

"Right." Beaming, she stood and put her hands on her waist while the boy held the knife out to Ben. Then she bent and kissed her son's cheek, and they both giggled.

Aware that Bertha glared at them, Ben couldn't help but wonder at her treatment of such a shy and delicate sister-in-law. Wanting somehow to make up for it, Ben held out a shiny new shilling to Corbin.

"Oh, you mustn't do that," Abigail said, not quite meeting his eyes this time.

"But I must. Small payment for your family's generous hospitality. When he tires of it, pass it on to your mother-in-law for me."

"Abby," Bertha said from the side. "The day's half gone. You should have been heatin' wash water. Me an' Ma can't do everything around here."

"Sorry," she breathed, turning away from Ben. "I didn't think about it."

"Ya never do. That's the trouble."

Clenching his jaw, Ben straightened. The lass had just finished Bertha's big pile of dishes. "Well, I'd best be going. I do want to thank all of you for your kindness. I appreciate everything you did for me." With a last look and smile at Abigail, he strode to the front door for his coat and boots.

All the while, Bertha trailed him like a shadow.

Outside in the barn, she insisted on helping Ben saddle up. When he buckled Rebel's cinch and reached for his saddle-bags hanging nearby, she beat him to it. "I'll get 'em for ya," Bertha said, her voice eager, her eyes wide.

"Thanks, but you don't have to. I like to do things a certain way, so I know where stuff is. You've done way too much already," he added politely. Taking them down, he slung them into place behind his saddle.

With a shrug, the girl busied herself with a hay rake,

straightening the straw-strewn earthen floor nearby. "Never could see why my brother, Ray, married up with that useless Abby," she began as though thinking aloud. "Gal had no dowry, barely knows how to cook. . . ."

Ben almost blurted out something in Abigail's defense, but he held his tongue. There was no point in making her lot in life any harder, since it was obvious she had more than enough to handle as it was.

"But no one could talk a lick o' sense into Raymond," Bertie went on. "Seems he always was a body to take in strays. Baby birds who'd fallen out of the nest, wild critters with no ma. Such foolishness." She shook her head, and the wool scarf she'd looped under her chin worked loose on one side. She tossed it back. "That boy wasted more time on worthless pets, never considerin' the pile of work waitin' to be done. On a farm, there's no end to the chores that need tendin'."

Ben nodded as he removed dry gloves from one of his bags and pulled them on, stretching out his fingers. Then, seeing her warm gaze fasten on him, he sought a change of subject. "I saw you and your mother fixing the chicken coop this morning. You sure have a fine place here. Big house and all."

"We'll do our best to keep it that way, too," she said firmly, "till some man comes along who'll care as much about it as we do and who'll want to help out. Got six hundred forty acres of good land. Biggest farm for miles." With one final sweep of the rake, she leaned it on its tines and met Ben's gaze. "Ma says if I stay once I'm wed, she'll give me half the place as my dowry. Course, I don't spread that around, or I'd have more suitors flockin' round me than flies in a milkin' shed. I'm waitin' for just the right one, ya see."

Relieved that all his gear was tied on now, Ben swung up into the saddle, giving not the slightest indication he'd noticed Bertha's rather broad hint. "Well, I'd best be off. Be sure and give your mother my deepest thanks, now."

"I will."

Clucking his tongue, Ben guided his mount out of the barn.

"You come back again, y'hear? Soon," Bertie called after him. "There'll be a bed an' a hot meal awaitin'."

Yes, but you will be too, Ben thought wryly.

Heading up the snow-covered road, Ben glanced back toward the house, where he thought he caught a glimpse of Abigail's slender form in an upstairs window. What a waste of her sweet life, living with her babies under the roof of two domineering females. She probably found precious few moments to play with them as she had that morning. He smiled at the memory of the laughter and love he'd witnessed before she'd discovered his presence.

The gentleness of Abigail's spirit and her acceptance of her fate reminded Ben of Susannah as he rode down the far side of a rise and lost sight of the Preston place. His sister-in-law's second babe would be born in a few months. And Dan had aided in the escape of a deserting officer of the Crown. If caught, his sentence would surely be severe. Perhaps he'd even be hanged. Would Susannah, too, end up alone without a husband to care for her, the way Abigail had? The more he thought about it, the stronger came the conviction that perhaps he'd been too hasty in trying to push Dan into taking unnecessary chances. Chances that could make his wife yet another lonely widow.

24

Yancy walked Felicia toward the stable the next morning. Mr. Thornton would be meeting them to escort them to the abandoned farm.

"I wonder what the place will be like," Felicia mused.

"No way of knowin' till we see it." Hands in his pockets, Yancy watched Matthew's blond head disappear into the barn, then emerge again as he took feed to the chickens. Yancy wasn't all that anxious for the day's venture, since staying alone in the forest with Felicia Blair was out of the question. Completely. Just the thought of it made his palms sweat. But he knew the lass thought of nothing save getting away from Skinner Thornton. And he could see to that, at least. Surely there would be a family along the way who would take them in. He'd just have to find one.

Reaching the stable, he opened the door for her.

She looked up at him as she went in. "Do you think we could go by and visit Papa later today? If there's time after we see the Wilkins cabin, I mean." Such a ray of hope lit her eyes, it was hard to ignore. And with her long hair tied back with a ribbon, she appeared much younger and more vulnerable than she'd ever seemed . . . vulnerable and very desirable.

An even greater weight of responsibility settled on his shoulders as her words sank in. "Do you think that's wise?" he had to ask.

Felicia's smile wilted, and she sighed. "We wouldn't have to

213

go very close. Just close enough to see that he's faring well. I . . . worry about him."

"Aye."

"Papa's never been good at looking after himself, you know."

Taking hold of Felicia's elbow, Yancy stopped and turned her to face him. "Look, we, uh, can't plan on stayin' at that farm together, alone. You know that, and so do I. So 'tis best ye not count on it."

Felicia searched his eyes, then lowered hers. "Well, I'm not about to spend one more night here with that loathsome Skinner Thornton leering at me every time I turn around. And you never know, the cabin might have two rooms. We could make do."

"Felicia." Yancy raised her chin with his finger, forcing her to meet his gaze again. "Do I have to say the words to ye? Even *two separate cabins* wouldn't be enough for us. How much willpower do ye think I have? I used a goodly supply of it last night."

She didn't answer right away. Then, obviously not taking him seriously, she giggled.

Giving her a withering look, Yancy shook his head.

She arched an eyebrow. "Well, you're the one who came up with that lie about our being married. Otherwise we wouldn't *be* in this predicament."

"You're right. I should've shot the pirate when I caught him molestin' ye."

"Oh, Yancy," she breathed, placing a hand on her hip. "A person doesn't go around shooting people, not even way up here in the frontier."

"Maybe not." He let his gaze rest on her dark eyes. Her smile made his insides ache. "But maybe 'tis time someone raised a few knots on that jughead of his."

A flash of horror crossed her smooth brow. "You can't be serious. Skinner Thornton is big. And mean looking. He might hurt you instead. Or worse."

Would the lass never stop questioning his manly abilities?

"I've spent me life on the docks dealing with all kinds of ruffians. I can take care of meself."

"But you can't truly be sure of how a confrontation would turn out," she insisted. "And if something happened to you I'd—"

"Be left to Thornton's mercy," he finished for her. "Or some other cur just like him." Not liking the thought one bit, Yancy felt himself tense as he saw her shudder.

"I hadn't thought about that. What I was going to say is I'd never be able to bear it if something bad happened to you because of me." She took his arm. "Please, Yancy. Don't do something that will put you in harm's way."

Almost afraid to believe the lass actually cared that much about him, he tried to make himself dismiss her request. But the sincerity glowing in her eyes and her expression sent his soul into flight. "I'd relish the thought of trimmin' Thornton's sails, ye know. But if it upsets ye so much, I won't."

"Oh, thank you. Thank you." Throwing her arms around him, Felicia gave him a hug.

Feeling her nearness, his mouth yearned to claim hers. He reached for her, barely stopping himself in time. Instead, he swallowed and gently pushed her away. "Don't. Don't . . . do that."

At her stricken look, he had to toughen himself even more. "And don't look at me that way, either."

Felicia's tempting lips slid into a knowing smile.

He couldn't help but return it. "Most of all, don't smile at me anymore."

Amazingly, her smile faded away. But as she looked beyond him, she moved closer.

Yancy swung around.

Skinner Thornton was coming toward the barn, a lazy grin smeared across his cocky face.

Yancy's fingers tingled. He wanted to plunge a fist right into the middle of that smirk. But he had made a promise to the lass. Noticing her frown, he reached up with his fingers and smoothed the deep line above the bridge of her nose. "Don't worry," he whispered. "We won't be spendin' another night here if we have to stop at every farmstead we pass. Someone's sure to have room for us. Come on, let's saddle your mare."

The trader's son came in. "Pa told me to take you to the Wilkins place."

And I'm the king of England, Yancy thought, more than convinced the scum had been an eager volunteer. He clenched both fists.

Felicia must have noticed, for she took one of them and unwrapped his fingers as she looked up at him beseechingly. She then turned to Skinner. "Thank you. That's very kind. My husband and I appreciate your taking the time to escort us. Don't we, sweetheart?"

False or not, the endearment calmed Yancy slightly. "Aye," he muttered, more for her benefit than anything.

The three rode to the abandoned farm a few miles from the fort almost in complete silence. Felicia did not acknowledge any of Skinner's innuendos or suggestive remarks, much less make a comment of her own. Yancy completely ignored him. They were unsuccessful at finding other accommodations in the few already overcrowded cabins they passed along the way, and Yancy's mood continued its downward spiral.

When they finally broke out of the woods onto the two acres of cleared land Mr. Wilkins had left behind, Yancy begrudgingly assessed the crude dwelling.

"Would you please help me down, sweetheart?" Felicia asked brightly.

"Glad to," Skinner offered, already striding her way.

Yancy stopped him with a glare.

"Kind of you to offer," she told the upstart. "But my husband takes singular pleasure in helping me down from high places."

Yancy saw her eyes sparkling with mischief as he went to her, and he recalled how she'd virtually thrown herself off the wagon at him on their way from Charlottesville. Taking in her impish expression now, he braced himself in case she tried that again.

This time she used just enough force to have to cling a little. For one brief second he held her close, then lowered her to her feet.

"Hmph," Skinner snorted, breaking the spell. "I see what ya mean."

Still savoring the tender moment despite himself, Yancy suddenly felt Felicia grab his hand and tug him toward the house. Reluctantly he went along, although he knew they wouldn't be staying. Besides, the place looked little more than a hovel.

His impression was confirmed as they went inside. Not even one glass window, he noticed. Rough furniture, too, what there was of it. Dirt floor . . .

"Not a bad fireplace," Skinner commented, bending to peer up through the chimney. "From the look of the ceiling, you can see it don't smoke much. And best of all, it's just a couple of miles from the fort. Makes it right neighborly." That sickening smile appeared again.

Felicia brushed off her dusty gloves and swept a glance around the cramped interior. She tilted her head at Yancy. "It's not really so bad," she said on a hopeful note.

The truth was the cabin was in pathetic condition compared to the others where they'd stopped while her father had been with them. And she had found plenty to criticize in all of those.

Yancy didn't bother to comment. He stared out the door and then began to smile. Skinner's horse had wandered a good hundred yards off. The fool had neglected to tie the animal. "Say, lad," he said with a grin. "Looks like ye need to take me horse and catch yours, before it gets much farther."

Grumbling under his breath, Thornton smacked his hat against his pant leg and slammed it back on his head as he stomped away.

"The place has possibilities, don't you think?" Felicia said as Skinner took off on Yancy's horse across the clearing. "I don't feel any drafts."

"Like I said, we're not stayin' here."

"Of course not. Not now. But when Papa is able to leave the Richardses, perhaps we could come here then. Stay until spring. Wouldn't it be nice to get warm and stay that way for a while?"

Yancy merely stared. It was no use informing her that anywhere in proximity to her was plenty warm enough for him.

Felicia strolled to the wooden table and checked to see if it rocked. "Mistress Thornton says there's a real need for a preacher around here."

Yancy watched her movements as she picked up a discarded mixing bowl. He rolled his eyes. "Wasn't it just a couple of weeks ago ye were beratin' your pa for preachin' without a license?"

She met his gaze evenly. "A few weeks ago, I said a lot of things I didn't mean. Anyway, no one way up in these mountains is going to care if he has legal papers or not, as long as he brings God to them."

"Felicia—" The trader's son was already returning with the straying horse in tow, and Yancy shook his head. "In the meantime, this doesn't solve anything. There's still no safe place for ye to spend tonight."

"I always feel safe," she said with a flirty smile, "when I'm with you."

"I told ye to stop that!"

"Stop what?" Skinner asked, just outside.

"Stop bein' so nosy." Yancy aimed a hostile stare at the shiftless lummox, who swung down from Yancy's horse, then mounted his own.

Felicia moved closer to Yancy. "Would you mind giving me a hand up, darling? It must be miles and miles to where Papa is. You did say it was in the opposite direction, didn't you, Mr. Thornton?"

Her innocent tone only added to Yancy's irritation.

"It is. That's a fact," Skinner returned, not shifting his gaze from Yancy's own combative one. "But I'd just as soon keep my distance from a pox house. You know the trail to take once we get back to the fort."

As he and Felicia took their leave from the last homestead between the fort and the Richards place, Yancy felt his panic mounting. The first cabin along the trace had been crowded and overrun with children, not to mention smelling of too many unbathed bodies in such confined quarters. And the second had someone down sick with what could easily be the start of smallpox.

He could tell from Felicia's demeanor that she was beginning to worry, too. But from the look of her after they'd left the last place, he didn't know which bothered her more—spending another night with the Thorntons or her fear of the spreading disease.

At a loss, with nowhere else to turn, Yancy yanked his hat down so she wouldn't be able to see his face and lowered his eyelids to almost closed. *Lord, it's me again, comin' to bother ye. I know it was just last night I asked ye to help me. Ye did, and I thank ye for that. But now tonight's looming upon me, and I'm in a real mess again. I don't know what to do. You've got to find this lass a safe place, Lord. Safe from anyone who'd harm her—and that includes me. You know I'm not strong when it comes to facin' temptations . . . particularly when it's of the female sort. And the lass, well, she's the worst temptation I've ever faced in me life. Maybe this is punishment for that lie I told. But, Lord, ye know I did it with her welfare in mind. And if I confess we're not married now, she'd only be branded a wanton . . . and have all the more hungry wolves like Thornton snappin' at her heels.*

"Look!" Felicia cried.

Yancy jerked his head up and followed the direction she pointed, searching the trail ahead. A trio of fox kits tumbled about in play, their reddish coats a splash of color against the white snow. Glancing back at Felicia, he saw something even more delightful as she watched them . . . her sweet smile, which tugged all the more at his heart and tied his insides in knots.

He resumed his prayer. *You don't have to tell me, Lord, how caught the two of us are in my lie. But if ye could just help us through this muddle, I'd be beholdin' to ye forevermore. I'd never once doubt your power again. Ever. 'Tisn't as if I bore false witness against her, I was just tryin' to help. I just didn't think it through. And if her pa hadn't stayed behind in that pox house, we could've moved on, leaving the tale behind. Please, Lord. You've just got to help us. We don't have anywhere else to turn.*

25

As the horses started up the gentle slope toward the Richards farm, Mr. Blair came running out of the cabin, waving his arms over his head. "Stop. Don't come any closer."

Taking in the old gentleman's expression, Yancy nodded to Felicia, and they reined in their mounts a number of yards before reaching the dwelling.

"Are you well, Papa?" Felicia asked. "Is there anything you need?"

Mr. Blair smiled in response to her queries, a smile that continued to grow on his guileless face. "I'm just fine. Both Mr. and Mistress Richards have met the Lord."

"They're dead?" Yancy asked in shock. "Both of them?"

"Oh no. Not by any means. They've accepted the Lord as their Savior." He grinned even broader, his countenance aglow. "Isn't it wonderful? Now I'm all the more convinced I was right in my calling. I had to come here. This little family was waiting, in need of me."

Yancy had never seen a more angelic or more peaceful expression on a face in his life. He could only stare.

"Why, that *is* wonderful," Felicia said. "I'm so happy for you. But, Papa, smallpox most often claims the very young and the old as its victims."

The druggist chuckled. "And you think I'm so old. Is that it, Leece?"

She blushed a little, then recovered and placed her hands on her hips.

"You need to trust our heavenly Father a little more, my child," her father went on. "He truly is a wonder, as you'll discover if you put your trust in him."

The man never ceased talking about the Almighty, Yancy mused as he assessed the fading daylight with apprehension. "Mr. Blair, I need a private word with ye."

"*Again?*" Felicia blurted in exasperation. "What is it you two talk about that I'm not permitted to hear?"

Waiting until the older man's gaze returned to his own, Yancy reinforced his urgent look.

Mr. Blair nodded and motioned for him to dismount. "We'll be back directly," he told his daughter.

As Yancy strode off with Mr. Blair, keeping a safe distance between them, he didn't dare glance back at Felicia. He didn't want to give her further evidence of how completely she'd undone him.

Once they'd reached the seclusion of the grove a good stone's throw from the homestead, Yancy wasted no time in relating his woes. "I even ended up prayin' to God for strength, like ye said, to see me through," he finished.

"And did you receive the help you asked for?"

"Aye." Yancy scowled—the old gent was missing the point entirely. Didn't he have more concern than that for his beautiful and innocent young daughter? "I got through the night, that's a fact. Even managed to keep from breakin' Thornton's bones a time or two. But me real problem's still starin' me in the face."

"And what problem might that be?"

"Your daughter!" Yancy almost shouted, then lowered his tone. "Felicia. I'm having thoughts regardin' the lass that I've no right to. But I'm only human, ye know. I don't have to tell you how fetchin' the lass is . . . or remind ye that I've not always been exactly an honorable sort around females." He felt his neck redden, but he swallowed the huge lump in his throat and went for the last of his confession. "I ended up down on the floor last night, on me knees. Prayin' for strength."

Mr. Blair broke into a smile. "That pleases me immensely."

"Pleases ye?" Yancy asked incredulously. "I'm tempted to the brink of madness by your daughter, and you're *pleased?*"

"Why, yes, lad. Because you didn't give in to the temptation. You allowed the Lord to see you through, as I had faith that you would."

"That's all well and good, but what about tonight? And the one after? Do ye expect me to keep prayin' for the rest of me very life to get through every month-long night?" He turned and strode a few paces off, then came back as near as he dared as he searched Mr. Blair's face for answers. "I'll never make it. I'm even more tempted today than I was yesterday."

"Are you saying you care for my little girl?" the man asked with a gentleness that perturbed Yancy all the more.

"Care for her?" He shoved his hands in his pockets and let out a whoosh of breath. "I've discovered feelings inside me that I never knew I had. I would fight off a drunken mob for her. A pack of wolves. A tribe of warrin' Injuns. I would consider being a landlubber for the rest of me days, if . . . if . . ." He groaned and raised an open palm in a helpless gesture. "Listen to me. I'm startin' to sound like the worst lovesick fool I ever came across. Me! I don't believe it meself!"

Mr. Blair looked as if he were struggling to maintain a serious expression but losing the battle. "And Felicia. Is she aware of this?"

Yancy sputtered. "Aware of it! The lass baits me! Flutterin' her long eyelashes just so, sashayin' past me at every turn, teasin' me with promisin' little smiles . . . and I warned her to stop it all."

"That does sound like my Felicia," Mr. Blair admitted, obviously on the verge of laughter. He rubbed his jaw in thought. "There is, however, a solution to your problem that you might have overlooked."

"There is?" Yancy asked, seizing the hope like a drowning sailor.

"Yes. In God."

Yancy felt his spirit plummet.

Mr. Blair looked right into Yancy's eyes. "Tell me. When you talked to the Almighty last night, did you perchance repent of your sins before asking his help?"

"Aye. Every single one I could think of. Took me a good long time, too. Only seemed right, ye know," he added with a shrug.

"Afterward, how did you feel?"

"Calm. Kinda peaceful-like. At least after that I was able to get some sleep," he said sheepishly.

"And did you happen to make any grand promises while you were at it?"

Cocking his head, Yancy almost denied it, then relented. "Aye. I figured if the Almighty could help me with the lass, help me keep me sanity around her and all, then maybe I could trust him to keep me on solid ground the rest of the time, too. I know I'm not deservin' of it."

"Well, none of us is, when it comes down to that," the old gentleman said, eyeing him steadily. "But the Lord loves us all. He *is* love, you know. And he created love in us. The great apostle Paul said it best in his epistle to the Corinthians when he said that because of the need to love and be loved, a man should have a wife, and that the two of them should become as one in the eyes of God." His gaze turned heavenward with a sad and dreamy look. "A loving wife is a glorious treasure, lad."

Suddenly realizing all too clearly where this conversation was leading, Yancy's mouth dropped open. "Ye can't be sayin' you'd give your lovely, innocent daughter to the likes of me, a carousin' sea rat!"

"No, I'd never give her to a carousing sailor, that's true. But to a man who has proven himself to be a trustworthy friend, one who'll make a far better Christian husband than he ever did an undisciplined seaman, to him I would give my heartiest blessing."

Yancy was rendered speechless for several seconds. He

couldn't have heard right. But yet, the man was beaming at him in the most incredible way. "I'm . . . not the right man for your daughter, sir. She needs a proper home, one like she was raised in, where she'll be given all her heart's desires."

Mr. Blair met Yancy's eyes again. "The heart's deepest desires, lad, have nothing at all to do with riches or earthly possessions. Believe me. There are no riches greater than those which God, in his supreme blessedness, will shower upon both of you as you live for him. I could ask nothing more for my Felicia than that. Nor," he added more forcefully, "will I accept less."

Marriage! Yancy thought, his mouth going dry as the African desert. *To Felicia!* His heart leaped, nearly bursting from his chest. "But . . . would she have me?"

"There's only one way to find out."

Pacing a circular path around her mare, Felicia pressed her lips together and stopped to look for the hundredth time toward the grove where Papa and Yancy had gone ages ago. The afternoon sunlight was growing thinner by the minute, and they still had not secured a haven for the night. What on earth was taking the men so long?

In frustration she braided a section of the mare's mane. Anything to keep busy. She tapped the toe of her boot impatiently in the crusted snow.

Finally hearing their footsteps, she turned to face the men emerging from the stand of winter-bare trees, more than an arm's distance separating the pair. "Men and their silly secrets!"

Her father came toward her, smiling. But Yancy wore a curious expression on his weathered face.

She centered her attention on him. "From the looks of you, Papa didn't have the answers you sought."

"No," her father piped in, stopping a distance away. "Only you have those. I must go in and check the Richardses. I'll be back directly."

"My goodness," Felicia said facetiously. "Aren't we mysterious." She turned to Yancy, who remained a few steps off, stiff and awkward, tapping his fingertips against his leg. "Pray tell, what was Papa talking about?"

She saw Yancy's Adam's apple lurch as he swallowed. "A-are you leaving us?" she asked in a sudden surge of fear.

"Leavin'? Nay." He removed his hat, raked his fingers through his tumbled curls, then crushed the poor thing in his big hands. "That is, I don't know. Depends."

"On what?" Unable to decipher his strange expression, or allay her own apprehension, for that matter, she moved closer.

"On you." He averted his gaze and looked off into the distance. "Let's . . . um . . . would ye come with me to that log yonder and sit down?"

Curious, and a bit apprehensive, Felicia went along with him. She took a spot he brushed free of snow and snuggled deeper into her cloak.

Yancy appeared ready to take flight. It made her even more nervous. This must have been too much for him . . . her overzealous father, who spoke of nothing but religion day and night, her own short-tempered spitefulness and constant complaining. To say nothing of his being stuck with having to care for the two of them in the cold of winter. Then having Skinner Thornton to contend with. Her eyes stung with tears, and she blinked them back as she tried to concentrate on her hands clasped together in her lap.

An eternity seemed to pass as Yancy neither breathed nor moved. "Felicia, lass," he finally said, his voice low and foreboding, "I know ye expected more. Lots more. But—" He expelled a lungful of air.

Not even wanting to imagine what was next, she turned toward him, all the while steeling herself for the worst.

Yancy's blue eyes darkened, and there was a slight tremor in his hand as it toyed with a frozen twig from the log. Slowly he met her gaze. "But I . . . love ye."

"What did you say?" A tear spilled over the edge of her lashes and warmed a path down her cold cheek.

With a deep groan, he wiped it away with his thumb. "I shouldn't have burdened ye with my feelings, I know. I-I'm sorry."

"You *love* me?" she asked, not recognizing her own voice. "You don't want to burden me?" Dazed with wonder, she threw her arms around his neck. "Oh, Yancy!"

A shudder ran through him as she raised her lips to his. His mouth touching hers so dazzled her, she heard nothing save the echo of his confession ringing in her heart. He loved her. He actually loved her.

When they finally broke apart, she saw that Yancy was as breathless as she.

The cabin door banged, and Papa came running, grinning from ear to ear. He stopped abruptly several yards short of them. "She said yes, I take it. The Lord be praised. I'd shake your hand if I could, son, but congratulations. Congratulations!"

"I, uh, haven't asked her yet," Yancy stammered.

"You haven't? But I thought—"

"Asked me what, Papa?" Felicia asked, as she stood up.

Yancy sprang up beside her. He took her hands into his. "To marry me. If ye'll have me. I can't simply pretend to be your husband any longer."

Seeing that the charmer was absolutely serious, Felicia somehow managed to keep her knees from buckling. "Even after all the horrid things I've said to you, the spiteful way I acted, you would give up your life as a sailor for me, Yancy?"

"'Tis not as if I have a choice," he blurted.

Felicia stiffened and pulled out of his grasp. "You mean Papa's threatened you?" She shot her father a stunned look.

"Nay. Not at all." Yancy spoke with utmost sincerity as he smiled at them both and recaptured her hands in his. "I meant that I love ye far too much to be parted from ye ever again. I know this is sudden. . . ."

Taking in his pleading, childlike expression, Felicia was

overcome with tenderness. How could she ever have been so mean to him as she had when he first came along? How could she hurt him now as he stood before her vulnerable, offering something as precious and beautiful as his love?

"Well, Daughter? What do you say?" Papa asked from the sidelines. "Do I summon Mr. Richards out here to witness a wedding? Do I record your names in the family Bible?"

"Now? Here?" Felicia looked from one to the other, astounded, then surveyed the barren wintry landscape, awash in the blue-purple shadows of dusk.

"Truly man could not build a more wondrous cathedral for a wedding, my child, than the one in which we stand this moment." Papa spread his arms wide, encompassing the surrounding clearing.

"But . . . look at me!" she cried, fingering the wrinkled poplin gown she wore beneath her stained cloak. "We've been on horseback this whole day. I probably even smell like my horse. Every decent gown I own was left in our chests at Staunton. My hair's a sight from blowing in the wind—"

"And you've never looked more bonny," Yancy said, cupping her cheek and turning her face to him. Gently he reached behind her head and untied the ribbon at the nape of her neck, then veiled her dark waves about her shoulders. "You've never been a more beautiful sight, my Felicia. Ye steal me very breath away."

Beginning to see in Yancy's eyes the feelings he was no longer trying to hide, Felicia felt a smile tug at her lips even as tears turned the lovely moment into one of blurry images and colors. She took his hand from her face and kissed his palm. Her own heart swelled with joy and wonder at the answering love deep within herself that she'd been trying to ignore since the day Yancy Curtis had walked into her life. There truly was a husband for her in this wilderness . . . and an abiding love.

Papa had been right all along. Papa and God.

26

As Ben rode down into Bennington, a village sprawled on a wide sloping rise along the flats of the Walloomsac River, he couldn't help but notice how the area differed from much of the surrounding grants. The land appeared more level and open, with low hills slouching away from the undulating plains in long easy rises.

He guided his horse toward Catamount Tavern, barely noticing the plumes of smoke coming from the great chimneys of the building known to be the headquarters for the Green Mountain Boys. His gaze was arrested instead by the twenty-five-foot pole standing before the wide front door. Atop it perched a large stuffed cat-a-mountain, the fierce snarl on its face directed westward, toward New York. Knowing the catamount symbolized the defiance of the settlers in the grants and their determination to keep their land, Ben chuckled.

He dismounted, looping Rebel's reins through an iron ring in the hitching post, then strode toward the ordinary, hoping to be on his way north to see Dan and the newlyweds soon after delivering the message from John Hancock to Landlord Steven Fay.

Just inside the door he stopped for a moment to let his eyes adjust from the brightness of the snowy landscape to the much dimmer interior of the inn.

"Ben!" a voice called out jubilantly. "Ben! Over here!" In a far corner of the room, Dan and Ted both sprang to their feet and rushed toward him. "We've been praying most fervently for your safe return," Dan said, releasing him from a bone-crushing hug.

"We expected you days ago," Ted added. "Did Alex, per-chance, have some men following you?"

"No more than I expected," Ben said with a grin. "Any postrider worth his salt has little difficulty shaking them off. Actually, Fontaine had me imprisoned for more than a week."

"You can't be serious!" Ted gasped.

Dan put an arm across Ben's shoulders. "Well, thank providence you're here now, little brother. You'll have to tell us every detail of what happened, plus how Susannah and Miles are faring. I trust they're well."

"Yes. They're both fine, holding up admirably."

"Have you news of Yancy Curtis yet?" Ted asked. "Surely someone must have heard something."

"Far as I know, aside from a notice I saw fastened to a lamppost offering a twenty-five-pound reward for his capture, there's been no word of him at all."

Dan shook his head. "Well, now that you've come in out of the cold, how about some good hot cider to warm your bones?"

"Not just yet. I've an urgent message for Landlord Fay to take care of first."

"Well, lad, you're in luck." An older man of medium build and age stood up at the table Dan and Ted had just vacated, along with a younger one who bore close resemblance. Both appeared jovial and more than interested. "I'm Steven Fay, and this is my son, Jonas."

"Ben Haynes." Shaking their hands, Ben noticed that Charles Warren was also present. He nodded. "Charles."

"I'll fetch you a hot drink," the landlord said while Ben removed his outercoat and draped it over a nearby chair. He strode to the bar and returned with a tankard of hot cider.

"I wasn't expecting to find you two here," Ben told Dan and Ted as they took seats.

x

"One of God's mysterious workings, I'm sure," Ted quipped, a grin softening the square contours of his jaw.

"Actually, Landlord Fay sent for us," Dan answered. "I wasted no time getting here in case it concerned news of you."

"As it turns out," Jonas Fay said, his youthful face serious, "we were hoping they had heard something."

"We also wanted Paul's opinion," the older man said, using Ted's assumed name, "on whether or not the fort at Ticonderoga could be taken, as Ethan thinks. Harrington was just getting around to telling us when you blew in. Don't see why we can't hold off, though, until we know if we need to. Do you have the message on you?"

"I wasn't given anything in writing," Ben said. "If something of this nature were to fall into the wrong hands, there wouldn't be rope enough in the Colonies to hang us all." Even as he spoke, Ben noticed that the spark of anticipation radiating from the eyes of the Fays was markedly absent from his brother's and Ted's. He exhaled slowly, admitting to himself that the pair had more personal experience with the might of the British.

He shrugged and went on. "Fortunately, John Hancock and the lawyer, John Adams, were successful in securing my release from the military stockade at Castle William. And hopefully," he added with a grin at Dan and Ted, "the lieutenant has faced a severe dressing-down from his superiors for arresting me without due cause or process."

Ted smirked.

"What about Colonel Allen's proposal to take the fort?" Landlord Fay asked, redirecting the conversation once more.

Ben met the man's impatient expression. "Mr. Hancock was very much for the idea. Quite enthusiastic. But Adams was more cautious, as you'd expect of a lawyer. He did say something encouraging, however. He knew his cousin Sam would be so eager at the prospect he'd probably want to lead the charge himself! He was jesting, of course. But neither gentleman had any doubt that Sam Adams—and any of the others who make up the Committee of Correspondence—

would be elated to know that the folks in the Green Mountain country will give such helpful support if the time comes."

Fay slammed his pewter tankard on the tabletop and nodded to his son. "See? What'd I tell you?"

Raising his drink to both, Ben grinned. "Hancock even went so far as to correct Adams by saying, 'Not *if,* but *when* the time comes.' And it's not merely Boston. Riding through Massachusetts, I twice saw angry mobs in the middle of tarring and feathering someone who'd spoken out in favor of the Crown."

Ben caught sight of Dan's appalled expression. Pouring hot tar over a man was not only humiliating, but torturous as well. He shrugged. "The whole countryside is on the verge of exploding."

"I can believe that." Mr. Fay stroked his jawline in thought while turning to Ted. "Well, now that we know tempers are on the rise throughout the land, maybe we can get down to some serious talk. What say you, Mr. Goforth, would be our best strategy in taking the fort?"

Ted smiled wryly at the use of his alias, but answered without comment. "Considering the battery of cannon at Ticonderoga, there's but one way. Surprise. Absolute surprise. That means there should be no unnecessary snooping around in advance. And as we were discussing earlier, no one—not even your trusted lieutenants—should be told before it's absolutely necessary. The fewer who know, the less chance word will get to the men at the fort. Don't even talk among yourselves of this until Colonel Allen returns in the spring, and then only to him."

Charles shifted his bony frame in his chair, his half-smile adding emphasis to his hooked nose. "Don't need to worry none about these folks. We're all good patriots out here."

"Well then," Ted answered, "such good patriots will understand the need for secrecy."

"We both give our word. It will not leave this table," Mr. Fay vowed.

"Capital," replied Ted. "We don't want the soldiers reinforcing their ranks or posting double guards."

With a solemn nod, Landlord Fay agreed. "As it is now, they leave the gates wide open every day into the night. And we'd sure hate having all those cannons primed and ready to fire."

"Now you understand," Ted said. "Since there's been no trouble with the Indians for some time now, very few soldiers relish being stationed so deep in the wilderness. They languish from boredom."

"That's one thing that cannot be said about Boston," Dan reflected sadly.

"Right," Ben said. "We keep it lively for all our own poor lobsterbacks." He tossed back the last of his cider.

A chuckle circuited the group.

Then Ted sobered. "The grants have one other advantage that Landlord Fay mentioned. Not only are its people loyal to one another, but they also have no appointed magistrates. No outsiders brought in who can't be trusted."

"Compared to the coastal towns, where rioting against Tory judges and such is becoming commonplace, you folks appear very peaceable," Ben had to admit.

"Unless another Yorker surveyor shows up—which shouldn't happen anyway until the snow melts," Charles said with a laugh.

"Nor should any further orders or proclamations be coming from England before spring," Ted added. "So for the next few months, at least, peace should reign in these mountain valleys and the fort across the lake . . . for which we should thank almighty God."

"And let us not forget to pray without ceasing for Boston," Dan suggested, "and our many loved ones and dear friends at the mercy of the regiments there."

Ben recognized the morose note in his brother's voice.

Across the room, the door opened, admitting several customers. Landlord Fay got up and went to tend them.

Jonas grinned at Charles. "Just bought myself a new squirrel shooter the other day from a hunter down on his luck. All carved and painted with Indian signs and everything. Come up to my room and I'll show you."

As the two friends strode off, a look of relief settled upon Dan. "What news do you have of Susannah, Ben?"

Immediate thought of her condition flew to Ben's mind, but having decided on prudence—since hasty action brought on by that news might lead to tragedy—he chose to abide by Susannah's wishes. He reached for his greatcoat and dug into an inside pocket. "I brought letters from her."

Dan desperately clutched his and couldn't seem to open it fast enough.

Unable to endure watching his brother's face while reading the private words from the wife he so longed to see, Ben rose. "Guess I'll go get myself some stew. I hope it's not bear meat. I hate bear."

Returning moments later and setting down his bowl, Ben saw his brother pale as he lowered the written pages. "She's with child," he mumbled.

Ted looked up from his own letter. "I beg your pardon?"

"With child," he repeated more forcefully. "Susannah is with child."

The expression on his brother's face was enough to make Ben's appetite vanish. He remembered how he'd threatened Susannah that he'd inform Dan of her condition. She must have felt compelled to confess the truth herself to keep him from doing just that. "She's fine, Dan. Just fine. All your church friends are looking after her, keeping watch day and night."

Utterly crestfallen, Dan slumped forward, resting his weight on his elbows.

Exchanging a look of concern with Ted, Ben swallowed. "She understands completely why you didn't feel it was wise to return. She even agrees. Wholeheartedly. She doesn't want you to do anything you're not absolutely certain was—how did she put it? Oh yes . . . led of the Lord."

A rush of air came from Dan's lungs. "Pastor Griffith's broken leg turned out to be far worse than any of us expected.

(continued)

It is now infected. And whether I choose to be here or not, I know this is where I'm supposed to be, where I must be, at this time. I've been attending to the pastor's duties as well as preparing Ted for ordination orals—not to mention teaching him the rudiments of farming."

Hoping to lighten the moment somewhat, Ben sputtered into a laugh. "And just how do you do that with the ground frozen?"

Ted grinned broadly. "Believe it or not, your brother's had me out plowing the snow for practice. Then there's milking, mending harnesses, whittling new handles for the broken tools, training the filly . . . anything he can come up with to keep us both working sunup to sunset."

"Well," Ben said, scratching his head, "I suppose if you have a notion of becoming a pastor in a wilderness neighborhood, it would behoove you to know how to farm. A minister could get mighty hungry, since there's not a whole lot of cash money passing hands in the deep woods for tithes or anything else. Of course," he added, jesting, "with your knowledge of weapons, you could take to hunting."

Ted appeared to take the last remark seriously. He shook his head. "Hunters are gone from home far too much. I rather doubt Jane would like that. And truthfully, I'm enjoying what I'm learning about farming. Building something out of the wilderness with one's own hands seems quite the exciting challenge . . . to Jane as well as to me."

"Are you speaking about *our* Jane?" Ben asked, dumbfounded. "If that's true, she certainly has changed, hasn't she—" Flicking a look in Dan's direction, he realized his brother's thoughts were hundreds of miles away, as he devoured Susannah's letter again. Utter dejection etched creases alongside Dan's dark eyes.

Ted apparently observed Dan's preoccupation as well. He went on in a casual tone, "That's precisely what we've been trying to tell you, Ben. Your sister has changed. Grown up and learned the joys and blessings that come from obedience to the Lord."

"Yes," Ben said with a laugh. "One of the blessings being you, no doubt."

Ted merely grinned. "Just wait until it happens to you, that's all I can say. One of these days when you're least expecting it, you'll meet a sweet maiden who will affect you so deeply that henceforth you, too, will feel a great lack whenever you aren't with her. And speaking of sweet maidens, I want to go to the settlement store and buy mine a gift—a belated wedding gift."

A vision of Abigail Preston drifted across Ben's mind as it had amazingly often during the past several days. He couldn't imagine a sweeter maiden than she, with the silky hair like finest gold, the loving nature that, even amid her thankless existence, poured forth joy to her little ones. "I just might keep you company, Ted. I wouldn't mind making a purchase or two myself."

Ted gave Ben a quizzical glance and smiled slyly.

"Toys," Ben blurted out, covering his blunder as he rose. "I nearly met my demise in a blizzard during the trip up here, but a kind family took me in. There are two little ones who could use some nice playthings, and I intend to see that they get them."

"Whatever you say," Ted said, not relinquishing his intent gaze.

Ben turned to his brother. "Care to come with us, Dan?"

"Hm?" Dan looked up blankly, his mind obviously otherwise occupied.

"Ted and I are going over to the store. Would you like to come?"

Folding the sheets of Susannah's letter and tucking them in his inner pocket next to his heart, he got up. "No, I think I'll go to our quarters for a while. Perhaps read my letter again, do some praying."

"Whatever you say."

On their way to make their purchases, Ted turned a thoughtful glance to Ben. "Dan hasn't been quite himself for some time now. I rather wish he'd never gotten caught up in our troubles, Jane's and mine."

"No use in trying to blame yourself or anyone else, Ted. Dan couldn't have done anything but what he's chosen to do."

"Aye, but he seems now to be losing his joy, his exuberance in being a Christian. I see it happening by the hour, yet there's nothing I can do to stop it. He never laughs, and every smile seems an effort. What if his faith is the next thing to suffer?"

The question disturbed Ben deeply. Dan did seem subdued and quieter than usual, but could his brother actually be losing that deep, abiding faith . . . that faith that until now Ben hadn't realized he himself depended on?

He tried to still the nagging fear that began to eat at his insides. It couldn't happen. Not to Dan.

27

Convinced that no word would come of Britain's retaliation until April at the very earliest, Ben argued with himself as he headed east toward Boston rather than south to Salisbury, Connecticut. He had left word with Landlord Fay—there was plenty of time to contact Ethan Allen later. February had barely made its appearance. With two feet of snow on the ground and freezing temperatures, nothing much could possibly be accomplished anyway. He refused to dwell any further on the possibility that the Green Mountain colonel might want time to plan the assault with his lieutenants. After all, Ted had said that utmost secrecy was a must. Ben was merely ensuring that secrecy.

And besides, he had some new toys to deliver.

Coming within sight of the Preston farm, Ben felt the pace of his heart pick up speed even as he nudged Rebel's flanks into a canter.

No one was around as he turned up the partially cleared path onto the place, but since it was nearly noon, he hadn't expected to see activity on the grounds. The cold snap would keep folks inside except for whatever duty or daily chore necessitated coming out.

Smoke rose from the east chimney, ascending like a prayer to heaven. It was probably too much to hope that Abigail would be the one to greet him. A mere moment alone in her presence before Bertha clomped onto the scene would be enough to treasure through many a lonely night on the road. As he poised a foot on the bottom step, he gave fleeting thought to praying that Abigail would answer the door.

Then guilt assaulted him as a bevy of faithless remarks he'd made to Dan and Jane and their mates flashed into his head. What was he doing here, anyway? Obviously a few too many hours spent in the glow of honeymoon bliss shared by Jane and Ted had caused him to take leave of his senses. No man with all his faculties would willingly come to a place where a determined female like Bertha Preston was waiting to pounce.

In all likelihood the snow had muffled the sounds of his approach. Ben turned back toward his horse, intending to make his escape, then stopped. He did want the children to have the new playthings. The least he could do was see that they got them, now that he was already here. With a nervous look toward the house, Ben removed the brown-paper parcels from his saddlebag. He drew a fortifying breath, went to the door, and knocked.

In seconds it opened. Cassandra's round blue eyes peered shyly upward, then a bright smile of recognition lit up her face. "Mama!" Leaving the door standing wide open, she ducked her head and ran right past her brother playing with a beanbag at the bottom of the stairs. "Mama!" she yelled again as he tossed it after her.

Even though he felt like an intruder, Ben decided it would be prudent to keep as much warmth inside as possible. He removed his hat and tucked it under the arm holding the packages, then stepped inside and quietly closed the door.

The beanbag sailed into his chest as he turned around, and he caught a glimpse of Corbin darting into the shelter of the stairway. Chuckling to himself, Ben retrieved the offending object and dashed after the boy. "Good shot, lad!" he said, scooping the laughing child up with his other arm.

Hesitant to venture farther uninvited and possibly encounter Bertha, Ben carried the boy back to the door and deposited him on his feet just as footsteps approached from the rear of the house. He felt the boy snuggle against his leg.

Cassandra reappeared, her mother in tow.

"Postrider Haynes," Abigail murmured, not entirely able to subdue the sparkle of delight that sprang into her blue-green eyes. Freeing herself from her daughter's grip, she dropped a feather duster into an upholstered chair in passing and reached up to brush some errant tendrils of hair aside.

"Mistress Preston." Ben's gaze remained fixed as he gave a polite nod. Even with a white mobcap hiding most of her golden hair, she was lovelier than he remembered. A crisp bib apron clung to her slender form, revealing alluring curves that would have otherwise been hidden beneath her shapeless, nearly colorless, work dress.

A fragile rosy glow highlighted Abigail's fine cheekbones. She didn't quite meet Ben's eyes. "What brings you by on such a cold day? You were headed for the grants, or so you said."

Aware that he was concentrating more on her whispery voice than the words she'd spoken, Ben cleared his throat and observed Cassandra, hiding again behind her mother's skirts the way she had during his other visit.

He winked at the little girl. "I've already been there and made my deliveries."

"My goodness. You must have a very swift horse."

"Swift, yes," Ben said with a smile. "And surefooted, even in this poor weather. Actually, I came because I had some things I wanted to bring by. One of them," he said with a tap on Corbin's nose, "is for you." He handed the boy a round package, then stepped closer to Abigail and held the other out to Cassandra. "And this is for you."

The child took the gift and stooped at once to tear the wrappings open. Seeing Cassandra, her younger brother did the same.

Their enthusiasm was gratifying. But Ben found his attention centered on the young mother. She watched her little ones, a dreamy smile on her face.

Corbin, holding up a brightly painted ball, grinned from ear to ear. Cassandra tilted her head and studied the satin-garbed wooden doll with its porcelain face for a second before giving it a fierce hug.

"They're wonderful gifts," Abigail said breathlessly as the pair ran off to play with their treasures. "Perfect."

Ben's heart caught as she blinked back tears. "I, er, wanted to do something to repay you—and your family, of course," he added quickly. "You were all so kind the night of the blizzard."

"We did far too little to deserve such a grand reward, I'm sure." She slowly slid her gaze to his face.

He raised his brows in mock dismay. "You don't consider my life worth the price of a little dolly, Mistress Preston?"

Abigail blushed profusely and lowered her head. "That's not what I meant."

"I know." Boldly Ben lifted her chin with the edge of his index finger and smiled gently. "I was just teasing."

The tots burst into the room again, Cassandra chasing her brother as he held the doll just beyond her reach and ducked behind Ben's legs. "Mama, make him give it back," she whined.

Disentangling himself from the little fingers clutching the bottom of his greatcoat, Ben rescued the toy from Corbin's other hand and restored custody to the new mommy. "Do you like the dolly, Cassie?" he asked, gazing down into expectant eyes the exact color and shape as her mother's.

"Mm hm," she mumbled, nodding.

"Ball!" the boy piped in as he rolled it across the room. He gave a whoop and charged after it.

As he returned, his mother caught his hand. "What should we say to Mr. Haynes for giving us these wonderful gifts?" she prompted, looking from one child to the other.

"Thank you," they said together, then Corbin flung the ball again. As it bounced off the wall, both children ran after it.

"I suppose you can tell which is my shy one," Abigail said.

Ben had already decided that the little girl, being such a miniature of her mother, was no more bashful than Abigail must have been at that age. "I think we'll do fine, once we get to know each other a little better," he said, hoping she'd include herself in the statement as well.

"Oh, faith!" Abigail gasped. "Where are my manners? I haven't taken your coat as yet! Won't you come into the kitchen by the fire while I fetch you something to warm your insides? We were about to have dinner. You must join us."

"Are you certain it won't put you out?" Ben asked, wrestling out of the heavy garment and handing it over. "I know you weren't expecting an extra mouth to feed."

She hung the wrap by the door and turned. "I'd like—that is, the children would be most pleased to have you to eat with us," she amended quickly.

"Stay. Stay," Corbin said, racing back. Grabbing a hand, he tugged Ben.

"Well, I certainly wouldn't want to disappoint *the children,* now, would I?" he said teasingly.

Her color deepening, she swept Cassie into her arms and led the way through the homey parlor and on toward the kitchen beyond.

"Where is . . . everyone?" he asked, taking the chair she indicated. He had expected to have to contend with Bertha and Ma Preston the instant he arrived.

Across the room at the hearth, Abigail smiled over her shoulder. "Mistress Canfield, Ma's old friend on the next farm, took a chill. Bertie and Ma took her some herb tea and fresh bread. Most likely," she added wistfully, "they'll stay to dinner there." Immediately she averted her eyes and tended to the kettle.

Ben could have leaped for joy. But just as quickly, his joy plummeted as the front door creaked open, immediately followed by the pounding of boots coming their way.

"I knowed it was you!" Bertha guffawed, her feet still caked with snow as she exploded into the room. "Ma! I told ya it was him. He's back!"

An hour later, Ben rode away, intensely relieved that he'd escaped with his life. He called himself all kinds of fool for setting himself up for another downright mauling by overeager, overzealous Bertha. Who would have believed the girl could have been blatant enough to attempt to entice him out to the barn, of all things. It was bad enough she'd plunked herself between him and everybody else in the room—even the children.

Abigail had been all but banished from the kitchen, but Ben consoled himself with the memory of how Cassie and Corbin had finally climbed up on his lap and snuggled close, their tender little bodies clingingly soft and huggable. Ma and Bertie blustering around had turned them both shy and quiet.

Ben emitted a deep sigh as he crested the far hill. He swiveled around for a last look at the Preston house jutting up imposingly against the stark leafless trees.

No doubt he was becoming completely enamored with Abigail Preston and her two offspring. Sinking fast. He should count himself fortunate that the two women arrived when they did. Why, as befuddled as that beguiling threesome was making him, he might have found himself down on one knee within the hour, proposing marriage! And this was no time to let fanciful visions of hearth and home distract him from his duties.

He tried to cast aside his tender remembrances of Abigail Preston, the wonder of what it might be like if she were his love. But his wayward thoughts shifted to the silly secret smiles he'd seen pass between his sister and Ted. And Emily. He could not forget the expressions of love that gave life to her and her Scotsman's face the day Dan had married them, the light radiating from their eyes.

That same light had shone in the children's faces today. Ben grimaced at the jolting realization. "But of course they'd smile when someone presented them with gifts. Who wouldn't?" The sound of his voice in the winter hush brought him back to reality. He urged Rebel to a swifter pace as they neared a forested hill.

But his mind would not take a different route. Try as he might to force his thoughts to business at hand, to missions yet ahead, within moments they had rambled backward that mile or so. And a loneliness descended upon him. He took off his hat to wipe his forehead on his sleeve, then quickly resettled the hat firmly in place.

What he needed more than anything right now was people. Lively, noisy people. Lots of them. Coming up to a crossroad, Ben purposefully took the southward turn. His sisters' households in Worcester never knew a dull moment. Perhaps if he plunged into the joyous confusion they called everyday life, some of the ache inside would ease.

A feathery gust of late afternoon wind sighed through the countryside, breathless and light. *Just like her voice,* Ben thought. He looked back one more time.

Nothing was there but a barrier of trees. Evergreens heavy with snow stood mutely on the white, white hills. And all around them the world was still. Silent. Empty.

A mild salty breeze stirred the rows of budding trees that lined the Boston Common as townspeople strolled the mall in the spring sunshine.

Susannah spread a blanket in the shade of the great elm and set her picnic basket on it. "Stay by Mama, now," she told Miles. "I can't be running after you."

He smiled as he gave his rubber ball a toss, then ran to fetch it.

Watching her tawny-haired son for a moment to be sure he didn't wander far, Susannah gingerly lowered her cumbersome body to her knees and opened her picnic basket, setting out some sliced bread and cheese.

"I hope we haven't kept you waiting overlong," Beth Morgan said, hastening over with her two little daughters. Putting her own basket near Susannah's, she untied her bonnet and set it down.

Susannah smiled up at her auburn-haired neighbor. "Not at all. Miles and I came only a few moments ago, after he awakened from his nap."

"Splendid." Beth fanned herself with a lacy handkerchief. "I've been rushing about all morning, airing the house, beating rugs . . . it'll be delightful to have a rest." She sank to the ground and tucked her feet under her skirts.

"Mama," six-year-old Sarah said, tapping Beth's shoulder, "may we pick flowers?"

"Yes. But please remember to share with Sissie. She's not as old as you."

"Yes, Mama." Sarah's mouth curved into an enchanting smile as she and four-year-old Charlotte ran hand in hand across the grass toward a cluster of spring blossoms.

"Goodness, they're growing so quickly," Susannah remarked, wistfully admiring the ruffles and ribbons adorning their frocks. She bit into a slice of bread.

"Almost as quickly as your Miles. Seems only weeks ago you first brought him to church, a tiny wiggly bundle in blue. And now just look at him."

Hearing her son's giggle, Susannah shaded her eyes and saw one of her guards swinging Miles around in his arms.

"My, my. You've certainly made a pet of that lobsterback of yours, haven't you?" Beth whispered teasingly. "I suppose he'll be expecting you to feed him as well."

"Oh, Private Williams is a sweet lad," Susannah said, adjusting her position as the growing babe within gave a stout kick. "None of this ugly political business is his doing."

"Perhaps not. But if ordered, I'd wager he'd be right in line with the rest of them, bayonet pointed and ready." She motioned with her head further out in the field, where a company of uniformed men practiced bayonet thrusts during their daily marching exercises.

Ignoring the other soldiers, Susannah considered Private Williams' boyish face, the spattering of freckles across the bridge of his nose, the easy smile as he played with Miles. "Well, he might be capable of presenting a threat to an enemy, but he's quite tenderhearted, really. He'd not be one to inflict harm on weak and helpless folk. In fact, just the other day he and Corporal Barnes did me a great service. Lieutenant Fontaine had been away for several weeks, as you know."

"Yes. Who could help but notice?" Beth shook her head, the waves in her thick hair shining in the sun. "At least when he's not around we can all feel safe crossing the street without fear of being run down by him and that wild racing stallion of his. Sometimes I think the man is possessed."

"Perhaps obsessed might be closer to the truth." Susannah paused. "Well, the lieutenant had just returned from another of his futile trips . . . to Philadelphia this time, to search for my brother. He was in a rather black mood, which only worsened when the fact that I'm with child could no longer be hidden. Maybe he couldn't deal with the thought of the child he and Jane might have been expecting by now. Whatever it was, just seeing me drove him into a deeper rage. He grabbed me and started yelling all manner of mad things he'd do if I didn't inform on my family."

"I didn't know." Beth reached out a comforting hand and took Susannah's. "Did he hurt you?"

"Mama," Sarah said, running up to her mother. "Sissie thinks her wreath is better than mine. It's not nearly as pretty." Her lower lip gained prominence as she nudged the younger child aside and held out the lopsided crown.

"Oh, now, I'd say they're both lovely," Beth said in a placating tone. She smiled and examined each in turn.

"It's for you, Mama." Sarah offered hers.

Little Charlotte sidled nearer to Susannah and shyly deposited her ring of flowers.

"Thank you, sweetheart. I've never seen anything quite so pretty." Susannah winked at Beth, who was having trouble keeping a straight face as she looked at the pitiful handiwork.

"We'll go pick some more for you," Sarah said, taking her sister's hand.

Watching as they skipped away, Susannah couldn't help but wonder if her new baby would turn out to be a girl . . . one who would someday come all bright eyed, bringing flowers in the springtime. *What a joy it would be to fuss with curls and frills,* she thought. She absently rearranged the entwined wreath in her hand.

"So what were you saying about our mad lieutenant?" Beth prompted.

"Hm? Oh, that. There's not much more, really. Private

Williams came running to the door at that moment, reporting that Alex's horse had bolted off down the street and that he'd been unable to catch him. Of course, Alex was livid. He ended up having to go after the animal himself . . . and didn't return."

"Thank heaven. The Lord must have been watching over you."

"I've no doubt of it. But so was the private. He even winked at me when Alex turned to leave." Susannah giggled and gazed toward the young man who was still entertaining Miles.

Beth fingered the orchid ribbon ties of her discarded bonnet with a smile. "Hardly a surprise, you know. After all, the entire rotation of guards who stand at your gate are smitten with you—except for the twosome who volunteer for Sabbath duty, of course. They fall over each other flirting with that brazen Molly Stuart. That girl needs a good switching."

Susannah rested a hand on her bulging abdomen and tried to get more comfortable as she loosened her crocheted shawl. "Well, I wouldn't be the least surprised if one of these days, dear Beth, you'll have to be keeping a closer eye on your own sprouting angels. They'll likely turn more than a few heads themselves."

"Oh, not for years and years, I hope." Beth fanned herself again.

"Children grow up before we know it," Susannah mused. "Dan's youngest sister, Emily, was quite the tomboy when first I met her. But now she's a loving wife and mother. In a letter she managed to smuggle to me some days ago, she mentioned that Alex had been to Princeton in his desperate search for Ted. Honestly! He's still tearing through the Colonies even after four and a half months! One would expect the man to give up."

"I'm certain his superiors can't go on indefinitely endorsing the expense the search must involve—in men as well as time." Beth flicked a glance over Susannah's expanding middle. "I do hope he drops the effort before your time comes."

Susannah sighed. She didn't want to voice her growing apprehension over the possibility of giving birth alone this time. The experience with Miles had taken her to the very brink of death. Forcing the morbid thoughts aside, she plopped the flower wreath atop her head. "How do I look?"

"Probably," Beth said, doing the same with hers, "as good as I do!" She bubbled into a laugh, then gazed off toward her daughters.

"Wouldn't it be wonderful," Susannah said dreamily as she took off the flowers, "if perhaps, this Christmas, Dan's and my family could all be together, just this once?"

"They do seem quite scattered to the four winds, don't they?" Brushing a tendril of hair out of her eyes, Beth tossed her head. "But at least they all manage to write to you. You haven't lost touch despite the obstacles."

Susannah nodded. "And I'm grateful for that, as well as for other small miracles. Emily wrote that if she and Robert hadn't moved from the Lyons' Den Inn to a small house of their own mere days before Alex showed up, she might have been waiting tables when he arrived . . . and Robert would be in irons by now."

Beth shuddered.

A childish laugh carried their way, and Susannah turned to watch as Miles tried to catch Private Williams, who was pretending to run from him. "That should be Dan playing with our son," she said with a sad smile. "He's missed so many precious months."

"Do you hear from him often?"

"Yes," Susannah answered, her eyes still on her son. "And his letters are always encouraging. I'm sure that's for my benefit, really." She turned to her friend. "His sister Jane writes that she's worried about him. According to her, he's lost weight, is moody. She doesn't think he'll stay put much longer with the baby coming . . . God's timing or not. She wants me to try to reassure him more earnestly that I'm well. That *we're* well."

Feeling truly uncomfortable, Susannah lumbered to her

feet, rubbing her back. Then, noticing a commotion as people rushed past the graveyard and toward the street, she frowned.

"What's happening?" Beth asked, rising also.

The distant sound grew more clear as a drummer boy came into view along Common Street. She heard a second drummer coming from the opposite direction.

Susannah exchanged a worried look with the private, who scooped up the baby. She saw him scan the nearly empty Common with an expression akin to fear. The company of redcoats who'd been practicing drills earlier had departed, she noticed. Knowing a lone soldier would stand a good chance of being mobbed if something like the '70 riot reoccurred, Susannah went to him. "If you'll be kind enough to look after Miles, I'll see what the trouble is."

He nodded gratefully.

"Would you keep an eye on my girls, too?" Beth asked, rushing after Susannah.

They'd barely reached the edge of the gathering crowd when Susannah heard men shouting.

"They're gonna blockade the port?" came one angry voice. "When?"

"What about Philadelphia? New York?" yelled another. "Are they shuttin' them down, too?"

"They won't allow tea ships to unload there either?"

"No!" someone hollered in the center of it all. "Only Boston. The first of June. General Gage is on his way from England right now to enforce it—*and* he's bringin' more troops."

An angry rumble rolled through the mob.

"We'd better go, Beth," Susannah said over the din. The closing of the port would infuriate the townspeople enough, but the thought of another raft of soldiers tramping the Boston streets would take them to the boiling point. She nodded to the private and hurried back toward him, hoping no one had noticed his presence as he stood with Miles under one arm and the girls hanging onto his coattails. She and Beth seized the picnic things and threw them into the baskets.

"Best we use the backstreets," Beth said. "No sense taking any risks."

❦ ❦

Susannah had never seen such a turnout of church folk in her house as she moved quietly to the parlor doorway and leaned against it, head bowed. Even as she closed her eyes she couldn't shut out the dire expressions mirrored from one face to the next.

"Dear Lord," Elder Simms was praying, "we all have a special place in our hearts for this city on the bay. Even though we don't think the Congregationalists are as enlightened as we Presbyterians happen to be, we know they've done their best to honor thee through the years, observing the Sabbath faithfully, praying for thy guidance in all their public meetings. They teach their children in their schools and homes to fear thee. We ask that you take this into consideration during the dark months to come. Bad enough we had a governor appointed by the Crown, but now for them to make General Gage acting governor as well as commander of their forces in America, that's bitter medicine for us to take."

"Amen," someone said fervently.

"It's martial law, that's what," another man piped in.

The elder peeked through one eye at the offender, then bowed his head again. "Martial law not withstanding, we'll trust the God of the universe to keep us all safely in his fold. We ask these things humbly, in the name of thy Son. Amen."

An echoing *amen* rumbled through the room.

"Well, Mistress Haynes," Elder Simms said, making his way to her. "We sure do appreciate being able to come here and pray together at such a serious time as this. We'll be taking our leave, now, so's you can have some rest. Thank you most kindly for the hospitality."

"You're more than welcome," she said with a smile, nodding and shaking hands with various individuals as the gathering quickly dispersed. Squeezing through to the door to bid the rest good-night, she looked across the street. She could make out the guards there in the glow of the streetlamp.

"'Scuse me, missus," a tradesman said on his way out. "I was asked to give ye this. A sailor friend on a ship from Philadelphia delivered it this afternoon, but I couldn't get here before."

Susannah took the rather beaten-up letter and scanned the uneven writing, then slipped it into her apron pocket. "Why, thank you. We have family in that area."

Even as she bid the last person farewell and took the remaining coffee out to the guards, she wondered if the letter was from Rob MacKinnon. Emily's handwriting was much more precise. She wasted no time coming back inside, then locked up and extinguished the lights. She was dying to read the letter, yet she enjoyed savoring the anticipation.

When finally she had dressed for night, she turned up the wick of the bedside lamp and eased onto the bed, envelope in hand.

The wax seal broke easily, and out tumbled a sheet of fine paper. She unfolded it eagerly:

Dear Daniel and Susannah,

Yancy here. I am not much of a mate when it comes to writing. I pray you can read this.

Susannah hugged the paper to her bosom and laughed with joy. She could easily picture the dear, redheaded seaman bent over the paper, a quill in a death grip, carefully making his marks as best he could. With a sigh, she spread the page out again.

I am safe. I hunt now instead of being hunted. I provide meat for two tables. I planted a field of corn. The first sprouts came up today, thank the good Lord.

Their sweet smuggler, plowing fields instead of the high seas? However had that come to be? And when had he ever in his life mentioned thanking the Lord for anything? She looked once more at the written lines that barely resembled his usual spoken words.

I wish I could see your faces when you read this. I am far away. I found the Lord. I also found a most amazing woman to love, the most beautiful person in this world. We are married and very happy. The Almighty had a hand in it.

I have had no news of Jane or Ted. Fontaine caught them helping me escape. I pray for them every night. I trust things are well with you and your wee babe. I pray for you also. Lord willing, we hope to see you soon.

Your mate,
Yancy Curtis

A tear splashed the paper before Susannah realized that she was crying. So many people had been praying for Seaman Yancy Curtis since the night of his escape, but never had she dreamed she'd receive such a treasured letter from him.

Breathing a prayer of thanks for God's goodness, she dried her cheeks and got up to get her own writing materials. Dan needed to know this. Perhaps it would not only give him joy, but help to restore his wavering faith as well.

Wild azaleas and rhododendron blended their rosy hues with the banks of mountain laurel and fern as Yancy and Felicia rode down into the Cheat River Valley for a Sunday morning church service. All around them a gentle breeze mingled the heady scents together, wafting the sweetness through the forest.

Yancy watched Felicia drink in the wonders of God's handiwork as she rode just ahead of him on the narrow wooded trail. But his gaze could stray no further than the silky hair coursing over his wife's delicate shoulders. Mottled sunshine drifted through the leafy canopy now and then, gilding the waves into a shining halo. What had he done in his life to merit such an angel? He watched with wonder as she glanced first in one direction and then the other, trying to absorb the lavish glories of June.

"Listen to the birds, love," she murmured softly, as if not wishing to interrupt the chirps and trills being passed from treetop to treetop.

"Aye. 'Tis quite a melody."

"The loveliest one I've ever heard. There didn't seem to be half as many birds in Williamsburg with all the buildings and bustle. Out here there's nothing to frighten them off—except, perhaps, for Papa's new adopted grandchildren." She paused, then pointed ahead. "Look. I think I see Papa's cabin."

Another miracle, Yancy mused. Felicia's father had become enamored with Millicent Hawkins, a warm, openhearted grandmother of one of the settler families. Having had the smallpox herself, she had immediately taken up the fight against the disease, working tirelessly at Pa Blair's side until the scourge had passed. They had ministered to both physical and spiritual needs in three homes where the inhabitants had been afflicted. During that time, love had blossomed, and so had the affections of the neighborhood toward them. Yancy and Felicia had taken to the motherly woman immediately and had been only too happy to witness the short but emotion-filled wedding ceremony less than two months after their own.

Through a stand of pines, Yancy could see the new dwelling he and Pa Blair had helped raise for Millicent's married daughter and son-in-law. Situated a mere stone's throw from the older cabin where Pa and Millicent resided, the new house teemed with children—at this moment, playing about the clearing.

One of them, a lad of about six, ran to the older house. "Somebody's comin'," he hollered into the open door.

At once Pa Blair and his new wife stepped outside and waved as they started hand in hand toward Yancy and Felicia.

Love agreed with the man, Yancy decided as he returned his father-in-law's wave. He had put on a few pounds during the two months since he and Millicent had gotten married, and he nearly glowed from inside out in his preaching clothes. Today he was clad in a white shirt and black knee breeches, a long black vest hanging nearly to his knees.

A welcoming smile plumped out Millicent's round, pink face beneath her lace-trimmed mobcap.

"You're early," Pa said. "We're pleased you made it so soon."

"Yes," Millicent added. "Come on down off them horses and have some fresh coffee, just made."

Yancy dismounted, then went to assist Felicia, and they followed the obviously adoring pair into the cabin, which forever emitted the delicious aromas of baked goods and rich soups.

On the way in, Yancy had noticed half a dozen rows of logs lined up in a clearing framed by dogwoods in preparation for Pa Blair's open-air service. Everybody within traveling distance attended, and the gathering gave Yancy a feeling of security, of togetherness. He no longer saw much significance in the poverty of the locals. Even though they lacked an abundance of worldly goods, the freedom and neighborliness they all displayed made them appear rich indeed, and not a one was ever slow to help another in need.

"The Lord bless you both," Pa Blair said, holding the door open for them. "In fact, may he bless us all!" He tilted his graying head in his wife's direction and beamed with pride.

"We had such a lovely ride, Papa," Felicia said, hugging him and kissing his cheek as she passed. "The woods are bursting with flowers and bird song."

"Yes, aren't they?" Millicent said at the hearth, filling a teapot. "The young'uns bring me violets near every day. Wildflowers are the treasure of spring and summer."

On his way to one of the sturdily crafted wood chairs at the dining table, Yancy caught the sound of swiftly approaching hoofbeats. He and Pa stopped and swung back to the doorway.

Three riders cantered into the clearing. Two of them Yancy had seen at the settlement store, trading furs and regaling everyone within earshot of the bountiful wonders of the Ohio River country. The third man, another frontiersman in the typical fringed garb and moccasins, was a stranger. His swarthy complexion seemed even darker from constant exposure to sun and weather.

"We're so glad you could come to service," Pa Blair said, extending his hand after they'd reined to a stop and dismounted.

"More comin' a little ways back." One of the two Yancy recognized, a rake of a man with a scruffy face, smiled brightly despite some rather large gaps between the few teeth he possessed. "Jed and me, we give a invite to our pal, Brady. Brady, this here's Preacher Blair."

"Glad to have you all," Felicia's father said with a nod.

"Tell him what you told us, Brady." The stouter one called Jed nudged the man in buckskin. "'Bout the Brits."

The fellow whipped off his wide-brimmed brown hat. "I got here quick as I could with word from up north. Some representatives from Boston came to see the Lees and some of the others that sit in Virginia's House of Burgesses. Those bigwigs in England finally did it. They're givin' all the land west of the Appalachians to the Frenchies."

"No!" Pa Blair said. "That can't be. The British would never give back what they won in the French and Indian wars."

"Ain't what I mean," the stranger said. "The Crown, of all fool things, ceded all the territories down to the Ohio Valley, not to Virginia or Pennsylvania, nor to the colonies borderin' the frontier, but to the Canadians instead."

"And that means us here. They sent a charter to the Frenchies that won't even let us elect our own assembly," the first man added. "It's a slap in the face to us, even if it isn't to them ignorant Frenchies. The charter says we won't be English subjects with basic English rights."

"That ain't all, Preacher," the third one cried. "They're letting the Frenchies keep their Catholic bishop and all that superstitious mumbo jumbo of theirs. What do ya say to that?"

Pa Blair scratched his head thoughtfully, worried creases deepening in his face. "Our wonderful land seems filled with trouble and dissension—more with each passing year. When the rest of our little flock arrives, we'll pray for God's guiding hand."

After the little assembly had gathered in the June sunshine and Pa Blair had broken the latest news, Yancy still felt no less shock and anger than the settlers who even now mumbled under their breath and shook their heads. Even as Millicent attempted to calm them by leading them in a hymn, it was more than evident that few would be able to concentrate on Pa Blair's sermon . . . if he even got to it.

Felicia gave Yancy's hand a reassuring squeeze, and he looked at her and warmed to her smile. Her attitude toward life in general had undergone a vast change, one that only added a new beauty to her spirit.

"Dear friends," Pa Blair said, raising a hand at the end of the song. "My sermon for today, providentially, will be from the first chapter of Joshua, a passage which the Lord has repeatedly called to my mind during this past week. I pray that the Lord will speak to us all from these words:

> Now after the death of Moses the servant of the Lord it came to pass, that the Lord spake unto Joshua the son of Nun, Moses' minister, saying, Moses my servant is dead; now therefore arise, go over this Jordan, thou, and all this people, unto the land which I do give to them, even to the children of Israel. Every place that the sole of your foot shall tread upon, that have I given unto you, as I said unto Moses. From the wilderness and this Lebanon even unto the great river, the river Euphrates, all the land of the Hittites, and unto the great sea toward the going down of the sun, shall be your coast. There shall not any man be able to stand before thee all the days of thy life: as I was with Moses, so I will be with thee: I will not fail thee, nor forsake thee.

While his father-in-law read the Scripture, Yancy observed the men becoming increasingly cheerful, beaming and nodding to one another. Even the womenfolk, somewhat more reserved, were wearing broad smiles and displaying hope in their expressions.

> Be strong and of a good courage: for unto this people shalt thou divide for an inheritance the land, which I sware unto their fathers to give them. Only be thou strong and very courageous, that thou mayest observe to do according to all the law, which Moses my servant commanded thee: turn not from it to the right hand or to the left, that thou mayest prosper whithersoever thou goest. This book of the law shall not depart out of thy

mouth; but thou shalt meditate therein day and night, that thou mayest observe to do according to all that is written therein: for then thou shalt make thy way prosperous, and then thou shalt have good success.

The congregation's spirits seemed slightly chastised by the time the end of the passage had been read, but it was more than apparent to Yancy that they were of one accord. As far as they were concerned, they'd just been given God's blessing to resist. And he was in complete agreement with that conclusion.

At the end of the service, Yancy helped the men rig some tables out of planks and barrels while the women brought an assortment of food to one already set up near the cabin.

"That's a familiar accent you have, lad," the newcomer remarked as he and Yancy placed one of the few remaining boards.

"Must be 'cause he's from up Boston way," his crony said. "You're a sailor, right? Must've read your stars wrong to end up this far inland—turned right when you shoulda turned left."

The third hunter guffawed loudly and whacked Yancy's back. "None too smart, I'd say, if ya didn't have sense to stop till ya got here."

An arm's length away, the frontiersman looked Yancy up and down. "Boston, you say? Might be interested to know the Crown closed the port the first of June."

"Are ye certain?" Yancy asked, not sure whether he was more surprised or dismayed at the news.

The stranger nodded. "Ordered General Gage back from England to see to it himself—along with a whole 'nother passel of redcoat dogs."

"I don't think the Canadians will throw us off our farm, do you, love?" Felicia asked, riding homeward later that day.

Lost in his own troubled thoughts, Yancy heard her question as though from a great distance. He had tried to ignore his twinges of longing for the coast since they had gotten married. He had made a concentrated effort to settle into life as a farmer. But all the while, the sight of the night stars, the way the wind would whistle through the forest as though the trees were masts and spars of great ships moored to the docks only added to his yearning to smell the salty brine once more. He sighed.

"Yancy?" Felicia cast a quizzical glance over her shoulder. "Is something troubling you?"

Yancy looked away and shrugged. *Where to start?* Finally he could restrain the words no longer. "I think 'tis time we went back to New England."

"What did you say?" Her lips parted in shock.

"Ye heard me."

"But—we'd be leaving our home. Papa and Millicent."

"Aye. But your pa is doin' fine with his new wife and his flock. And I'm needed up north. I know it."

Felicia's disappointment was obvious as her shoulders sagged. She didn't even answer at first. Then she slowed her mare and let him catch up. "Are you sure that's where the Almighty wants you to be?"

The question put him at a loss for words. He hadn't even asked the Lord's guidance. He'd just felt the deepest need to go aid his people in their resistance to the Crown's latest measures. He turned a weak smile to his wife. "When we get home, we'll seek God's will together." The statement sounded strange coming from his mouth, but it also brought with it a profound peace. He had discovered, since giving his heart to the Lord, that God was the one true Mate in this life. And come what may, Yancy would follow his orders.

Grasping the smooth brass rail of the coastal packet, Felicia looked across the rippling water of Narragansett Bay as the vessel neared the colony of Rhode Island. The farther they sailed, the more she felt Yancy's excitement.

"See off to the south?" he said at her side, indicating the direction with his finger. "Behind that sand spit there's a wee cove where we unloaded more Dutch tea than ye could shake a stick at. I don't know if the British ever found out it was there."

"You jest!" Turning to him, Felicia shot him a look rife with disbelief. "Why, I see nothing but shoreline."

"Appears that way, doesn't it?" Yancy said cheerfully. He took her arm and guided her past coils of heavy rope and barrels lashed to a mast. Reaching the other side of the ship, he nodded toward a cluster of whitecaps ruffling a patch of otherwise calm bay water. "Just below the surface there's a sandbar. Of course, with it bein' high tide right now, ye'd never know 'twas there. That's where the *Gaspee* met her fate."

"Under your very nose, I'm sure," Felicia said with a knowing smile.

"Aye. Meself was among the lot that set her afire. Ah, 'twas great fun."

She laughed lightly. "I never had the slightest doubt. And Daniel Haynes, the friend you've spoken of so often . . . his family's home is just five miles inland, you say?"

Yancy nodded. "A fine horse farm, they've got. They breed Narragansett Pacers, sturdy little horses known for their easy gait and stamina when carrying double."

"Why would anyone breed an animal for the purpose of carrying more than one person?" Felicia asked, arching her brows in curiosity.

"Because of the back roads. Fine carriages may fare well enough in Virginia, but here they're not so practical—even if folks had the money to waste on them. The roads here in wintertime aren't fit for much more than a sled. Then when spring melt comes, they turn into muddy bogs. I tell ye, though," he added, his mouth spreading into a grin, "there's nothin' more cozy than ridin' double." Yancy's arms slid around her from behind and drew her against himself and nibbled the tender skin beneath her summer bonnet. "See what I mean?"

Felicia laughed as his breath tickled her, then straightened to watch the pilot-skiff off the bow steer their vessel around a sandbar. Beyond that, the channel narrowed twice as they drew closer to their destination—Providence.

"You like Providence, don't you," she said.

"Aye. Always gives this old salt a friendly welcome, she does."

"You mean old smuggler." Twisting in his arms so she could see his face, Felicia smiled teasingly.

Yancy chuckled. "That, too. We're all in it together here in Rhode Island. Come to think of it, it's nigh onto two years and a month to the very day since the whole town cheered the burnin' of that devil ship. That was also when Dan came home from college in Princeton, after havin' been away for more than a year. What a day that was. Him bringin' his pretty wife to meet his family for the first time, and me showin' up with young Rob MacKinnon, a deserter from the *Gaspee*. I barely had time to hide the lad from two redcoats that Dan's sister Jane had invited to dinner. One of them happened to be Susannah's brother, to top it all off, an' the two of them weren't seein' eye to eye at the time."

"That must have been quite the volatile gathering."

"Aye. You've no idea. By the end of the day, Dan's youngest sister, Emily, helped the deserter escape and ran off with him. Besides makin' their mother nearly perish, the older sister, Jane, was fit to be tied over havin' her chances of marryin' the English officer ruined. She harped about nothin' else for more than a year." Yancy wagged his head. "Yessir, that was quite a day."

"And now, after all that chaos, you'll still be welcomed by Mr. and Mistress Haynes at the farm?"

He rubbed his jaw in thought. "Well, the lady herself might raise a haughty brow, but Dan's father will welcome us to home and hearth without a second thought. He's quite friendly and kind. Dan's a lot like him."

Smiling to herself, Felicia wondered if anyone could be more kind and friendly than her own handsome sailor. He looked especially dapper in his richly tailored three-piece suit and new tricornered hat. *And even more handsome when he is full of mischief,* she added inwardly as a young seaman passed them carrying a thick rope and Yancy purposely set a foot on the trailing end of it.

As they disembarked a short time later, Yancy kept a firm hold on Felicia's arm. Since they'd arrived from Virginia and the customs agents would be dealing only with the cargo down in the hold, he figured none of the soldiers milling about would likely notice his arrival. He certainly didn't look like his old self in his gentleman's clothing, but one never knew for sure. Not wanting to show fear for Felicia's sake, he stepped confidently onto the wharf.

"Yancy! As I live and breathe!" a voice yelled from off to one side. "Hardly recognized ya in that fancy getup."

Yancy shot a glance toward the guards at the customs table set up on the next wharf, then relaxed. "Aye. Well, 'tis me, in the flesh," Yancy quipped with a jaunty wave, recognizing Burt Posten, the wiry dockworker who'd spoken.

Posten, along with a blur of other familiar faces dressed in similar working garb, rushed toward Yancy and pounded him on the back exuberantly, all speaking at once—and thankfully blocking the lobsterbacks' view.

"Where've ya been? It's been a dog's age since we seen ya."

"And no wonder," another said, eyeing Yancy's attire, "if that's how you're dressin' nowadays!" He sputtered into a belly laugh.

When the jabbering and laughing subsided, a moonfaced man in the group checked first one way and then the other before stepping closer. "Don't worry, mate," he said in a conspiratorial tone. "Whenever we spy one of them broadsides on ya, we rip it right down."

"Of course," Burt Posten quipped, "ever'time we see a new one go up, at least we know they ain't caught ya yet!"

Yancy opened his mouth but didn't have a chance to reply.

"Sure must've twisted Fontaine's aristocratic tail, the way the lieutenant's been down here so often tryin' to find ya."

A crony nudged him. "Oh, I don't think he'll be doin' much more o' that. Lobsterbacks aren't bein' made too welcome outside of Boston these days. Thickheaded as they are, methinks they're finally gettin' the message that we don't want 'em around."

"Enough of this redcoat talk," Posten said, sweeping an assessing glance over Felicia. "Who wants to discuss them when there's a ravishin' beauty hangin' on your bony arm?"

Puffing out his chest with pride, Yancy pressed Felicia's hand where it was tucked into the crook of his elbow and smiled at her. "This, me *deprived mates,* is me lovely wife, Felicia."

"Your wife, ya say? Can't be! Not our Yancy of the rovin' eye."

"Now, don't be spinnin' tales, lads," Yancy quipped. "Me lady is far too delicate to be exposed to your waterfront yammerin's."

Felicia gave Yancy an overly sweet smile and fluttered her lashes. "On the contrary, darling, I'd be most interested in whatever tidbits these gentlemen might wish to tell me. Truly I would."

"Then I'll be the first," the rowdiest one of the lot offered. Sweeping off his knit cap with a twinkle in his eye, he bowed elaborately and moved closer.

"No, ye won't," Yancy said, quickly steering Felicia toward the thoroughfare teeming with carts and pedestrians. "These scoundrels, sweetheart, are leagues from bein' gentlemen. Besides, I'd like to get our trunks to the inn and ride out to the Haynes farm before it gets too late."

"Well, lads," he heard one of his mates grumble as the group turned and walked the other way, "looks like that's one pretty lady ol' Yance won't be lettin' go of any time soon."

"Hey!" Burt Posten yelled suddenly. "Yance, wait! I need to talk to you about some local goin's-on."

Yancy stopped and looked back with a lopsided grin. "Ye mean smugglin'?"

"Aye. Now that British tubs are blockin' Boston harbor, there's more need than ever before."

"How 'bout later this eve, at the ordinary?" another fellow suggested. "If your wife'll let ya, that is." He gave an insinuating wink to his pals.

Yancy swallowed and looked from his friends to Felicia, whose elegant bearing seemed all the more imperious in her fashionable green traveling gown and hairpin lace shawl.

Abruptly and unaccountably, her expression turned to one of horror. "You would actually leave me, a poor, delicate, defenseless creature, all alone? Helpless, while you go off gallivanting with your friends?"

If Yancy hadn't known how phony that coy whine was, the theatrical near swoon she effected would have been proof enough. Several wide grins broke out on the faces of his mates.

Felicia dipped her bonnet toward the men with her most charming smile. "Of course my husband may join you . . . *if* I have your solemn promise to have him home at a respectable hour."

They stared at her as if dumbfounded.

"Well?" she prompted.

"Yes, ma'am," several of them chorused.

"Splendid. I wouldn't want my husband to keep company with fellows who were any less henpecked than he."

Their mouths all dropped open, and Felicia laughed outright, with Yancy and his friends joining in.

"Got yourself some woman there," Burt Posten remarked in all seriousness. "Quite a woman."

"You're not tellin' me somethin' I don't already know, mate."

As he was about to knock at the Hayneses' door, Yancy felt Felicia's grip tighten on his arm. He took a fortifying breath and attempted a smile, then rapped.

Beside him, Felicia turned and swept another glance of admiration over the lovely fenced grounds and paddocks where horses grazed and frolicked.

Within seconds, footsteps approached from within.

Dan's mother opened the door. She looked from Yancy to Felicia and back. Then as recognition dawned, her fine brows arched skyward over clear green eyes, and she raised her chin a notch.

"Good day, Mistress," Yancy said.

"Mr. Curtis." Not a muscle in her stiff face moved.

"Who is it, Sophia?" Mr. Haynes called from another room as he moved up beside his wife. Catching sight of Yancy, a broad smile deepened the laugh lines beside his mouth, and he stepped out to grab the sailor's hand in an enthusiastic handshake. "Praise be! You're alive! No one's heard word of you for so long we were beginning to fear you were dead. And just look at you . . . all dressed up, looking more robust than ever."

With a grin at Felicia, Yancy reddened slightly. "Must be me wife's good cookin'."

"Your *wife?*" Dan's mother asked, a hand at her mouth in amazement.

"Aye. That I did."

"And you'll be settling down now?" She continued to regard him with a puzzled look.

"Well now, as to that, ye see, I . . . er . . . What I mean is, I'm not sure. When I heard of the troubles up Boston way, I felt led of the Lord to come back."

"Led of the Lord?" A dubious smile quirked a corner of the older woman's mouth.

Not bothering to wait for Yancy to reply, Dan's father took Felicia's arm and drew her inside. "Well, let's have a look at the fair maiden clever enough to steal the barnacled heart of our roving sailor. Come along, lad," he said over his shoulder. "You, too, my dear. I'm sure the lovely lady would appreciate a nice cup of Dutch tea."

"Certainly." With a nod of her silver-streaked auburn pompadour, Sophia Haynes glided out of the room.

"Tea, I fear, is much harder to come by since you abandoned us, Yancy," Mr. Haynes said wryly. "But now I see what made you stay away so long." Smiling, he led the way into the parlor and gestured toward the settee. "What might your name be, my dear?" he asked as Felicia settled her skirts about her.

"Oh. I'm forgettin' me manners," Yancy blurted. "This is Felicia, sir. Sweetheart, Dan's father, Mr. Haynes."

"How do you do?" she murmured, offering a hand.

The older man grasped it warmly and bowed over it. "I'm honored to make your acquaintance. We think a lot of this seaman of yours. Most of us, at any rate," he added with a wink as he and Yancy sat down also.

Yancy grinned, while in his mind he tried to formulate a question about Ted and Jane. Their fates had been in as precarious a state as his the last time he'd seen them.

"So where have you been keeping yourself, lad?"

"West of Virginia, the mountain country."

"Hm. Still wilderness for the most part, is it not?"

"Aye. But I'm a real frontiersman now. Got me a Pennsylvania flintlock, a fringed leather shirt, and a good huntin' knife. You'd have trouble tellin' me from a seasoned trapper, that's a fact."

"You don't say." Mr. Haynes' easy smile flashed as he slapped his knee. "That is something I'd dearly love to see."

The lady of the house returned then with a tray, which she set on a low mahogany table. "Fringed leather shirt," she repeated, again looking from Felicia to Yancy with an elevated brow. "Well, I must say, I've never seen you dressed so respectably as today. Your good wife's doing, no doubt."

"Aye," he admitted with a grin, recalling the standoff he and Felicia had weathered over that very subject. When they had reached Williamsburg, they had gone to Felicia's home to leave their horses and retrieve the clothes she had left behind when she and her father set out for the wilderness. She had given him an ultimatum: either purchase a suit and wear it, or she would not board the ship. "I'm proud to have ye meet Felicia, a lass who's out to prove it's possible to turn a sow's ear into a silk purse after all."

Despite herself, the older woman actually smiled.

Felicia tilted her head at Yancy. "But, sweetheart, you are so wonderfully pliable."

At this everyone chuckled, even Dan's mother, who joined in after only a slight hesitation. The atmosphere seemed remarkably lighter.

"From where do you hail, my dear?" Mistress Haynes asked Felicia with apparent interest.

"Williamsburg."

"Oh. A charming city. I visited there when I was a child. My family comes from Philadelphia."

"An equally fine city."

"Do you take cream and sugar, my dear?"

Yancy had never dreamed the day would come when he'd be pleased to have a wife from a much more refined background than his own. Seeing how at ease Felicia was in this elegant parlor and with this regal matron as well, he breathed easier. But he couldn't help wondering how long it would last once he broached the real reason for the visit. He cleared his throat and looked at Mr. Haynes. "I've been concerned for some time about your daughter Jane. Since the night I took such hasty leave from Boston, in fact. I trust you know she aided me in the escape."

Mistress Haynes held a cup of tea out to him. "Not only do we know, but thanks to that reprehensible Lieutenant Fontaine, so does everyone else from Philadelphia to Maine. Do tell him, dear, while I pour ours."

By the time Dan's father had finished and Yancy took the first sip, his tea had grown cold. And despite the mild July temperature, his insides more than matched the chill of it. Dan, Ted, and Jane, all on the run because of him? Susannah a virtual hostage while with child because of him? How could so many lives now be in jeopardy for trying to save him? "I'm beginnin' to understand why the callin' to come back felt so strong." He didn't realize he had voiced the thought, until Mr. Haynes responded.

"You must not feel in any way responsible for the choices each of them made, lad. Besides, Jane and Ted are now man and wife, at long last, leading the life God intended for them all along. And Dan is not wasting his time either. He's helping Ted prepare for his orals at Princeton, for whenever life once again returns to normal."

Yancy glanced at Felicia. "God's ways truly are unfathomable, wouldn't ye say?"

"Is there, perchance, some change in you that you haven't told us, Yancy?" Dan's mother asked.

He felt himself redden. She had known him at his worst.

But to his relief, Felicia stepped in. "Yancy has given his life over to the service of the Lord."

To his utter amazement, the most profound transformation Yancy had witnessed in his entire life took place before his very eyes. Dan's mother all but dropped her china cup and sprang up to give him a teary embrace.

"Why, my goodness," she stammered, remembering herself

and stepping back, fingering a fold of her plum skirt. "What wonderful and exciting news!"

Finally recapturing his own voice, Yancy reached for Felicia's hand and grasped it tightly. "And who would've guessed the Almighty would give me, a sinner such as I was, a lady so gracious and beautiful as me dear sweet Felicia to love?" He paused. "But—Dan and Susannah! Isn't there anything we can do for Susannah, at least?"

31

The summer air was heavy with floral sweetness as Yancy and Felicia rode back across the sea plain to Providence. The beauty of the day made the ride seem like a jaunt through Eden's garden.

"Dan's parents were quite friendly, I thought," Felicia mused as her mount navigated around a rut in the road.

"Aye. Much more so than I expected. 'Twas pretty decent of them to offer ye a place to stay while I try to find a way to help Boston—and maybe Dan's wife in the bargain." Even as he spoke the words, Yancy couldn't imagine leaving Felicia now. The sight of her smiling face first thing every morning was a blessing he wasn't ready to relinquish so soon. But the fact was he'd gotten to know every nook and cranny of the coastline from his smuggling ventures. He could help immeasurably in getting badly needed supplies through—supplies that the British would never allow entrance.

As the animals plodded steadily over the dirt road, Yancy drifted into silent prayer—something he had been doing more and more lately. *There has to be many a ship in need of an experienced coastal pilot, wouldn't ye say, Lord? If ye wouldn't mind guiding my steps and leading me in that direction, I'd be truly thankful.*

"It must be frightful for Susannah," Felicia said, breaking into Yancy's thoughts, "all alone in her house with a small child to look after and another birth looming before her. I don't know what I'd do if I were in her place."

"I'm sure Dan's church members have been a big comfort to the lass. And she's quite a strong sort, really." Yancy vividly recalled the long agonizing night when Miles was brought into the world and how vulnerable Susannah had been throughout the ordeal. He supposed that no woman was ever truly certain she'd survive giving birth. But Susannah had always found a deep inner strength in the Lord.

"Yancy?"

Yancy was caught up in thought, aware that his own dearest wife would most likely face that same danger one day. "Aye?" He met her thoughtful expression. A strange light shone from the depths of her eyes.

"I've been going over something in my mind concerning Susannah's plight. I'd like to go and stay with her."

"Eh? What are ye sayin'?"

"She needs someone desperately. Her time is growing swiftly near, and she shouldn't be alone right now." She caught his expression of disapproval, and her eyes took on the old flash and fire that had both attracted and infuriated him when he had first met her. "Don't give me that look, Yancy Curtis," she went on. "You have things you feel you must do without me. This is what I feel *I* must do."

Had she gone mad? "What?" Yancy demanded.

"Just as I said. I want to go stay with her and her son."

"In Boston?"

Felicia tossed her head and set her jaw in determination. "Well, after all, I'll be worrying about *you* while you're off saving the day. It's only fair that you have someone to worry about, too."

"Never!"

"So this is Cambridge," Felicia said airily appraising the pleasant, attractive town. "It's quite lovely." They approached Harvard, the first institute of higher learning established in the Colonies, and the bells tolled as they passed the imposing structure.

His teeth on edge, as they had been since departing Providence, Yancy shot a sidelong glance at her as they guided the Haynes's pacers along the cobbled street.

"Where did Mr. Haynes say Benjamin has a room? With the cooper, was it?"

"No," Yancy said on a sigh, willing himself to be patient. "A wheelwright. The man's a loyal patriot. And just because I brought ye this far, don't be thinkin' I'm about to allow ye to go across the Neck and into Boston." He gave an emphatic nod.

"Yes, dear." A maddening smile made her eyes twinkle even as she spoke in that patronizing tone. "You were right about these horses, though," she went on in an obvious ploy to change the subject. "They are quite comfortable to ride. It's hard to believe we've been sitting on them for two days."

His wife did appear fresh, despite the hard travel, and quite beguiling. Yancy nudged his mount ahead to make way for a team of horses, then slowed to let her catch up. "I've never seen so many freight wagons on the roads. The closer we get to Boston the thicker they get. One of the drivers at the coaching inn last eve said there were even more comin' down from Salem port."

"I think it's just wonderful the way all the Colonies are rallying around and donating food and supplies to Boston. It's as if the Virginians and the other southern colonies have become equally involved as New Englanders in the standoff with Britain." She nodded her head at a couple passing in an oversized cart.

"First time I've ever known all the colonists to band together to help a neighbor in need."

"It seems so Christian, don't you think? Colonies of Good Samaritans. And, of course, I can do no less."

Yancy filled his lungs and expelled the air in one surge. "The matter is far from settled, woman." He added a scowl for good measure. He'd never known anyone as stubborn as Felicia. He couldn't believe he had even allowed her to come this far with him.

They moved toward the center of town, where various

shops lined either side of the main street. Busy at work, the sounds of the tradesmen's hammers and saws echoed from building to building. When they finally reached the two-story establishment housing the wheelwright's shop and upstairs apartment, Yancy dismounted and helped Felicia down before entering.

Sean Burns paused from pounding an iron rim onto a wooden wheel and wiped sweat from his brow. He replaced his kerchief in the pocket of his big leather apron, then looked up and caught sight of them. "Yancy Curtis!" The stocky man strode quickly across the dirt floor, his large hand extended.

Yancy pumped it in greeting. "Sean."

The wheelwright assessed Felicia, and he smiled. "So this must be the lass who caught and tamed ye, eh? Ye must be quite a woman, mistress. We thought this lad would still be a bachelor when he met his Maker." The *r*s trailed from the Scotsman's brogue as he grinned.

She smiled and dipped her head. "Life quite often takes an unexpected turn."

"How'd ye hear about us, Felicia and me?" Yancy asked, puzzled.

"Have me spies just about everywhere," Burns said with a lift of his shaggy brows, then sobered. "Actually, Charlie Pringle, the cobbler a block away from Dan's house, told me. He's the one—" he paused, casting a furtive glance in either direction—"who passes secret correspondence out to me. And I tell ye, folks here in Cambridge have the most well-maintained shoes in Massachusetts, since we're obliged to keep a steady flow of 'em goin' and comin'!"

Yancy started to chuckle, then contained it as they heard someone hurrying their way.

The sight of two pacers bearing his family's brand had piqued Ben's curiosity, and he left the bright sunlight and entered Burns's shop. "I saw two horses outside—," he began, then the three shadowy figures came into focus. "Yancy!" He lunged for the seaman and hugged him. "It's about time you came back!"

While thumping the redhead's shoulder blades, Ben's gaze came to rest on a dark-haired beauty standing off to one side. He eased away. "Now I see why you've been off playing house while the rest of us are in the middle of a war—and in need of your particular talents."

"*War?*" the young woman whispered, her eyes wide.

"Just about." Automatically, Ben reached up to remove his hat, discovering he'd forgotten it. He took her fingers lightly and swept into a bow instead. "I'd be most pleased to make your acquaintance, m'lady . . . if this sailor will have the courtesy to introduce us, that is."

"Ye can put your eyes back in your head first," Yancy said evenly. "And unhand her."

Ben kept his hold. "Always been full of surprises, haven't you?" he said to Yancy.

Felicia gently withdrew from Ben's grip. "Since my husband seems to be remiss, my given name is Felicia. And yours?"

"Ben Haynes, courier for the Committee of Correspondence, at your service."

She nodded politely. "And what precisely did you mean a few moments ago when you said you're at war?"

Sean Burns stepped forward. "How 'bout the three of ye go upstairs an' let Maggie make ye some tea while I close up down here. Never hurts to guard against any bootlickin' Tories who might be lurkin' in the shadows."

"Can't be many of 'em left," Yancy quipped.

"Not anywhere near what there were," Ben answered. "But even Jesus had his Judas. There's always someone who can't resist the jingle of those thirty pieces of silver." Smiling at Felicia, he gestured for her to precede him.

A short time later, they all sat at the table enjoying Mistress Burns's hospitality as she bustled about serving refreshments.

Ben watched the plump, jovial older woman pour the rich tea into her best china cups and set one before each of them. "I'll not be havin' ye goin' hungry," she said, setting out a plate of delicious-looking scones. "Eat up whilst ye do your talkin'. I'll not be botherin' ye."

"Thank ye, my dear," Sean Burns said with a loving pat on her pudgy hand.

"Yes, indeed. Thank you, Mistress Burns," Felicia said with a smile. "We so appreciate your kind hospitality."

"Least a body can do for those helpin' the cause."

"Ye know," Yancy said as the older woman settled into the corner rocker and picked up some mending, "we didn't pass a single redcoat on the road from Providence."

"That's because we're keeping the general and his boys too busy right here," Ben said, laughing. "At the moment he's trying to foist a new government on us. And you've probably heard how stiff-necked we New Englanders can be. Poor man," he added facetiously. "He's invited our assembly to meet with him in Salem next week. But nobody's accepted his invitation."

Yancy nodded in understanding.

"Then there's that little problem up in Worcester," Ben went on. "He appointed new judges to hold court, but folks there won't let them anywhere near the courthouse. Yessir, the man has his hands full." A broad grin broke forth.

"I don't see that as bein' the end of it, though," Yancy said, spreading a dollop of cranberry jam onto a scone. "Leastwise from the temperament of the people we talked to along the way." He popped the treat into his mouth.

Ben cocked his head thoughtfully—Felicia Curtis seemed equally interested in the discussion as she sipped her tea. Ben began, "You couldn't have spoken truer words. I just got back from Philadelphia. I heard all the Colonies will be sending representatives to meet there in September. The Continental Congress they're going to call it. Got a nice official ring to it, what do you say?"

"A congress?" Yancy brightened. "Then all the Colonies truly are goin' to be behind us."

"Not going to be. Already are." Ben gulped some of his drink, then set the cup down. "The Crown, I'm sure, was counting on the Colonies' greed to isolate Boston. It never dawned on them that instead of the other ports smacking their lips at the thought of devouring whatever trade Boston would be missing, they'd come to our aid with desperately needed money and supplies. Sam Adams doesn't think there'll be any turning back now. The British have rendered their last proclamation."

"Pardon me for interrupting," Felicia said quietly. "But how can you sound so happy? What of your sister-in-law, trapped in the midst of Boston?"

Ben sighed. "I am concerned about her, true. But there are other members of my family in worse jeopardy, fleeing the Crown—as is your husband."

"Me dear wife," Yancy explained, "has taken it upon herself to think she should walk right into the lion's mouth to—"

"And men seem to think," she said, shooting him an angry glare, "they're the only ones the Lord can possibly use to do his work."

Ben saw Yancy open his mouth, then promptly clamp it shut. It was the first time he'd ever seen the sailor speechless, especially with a mouthy woman in close proximity. He winked at the wheelwright.

"Well?" Felicia asked.

Ben sat back, savoring the knowledge that Yancy had at last met his match. "Yes. Well?" he parroted.

The seaman turned to him, hands lifted in frustration. "Talk some sense into her, will ye, Ben? She thinks she needs to be with Susannah until her new babe arrives."

The announcement sent renewed hope surging through Ben. "You'd do that?" he asked Felicia. "I can't tell you how grateful I'd be, to say nothing of how it would thrill Dan!"

"Ben!" Yancy growled. "She doesn't need encouragin'."

"But, Yance. Think about it. No one in Boston knows who she is. Especially Fontaine. He'd have no reason to harass a newly hired servant, would he?"

"A very beautiful one, she'd be. And at his mercy."

Felicia snuggled up to Yancy and toyed with the edge of his

sleeve. "Oh, sweetheart, we've nothing to fear if we trust the Lord."

"Maybe not—but the last time ye were in trouble, I was there."

"Only by the grace of God," she added.

"But I won't be there this time. And if that blackguard so much as looks at ye—" He turned desperately to Mistress Burns. "Won't ye tell me foolish bride she must not go?"

"Methinks I hear a pot boilin' over," the older woman murmured with a sheepish look. Rising from the rocking chair, she hastened to the hearth.

Ben saw Felicia hide a smile. "Trust me, Yancy," he said comfortingly. "I have far more reason to dislike Fontaine than you have. But I'm certain both women would be quite safe. The neighbors keep constant watch over Sue, and whenever Fontaine pays her a call, one of them manages to find a reason to go and visit her at that very moment."

"If it's so *safe,*" Yancy grated, "why is me wife needed?"

"Because . . ." Ben hesitated, then spoke firmly. "Because my sister-in-law is so stubborn she refuses to let us hire anyone to stay in the house with her as her time nears. But if Felicia were to show up on her doorstep out of the blue, with nowhere else to go . . ." He raised his brows with hope.

"And look at it this way, sweetheart," Felicia added. "You are going to be far too busy and in far too much danger yourself to be my constant protector now, no matter where I am. You know that as well as I." With a shake of her head, she turned to Ben. "I had no idea how popular my dear husband is. At every public house where we stopped for lodging or a meal, he was greeted like the Prodigal Son. *And* asked to join some dangerous venture to smuggle not only tea into Boston but weapons and gunpowder, as well."

"Ye wouldn't ask me to shirk me duty," Yancy said. "We're all in this together, right, Mr. Burns?"

The stocky older man raised his palms as if to ward off any involvement in the dispute.

"And you shouldn't ask me to shirk mine," Felicia countered.

Yancy's bullheaded expression crumbled. Rising, he drew his wife up and into his arms, brushing a tendril of rich brunette hair off her forehead. He pulled her close, rocking her in his embrace. "I never thought me faith would be tested more than it's already been in the past. I don't know if I can do what you're askin' of me. Not when I love ye so much."

"And I love you." She took his weathered face into her hands. "But God will see us through. Both of us."

The agony in Yancy's eyes diminished. Taking a deep breath, he nodded. Then he took one of her hands and pressed a kiss into the palm. "As you wish, Felicia, me love. We'll trust the Lord together."

Ben had to remind himself to close his mouth. He had heard that the seaman had fallen hard for the lass he married, and Susannah had told him that Yancy had become a Christian. But this was almost unbelievable. Now witnessing the sailor and his wife gazing upon one another with such love and trust, he felt his chest constrict painfully at his own lack, his aching loneliness. Unable to endure the sight of such tenderness for one more second, he shoved back his chair and got up. "I . . . think I'll go see to the horses."

"Well, I, for one, think this is outrageous," Ben heard Felicia mutter as the toe of her buckle shoe tapped a rapid staccato against the ground. "Having to wait in line in the hot sun merely to enter Boston. And all these carts and wagons ahead of us, too. We'll be here all morning." She tugged the brim of her summer bonnet forward and ducked her face into its shade.

Ben glanced at Yancy and grimaced. "I'm sure it gives the lobsterbacks great satisfaction being able to lord it over us, searching all incoming wagons, taking a little here, a little there."

Yancy craned his neck and peered the hundred-yard distance still between them and the sentries. "Aye, I'll warrant they do."

Following the seaman's gaze along the narrow stretch of water-bracketed land, Ben set down the heavy satchel of Felicia's he'd been carrying and stretched a kink out of his muscles. "You know, Yance, it might be smarter for you to leave now, not go any further. We haven't been able to rip down the broadside about you they have nailed to the guard shack. No sense pressing your luck."

Yancy's shoulders sagged. "You're right." He put the other bag down and took Felicia into his arms, burying his face in the thick dark curls beneath her hat as he hugged her fiercely. "Ah, but it's so hard to leave ye."

Even with her eyes squeezed shut, tears escaped Felicia's thick lashes as she clung to him desperately, wordlessly.

Trying not to let the obviously emotional parting get to him, Ben couldn't help wondering why the girl had been so insistent upon going to be with Susannah when she'd never even met his sister-in-law or Dan. If this had been his fragile, sweet Abigail who'd taken this notion, Ben knew he would never have allowed it.

When the pair finally separated, Yancy's eyes were filled with unshed tears. With a watery smile, Felicia touched her handkerchief to her husband's eyes while he brushed her tears away with his thumb.

Ben averted his gaze as he picked up Felicia's bag and moved another step ahead. Women sure could take the starch out of a man. Yancy's talents and experience were sorely needed now more than ever, yet the seaman had become as lovesick as Dan and Ted. In fact, now that Ben thought about it, the last time he'd seen Dan, nothing could pull his brother out of his doldrums—not even the plans to take the fort and its large battery of cannon. He had even pleaded sick the Sunday before Ben had arrived, leaving Ted to take Dan's notes and prepare a sermon for the three meetinghouses on Pastor Griffith's circuit. Men should have more sense than to marry at such a critical time. Women and war did not mix, and soon enough the Colonies would find themselves in the middle of open rebellion against that high-handed Lord North and his Parliament.

"Here, you'd better see to this one, too," Yancy said, handing over his wife's carpetbag to Ben. "I'm countin' on ye to see her safely to Susannah's doorstep."

"Don't worry, I'll keep my word," Ben said in a flat tone as he took the extra burden. By the time he lugged those two valises the rest of the way, his arms would be ready to drop off. "Come along, Felicia."

Reluctantly she started toward him, then turned and flung herself into her husband's arms for a last embrace. "Be careful, my love," he heard her whisper. Her voice caught on a sob as she dragged herself away from Yancy and all but ran ahead, passing Ben by.

"Hold up," he called after her.

She stopped while he caught up, but kept her face turned away.

Fine with him, he decided. Her sniffing was getting on his nerves anyway, and Ben could imagine her woebegone demeanor without seeing it.

No more than a couple of minutes later, he dropped the valises at Felicia's feet. "I'm going to check ahead now for a wagon to hitch a ride into town on. As I said before, I'll be less likely to be noticed if I'm not on a horse. And it's more than two miles to Milk Street once we've passed through the entry."

"Whatever you say. My shoes aren't suited for walking far."

Nor my shoulders for toting two-ton bags, Ben thought grimly.

Coming up on a wagon loaded with bushel baskets of potatoes, carrots, and green beans, Ben noted that a lone driver occupied the wide seat. He removed his hat. "Excuse me, sir."

"Yes? Can I interest you in something?" A farmer who appeared in his middle fifties turned his head. Beneath his floppy hat, his large ears stuck out like jug handles as he scrunched up his face in thought. "You look a mite familiar."

Ben grinned and lowered his voice. "I'm a courier for the Committee of Correspondence, and—"

"Oh. One of Sam Adams' boys, eh?" A smile broadened the man's cheeks. "Without a horse?"

"That's a long story. I'll be glad to tell you, though, once we get through the Neck."

"Well, hop on, then."

"I've a young lady with me, as well, whom I'm escorting to my brother's house. Do you mind?"

The farmer gave a careless shrug. "The more the merrier." He scooted over on the seat to make room. "Hurry up, though. Don't want to lose my place in line to some fast-ridin' rascal. Been here half the mornin' already."

Ben went back for Felicia and her luggage, then helped her aboard before climbing on.

Half an hour later, as they neared the guard booth, he pulled his hat low. This would be the first time Ben had approached the city by land since his arrest, though he'd rowed over twice on moonless nights to check on Susannah. There wasn't a wanted flier out on him as far as he knew, but there hadn't been one the day the soldiers had nabbed him for Lieutenant Fontaine.

Sitting beside him, Felicia appeared quite calm as the driver moved the wagon alongside the guard shack and stopped. "Comin' in from Lexington with a load of vegetables," he offered in the weary tone of the experienced before any of the half dozen soldiers had posed the first question.

Ben watched from the corner of his eye as two soldiers hopped onto the rear. They speared carrots with the bayonets on the end of their muskets and started munching, then poked recklessly through the barrels without regard for the vegetables.

Fighting his own rising irritation, Ben turned back and saw a muscle twitch in the driver's jaw. For a fleeting second he wished he could tell these king's puppets exactly what he thought of them. But it would serve no purpose other than to draw undue attention to himself—which he could ill afford. He clamped his teeth together.

"Sirs," Felicia said as she swung to face the soldiers, "would you mind hurrying? I'm on my way to a *tea party*, and I wouldn't want to be late."

One of the men in the wagon behind them snickered, but Ben groaned as the two privates stopped searching and stared at her.

Then the eyes of the other soldiers trained on Ben.

He hunkered down into his turned-up collar.

"Keep searching, men." A beak-nosed sergeant stepped away from the guard shack and headed over toward the farm wagon. He stopped and eyed Ben. "Take off your hat, farm boy. Get down. I want a closer look at you."

Ben stared blankly ahead for several seconds, then reluctantly complied with the order.

"Just as I thought," the sergeant said with a gloating sneer. "You're that upstart postrider Lieutenant Fontaine locked up last winter. And without your horse. My, my. A postrider without his horse. Sound suspicious to you, Corporal?" He turned toward another redcoat.

"About as suspicious as him tryin' to sneak in usin' a pretty wench to distract us," the other soldier said, leering at Felicia. "We should make her get down, too. Search her *real good.*"

The sergeant broke into a grin. "Aye. No telling how many secret messages she's hidin' up in them skirts."

"You'll do no such thing!" Felicia cried, voicing her own enraged determination as she began to rise.

Ben edged toward the nearest rifle.

Felicia stood up, her hands on her hips in fiery challenge.

The farmer tugged her firmly back to the seat. "Stay where you are." Gathering his horse whip, he stood. "The first one to lay a hand on my daughter will lose it."

The two soldiers circling the wagon froze, while the ones in the back crouched low.

Other colonists in the long line came forward with grim expressions, and from the rear, Ben saw Yancy charging through.

"What's goin' on here?" someone asked accusingly.

"These British dogs are threatenin' to molest my daughter!" the farmer bellowed. "That's what's goin' on."

"That right?" another driver challenged.

Ben saw that Yancy was almost upon them. He waved him off.

"Mebbe we need to see she gits through safe," another voice said as the others closed in around the soldiers.

The sergeant lifted an arm, worry more than evident on his face as his eyes darted to the forming mob. "There's nothin' to get upset about. We suspect she may be carrying treasonous messages on her person. We just want to search her."

"You'll not be touchin' her," a burly colonist said, already rolling up his sleeves.

Ben, fearing that Yancy would break through, hastily spoke up. "I'm sure the sergeant has had a change of heart. That's right, isn't it?" he asked, hoping the beak-nosed man would realize the crowd could overwhelm the soldiers at any second, despite their weapons.

The redcoat's ferret eyes assessed the horde, then flicked a glance at Felicia. "The young lass seems like a bold one. Perhaps she'd be willing to swear that she has nothing illegal hidden on her person or in the wagon."

Relieved that the sergeant had chosen wisely, Ben and everyone else turned their attention Felicia's way.

Ben could tell by Felicia's wistful smile the precise moment when she located Yancy in the mob.

His heart stopped. Didn't she know she was fingering her husband?

She raised her chin and turned to the sergeant. "I have a Bible in my satchel. Do you wish me to get it and take a proper oath?"

"That won't be necessary," he growled. "Just tell me if you have anything illegal on the wagon."

"Absolutely nothing," she said with a triumphant smile. "And I say this in the name of King Jesus."

"No king but King Jesus!" someone in the crowd echoed with force, and the chant was then taken up by the others and repeated over and over with gathering intensity.

In the eye of the deafening rally, the sergeant nervously motioned the wagon through the gate.

Ben started to climb aboard.

The sergeant grabbed him by the back of his collar. "Not you." Again the soldier motioned for the wagon to move.

The farmer hesitated. He looked from Ben to the sergeant.

Ben met the driver's doubtful expression and Felicia's fearful one and waved them on.

Panic filled the young woman's eyes. He couldn't hear what she tried to say as they drove away, but for a few seconds he feared she would leap off. Then the farmer grabbed her arm and stopped her.

The crowd filled the empty space left by the departing wagon. They surrounded the soldiers in far greater numbers. Threatening numbers.

"You better have a real good reason for detainin' the lad," one man said evenly.

Flushing, the sergeant inflated his chest. "He's . . . he's—" in one burst, the lungful of air was released—"free to go."

Ben started past the crowd. He'd have to run to catch the wagon.

"Not that way," the sergeant barked. He grabbed Ben's arm and forcibly pulled him back, giving him a shove in the opposite direction. "That way."

"We must do something!" Felicia cried as, half standing, half sitting, she stretched to see over the nearest heads.

"There's nothing we can do about that, lass. You're lucky you got through yourself, just bein' with him."

Spotting Yancy's bright hair, she stared at him helplessly. The sight of her husband throwing up his hands, then walking away dejectedly with Ben was disheartening. "But . . . what do I do now?" Defeated, Felicia swallowed and turned to the farmer. "I haven't the slightest idea where Susannah Haynes lives."

"Know what street she's on?"

"Milk Street, they said."

"Well, then, that gives us some place to start, lass." With a comforting pat, the older man smiled as the workhorse clopped down the busy, narrow strand.

Soon the peninsula widened markedly, and buildings of brick and stone lined both sides. Felicia turned this way and that at each corner, peering as far as she could into crooked streets and lanes as they passed them by. How would anyone find the correct house in such a maze? She sighed.

"No use your bein' upset, miss. I'll do my best to locate your friend Mistress Haynes. Her street is well known. It intersects the one we're on. There's not a man around who can't find his way to that corner—it's where the Old South Meeting House is located. Me and thousands of other gents spent a number of days there last December decidin' what to do about that blamed tea ship."

"Yes, my husband told me all about that." Even the mention of Yancy made Felicia feel incredibly lonely without him.

"Milk Street runs down to the harbor and Castle William," the farmer went on, "so it's a busy one. But if we have to knock at every door along the whole length of it, we'll find her house for you."

"Oh, thank you. Ben says there are soldiers standing guard at it day and night. Maybe that will help."

He grunted. "Can't say as I want that kind of help."

Felicia tried to still her quaking heart as she concentrated on the well-kept brick homes and business establishments lining the thoroughfare. "My goodness. I had no idea there'd be so many men loitering about. I'd always heard you Puritans were an industrious lot."

"This is a port city, miss. Not only did the blockade cost the dockworkers and sailors their livelihoods, but all the businesses that outfitted and supplied the ships are suffering as well. Must be a thousand men out of work. And," he said, clearing his throat, "you know what they say about idle hands."

Turning forward again, Felicia became aware of the regulated cadence of a drum growing nearer. Seconds later she saw a company of redcoated soldiers marching across the road ahead of them.

The farmer stopped the wagon and sat back, waiting.

"Only good lobster's in a boilin' pot," came a voice from the side.

Felicia swung her attention to a man lounging against the outside wall of a shop. He spat on the street.

Some of the soldiers obviously had heard the remark. Their lips tightened and the knuckles on the butts of their rifles grew white. But they maintained their attention straight in front as they headed down a street to her right, save for a few appreciative glances that slid her way and a wink from a particularly rakish private.

Her driver must have also noticed. He bristled, and his fingers curled around the handle of his whip. But when the last man had gone by without further incident, he relaxed. Then he continued to wait long after they had passed.

Wondering why he hadn't started the team again, Felicia sent him a questioning look.

"This is Milk Street," he said, nodding after the redcoats. "Thought I'd best wait a spell, till they're further on." He nudged her elbow. "That there's the meetin' house," he offered, indicating a huge white building on the corner. "The one I mentioned earlier."

Two men came out of a tobacco shop nearby the imposing structure.

"Say, lads," the farmer called with a jaunty wave, "can either of you tell us how to locate the Haynes household? This wee lass is headin' there."

One of them grimaced. "That'd be the poor young thing hounded every minute by Lieutenant Fontaine," one answered. He gestured with his thumb down the street. "On the right, two or three houses before you come to Long Lane. About the only one on the whole street that isn't brick."

"Yep," the other said. "There'll be guards out front or just across the street. You can't miss it."

"Thank you so much," Felicia said, forcing a polite smile. Suddenly the whole idea of descending on a total stranger was beginning to seem incredibly presumptuous.

"Tell Mistress Haynes we're prayin' for her," the first man said as he and his companion turned the corner.

As the farmer snapped the reins and the wagon slowly began to roll along Susannah Haynes's street, he maintained an adequate distance behind the marching soldiers. At last Felicia spied guards several homes ahead.

"Perhaps I should get off here," Felicia offered, "so they

won't know I came from outside the city. I wouldn't want to arouse suspicions again."

"That might be wise," the farmer agreed. Halting the team, he hopped down and helped her, then lugged her bags to the side of the street.

Some women in the immediate area came out of their houses, eyeing the fresh produce in the wagon bed. With a smile their way, the farmer motioned for Felicia to follow him to the back of the conveyance, where he took out a large kerchief. He filled it with fresh vegetables and handed it to her with a kiss on the forehead. "Take care, *daughter.* I won't be leavin' this spot till I know you're safe inside."

Felicia rose on tiptoe and kissed his cheek. "I thank you for your help, Mr.—"

"Black, ma'am."

"Mr. Black. God be with you." Placing his gift atop one of her satchels while the man attended his customers, she grasped the handle and heaved it for all she was worth, lugging it to the yard of Susannah Haynes' white clapboard house. She set it just inside the wrought-iron gate, then went back and did the same with the other. How could they possibly weigh so much?

All the while, the pair of soldiers had watched her. One even seemed ready to come help, but the scathing look she gave him stopped him cold. She grabbed the vegetables and hurried up the brick walk toward the black-shuttered home and knocked.

A very pregnant young woman who appeared only slightly older than Felicia's twenty years answered the summons. A toddler dangled from one hip. "Yes?"

"Sorry I'm late, Mistress," Felicia said in overly loud tones as she held out the kerchief bulging with produce. "Me mum wouldn't let me leave till I'd finished the wash."

"Mothers are like that," Susannah said, not quite able to hide the curious light in her smoke blue eyes. "Do come in, won't you?"

"I'll just get me bags, Mistress." Bringing each one separately, she finally managed to get them inside and closed the door. Then, struggling to catch her breath, she straightened.

Susannah Haynes set the little boy down and went to peek out the sitting-room windows. After a moment she turned back to Felicia. "Might I ask who you are? And what I might do for you?"

Wishing she had thought ahead and formulated a rational-sounding speech, Felicia decided simplicity would be the best tack. "I'm Felicia Curtis. Yancy's wife. Actually, I've come to help you. I'll be staying at least until after the new baby arrives."

Mistress Haynes stared mutely, a peculiar expression on her delicate oval face, then she opened her mouth as if to speak.

"Before you start protesting," Felicia broke in with a cheery smile, "as I was told you might be inclined to do, I must assure you that I've come because of the Lord's leading. If Yancy had had his way, I'd still be in Rhode Island with your husband's parents."

Susannah gawked a moment longer, then suddenly she smiled, and the radiance heightened the peaches-and-cream of her delicate British complexion.

"Well, then, Felicia, who am I to argue? Welcome to my prison."

33

In a stuffy upper room of the Red Bird Coaching Inn, Ben peered at Yancy over the rim of his tankard of flip. The seaman had chosen a seat by the open window and was obviously adrift on a sea of thoughts as he gazed toward Boston. It was doubtful Yancy had heard a word of the conversation that had been going on for the past half hour. Ben rolled his eyes and shook his head at the other men in the room, two of whom were crew members of the *Seven Winds,* moored in Salem.

Reuben Shields, first mate of the vessel, followed Ben's glare and leaned forward, resting his angular elbows on the tabletop. "Thought it was *his* idea to have this meeting. Me and the other mates do have other things we could tend to, ya know, if all he's got in mind is wastin' time."

"Aye," Yancy said absently. "Sounds good to me."

"You fellows will have to make allowances for Yance these days," Ben muttered, throwing up his hands. "He isn't suffering from a lack of enthusiasm for the cause. His wife's just gone to stay in Boston with my sister-in-law, right under the nose of that blackguard Lieutenant Fontaine. He can't help being concerned for Felicia's safety."

At the sound of her name, Yancy straightened and turned as if he'd just awakened. "Beggin' your pardons. Guess I missed what ye were sayin'."

"We noticed." Reuben Shields smirked. "Ready to get down

to business? We're due back in Salem before high tide. We're sailin' down to the Carolinas for a good lot of gunpowder an' other things they're donatin'. It would help to have a mate who could help us find a quiet little cove to unload the merchandise on our return."

Yancy narrowed his eyes in thought. "Don't think I can set somethin' up before nightfall. I just got back here, ye know, and it'll take me a day or two to round up more of me friends. But we'll post lookouts for ye and catch ye on the way back. You've me word."

"You're pullin' my leg, right? We need you to sail with us!" First Mate Shields looked askance at his two crewmates. "The least bit of fog and you'd miss us. And this cargo cannot be confiscated. There's not near enough gunpowder in Boston Town if trouble erupts."

"Except for what the lobsterbacks have," another of the seaman added.

"What do you say, Yance?" Ben tried to read his friend's expression.

"You know I can't be gone that long," Yancy said. "I have to stay close enough to Boston to keep tabs on me wife, know she's safe. I can still keep me hand in the pot by unloadin' contraband from the ships headin' for Salem port." He looked hopefully at the wiry compatriot sitting opposite him at the table. "Mebbe Marty Links, here, could take me place on ship."

"Who, me?" Links cocked a light brow. "I'd rather stay here in the thick of things than be stuck for weeks on some boring tub."

"Might behoove you, mate," Shields said, "to tag along with us. If we pull off the Cap's plan, you'd be the most famous smuggler on the coast."

Another smaller man perked up, a light in his shifty eyes. "I'd jump at a chance like that myself, Links. But my mother's ailin'."

"Last week it was your father, Collins," Links said. He

looked from one face to another, then nodded at Reuben Shields. "All right. I'll go."

Collins slanted a grin at Yancy. "So how 'bout comin' with me, then, mate? I'm takin' a wagon up to Newburyport at first light to pick up some long rifles a gunsmith is donatin' to the cause. I could use the help gettin' 'em into Boston. We'll be gone only five days."

"Five days!" Yancy frowned. "Shouldn't take ye that long."

"Not on the Salem road, it wouldn't," Collins returned. "But I'll be takin' the Haverhill Road. The Salem one's slated for a lot of military traffic now."

Ben gave a nod of agreement. "He's right. General Gage is supposed to leave Boston tomorrow to start playing governor in Salem—for all the good it's gonna do him."

"And I can't see him headin' out without at least a full regiment along," another smuggler said, a cocky grin widening his mouth. "Protection from us ungratefuls, ya know."

Collins tipped his swarthy head Ben's way. "You're welcome to come along with us to Newburyport."

"Wish I could. But I need to stay here in case I'm needed to deliver correspondence." Even as he answered, Ben's glance drifted in Yancy's direction again. The sailor's attention had strayed out the window once more, and a sad longing drained the life from the sailor's normally jovial demeanor. Lonesome himself of late, Ben couldn't help hoping that whatever messages sent him forth again might lead toward Millers Falls.

Checking to make certain that Miles was happily occupied with the toys in one corner of the kitchen, Susannah plunged her floury fingers into the soft bread dough and began kneading it.

"How do you know when it's done?" Felicia asked.

Realizing the dark-haired young woman was completely sincere, Susannah smiled. "It just feels right. I spent a lot of hours helping Mistress Lyons at the coaching inn where I was

bonded for a year after I arrived from England. She was a
wonderful cook. Most of what I know now I learned from
her."

A wistful smile softened Felicia's features as she peeled
potatoes for the soup. "I'm all but useless in the kitchen, I'm
afraid. Most of the cooking has been left to Yancy since we've
been together. I was raised in a quiet, proper home in
Williamsburg. We had servants to attend to all the mundane
tasks."

Susannah sprinkled flour on the board and turned the
dough again. For someone who had arrived on her doorstep
supposedly to be a housemaid, the girl possessed some of the
finest frocks and slippers Susannah had seen for quite some
time. Yet there seemed nothing the least superior in her
attitude, and she did try to be helpful. "And you said your
father is a minister? He must have had quite a huge church."

"He wasn't a minister then. He was a druggist. We attended
a large Anglican church, though. It wasn't until last year that
Papa got caught up in the Baptist revival. At first I thought
he'd lost his senses."

Susannah giggled at Felicia's comical expression as she
shaped the dough into two loaves. "I understand only too
well. My father was an Anglican pastor, so that structured,
orderly manner of worship was all I had known until I arrived
in the Colonies. When I witnessed firsthand the sort of enthusiasm for the Lord that seems so prevalent here, I thought
everyone had gone quite mad."

"Actually," Felicia said with an impish smile, "that's not the
story Yancy tells."

Susannah blushed with chagrin as she lifted one of the
loaves and placed it in a waiting greased pan. "Did he mention the day Reverend Whitefield came to Princeton? Now,
mind you, it wasn't my idea in the least, but some students at
Nassau Hall were so intent on my seeing the great evangelist,
they forcibly perched me atop their shoulders for all the
world to see. And when my gaze fell upon Dan—handsome,
dashing Dan, whom I'd met only twice before in my life—

standing on the college steps with Reverend Whitefield, I
wanted to die on the spot."

Felicia chuckled.

It made Susannah smile, too, and then she continued with
the tale. "But somehow, as I listened to the man preaching to
that vast crowd, I found my heart so touched by his message
that I forgot my embarrassing predicament completely. I
finally understood, that day, God's grace and the love that
comes with it. I've never been the same since then."

"It took me a bit longer," Felicia admitted. She rinsed the
last potato and cut it in half before adding it to the pot. "I had
a lot of arrogant words to eat before I came around to
realizing the truth of God's love. And Yancy took great delight
in hand-feeding each and every one of them to me."

The baby's ball rolled Susannah's way. Looking over one
side of her conspicuous abdomen, she stuck out a foot and
gave the toy a gentle push back to him. "How did you happen
to meet our Yancy?" Susannah asked.

Felicia smiled sadly and averted her gaze. "He came to our
rescue, Papa's and mine, when the wheel had broken on our
wagon. I was in a fit of temper, berating poor Papa, when
along came this gangly, whistling *clown*. I thought he was the
most useless, pathetic excuse for a man I'd ever seen." She
sighed wistfully. "Looking back, I realize I was the useless,
pathetic one . . . judging people by possessions, fashionable
clothes. And Yancy, he . . . well, he was a jewel just waiting to
be polished." Sudden tears misted Felicia's dark eyes, and she
blinked them away.

Susannah reached over and patted her arm. "Why don't I
put on some tea? You might be interested in hearing the story
of how I happened to become acquainted with Seaman Curtis."

Even as Felicia's face brightened, the rat-a-tat-tat of drums
carried from outside.

Instantly Miles sprang up and trotted away to the front-
room window. Felicia and Susannah followed, and they all
peered out toward the street as the boy squealed with glee.

Susannah rubbed her back absently as the redcoated drummers beat cadence for troops marching up Milk Street. All the soldiers were in full gear, including their knapsacks and haversacks. "General Gage," Susannah said over the ruckus. "He's leaving today for Salem."

Felicia nodded with interest and watched them pass as Susannah scrutinized every officer's face, hoping against hope that Alex Fontaine's would be among them. She wouldn't be sorry to see him depart the city.

An open carriage rolled by containing the general and another high-ranking officer, both resplendent in their dress uniforms. Supply wagons and additional troops and officers followed.

As the last marched by, Susannah let out a disappointed sigh.

"I should think you'd be glad to see so many of the king's men marching out of Boston."

"I am, and no doubt the rest of the town feels the same. But the most infamous one of the lot was not among them. Lieutenant Fontaine."

"Oh, I'm sorry." Felicia put a comforting arm around Susannah. "I've heard some rather disturbing tales of that man from Yancy and your family." Leaning nearer to the window, Felicia took a second look outside. "How odd. I just noticed there aren't any townspeople along the street watching the parade."

Susannah nodded. "The residents make it a point never to give the general the impression that his comings and goings are of the slightest consequence to them, nor is anything else he may be planning for the colony."

As the late afternoon shadows stretched across the meadow, Felicia accompanied Susannah and Miles to the stable behind the house, where two pacers stood in stalls, their big brown eyes patiently observing the arrival of the humans. The little boy reached up with a carrot for each, then toddled to a mound of clean straw at the far end, where he flung himself down and rolled around in childish delight.

Susannah smiled and took Felicia by the hand, drawing her to one side. "Over here is where we keep the grain and hay. Of course, if the horses have been staked out in the meadow during the day, they only need grain. And we share a well with our neighbors, at the edge of the property." Reaching for the hayfork, she began awkwardly pitching some fresh hay into the feeding troughs.

"I think it would be best if I take over these duties," Felicia said, removing the tool gently but firmly from the expectant mother's grasp and continuing the task. "I have quite a nice mare of my own. I had to leave her behind when Yancy and I left Virginia, but I'm sure my old servants, Tisha and Seth, are taking fine care of her."

When the mangers had been filled, Felicia scooped up Miles and grabbed the empty bucket, and the three headed for the well to water the horses.

After the first had been watered and they were about to make the second trip, two uniformed men came around the corner of the house.

Susannah stayed Felicia with her hand. "I'll see to Lieutenant Fontaine if you don't mind getting the rest of the water."

Recognizing the infamous name, Felicia hesitated and flicked a wary glance toward the scowling officer. The man's expression relaxed as he caught sight of grim-faced Susannah. "You can go back to your post," he told the soldier accompanying him.

Still leery of going as far away as the well, Felicia tightened her hold on Miles' hand and reluctantly trudged over to it, uncomfortably aware of the redcoat's gaze fastened to her.

"I was concerned when there was no response to my rap on the front door," the lieutenant said matter-of-factly as he approached.

"No doubt," Susannah muttered on a wry note.

"I'd heard you'd hired a servant." He altered his direction slightly, veering again toward Felicia.

She pretended to mind her own business as she drew a full pail from the well.

Susannah waddled doggedly behind while Miles peeked around Felicia's skirts at the officer.

A few long strides carried Alex swiftly to them. He cupped a hand over Felicia's. "Allow me."

She snatched her hand away and glanced nervously at Susannah. The redcoat made short work of the chore and tipped the water into the stable bucket.

"Obliged," Felicia said. She nodded to Susannah. "I'll finish me chores, mum." Then, grabbing the pail, she started back toward the horses.

Susannah swept her son into her arms. "Is there something you require, Lieutenant?"

"Not at all." He fell into step with her as she trailed after Felicia. "I was merely curious to see how my favorite guest in Boston might be faring. Now that I have, I shan't stay away so long again." Lengthening his strides, he passed Susannah and caught up to Felicia at the stable entrance. He took the bucket from her, leaning overly close as he filled the water trough. "How thoughtless of me to miss the fact you'd been left with all these dreadful barn duties in your delicate condition," he said, glancing over his shoulder at Susannah with a smirk. "I've been woefully remiss. But I shall take care of the matter posthaste."

Felicia watched the lieutenant stride out as far as the corner of the house and draw his saber from the scabbard, waving it in the direction of the guards.

He turned back to Susannah and Felicia. "I must apologize for neglecting you both. Beautiful women should not be burdened with such coarse duties."

Felicia exchanged a dubious look with Susannah.

At a dead run, a soldier rounded the corner of the house and came to a halt in front of Alex, snapping a salute.

"Halter the horses and take them to the corral on Fort Hill."

"Yes, sir."

Unable to believe the man's arrogance, Felicia struggled to think of a sharp retort, but Susannah spoke first.

"Unless I'm given a written receipt for the confiscation of my animals, Lieutenant, I shall consider your action theft. I'll take the matter up with the authorities immediately."

Alex chuckled, a smug twist to the side of his mouth. "It matters not. General Gage is now the highest authority of the land, and I am one of his most trusted officers."

"Trusted!" Felicia flung at him, forgetting herself as she put a hand on her hip. "We'll just see how *trusted* you are when our lawyers descend upon you. I understand that Boston has some very convincing men of law."

His eyes hardened to the cold shade of steel. "I take it, wench, that you're not from Boston."

"No," she admitted, regathering her composure. "I've come from Rhode Island to be with Susannah. And I'll be here keeping close watch over her until well after she gives birth."

"I had a feeling you weren't a serving wench," Alex said evenly.

Felicia met his gaze and hiked her chin. "And it would behoove you to remember that fact. I'm not without friends in very high places."

"Horrors!" Alex raised a hand in mock fright. "And would those highly placed friends of yours be in Boston, may I ask? Or that oh, so great and powerful city of Providence?"

Felicia could almost feel Susannah staring holes in her back, but she could think of no way to back down gracefully. "Suffice it to say I've warned you."

The fresh-faced soldier emerged from the stable leading the pacers that had been left behind months ago by Dan and Jane. He could not hide his guilt as he slid a helpless glance at Susannah.

She smiled at him and shrugged, then looked sternly at Alex. "I suppose you'll require ink and a quill in order to draw up my receipt."

"And perhaps a spot of good East India tea," he said flip-
pantly as he swung around and led the way to the back door.
Susannah switched Miles to her other hip. "Felicia, would
you mind running upstairs for my writing instruments while
I show Lieutenant Fontaine the remainder of our possessions
out here? He might just have missed something else of which
he is in dire need."

Admiring Susannah's spunk and ingenuity at keeping the
blackguard out of the house, Felicia hurried away. She didn't
want to leave the vulnerable young woman alone with the
officer any longer than necessary. She returned within seconds, making an effort to hide the fact she was out of breath.
She seized a piece of scrap wood from a stack by the door to
use as a makeshift writing surface and arranged the accoutre-
ments on it, then held it out in front of him.

Only a corner of his mouth curled upward, the smile not
reaching his eyes. He took the quill and dipped it into the ink,
stepping much too close, then penned a few words, stopping
to peer up at Felicia suggestively during the process. "Yes, yes.
I've been far too remiss. I shall come by much more often
now. Much more often." Then with utmost impudence, he
ran the plume lightly over Felicia's fingers where they held
the improvised writing table.

She gasped as if the feather tickled and tipped the board
toward him, sloshing ink down the impeccable redcoat he
wore so proudly.

Alex knocked the writing things away, his eyes glittering
with fury. The partially written document fluttered to the
ground, and he twisted his heel into it. "Tomorrow," he
roared, "I shall bring my uniform here. And you *will* remove
every last speck of ink or pay for a replacement. And it would
behoove *you* to bear in mind that I have no need of a lawyer
to enforce *my* will." With that he wheeled around and
stomped away.

She swallowed. What had she done? She shouldn't have
been so hasty or hotheaded. Guilt-ridden, she mustered the
nerve to meet Susannah's gaze.

Susannah, her eyes twinkling, bubbled over with laughter. "Did you see that?" she sputtered. "His face turned every bit as red as his coat used to be!"

Felicia threw her arms around Susannah and collapsed into laughter as relief washed over her.

When finally their hilarity began to subside, she retrieved the soiled paper, then did her best to smooth it out.

"I suppose we can safely assume by your merriment that the two of you are unharmed," came a voice from the side of the house.

Felicia looked toward the sound and saw one of the guards and a civilian, both smiling at them.

"For the moment," Susannah said, overcome by another round of laughter. "For the moment."

34

Ben inhaled the sumptuous aroma of new leather that permeated the interior of Nelson's Saddle Shop, where he helped out between his courier duties. He and Yancy stood across from each other at a worktable, painstakingly slicing tanned hide into even harness strips.

"What's takin' Fred so long to bring back word of me wife?" Yancy muttered, adding another long piece to the growing stack between them. Expelling a disgusted breath, he set down his tool and crossed to the open door, where he leaned out and peered up and down the Cambridge street for the tenth time. He returned dejected, hands in his pockets, and slumped down onto the bench. "Shoulda never let her go."

"I'm sure she's fine, Yance," Ben said. The empty platitude was probably of little comfort, but it was all he could think of to say. "Mr. Nelson will probably be back any time to calm your fears, then you can hurry down to the waterfront and tar that rowboat before tonight's smuggling operation."

"Hope you're right." The seaman ran a hand through the wild disarray of his red hair and took the leather cutter again, setting back to work.

"I sure hope the saddler brings more letters for me to deliver. I'm not used to sitting in one spot for a whole week when so many people need to be kept abreast of the latest developments." Ben noticed Yancy's work as he put another strip on top of the pile. "Better put a little more muscle to that batch. The saddler wants all clean cuts."

"Aye." Yancy rolled up his sleeves, but he had barely sliced into the next skin when Fred Nelson's cart drew up before the establishment. He dropped the worn knife and rushed to the door. "Have ye news of Felicia? Have any lobsterbacks been harassin' her?"

"She's fine. Just fine." The tradesman slanted a grin beyond the sailor as Ben emerged from the shop with a helpless shake of his head.

"Are ye sure? Did ye see her yourself?"

Mr. Nelson wrapped the horse's reins around the brake lever and climbed out. He laid an oversized, calloused hand on Yancy's shoulder. "Thought you was supposed to be trustin' the good Lord for her safety, you bein' a believer now and all."

"You're right." Yancy colored slightly. "I try to. But—"

"But?" Ben asked, still having problems of his own believing the radical changes in his friend.

Yancy's flush intensified. "I need to do better, I know. With the Lord's help, I'll do me level best to keep from imaginin' all sorts of evil lurkin' about me wife. At least until tomorrow." He chuckled at his own remark as he hefted a heavy wooden crate from Mr. Nelson's cart. "Did ye say you'd seen her?" he asked the saddler.

"No, lad. We try not to show any more links between the Haynes house and here than necessary. Wouldn't do for the redcoats to start getting curious. We let the church members get the information out to us, since they come and go regularly."

"And do they say she's settled in, at least?" Yancy stood with the crate balanced atop his shoulder.

"Yes, all settled." He picked up a bulging sack. "And I know you're concerned about that crazy Lieutenant Fontaine, too. Well, you can forget about him for a while. This mornin' he was ordered to Salem to replace another lieutenant who'd fallen ill." That said, he carried his burden inside.

Yancy exchanged a look of relief with Ben, then followed the saddler. "Then Felicia an' Dan's wife are gettin' along?"

"Yes." The word came out on a weary breath.

"Guess you can start thinking about caulking that boat, then. Right, Yance?" Ben said.

"Aye. I'd best get to it." Looking years younger now that his mind was somewhat eased, Yancy set down the crate, then grabbed a tar bucket and brush near the door. He glanced back one more time before leaving. "Thank ye, Fred. For bringin' word."

"Sure thing, lad." As the saddler watched the sailor stride away, his chuckle turned into laughter. After a moment he craned his neck to make certain Yancy was out of earshot, then nodded at Ben. "Didn't want to say this in front of Yancy, but the way I heard it, that was one fit-to-be-tied lobsterback lieutenant who hightailed it outta the Haynes place last night, drippin' ink from head to toe. The two little ladies about collapsed, they was laughin' so hard. Course—" his face sobered—"the redcoat is demandin' they set his uniform to rights, or else."

Ben's own expression tensed in the middle of a grin, and he dropped the broken harness he'd just brought in. "They poured ink on him? That puts Susannah and Yancy's wife in far worse jeopardy. I'd better go check on them—even if I have to swim the river to do it."

Fred Nelson raised a hand. "Like I said, Fontaine has been called away. The corporal who brought the ruined uniform to Mistress Haynes told her so. Anyway, a tailor down her street has already offered to replace the damaged sections of the coat before the lieutenant gets back to Boston even if he has to put all his other work aside to do it—you know nobody on Milk Street is gonna let any harm befall your ladies. Now, come on and help me get the rest of the truck outta that cart. There's a pouch of letters for you at the bottom."

The two made short order of the task. When they finally came to the mail, Ben grabbed it and opened the sack to glance through the wax-sealed envelopes. A smile drifted across his face when he saw addresses that would take him through Massachusetts to New Hampshire and even Bennington. It had been far too long since he'd gone in that direction.

In the shadow of the Green Mountain countryside, Ben reined Rebel to a stop before the Griffith cabin.

Tending several rose bushes at the edge of the yard, the pastor's wife moved to her feet, her lined face crinkling into a wide smile as she tucked a wisp of gray hair inside the ruffle of her mobcap. "Why, young Ben. How nice to see you."

"Good day, Mistress Griffith. Does my brother happen to be about?"

"He and the others are across yonder meadow," she said, indicating the direction with a hand. "They're all busy putting up a cabin for your sister and Ted with the dowry from her father that you brought last month. The newlyweds decided to purchase the farmstead plot adjoining ours."

"They've bought land way out here?" Ben could hardly believe it. It was so unlike Jane to choose willingly to settle in a place so far from her family and friends—or from a city, for that matter.

The pastor's wife smiled with understanding. "When young people are first married, all they want is to be alone together. Later on, after things have settled down, they may view things differently and decide to return home."

The thought of being alone with sweet Abigail even for a few precious moments flickered in Ben's mind. But then he remembered Bertha always pushing herself between them and sighed. Still, he had purposely completed his other deliveries already, and only those in Abigail's vicinity remained. Once he finished, he might manage to get her alone—with some luck and a lot of patience. Ben tipped his tricornered hat and started turning his mount. "My thanks, Mistress Griffith. Guess I'll go see the others."

"Wait, lad." She put a hand on the horse. "I'm afraid your brother shows no improvement since your last visit. He tries his best, mind you, to say all the proper things, to preach a good sermon and all. But unless one of us is speaking directly to him, he just mopes around, hardly saying a word."

Ben's heart contracted painfully, but he forced a smile. "Well, I've brought him a letter from Susannah. Perhaps that'll perk him up."

"Let's hope so. The pastor and I pray for him constantly."

With a thankful pat on the older woman's gnarled hand, Ben nudged Rebel forward toward a wooded hill at the edge of the clearing. He maneuvered his mount along a well-worn path through the thick trees, a testament to the daily trips back and forth from the Griffith place. Cresting the knoll, he saw a nearly completed cabin. Dan and Ted were busy hanging the door as Ben rode up.

"Ben!" Jane hiked her navy calico skirts and ran toward him, her face rosy with happiness.

Dan and Ted dropped what they were doing and followed.

Ben jumped down and gathered Jane into a hug. Pastor Griffith emerged from the cabin, walking with barely a limp.

After gripping Ben's hand in greeting, Ted stepped aside.

"Any letter from Susannah?" Dan blurted.

"Good to see you, too, Brother," Ben chided. Smiling, he dipped into a saddlebag and drew out letters for all three.

Dan seized his and hurried away.

"He's getting worse by the day," Jane whispered, squeezing Ben's hand as she watched Dan sit down behind a tree several yards away and tear open his missive. "I always thought his faith was so strong and unshakable. But he's as morbid now as he was the night Susannah gave birth to Miles."

"No doubt she'll be doing that sort of thing again very soon," Ted added. "And Dan's not the only one who'd give anything to be there to see her through that dark valley."

Ben nodded. "You'll be glad to know, then, that Yancy's wife has gone to Boston to be with her through it all."

Jane's fine eyebrows rose. "Yancy's back?"

"That's right. And with a wife who's as willful as she is beautiful!"

"She would have to be!" Jane gave a delighted nod.

"Her name, by the way," Ben went on, "is Felicia. When she heard Susannah had been all but deserted in Boston, she immediately got the notion to go and stay there until the new babe arrives. Nothing any of us could say would dissuade her."

"I must go tell Dan!" Jane whirled around and ran to her older brother, sinking down beside him. "Did you hear? Yancy's wife insisted on going to Boston to look after Susannah, to make sure she wouldn't be alone during childbirth."

"I'm the one who should be doing that. No one else." Dan rose and started back toward Ben. "I'm going home."

"Don't do something that might get you arrested," Ted cautioned. "Sue needs her husband, that's more than certain. But she needs you alive, not dead."

"You're right, Ted," Dan retorted. "Susannah needs her husband. Now." He switched his attention to Ben. "Are you coming with me?"

Ben shifted his stance. "Well, actually, I was hoping for a meal before starting on the long ride back. I'm starving."

"Don't take all day. I'm going to pack my things."

As Dan walked toward the other cabin, the pastor stepped forward and shook Ben's hand warmly. "We'll all be prayin' for the boy's safety. Who's to say he's not being led of the Lord to go back now? Could be his desire to go has been so fierce all along that he thinks it's his own will, not God's. But our heavenly Father cares deeply for us; he wants us to reap all the joy he has waiting for us."

During the next two days, Dan set a grueling pace for Boston. Nonetheless, the deep lines of care carved in his face had eased.

As they passed through the hamlet of Millers Falls, Ben had yet to broach the subject of stopping off at the Preston farm. He was certain his older brother would balk at the delay. But, Ben argued silently, he couldn't pass by without seeing Abigail for a few minutes at least. He drew sweat-lathered Rebel alongside Dan's horse. "I know a place not far ahead where we might get some fresh mounts."

"Is that right?" Dan checked the angle of the sun, and his expression brightened even more. "With rested horses we could make Boston by tomorrow night."

"Cambridge, maybe," Ben said grudgingly.

Dan set his jaw. "Boston."

"Let's see about getting the horses first."

"And how far away might they be, the ones you mentioned?"

Ben smiled as he focused his gaze on the farm that was now a speck in the distance. "See that place?" He pointed straight ahead, and Dan nodded. "I got caught in a storm one night, and the folks there took me in. Real friendly, too. Women. They don't have a man on the place anymore."

Dan's quizzical look was reminiscent of his old self as he tipped his head Ben's way. "Just women, you say?"

"Now, it's not what you think," Ben said quickly, aware of the sudden rise of heat inside his collar. Nevertheless, his spirits made a rather swift climb. "Now that I think of it, you just might come in real handy."

35

Ben was hard pressed not to kick Rebel into a full gallop when he and Dan came within shouting distance of the big Preston house. The mere sight of the huge, rambling dwelling, its curtains billowing from several open windows, made his pulse throb faster. He was eager to set his eyes on Abigail's lovely face, to hear her whispery voice. He searched the farmyard for a glimpse of her.

"Let me see if I've got this right," Dan said, his words cutting into Ben's musings as they turned onto the wagon path. "You want me to divert the sister-in-law to give you smooth sailing with the young widow, huh? Are your intentions matrimonial? Otherwise, it doesn't sound very—"

"I can't take on that kind of responsibility," Ben snapped. "Not with war about to erupt."

Dan gave him an older-brother stare. "You don't know that for a certainty. Tempers have been high since England tried to foist their stamp tax on us back in '65. And, as I recall, three or four years ago you couldn't wait to marry me off so you could take over my postriding position."

"That was different. Then was nothing like now."

Dan slid him a sideways glance. "You don't think five Boston citizens lying dead and bleeding in the snow created a tense situation in '70?"

"Yes. Yes, I do. But that was merely a prelude. London's continued refusal to treat us as anything but a bunch of disinherited stepchildren has drawn a very clear battle line. We'll be stepping up to the mark soon enough, wait and see."

"Remember, baby brother," Dan reminded him, "Parliament backed down for the most part from that Stamp Act. It's entirely possible they'll do the same again once they see how all the colonies are rallying to Boston's plight."

Ben grimaced. "Even if they do, England will just come up with something else to shove down our throats. We're not going to sit still for it any longer."

Dan shrugged, then pointed toward the garden. "Looks like someone's out hoeing weeds."

Trying to still the ridiculous pounding of his heart, Ben followed Dan's line of vision. His spirits sank. Bertha. "That's the sister-in-law I was telling you about. Bertha Preston. If you could just occupy her for any length of time, I'd owe you. Ask her about the farm. She loves to show it off."

"As long as we're gone from here within the hour."

As if she'd heard them talking about her, Bertie looked over her shoulder and saw Ben and Dan. She tore off her sunbonnet and gloves and raced for the back door of the house.

Dan chuckled. "It would appear she wants to make herself presentable for you before you see her."

"More like she's running for a rope to tie my feet and hands," Ben muttered wryly.

Reaching the edge of the yard, they dismounted and tied their horses to a tree branch, then walked to the door.

It was wrenched open before Ben's knuckles connected with the smooth wood. "Well, howdy, Ben!" Ma Preston bellowed, grabbing him in a hug that would crush a logger's bones. "Right good to see ya!"

"Ma," Ben croaked, inhaling stray hairs from her loose topknot until she let go. "I wanted you to meet my brother, Dan. Dan, this is Mistress Preston."

"Horsefeathers!" Ma said, her gravelly voice echoing off the barn. "It's Ma. Just plain Ma. Nice to meet ya, Dan. So you're our Ben's brother, huh?" She straightened, hands on her hips, and looked him up and down.

"That's right." Dan's expression barely hid his mirth.

Ben searched past the formidable woman for Abigail as clunking noises came from the upstairs bedroom. He imagined Bertha shucking her old work boots. Beyond the parlor, he heard the back door squeak open and shut.

Ma kept her eyes glued to Dan as she cocked her head toward the sound. "Hey, Abby. Come look who's here." Then she frowned. "You that Presbyterian preacher Ben told us about?"

Barely hearing his brother's response as Abigail appeared, a vision in periwinkle blue, Ben's heartbeat throbbed in his throat. He swallowed and stepped past Ma, meeting Abigail beside the foot of the staircase. Removing his hat, he took her slender fingers in his and smiled into her shining blue-green eyes.

"Ben," she whispered. "I'm so glad to see—"

Bertha's footfalls drowned out Abigail's airy voice as the stocky girl clambered downstairs.

Ben gritted his teeth and maintained his hold on his lovely lady. He drew her toward Dan.

Bertie caught up to them there, breathless, her close-set eyes sparkling with unconcealed delight. Just-scrubbed cheeks matched her crisp rose calico frock, and her hair appeared freshly braided as she stepped between them and Dan.

Ben cleared his throat. "Dan, this is Bertha Preston, the young woman I told you about, who almost single-handedly is managing this huge farm." He cocked a brow, prompting his brother to pick up the cue and ask Bertie to show him around.

"I'm very happy to meet you, Miss Preston." Dan then turned his warm smile on Abigail. "And who might this be?"

"This is *Miss* Preston's sister-in-law," Ben said, extending another broad hint. "Bertha, tell my brother how many acres you have in corn and how many in beans this year. He's very interested in all you've accomplished."

A blush pinkened Bertie's glowing cheeks. "Better to show ya," she said, grabbing Dan by the arm and starting for the open door.

Ben almost laughed aloud in heady elation over the successful ploy. He started to expel a breath of relief.

But Bertha swung his way and latched onto his elbow as well. "Might's well show both of ya. We wouldn't wanna leave you behind, now, would we, Benjamin?" She fluttered her sparse lashes beseechingly.

With a silent plea of helplessness at Abigail, Ben tipped his head. "Ma, why don't you and Abigail come with us. I haven't seen either of you for some time. Besides, I have a favor I need to ask of you."

"We'd be right pleased," Ma said with a grin. "The babies should be fine for a spell. Come along, Abby." She waved her daughter-in-law ahead, then followed her out, catching up with the group in a few strides as they started across the grounds, lush now with summer growth. "Now, what was the favor you were wantin'?" She looked questioningly at Ben.

He smiled, easing into his request. "My brother and I must be back in Boston by tomorrow night. Would you happen to have a couple fresh horses we might borrow?"

"Why, sure! I thought mebbe it was somethin' important!" She fanned herself with a corner of the long work apron covering her plain cotton dress. "Bertie, we might's well head for the barn first so's Ben can choose a horse or two to suit himself."

Ben nodded his thanks, then he turned an encouraging smile on Abigail, who walked a step or two behind.

Dan politely removed Bertha's hand from his arm and strode toward the mounts he and Ben had ridden in. Untying the reins, he handed them over to Ben. "Why don't you see to the horses while Miss Preston shows me around the rest of the farm?"

"Sure." Bertha's initial dismay melted beneath the flattering attention a good-looking young man was willingly showering upon her. Ben smiled to himself as he waited for Abigail to come alongside, then led the animals toward the stables.

When the sound of Bertie's voice raving about the corn patch faded into the distance, Ben grinned at Abigail. "Where are the children today?"

"I put them down for a nap just before you arrived."

"Oh. Too bad. I was hoping I'd see them before I had to hurry away again."

"That's one fine boy child I got me," Ma boasted from Ben's other side. "Yessir. Spittin' image of his pa, ain't he, Abby?"

"Yes, Ma. Corbin looks very much like him."

While the conversation centered on Abigail's dead husband, Ben patted Rebel's muscled neck to mask his disappointment. But the sweetly apologetic smile Abigail turned his way made the discomfort vanish as quickly as it had come.

They reached the barn, and Ben led the pacers inside, enclosing them in two empty stalls. Then he followed Ma to the three horses she stroked proudly in passing.

The animals could hardly be compared to the mounts he and Dan had arrived on, but he knew they'd have to do. At least they looked rested and well fed. Looking them over, he made his choices. "We'll take the bay on the end and this gelding, Ma, if that's all right. And we'll have them back first chance we get, though with things in Boston being the way they are, it may not be for several weeks." He caught the sadness in Abigail's eyes.

"Ain't no rush. Yours'll do just fine in the meantime." Ma strolled over to examine the spent pacers. "What's the latest from over to the coast?" Ma asked, rubbing Rebel's velvety muzzle.

Ben followed and began unsaddling his horse. "General Gage has gone to Salem to preside over the Massachusetts Assembly. But—"

"Oh, pshaw," Ma said with a flutter of her hand. "That's old news. How long you been gone, anyway?"

"More than two weeks. Why?"

"Then I'll tell *you* the latest. Not one single representative showed up for Gage's little powwow. So General High-and-Mighty says he's dissolvin' the assembly. Now, wouldn't that be a sight." She whacked her leg and laughed. "Him, standin' in front of an empty room, announcin' he hereby dissolves the assembly. Wouldn't surprise me none if he tries to find himself a whole new bunch. Boot-kissin' lackeys more suited to his kind, like as not."

Ben grinned. "Those are getting harder to find all the time. Especially with Governor Hutchinson escaping to England."

"And good riddance," Ma said with a snort.

Abigail moved to Ben's side and picked up some straw. "Since you and your brother are in such a hurry, I'd best help with the horses." She began rubbing down Rebel's lathered coat as she looked beyond the animal to her mother-in-law. "Ma, I'll wager the men would dearly love some of that wonderful nut bread you made yesterday. Perhaps you might wrap up several pieces for them while we finish out here. And maybe some of your sausage, too." She turned a sweet but conspiratorial smile toward Ben. "Folks are partial to the way you spice it up."

"Why, that's a right fine idea," Ma said.

Ben stood speechless for a few seconds while the older woman actually returned to the house, leaving him and Abigail alone. At last. Then suddenly aware of how quickly that could change with Bertha traipsing around out there, he grabbed some straw himself and started helping Abigail.

She offered a timid smile.

"I've been wanting to speak to you," Ben said.

"You have?"

The look in her eyes made all reason take swift flight. Ben couldn't even remember what he'd hoped to say. But one thought did come to mind. "I think about you all the time." Surprised that he'd had the courage to admit that small truth, Ben took heart as a fragile pink settled on her delicate cheeks. "In fact, you're all I do think about. When I'm riding through the woods and the wind rustles through the leaves, it's the same soft sound as your voice. Did you know that?"

She paused in her work, and her eyes shimmered. "I . . . think about you, too."

"Do you really?" When she nodded, Ben took her hand and brushed away the straw as he lifted her fingers to his mouth and pressed them with a kiss. He was elated when she didn't pull away. "I wish it were possible for us to see each other from time to time without your in-laws around."

"From time to time?" she whispered.

Ben noticed her dismay and wondered if he had spoken too quickly. He lowered her hand but didn't let go. "I meant I'd like to get to know you. Maybe when I return the horses I could pretend to leave . . . and you could meet me on the other side of the hill. We could talk for a while. Just talk. I promise."

"I see." Withdrawing her fingers from his, Abigail picked up some fresh straw and moved to Dan's horse. She began working in earnest.

Her action and expression left Ben utterly confused. Had he offended her? He opened his mouth to ask, then noticed movements outside as Dan and Bertha neared the barn. "I'd be a perfect gentleman," he blurted in desperation.

Abigail shot him a withering look.

"Which horses are we taking?" Dan asked as he and Bertie came in.

Ben couldn't tear his gaze from Abigail's. What had gone wrong? "The bay and the chestnut."

"Good. I'll start saddling up."

"I'll give ya a hand, Dan," Bertie offered, appearing completely taken with him.

Exhaling, Abigail wiped her hands on her apron. "It seems you have plenty of help. I'll be going now."

❧ ❧

After a good half hour of silence, Dan nudged his mount to increase the pace so he could catch up to his stony-faced younger brother. Ben had barely uttered a word since they'd bid good-bye to the Prestons. "Don't you think the animals could use a rest? They're merely farm horses, not used to this steady speed."

Expelling a long breath, Ben reluctantly guided the bay off the wagon road and drew up next to a stand of birches.

Dan dismounted and hurried after Ben, who was already striding several yards ahead. "You might as well spit it out."

"What?" Ben growled.

"You know very well what. I take it the fair damsel doesn't have the same affection for you."

Ben stopped and turned. He shook his head and gestured helplessly. "I don't understand. I really don't. She said she'd been thinking of me too. But when I asked her to meet me in secret the next time I come, she turned icy cold on me."

Dan spent great effort restraining his chuckle. "You asked her to sneak out to see you, Ben? A young widow with two small children, living on the charity of her mother-in-law?"

Guilt stiffened Ben's already hard-set jaw. "You don't have to tell me Abigail's circumstances. I'm more than aware of them. But how else can I expect to see her without Bertha always nosing in?"

"The same way every other young man does, runt. You should've spoken to Ma Preston first, offered for Abigail properly."

"Yes, well, like I told you before, I can't think seriously about marriage right now. I have no intention whatsoever of ending up like you and Ted . . . both too worried about your wives to be of any use to the cause. And, I swear, Yancy's even worse." With a disgusted huff, Ben turned away.

Dan grabbed his arm. "If only you'd learn to trust God, you'd see that—"

"*Trust?* You, who have been moping around for months because you've been forsaken of God, are lecturing me about trust?"

Dan felt the blood drain from his face. He opened his mouth to protest, but no words would come. He thought about the days and weeks of his separation from Susannah, the empty ache inside him that not even God could fill. He hadn't prayed—except for her safety. He hadn't even tried to let the Lord meet his needs. He hadn't sought the Lord's peace. He had simply given in. Suddenly he realized—Ben was right. What a wretched example he'd been to his brother. To the rest of them. What a miserable mess he'd been altogether.

"Forgive me, Ben. I've wronged you these past months. I see that."

Ben scowled. "What do you mean?"

"When I should have been trusting God's wisdom and reaping the peace—and yes, the joy—our Lord spread before me in the grants, I cheated myself and all those around me by not embracing it. All you saw was a self-pitying, angry man so intent on bombarding God for just one thing that I let each day and its blessings pass unnoticed. I wasted all that time, and now it's gone and I'll never have it back. Ben, please remember this. God gives us our lives to live one day at a time. Each day is important. Each day."

"That's what I've been saying all along," Ben argued, pulling away. "And we mustn't let anything distract us . . . particularly not some silly female affliction. There's too much at stake." Stubbornly he strode off.

Dan could see Ben was far too upset to accept his words just yet. But he knew without the slightest doubt that God had intended for him to be here at this moment with his brother to say the words he'd said as much for Ben as for himself. And with no less doubt he knew that returning to Boston now was in God's timing, despite the fact he'd run off half-cocked, not taking so much as a moment to listen, to hear . . . another blessed moment he would never again retrieve.

Still, he was on his way home now, at long last.

Thinking of the two very precious people awaiting his return spurred him back to the present. "Let's mount up. I'm sure the horses have had enough rest."

36

"Good night, dear friends," Susannah called after the departing church members. "May the Lord keep all of you."

"My goodness," Felicia remarked as she closed and bolted the front door. "I never knew one little house could hold so many people. The place was fairly bulging at the seams."

"Yes, wasn't it." Susannah smiled and returned to the parlor, brushing crumbs from the settee, gathering the used teacups, and stacking them on a tray. "Since the flock first began meeting here for prayer, things have changed. Now they're not merely rallying around me. They, too, are starting to feel as cut off from the outside world as I do from Dan. It's no wonder so many more are turning up for evening vespers."

"I'm certain the congregation draws as much comfort in merely coming together like this as they do from being able to unite their prayers on Boston's behalf." Felicia picked up a chair to return to the dining room. "Of course, a few of your loyal members are beginning to show their annoyance at that special prayer request you insist upon making each night."

Susannah straightened the lace-edged handkerchief in the bodice front of her muslin gown. "Which one is that?"

Felicia looked askance at her. "The one for Lieutenant Fontaine, as I'm sure you know."

With a shrug of one shoulder, Susannah resumed her tidying. "Oh, but when I first met him, he was such an amiable, jolly sort. It disturbs me now to see how tormented he has become. Even his face has taken on a twisted appearance, and there's such a hardness to his eyes."

"Well, if you don't mind," Felicia said with a shudder as she rested the chair on two of its legs, "I can't help feeling grateful that I haven't had to see the man since that last rather *blackening* incident here."

Susannah couldn't quite smile at the memory. She lifted the tray of dishes and propped it against one side of her bulging abdomen. "It's really quite sad that you never met the old Alex. He was such a good and generous friend to my brother and ever so entertaining with his sublime humor and wry smile. In some ways I feel I also lost a friend since all this political trouble came between us."

Felicia's expression became thoughtful as she picked up the chair again and started for the open-beamed dining room. "I truly hope that one day I'll be gifted with the same forgiving nature you have, Susannah."

Susannah would have hugged the girl if their hands hadn't been otherwise occupied. Instead, she followed along to the homey dining room. "Don't lose sight of all the wonderful gifts the Lord has bestowed on you, Felicia. I must tell you, I could not have asked for a more companionable *sister* since you arrived. Just please try to remember that Alex needs our prayers desperately. He's been weighing heavily on my mind of late."

"If you ask me, it's that babe who's doing most of the heavy weighing."

Susannah laughed lightly and continued on to the kitchen. She put the dishes on the work counter, then returned down the hall to the parlor, a hand on her stomach.

Her friend removed a candle and holder from a drawer by the stairs and went back to the front room. She touched the wick to the flame of the table lamp, then bent and blew out the larger light.

"I think I shall stay up a bit longer," Susannah said. "I'm a little too restless to retire right now."

Felicia's eyes grew wide. "Are you having pains?"

"No, dear, I'm just uncomfortable."

"How about if I help you upstairs and then bring you a cup of tea? Wouldn't you be more comfortable in your room instead of down here all alone?"

"Thank you, but no. It gets so stuffy up there. Perhaps I'll step outside, take a short walk in the meadow out back."

Worry lines feathered her friend's expression. "You're certain you're all right?"

"Yes, truly, I'm fine." Susannah smiled reassuringly.

"Well, then, I'll go with you. You shouldn't be out there by yourself." Setting the candleholder down, Felicia started toward her.

Susannah raised a hand. "Felicia, dear, you've been so busy all day. I can see you're tired. Run along to bed. I promise I'll not go a step farther than the backyard. And I'd really like some time alone."

Felicia's dubious expression changed to one of understanding tinged with relief. She picked up the candle again and turned toward the staircase. "Please call if you need anything."

Susannah smiled and gave her a gentle push. "I will. Now, good night."

When Felicia's door closed after her, Susannah made her way to the kitchen, an uneasiness creeping through her. As the dangerous hour of birthing was drawing steadily nearer, she couldn't help but wonder if all the platitudes she'd been saying to friends and God alike were just that . . . a brave but hollow front. She sighed at the thought. Perhaps some warm milk would help her restlessness.

In the kitchen, Susannah noticed the lamplight sputtering. As she turned up the wick, she recalled hearing one of the men mention earlier that the supply of oil in Boston was rapidly shrinking. How many more things that people took for granted would diminish as the seaport was slowly strangled? Feeling stifled herself, Susannah walked to the back door and opened it wide, then stepped out onto the landing.

Sea-scented air mingled with the fragrance of summer

roses as the balmy August breeze stirred her skirt and hair. Hands at her spine, Susannah leaned against the house and looked up at the sky. There was not much of a moon, but the night was aglow with sparkling stars as she peered into the distance toward the Neck. Even at this hour she could make out the glow from the torches at the guard post where the ever-present stream of wagons stood lined up and waiting to come into the city.

But Susannah's thoughts didn't stop there. They went far beyond, into the nameless unreachable distance. Somewhere, Dan might even now be gazing up at the very same stars. She imagined his sable eyes and how they, too, twinkled whenever he smiled. It had been so long. So long. How she yearned to reach out and touch him. With a wistful sigh, she extended her arms, pretending she could do just that. If only she knew where he was! But Ben had never told her.

"Oh, Dan," she murmured into the stillness. "Where are you, my dearest? Where are you?"

"I'm here, love."

She froze. Surely she had imagined that voice coming to her in the dark.

A familiar figure moved out of the velvet blackness beside the woodshed.

Susannah's heart nearly burst. "Dan?" she whispered.

She barely managed to take a step toward him before he engulfed her in his hungry embrace, holding her as tightly as he could with her unborn child between them. They clung to each other, their tears intermingling as their lips met for a breathless eternity.

Yancy was nudging Felicia's shoulder. Toying with her. Teasing.

"Wake up. Please, wake up."

Her eyes fluttered open. But it wasn't Yancy. A strange man in a white shirt and tan breeches, his hair drawn neatly back in a queue, was standing over her, his hand still on her upper arm.

"Susannah needs you."

Felicia gasped and bolted upright, clutching the sheet to herself as she peered up into brown-black eyes as dark as her own. "Wh-who are you?"

"Dan. Susannah's husband. We can talk later, but right now I need you to go fetch the midwife."

"Midwife?" Felicia said, still trying to gather herself together. "The baby is coming? What time is it?"

"Almost four."

"In the *morning?*" She shook her head to clear her mind.

"Yes. And there's no time to waste." In two strides he was at the door and cast an urgent look over his shoulder at her. "Please hurry."

Felicia sprang out of bed and grabbed the nearest clothes. All the while, her heart raced with excitement and fear. How wonderfully good of God to have brought Susannah's husband home at the exact moment when she needed him the most. It was nothing short of a miracle. And neither was the bringing of a new life into the world. Fumbling with the lacing of her frock, she finally finished, then hurried out into the hall.

Dan met her there. "She wants to see you before you go." He stood aside and ushered her into the bedroom.

Susannah sat composed in the rocking chair, her face glowing with happiness in the pale lamplight as she smiled. "I'd hoped to introduce you both to one another in some ordinary fashion. But lately, what is ever ordinary?"

Swinging a glance to Dan, Felicia noted absently how much he resembled Ben and little Miles . . . and how distracted he appeared at the moment as he took her hands in his.

"I want to assure you that I deeply appreciate your coming here," Dan said. "When I found out you were with my wife, it helped ease some of my own anxiety."

Felicia started to reply, but Susannah's face twisted with pain. Felicia drew free and moved to her friend's side along with Dan, watching wordlessly until her expression relaxed.

"Felicia," Susannah said, drawing several deep breaths, "you know how to get to the midwife's house?"

Felicia nodded.

"I don't want you to go out alone at this hour," Susannah continued. "Take one of the guards along with you."

Dan frowned incredulously.

"Don't be alarmed, sweetheart," Susannah added, patting his arm. "They've actually become much more of a protection for us than a threat, believe me."

"And," Felicia said, "I shan't invite them in. Just stay well back from the windows. You'll be quite safe."

"Felicia, dear," Susannah said, reaching for her hand and gripping tightly. "Tell Midwife Brown that the pains are coming much faster than last time. Will you do that?"

She nodded. "That's not bad, is it?"

Susannah shook her head. "No. Not at all. But run along."

"Yes. Please!" Dan said, his voice hitting a harsh note.

Hastening to the door, Felicia took a backward glance and saw Dan kneel before Susannah, their hands intertwined. In the face of their unfathomable love, she felt like an intruder. She whirled and raced to the steps, more aware than ever of the lonely void within her own heart that continued to grow steadily with each passing day.

The hall clock chimed six times. Having just convinced Susannah to climb into bed, Dan arranged the sheet over her and gave her an encouraging smile. *Please, dear Lord. Where are they? They should have come by now.*

Outside, the iron gate squeaked on its hinges, then closed. Dan crossed to the window and cautiously moved the edge of the curtain aside just enough to see if anyone was coming.

The soldier across the way was clearly visible, and the other joined him as Felicia and the midwife came toward the front door.

Dan released the panel and dashed for the stairs, meeting

the two starting up. "What took you so long?" he whispered as loudly as he dared.

The older woman's plump face whitened as recognition and surprise fought for prominence in her expression. "Pastor Haynes!"

"Shh." Felicia put a finger to her lips and turned to her. "No one knows he's here."

"I didn't know you was back," the midwife finished softly.

"I only arrived last night."

"And just in the nick of time, too," Mistress Brown said as they ascended the remaining steps.

Dan tipped his head toward Felicia. "Did you lock the door?"

"Oh no. I forgot!" She turned and rushed back down.

"Mistress, my wife's pains seem to be different this time. It's only been three hours since the first small ones began, and already they're coming much harder and faster."

She nodded, her cap ruffle bobbing slightly. "I see. Did you start some water to heatin'?"

"Yes, ma'am. What there was in the house."

The heavyset woman retreated a few steps. "Felicia," she said quietly, "get one of them soldiers and have him fetch plenty of water."

"No!" Dan blurted in disbelief. "I can't have them in the house."

"Oh, now, don't you be worryin' none about them fellers," she said, pulling him along with her. "Circumstances bein' what they are, I'll let you stay with me this time. *If* you promise to behave proper and do as you're told. And most important, I won't have no swoonin'. Can't abide weak-stomached menfolk around when I'm busy with a patient who truly needs me."

Reaching the bedchamber, Mistress Brown blocked Dan with her arm. "Best you let me examine her first." That said, she went in and shut the door in his face.

Dan let out an exasperated breath and rubbed the bridge of his nose. He'd thought she meant he could be with Susannah the entire time, and here he was already barred from the room.

Soft stirrings carried his way from the nursery. Dan straightened and went to the door. Opening it silently, he peeked in.

Miles was still asleep, one small hand sticking out through the bars of the crib.

Dan swallowed and stepped into the room, crossing to him to have a closer look.

His heart wrenched at how much his son had grown. All those precious months missed, never to be recaptured. Gone was the baby he'd left behind, and in his place lay a little boy. Who had been here to watch him sprouting up, running at play? How did he sound when he talked? Dan gazed at the abundance of golden brown hair splayed about the small pillow, the straight white teeth that glistened between softly parted lips. And Dan mourned every wasted day.

Hearing the bedroom door open across the hall, he left Miles' side and went back into the hall, where Mistress Brown beckoned.

Susannah, when he went in to her, was propped up with pillows and appeared flushed, as if she'd run a footrace in his absence. Strands of her hair were damp and clinging to her cheeks and forehead. It seemed an agonizing repeat of last time.

She offered a weak smile.

The midwife moved closer and nudged Dan. "Before leavin' home, I sent my son to ask the elders of the church to come and pray while the missus is givin' birth. Thought I'd better tell you, in case you don't want to be seen. I hope it don't put you in further jeopardy, but I had no way of knowin' you was here. Besides, the more prayin', the better."

Trying desperately to derive some kind of comfort from her last statement, Dan instead felt chilled to the bone. He looked back at Susannah.

"But," the woman went on, "like as not, we prob'ly won't have as much trouble this time. Will we, sweetie?" She smiled broadly at both of them.

Dan watched as Susannah's face contorted in pain. She groaned from someplace deep inside and clutched one of the bedposts. Her eyes rolled back.

Struggling to maintain his own composure, he covered her whitened knuckles with the warmth of his hand and prayed hard.

37

"Pretty," Miles whispered. "Pretty sissy."

"Shh." Holding his son extra close, Dan gazed down at Susannah and their new daughter, his heart about to burst with thankfulness. Miles was right. Tiny Julia Rose was beautiful. As beautiful as her mama, dozing now amid fresh linens in the dark pine four-poster.

He studied them for a few more precious moments, then stole nearer, bending down so Miles could touch the tiny head of the babe cradled in his mother's arms.

"Soft," the boy breathed.

Dan filled his lungs and swallowed the lump forming in his throat. He stood up. Footsteps were coming up the walk. Giving Miles one more hug, he moved to the window and peered out.

Two elders from the church had come. Too late for them to pray for a swift and simple birth, Dan reflected. All was well, and the hall clock had yet to chime seven times. But it was thoughtful of them to stop by.

He carried Miles out into the hall and started down the stairs while Felicia admitted the men.

"How's the little missus?" he heard one of them ask.

"She's just fine, we're happy to say," Dan said, unable to suppress a huge grin.

"Why, Pas—," the man blurted exuberantly.

Felicia quickly smothered the word with her hand as she

tilted her head toward the guards outside. After closing the door, she hurried to the window to see that they remained at their posts, then turned back with a smile.

"Well, what a surprise to see you, Pastor Haynes!" Elder Simms said on a quieter note, administering a stout clap on Dan's back. "When did you get home?"

"Last eve. Just in time."

"And how is your wife?"

"Fine. Just fine. God has blessed us with a strong, healthy daughter, and we couldn't be more thankful for the Lord's goodness."

The older man nodded thoughtfully.

"Well, where have you been?" Elder Calloway asked, still appearing stunned. "Your brother wouldn't tell any of us your whereabouts, not even the most trusted elders."

"Well, neither will I," Dan said with a laugh as he beckoned them upstairs. "In fact, I haven't even told Susannah. After all, it would be a burden on the lot of you, don't you think? Having to lie, worrying that you might let something slip to the wrong person."

"I suppose you're right." Stopping at the top landing, Elder Simms stroked his dark beard reflectively. "Your wife was kind enough to read us portions of the letters you and your sister wrote home. All of us at the church are thankful to know Jane and Ted are safe with some good Christian patriots now and happy as well."

Dan smiled at both of the men and put his free hand on Mr. Simms' shoulders. "Although I missed my wife more than words can say, I now count it joy, being able to watch my sister and Ted growing together in the Lord during these past months. Ted is going to make a fine, loving pastor one of these days. Every bit as compassionate as Susannah's father once was."

"I'm glad to hear that, lad."

"And Jane!" Dan went on. "You wouldn't believe my sister is the same girl who spent every moment she could possibly steal last year with that arrogant British officer, snubbing her nose at everything the rest of us hold dear. An incredible rebirth. Incredible."

"Speaking of that officer," Elder Simms said, narrowing his eyes, "Fontaine and General Gage are still in Salem tryin' to set up a new government, but to no avail. Israel Schuster, a farmer outside of Salem, came into Faneuil Hall the other day. A cleaning woman he knows overheard one of Gage's officers tryin' to talk the general into sendin' a company of soldiers to Worcester to force the people to allow his new judges to hold court. The woman reported that Gage considered the idea, but then thought better of it. He must know it would spark open rebellion before he's ready to deal with it. He's not that stupid. He'll wait for reinforcements first."

With a grin, Elder Calloway laced his fingers together over the front of his frock coat. "Nothing has gone well for the general since he arrived."

Simms shook his balding head. "But from what Schuster up in Salem said, nothin' has riled Gage more than hearing it bandied about that he'd tried to bribe Sam Adams to bring us ignorant sheep back into the king's benevolent fold."

Calloway gave a huff. "Well, I think he's gotten our message. Schuster noticed that the soldiers were startin' to break camp up north. All of them. He's pretty sure Gage is returnin' to Boston."

"Like a dog with his tail tucked between his legs, if you ask me," Simms added. "They're not feeling too safe up there all by themselves."

The church bell reverberated at Faneuil Hall. Its knell was picked up and echoed by the one at South Church, then others all over Boston joined the tolling. The sound of distant cheering, faint at first, gathered strength.

Dan exchanged curious looks with the church officers, and they all strode into the nursery, where Dan set Miles down to play with his toys.

One of the elders opened the window and leaned out. The other stretched to see over the first one's head. They both ducked back inside and grinned. "Looks like our delegation is leaving," Elder Simms said.

Dan was completely confused.

"It's our delegation to the Continental Congress in Philadelphia, Pastor," Calloway said with a chuckle. "They'll be going to thank the other colonies for supporting Boston—and they're planning to ask for *us Americans* to boycott all English goods again. If I know Sam Adams, he'll convince them to band together and stay that way this time."

Simms nudged Elder Calloway in the ribs. "What say we head on up to Marlborough Street and do our part to give them a proper send-off?"

"Yes. A proper send-off," Calloway repeated with enthusiasm. He extended a hand to Dan. "Well, Pastor, you take care of that new daughter of yours while we're gone. We'll take a peek at her when we come back. I want to talk some more."

Dan nodded and watched the men leave. Then concerned that all the ruckus had disturbed Susannah, he went in to her.

A slight frown lined her forehead as she leaned up on one elbow, a question in her eyes.

"Everything's fine, sweetheart."

"Good," she breathed, lying back down. "I dreamed the bells were for me and the baby."

"In a way they are, love. In a way they are."

Using the brilliant red-orange glare of the setting sun as a cover, Yancy rowed toward the marshy mouth of the Charles River. It was getting more and more difficult to outsmart the lobsterbacks, but he was certain none of them would expect someone to attempt an escape from Boston at this time of day. A smug grin broke free.

During the last week, he'd managed to deliver every single case of rifles to the Copper Works on the northwest tip of the peninsula. But even though his missions had taken him within two miles of Felicia each time, it might as well have been two hundred for all the good it had done. Particularly today. With the delegation's departure sending every one of the troops into the streets, it had been impossible for Yancy to sneak to Dan's house.

Maneuvering the rowboat to the right of the strong currents at the river's mouth, Yancy pulled hard for the marshes, tall with reeds. He would far rather have been in his wife's warm embrace than returning to Cambridge again to report another success to the Sons of Liberty, but nothing could be done about that now. For a fleeting second he held the oars aloft and allowed sweet remembrances of Felicia to tease his mind . . . the way the soft contours of her body molded to his, the way her voice sang across his heartstrings. Even though she was shut away from him now, he could still smell the fragrance of her hair whenever he closed his eyes and drew in a long, slow breath. He exhaled on a sigh.

He caught movement against the blinding glare of the sun, and the hairs on the back of his neck bristled in alarm. Shading his eyes, he squinted into the light.

A longboat full of soldiers appeared from nowhere. Leaning into their oars, they were rowing hard. Straight for him.

Ben's stomach growled. Would Yancy never get back from smuggling those fool rifles? The two of them had planned to have supper, and here it was already an hour past dark. Yancy should have been here ages ago.

Opening the door of the rooming house where he was boarding, Ben leaned out and looked toward the marsh. The sailor was nowhere in sight, but he did see the cobbler coming his way. He waved.

A broad grin widened the tradesman's mouth as he lifted a beefy hand.

"Good to see you, Mr. Pringle. Come on up to my place, where we can talk privately." Ben stood aside while the tradesman entered, and they mounted the stairs. "Care for some cider?" he asked, closing the door of his room behind them.

"Sure thing." The stocky man took a kerchief from his back

pocket, wiped his brow, then replaced the cloth. He seated himself at the small table in the far corner of the stark room.

Ben brought over two tall glasses of the cool drink and took the opposite chair.

The cobbler raised his glass. "It's a grand day for celebratin', lad."

"So I heard. Every bell in the county was clanging." He took a long sip, then set down his cider.

"Makes a body wish he had his own bell rope to pull, don't it?"

Ben nodded with a wry grin and brushed imaginary lint from the sleeve of his off-white shirt.

"But fact is, I came with good news from Dan."

"Is that right? He made it home safely, then?"

The tradesman nodded, his balding head shining in the light of the lamp Ben had left burning. "Just in time, too. He's now the proud father of a new baby girl."

"Is Susannah all right? She had such a difficult birth with little Miles—"

"She's fine, lad. Nothing to worry about."

Ben let out a sigh of relief. "Girl, huh?" His thoughts turned to a little blonde sweetheart with huge eyes peeking around her mama's skirts. "What did they name her?"

"Nobody told me. Let you know next time I come around." He took a gulp of his drink, then wiped his mouth on the back of his hand. "But that wasn't the reason I came today. After the delegation left for Philadelphia, some of the men down at Faneuil Hall got to thinkin' it might be wise for us to know what the congress decides before the lobsterbacks do. Know what I mean?"

"I agree. And if old Sam Adams has his way, he won't come back without a declaration of war."

The cobbler's laugh sounded more nervous than amused. "Precisely. So they want you to set up relay points with fresh riders and horses. Word will get to us faster if express riders can travel day and night."

Ben rubbed his jaw. "That'll take at least a dozen horses. If we can get them."

"Well, the Holbrooks offered the use of four quarter horses. Of course, we were hopin' your family might be able to provide a string from Providence south to New Haven. And with all the time you've spent in the Middle Colonies, you must know some willin' patriots there who'd part with some horses for a few weeks."

"I do. And some of my postriding pals will jump at the chance to help out."

"Good. Good." The cobbler drained his glass, then rose. "Knew we could count on you, lad."

"Say, friend," Ben said. "Find out for me if Dan would consider being part of this, would you? I'd like him to help me with the relay."

"Splendid idea. With both you Haynes brothers involved, it's sure to be a success."

Ben grinned. Then as the man crossed to the door, he remembered Yancy and followed. But he was reluctant to worry anyone else just yet. "Had supper yet? I was just about to eat."

"Sorry, but fact is, Sean Burns and his missus invited me to eat with them."

"Oh, well. Just thought I'd ask."

Reaching the ground floor and front door, they parted company, and Ben set a course for the tavern a few buildings away while he kept an eye out for his overdue friend.

"Hey, mate," a voice whispered.

"Yance?" Moving into the deep shadows between two shops, Ben grinned at the dripping-wet seaman skulking in the darkness. "What'd you do, swim back from Boston?"

"Very funny," the sailor grated, tossing a glance over his shoulder. "Those redcoats are gettin' thicker than maggots on a carcass. I had to wade ashore in the reeds to keep out of sight. Have ye seen a patrol come this way?"

"No. But then, they don't feel all that welcome."

"Good. But to be on the safe side, I need to change before anyone sees me."

Ben let out an exasperated breath as his stomach protested again. Turning back to the door, he waved Yancy inside. Then, after tossing a glance up and down the street to make sure the sailor hadn't been followed, Ben went upstairs after him. "Make it fast, will you? They're serving kidney pie tonight. I don't want to miss out. By the way, do you want to join Dan and me as an express rider?"

"Eh?" Tugging the sopping shirt over his head, Yancy shivered and dropped it to the floor.

Ben groaned. "I asked if you'd like to join Dan and me as an express rider. The caucus at Faneuil Hall wants to set up a relay system from Philadelphia to Boston to bring the news from the meeting of the Colonies."

"Dan's back from Boston?" Yancy returned, shucking his britches.

"He's still with Sue. She had a baby girl this morning."

The color fled the seaman's face. "Is she all right?"

Remembering that Yancy had been present during the long ordeal when Miles was born, Ben nodded. "Fine."

"And Felicia, then. How's she?"

"Sorry, I forgot to ask. But if anything were amiss, I'm sure the cobbler would have said something."

Rummaging through his cinch bag, Yancy found a pair of dry stockings and pulled them on, then some fresh breeches. "If Dan's still in Boston, how do ye know he'll agree to set up that relay with ye?"

"No reason for him to refuse. He isn't needed any longer in the grants, and the way the king's men are closing ranks, there soon won't be a single one roaming the countryside to threaten him or anybody else."

Yancy nodded. "Kidney pie, ye say. Hm. Right after supper I think I'll float on back to Boston Town. See if he's interested."

"You haven't said *you* are yet!" Ben shook his head in disdain.

Yancy shot him a wry grin. "I'll tell ye, young Ben. After spendin' every night of the last two weeks rowin' boats to and fro across the Charles, the idea of ridin' across some dry land for a spell sounds mighty temptin' even for an old sea horse like me . . . providin' I can go tell Daniel and spend some time with me wife first."

Ben threw up his hands. "Why don't you hire a drummer boy to go along with you?" he said sarcastically. "You just got finished telling me the harbor is swarming with lobsterbacks!"

"Aye, that it is. But—"

"I'll give you *but*. I'm not gonna be the one who has to tell your wife you got taken prisoner just because you were feeling lonesome for her. Tomorrow morning when the cobbler returns, he can tell Dan. And tonight you and I are going over to the tavern and having some kidney pie. That's the most the likes of us can expect these days."

From the back landing of the house, Dan stared reflectively at the night sky. An ominous glow lit the distant darkness above the Neck, adding to his reluctance to leave Susannah again after only three weeks.

The door opened quietly, and Felicia moved to his side. "Susannah has nearly finished nursing the baby. She expects to come down soon." Her attention followed Dan's. "From the look of things, it would seem that our General Gage didn't appreciate his homecoming overmuch."

"No, I assume not, with the entire town shut up behind closed doors instead of out cheering his parade." He let out a slow breath. "I seriously wonder if the man even feels safe."

She nodded, then after a few seconds spoke again. "How long do you think it'll take for the military to finish the barricade across the Neck?"

Dan shoved his hands into his pockets and shook his head. "Not long at the rate they're going. No doubt they're hoping to have it done by the opening day of the Continental Congress, September fifth. Their answer to Boston."

"That's only four days away."

"Yes." He sighed. "I hate having to leave Susannah mere weeks after she's given birth, but aside from the danger I've put upon you both, I've already delayed far too long. Now in order to reach Princeton by the morning of the sixth, I'll have to ride night and day."

"Do you actually think the congress will come to any decisions on their first day, Dan?" Felicia asked, toying with the edge of her work apron.

He chuckled. "I'm hoping not. But just in case, I must be there waiting. I probably shouldn't have chosen faraway Princeton as my relay post, but I wanted to spend some time with my baby sister."

"Oh, yes. Emily." Felicia smiled wistfully. "Susannah mentioned you haven't seen her and her husband since they fled to New Jersey last year."

"Actually, it's nearly two years now, come December."

"That is quite a long time. Well, let's pray that our congress and the king's Parliament will find the way to peace by Christmas. It's Susannah's dearest wish for all the family to be together by then. Of course, seeing Yancy again wouldn't upset me one bit, either."

Grinning down at the girl, Dan slipped an arm about her slender shoulders and hugged her. "You know, I've tried to express my gratitude for the way you've sacrificed your own happiness to come here. But I want to tell you something. I've come to think of you as family, just as I do Yancy. And if there's ever anything I can do for you—anything at all—please, don't hesitate to ask."

With an embarrassed smile, Felicia lowered her gaze. "There is one small thing. . . ." She nibbled her bottom lip and raised her lashes.

"Name it." Even as he spoke, Dan feared that he might have made the offer too soon. He had to escape from the peninsula tonight.

She reached into an apron pocket, withdrew some stockings he'd seen her knitting the last few weeks, and pressed them into his hand. "When you ride south, stop at New York and give these to Yancy. I know he left for his post days ago."

"I'll be glad to." With another small hug, Dan handed them back. "But if you don't want them all soggy and smelling of seawater, you'd better wrap them in oilcloth. They might have to go for a swim with me tonight."

"Let's pray you don't." Felicia smiled, then pulled gently away, heading for the door. She turned. "Dan, when you see Yancy, would you tell him for me to please be careful. Very careful. And—" her voice lowered to a whisper—"tell him I love him." She whirled and dashed inside.

Dan didn't miss the catch in Felicia's voice or the sudden glint of tears shining in her eyes. She was a sensitive young woman, and despite the very brave front she put on, she probably cried herself to sleep many a night.

Feeling a stinging behind his own eyes, Dan swallowed. The longer it took Susannah to come downstairs, the longer their parting would be prolonged. He gazed slowly around at the house and its surrounding grounds, imprinting them once more upon his mind. Some of the happiest moments of his life had been spent here—his first parish home, where so many of his flock had come for advice or comfort. His two sweet children were born here. His baby sister had gotten married in this house. And now, if events continued in their headlong rush toward war, what would become of it, of Boston . . . or all of America, for that matter?

The sound of Susannah's voice drifted to Dan's ears through the open window. His heart contracted. How he would miss its sweet sound in the days and weeks to come—her charming British accent, the lilt of her soft laugh. How empty his world seemed apart from Susannah! But his presence here put not only his family and Felicia in jeopardy but also many of his church members who had helped shield him from discovery since his return. He had to go, for all their sakes.

It galled him to be forced to leave Susannah behind. But it had been dangerous enough to try to spirit her out of Boston months ago, when the only other consideration had been Miles. Now with the addition of another delicate new life, it seemed all the more impossible . . . unless God were to intervene. Dan turned his gaze skyward, searching for answers.

The door swung open, and Dan turned to see Susannah standing there, silhouetted against the kitchen light, its golden radiance haloing her hair. A sense of impending loss swept over him.

Coming to him with a troubled smile, Susannah handed him the oilcloth packet for Yancy, then wrapped her arms around his neck. "I told Felicia to take some cider and cookies to the guards to distract them while you leave."

Dan tucked the small parcel into his belt and slid his arms around his wife's waist, drawing her close. He gulped down the weight of his grief and mustered great effort to lighten the moment. "You've become quite the military thinker, haven't you, my love?"

Susannah turned an overbright smile up at him, tears already glistening in her eyes. "Do remember that the next time the Massachusetts militia is looking for an officer."

"And I suppose you'll want a uniform with lots of shiny buttons and miles of braiding, too."

"Just don't forget the fur hat. I expect the very highest one *and* the fanciest crest."

Dan heard the front door slam and figured Felicia must be on her way out to the soldiers. He could not delay his departure another moment. He gazed desperately at Susannah as she tightened her grip on his neck.

"Take care," she whispered, the house lights dancing in her moist eyes. "I shouldn't want to live if something were to happen to you."

"I love you, Susannah Harrington of Ashton. It was the fairest of winds that blew you to our shores. To me." He crushed her to himself, burying his nose in her fragrant hair.

"Yes, the fairest of winds." She rose to tiptoe and pressed her lips to his.

Somehow, Dan managed to break away, despite a heaviness inside that made it all but impossible to breathe.

Susannah backed toward the house. "That fair wind is waiting just beyond the horizon. I shall pray day and night that it will soon return you to me."

"Soon, love." He took a few steps, widening the gulf between them, then rounded the corner of the house, her soft words following after him.

"Soon, my dearest husband."

After Susannah finished dusting the parlor tables and lamps the next morning, she moved to the mantel and did the Staffordshire porcelain figurines. The curtain fluttered at the window, open now that Dan was safely gone. Susannah drifted to it and gazed out.

In a frock the same shade as the peonies, Felicia was weeding the front flower garden. Miles played happily near the lilac bush. When one of the sentries leaned over the fence and began chatting with them, Susannah decided to join them. Anything to keep her mind off her loneliness. She pocketed her dusting rag and stepped out onto the stoop.

The guard smiled, then stiffened with a look of panic as he hastened back to his post, motioning to his comrade to do the same.

Puzzled, Susannah wondered what was amiss. She walked to the gate and peered down the street, barely aware that Felicia had joined her.

Alex Fontaine, on his infernal prancing stallion, was heading their way, followed by two horse-drawn wagons and a pair of foot soldiers.

He was back. Susannah uttered a thankful prayer that Dan had departed when he did. But nonetheless, her spirits sank.

Felicia slid her arm around Susannah. "We'd better go inside. It appears he has business to attend, and we wouldn't want to delay the man, would we?" She hurried toward the house.

But before Susannah had time to grab Miles and reach sanctuary, Alex had spurred his mount and come abreast of the yard.

"Susannah!"

His harsh tone stopped her. She shot a quick glance toward Felicia, whose hand poised midair at the latch of the door.

"Alex," Susannah finally managed, trying to sound casual even as a dreaded certainty closed around her. Either the lieutenant had learned that Dan had been home, or worse— had captured him. "It's been awhile."

The officer dismounted stiffly, then secured his horse. "Inside!"

Hugging Miles to her, Susannah complied, following Felicia into the parlor.

"Sit!" Alex ordered, a mere step behind them.

Susannah maintained her hold on her little son while she sank onto the settee. She forced herself to look up at the tall, rigid redcoat looming over them, his hand toying with the saber at his side, his gunmetal eyes hard and glittering.

"It's over," he said with finality.

Susannah's heart quaked crazily as she struggled to breathe. He had captured Dan. Or killed him.

"I'm giving you one last chance," Alex said ominously, "to tell me what I want to know. I'm no longer required to coddle you. Martial law is in full effect, and I am now free to take whatever measures I feel are necessary. Where are they?"

The mere fact that Dan was still safe snatched the teeth from Alex's threat. "Would you care for a cup of *coffee*, Lieutenant?" she asked, ignoring his query.

Alex swiped in fury across the nearest table, knocking everything to the floor in a loud crash. "No. I would not."

Miles clutched Susannah and whimpered in fright, and upstairs the baby wailed, obviously having been awakened by the racket.

"Felicia, dear, would you please see to Julia?" Susannah never took her gaze from Alex, but she held Miles closer.

"I did not say she could leave," Alex barked as Felicia began to get up.

The crying grew steadily louder.

"Just as well," Alex said through gritted teeth. He waved Felicia out of the room.

"I'll be right back," she said, looking pointedly at Susannah as she swept away and up to the nursery.

"I'm waiting," he said, moving directly in front of Susannah.

She sighed. "Truly, Alex, even if I wanted to help you I could not. I've only received word that Ted and Jane are happy and well, nothing of their whereabouts. I swear that before God and on the life of this child in my lap."

"You don't say," he said on a dramatic note. "And we all know what a religious woman you are, with your nightly *prayer* meetings." He tapped his fingers against his leg impatiently. "Very well. Have it your own way." He pivoted. Then, kicking over any furniture between him and the entry, he stomped out of the room.

Miles started with fright at every crash, gripping Susannah harder as silent tears streamed down his face.

Attempting to calm her son and herself, she bent and hugged him, bestowing a kiss to the top of his head. The lieutenant was completely mad with rage. Urgently she began praying for strength and wisdom and for God's protection on the household.

"You. Men!" she heard Alex call at the front door. "Come here!"

Instantly their running footsteps sounded as they hurried toward the house.

"You two, start upstairs. Remove everything," he ordered. "You and you, in the parlor."

"Sir, we have no crates or barrels," one said.

He swept his hand over the hall table, clattering candlesticks and vases to the floor. "No need to be concerned about that, just dump everything in the wagons. And be quick about it."

"Yes, sir!" Two pairs of boots clambered up the stairs as the other privates came into the sitting room. Without a single glance at Susannah, they began gathering armfuls of furniture and belongings.

Alex swung to face her. "It won't be quite so comfortable for you and your Presbyterian traitors to plot against us now

. . . in an empty house, without so much as a cup to stir your poisons in."

Susannah's mouth went dry. She tried to remain calm for Miles' sake, but she felt her pulse racing. "But, Alex, the furniture does not belong to us. It came with the house. It's the landlord's."

His lips stretched into a tight smirk. "Something more for you to explain, isn't it?"

Felicia came rushing downstairs, baby Julia safely in her arms, while Susannah led Miles out of harm's way. They huddled together against the wall in the hall as the soldiers hefted the dove gray settee and started out with it.

Miles' tiny hand trembled as it clutched hers, his eyes growing wider with each tick of the clock. She gave his hand to her friend. "Take the children over to Mistress Simms. And stay with them there."

"Yes," Alex snapped. "Get out."

"But—" Felicia swung a fearful glance from Susannah to Alex, then pressed her lips together. "I'll come right back," she stated firmly.

The soldiers upstairs started down carrying a chest of drawers between them.

Silently pleading for the Lord to intervene, Susannah turned to Alex. "Would you step into the dining room with me, Lieutenant?" She led the way, glancing back to make certain he followed.

Narrowing his eyes, Alex stalked after her. As he passed the tall clock off to one side, he put a shoulder to it and sent it crashing to the polished floor. The explosion of splintering wood and broken glass barely missed the departing privates.

Susannah hardened herself against the senseless destruction and the evil glint in Fontaine's eyes. "Please, sit down, Alex," she said evenly, motioning to a cherry-wood chair.

"You're too kind," he said facetiously, booting it straight at her instead.

She leaped aside just in time. Susannah fought rising panic, all the while trying to maintain her inner composure. "Look at yourself, Alex," she said desperately. "Look at what you've become. This is not the Alex I used to know."

He reached out and seized her arm, gripping it forcefully. "On the contrary, my *pet*—" he spat out the word—"you see before you Lieutenant Alex Fontaine come into his fullest power and glory." He shoved her up against the table, pinning her there. "I will be toyed with no longer. I will take whenever, wherever, and *whatever* I want." Clawing at the neckline of her dress, he jerked hard, his intent clear.

The material held.

Susannah felt the color drain from her face as her knees threatened to buckle. "Dear Jesus," she cried. "In the name of Jesus, get away from me!"

As if struck by lightning, Alex staggered away from her. He stared at her, his face contorted. Then whirling around, he slammed out of the room, down the hall, and out the door.

Susannah's legs gave way, and she sank, trembling, to the chair beside her. "Thank you, Lord Jesus. Thank you," she murmured as Alex's horse clattered down the street.

"Susannah!" she heard Felicia cry. "Where are you?"

"In here," she managed.

En masse, a number of footsteps thundered along the hall. Felicia and the two sentries ran through the doorway, their faces awash with relief.

"What on earth happened?" Felicia asked as she gazed at the shambles. "The lieutenant tore out of here as if he'd lost his mind."

Susannah clutched her friend's hand and dropped to her knees, pulling the dark-haired girl with her. "Oh, Felicia. Pray with me for Alex. Pray harder than you've ever prayed before."

39

Bone weary, Dan barely glanced at the massive stone walls of the Nassau Hall as he rode through Princeton. Only a scant few lights still burned in various rooms in the darkened building. The college students had retired from their studies and compositions hours ago. Recalling some of the treasured hours he had spent under the tutelage of President John Witherspoon and the other gifted professors, he sighed.

Just ahead loomed the Lyons' Den, the three-story fieldstone coaching inn frequented not only by stage wagons but by college students and the townspeople as well. Dan noticed as he approached that the inn's yard appeared as neat as ever, the silhouetted shrubbery showing a few years' growth. Above the lamplit double door, the familiar sign shaped like a lion's head hung suspended on sturdy chains.

Despite the lateness of the hour, Dan knew he'd find, as always, a warm welcome and a clean bed for the night there. But there was no reason to cause more disturbance than necessary. He rode his horse, a long-legged English Thoroughbred he'd acquired at the last relay point, around back to the stable.

The full moon bathed the area in silver-blue glory. Dan didn't bother going for a firebrand to light the barn lantern, but dismounted and led the horse inside. No coaches stood parked near the entrance—a sure sign that it wasn't one of the nights when the stages from New York and Philadelphia stopped here to exchange passengers. All the better, he decided. There'd be plenty of room.

After tossing hay into the stall manger, Dan checked to make sure there was ample water in the trough, then took some clean straw and began rubbing down his overheated horse.

The back door of the inn slammed shut, followed by the sound of footsteps coming across the gravel.

That would probably be Jasper Lyons, the innkeeper, coming to see who was rummaging around in his barn. Dan's assumption was correct; the old man's shadowy form appeared in the doorway.

"Evening, Mr. Lyons. It's me. Dan Haynes."

The older man relaxed his stance and came forward. "Daniel. Figured it just might be you. Ben said you'd be comin' sooner or later."

The familiar gruff voice brought a grin to Dan's mouth as the man continued speaking.

"Fact is, we expected you days ago. We was about to give up. Come on inside and let me get a look at you."

"I'm just about finished here, Mr. Lyons. And I have a powerful thirst. How about going back in and fixing me some of that flip you're so famous for?"

"Right glad to, son. Don't be long."

Dan took care of the remaining needs of his mount, then headed toward the ordinary. The sight of it took him back to his student days and beyond. He could almost feel the awkward nervousness that had swamped him the first time he'd come here to see Susannah Harrington.

He opened the latch and went into the large common room, empty of customers at this late hour. He was elated to see that it hadn't changed. Behind the bar, the carved wooden head of a lion still hung between the shelves of glasses and tankards. As always, Jasper Lyons was in the process of filling a pewter mug with amber liquid and then inserting the hot tip of a poker. And on a perch in the corner, looking a little bedraggled in sound sleep, was Jasper's cockatoo, Methuselah.

As Dan swept a glance around the rest of the room with its long trestle tables and the empty fireplace against the far wall, he heard footsteps on the staircase. Esther Lyons descended in her nightdress and wrap, her face beaming.

"Daniel! Young Dan!" Her cheeks rounded with her huge smile, and her small hazel eyes shone as she grabbed Dan and hugged him. "Thought you'd never get here."

"That's for sure," Christopher Drummond said, nodding his sandy head in agreement as he came around the kitchen door.

Dan smiled at the older woman first and kissed her cheek, then shook hands with Chip, who had done an amazing amount of growing since Dan left three years ago. His voice had even deepened. "Good to see you both."

Mistress Lyons looked Dan up and down and shook her head. Then the fine crinkly lines of her face deepened in a frown. "Just look at you. You're a terrible sight. Skin an' bones, circles under your eyes. . . . You and Susannah need to get yourselves back here where we can look after you proper."

Dan chuckled and gave her another hug.

"Move aside, woman, so's I can give the poor lad his drink," Jasper growled, coming over with the tankard. "And let him sit down, too. Can't you see he's wore out?"

Barefooted Chip scrambled to the nearest chair and pulled it out for Dan, then seated the older woman and himself while Mr. Lyons took the last one at the table.

"How's our Susannah?" Mistress Lyons asked. "Ben told us she just gave birth to a little girl."

"Right," Dan said with a nod. "Julia Rose, named after her childhood friend."

"Oh, yes. Julia," the older woman said, nodding. "May she rest in peace."

"Mama and baby are doing wonderfully well, considering the trying circumstances in Boston at the moment."

Jasper rubbed a gnarled hand across his big nose, his wild

white brows flaring. "Young Ben filled us in on the goin's-on when he dropped off the relay horse. He said that carrottop sailor is farin' well, too. But the woes of Boston are terrible. Just terrible. Doctor Witherspoon and all the other men over to the college are behind Massachusetts 100 percent."

"That's good to know. We appreciate the support we've received from all the other colonies." Dan switched his attention to Christopher. "How's that sweet sister of yours doing these days, Chip?"

"Just great. I'm an uncle now." He puffed out his chest with manly pride.

"Yes, isn't that the most wonderful news?" Mistress Lyons added. "Mary Clare and Jonathan had their first wee one just last month. They say they'll bring my namesake, little baby Esther, to see us over Christmas." She paused, and an expression of sheer wonder erased a few years from her face. "Wouldn't it be simply perfect if you and Susannah could come then, too? What a celebration we'd have—all of us together, even Rob, Emily, and their little girl."

Dan had to laugh. "My poor mother is still waiting for us to spend Christmas with them! But I'll tell you what. If all goes well at the congress in Philadelphia, maybe we can plan a gathering sometime next year."

Slight disappointment reflected in her eyes, then she shrugged. "Well, we'll hold you to that, Daniel."

Jasper grunted, but a smile tweaked his mouth. "The wife means that. But for right now, drink up and get to bed. Your sister'll be arrivin' with the sun tomorrow—just like she's been doin' every mornin' for a week, hopin' to find you here."

Grateful, Dan downed his flip, then rose. "Which room do you want me to take?"

"Pshaw! Why, your old one, of course." Esther Lyons stood and grabbed Dan's waist in a hug. "I'll walk along with you."

Dan filled his lungs, realizing how much he'd missed this wonderful elderly couple who had treated him and so many other Princeton students like long-lost sons. And they had taken Susannah under their wing and made a home for her when she'd been alone and stranded in a new land. He and Susannah owed them a debt of gratitude.

Coming awake in the attic room, which once had been his and Susannah's, Dan felt something crash down on him, whooshing the breath out of him.

"It's about time!" Emily squealed.

Dan gave his exuberant youngest sister a hug. He sat up in bed and blinked the sleep out of his eyes. He groaned as he stretched his travel-weary muscles. "Morning."

Emily sank down onto the side of the mattress with a grin. "It's so, so good to see you. I've been coming by every day, hoping you'd arrived. Ben told us about our new niece—and if I have anything to say about it, Rob, Katie, and I will go to see her and Susannah very soon. We've had about as much hiding out as we can stand."

"I don't know about that, little sis. Boston is more dangerous than ever right now—and with you and Rob doing so well here, I might add—you'd be wise to stay put awhile longer." Dan's gaze made a slow circuit over Emily, noticing her soft green eyes, the same shade as their mother's. She still sparkled with youthful high-spiritedness, but there was an unmistakable maturity in her face. Although she had retained her appealing, slight figure, she now wore her hair in a becoming chignon.

"We do like it here in Princeton, of course, but that doesn't keep us from missing all of you." She pouted prettily and tousled Dan's hair. "And it was no surprise to me, you know, when Jane and Ted got back together."

"Oh, really?" He laughed and propped his chin in his cupped palm.

"Yes, really! I'm the one who had to put up with her ceaseless mooning over him for months on end before I left home, remember?" She brightened. "I hear even Yancy's gotten married. Now that *is* a miracle. The only one left to worry about now is Ben. Honestly, I thought he'd be elated by the rallying of the Colonies, since he used to be such a zealous patriot. But when he stopped by here setting up the relay, he was about as merry as a funeral. I wish he'd find someone to love, too."

"Well, his main problem is that he's taking the cause too seriously, acting as if the success or failure of it depends on him alone."

"It does seem like that, doesn't it? But somewhere along the way he's lost that adventure-loving part of him. And I miss that in him."

With a nod, Dan patted her hand. "He still hasn't learned patience, I fear. He has a way of wanting to run ahead of God, instead of waiting for the Lord and his purpose. And in doing that, he's missing out on the blessings God is trying to give him."

"That's our brother, all right," Emily said. "But didn't I hear something about you having some problems with impatience yourself while you were off in hiding?"

There was no denying his sister was right. "Guilty as charged," Dan said. "But at least I learned something through it all. If a person spends all his time bombarding the Lord with requests, it's almost impossible to hear God's answers. But amazingly, the Lord took good care of me despite myself, even when I was positive I was being rebellious." He shook his head, reflecting on the memories. "He brought me back to Boston the very night Susannah gave birth."

"So I heard."

"And by the way, Ben *has* found someone to love."

Emily's eyes widened. "Ben's in love? Well, he sure doesn't seem very happy about it."

"Nor will he be until he lets God shoulder some of the responsibility for the Colonies' future. At least enough," Dan added with a grin, "so that Ben can make room for a wife and children. He took me by the farm where the young woman lives. When we rode away, I had the opportunity to speak to Ben about his own lack of trust in God—a lack which caused him to say all the wrong things to the girl. He didn't think I had much right to say anything, considering the way I had been acting. But I truly hope he hasn't lost her because of his rashness. He's quite in love with her."

"Well, anyway," Emily said, scooting closer with a conspiratorial smile, "tell me about her. What's she like? What's her name? I just can't imagine Ben in love."

"Actually, she's nothing like you might expect," Dan began. Emily was beginning to look more like the little girl he'd always known—a smile curving her lips, her eyes dancing. "Her name is Abigail, and she's shy as a kitten. And I truly believe a strong wind could sweep her right up and whisk her off to the Ohio territories."

"You jest." Emily folded her arms across her bosom. "After growing up with two willful brats like Jane and me, how could he possibly be attracted to someone like that?"

"Maybe that's *why* he is!" Dan threw up his hands, anticipating a retaliatory punch. When none came, he peeked through his fingers and saw that same disgusted look his mother often used. He relaxed. "By the way, Abigail not only requires a good deal of care and protection herself, but she has two little ones who are in need of a father. Abigail is a widow."

Emily rose and stared down at him. "And you think our Ben, our ride-off-at-a-moment's-notice Ben, is going to settle down with that much responsibility when he's caught up in such an adventurous, dangerous life?"

Dan shrugged. "Well, now you know why he's in such a muddle. Love or liberty. He sees no other options, the poor blind fool." Reaching up, Dan gave his sister a playful shove. "How about getting out of here, so I can get dressed. Esther's bacon and fluffy biscuits are calling me."

She smiled wryly and started for the door just as footsteps filtered in from the hall.

The latch lifted hesitantly, and Rob stuck his head in. "Are ye decent? Katie couldna' be put off one second more."

Dan almost laughed aloud. "The more the merrier." He

grinned at his brother-in-law and the thirteen-month-old daughter he carried as they came the rest of the way in.

Rob set the little one down beside Dan, and Emily fairly beamed with motherly pride as she snuggled closer to her husband and watched their daughter tweak Dan's nose.

"Well, look at you, little miss." Dan's heart caught at the sight of the child's huge green eyes and cherubic face. Already she had an abundance of dark silky hair like her father's. How he wished Susannah were there to share this moment. "She's a real beauty," he told Emily. "I'd give her an official uncle's hug . . . if she and her mama would depart the room so I could get some clothes on."

"Oh, very well," Emily groused, sliding him an expression of feigned offense. "But at least be quick about it, will you?" She retrieved Katie from Rob's arms and went to the door. "I'll have a steaming hot breakfast waiting when you come downstairs."

"Thanks," Dan called after her as they left. Then he climbed out of bed.

"You and Emily are looking fit, very content," Dan said to Rob. "It appears you've made my little sister quite happy." He reached for a shirt and slid his arms into it.

"Ah, and how could I not, when she's the most blessed thing that ever happened along in me life? Has me blonde beauty told ye aboot the trip we're plannin' to see your folks?"

"She hinted at it."

"Well, just so ye know," Rob said, "I don't take their safety lightly. 'Tis where we feel our heavenly Father would have us go right now. We're aboot packed an' ready, have been for days. Just been waitin' for a tardy brother-in-law to show his face first."

Dan smiled, but otherwise ignored the barb as he sat down and pulled on some stockings. "Alex Fontaine is still searching for Ted. Did Mother write that he's been to the farm twice?"

"Aye. 'Tis why we'll be stayin' wi' the Websters, doon the road. But Ben says that most of the soldiers up north have

pulled back and are holed up in Boston for fear of the ragin'
hostility of the people, so we don't really expect to see the
lieutenant."

"You're probably right," Dan agreed. "The redcoats were
barricading the Neck when I left. It was very hard for me to
leave Susannah behind. I delayed so long, in fact, that I didn't
have time to stop by the farm and see my parents. Had no
time to look for Yancy, either, when I changed horses in New
York." He patted the packet of stockings on the night table.

Rob gave a thoughtful nod. "I'll be lookin' forward to
seein' him. He's visited only once since he brought Emily an'
me 'ere to Princeton. And we heard he'd given himself over
to the Lord—and married, to boot!"

"Yes. He's found a wonderful woman." Dan buckled one of
his shoes. "She's as spirited as she is beautiful, too. I think
she'll be able to keep up with him quite handily."

"'Tis a pity your Susannah and Yancy's wife wouldn't be
able to join us at the farm."

"Yes, I agree." A deep sadness wafted through Dan as he
stood and walked to the washbasin. "It's too bad."

Dan repositioned his ladder against the stone front of the Lyons' Den and climbed up a few rungs, pail and brush in hand. After dipping the bristles into the white paint, he applied it carefully to the trim around one of the many-paned windows of the inn. He looked at Christopher a few yards away, who was already hard at work at the next one, and grinned. "What a difference a little fresh paint makes, eh?"

"Yep. Been needin' it for a while. Seems every time we planned to start the chore, there'd be another couple days of rain."

"Perhaps with two of us we'll get finished before there's another storm."

The sandy-haired lad nodded. "I'll be glad when it's done, too. I'll be enrollin' at the college next term."

"That right?"

"Sure is. My pa and Mr. Lyons are each payin' part of the tuition, an' Doctor Witherspoon's been lettin' me split wood for the school on my days off to pay for the rest."

Dan paused in his strokes and eyed Chip. The lad might have grown taller, but he hadn't lost his boyish appearance. His face was longer and still as thin as the rest of him. But at least the old torment once visible in his blue eyes had dissipated when his father was delivered from his drunkenness and made peace with the Lord. "What will you be studying?"

"Engineering. Once when I was visitin' my pa down at the

gristmill, he showed me around all the machines. It was so interesting seein' how things worked. Then a friend from the college loaned me a book on engineering. I read it from one cover to the other. Twice!" The spark in his expression dampened suddenly. "Are you disappointed with my choice?"

"Who, me? Of course not." Dan wet his brush again and kept working. "I hope I never gave you or anyone else the impression that the only honorable vocation lies in the ministry. God imparts all manner of gifts and talents, and if yours happens to be in the field of engineering, Chip, then that's what you should pursue. The main thing is to be faithful to the Lord wherever he may put you, whether it be digging a canal or building a bridge."

Noticing the look of relief that brightened the lad's demeanor, Dan chuckled. "Speaking as a former postrider, we certainly could use some better roads—and a lot more bridges. You should never be at a lack for work."

Christopher laughed. Setting down the larger of his two brushes, he switched to a narrow one and started on the trim between the panes.

Dan did the same, whistling softly under his breath as he worked at the painstaking task.

Suddenly Chip let out a yell. "Hey! It's him!"

Dan glared at the white streak he'd smeared on a section of glass, then took a rag from his pocket and wiped it as an approaching rider galloped toward them on a lathered horse. "Run around back and get my horse while I tell Jasper and Esther the courier is here."

They both dropped their brushes and clambered to the ground, and while Chip rounded the corner of the inn, Dan dashed to the front door. He swung it wide and saw Jasper Lyons behind the counter drying mugs. "The express rider just got in," Dan called. "I have to go."

"Esther!" the older man bellowed as several late breakfast customers lurched up from their seats.

Dan raced to the rider.

"You my replacement?" Sporting a day's growth of beard, the exhausted-looking young man dismounted and brushed road dust from his fawn coat.

"That's right."

The horseman unhooked a leather pouch from the saddle and handed it to Dan. "Would've been here sooner, but I had to wait last night for broadsides to be printed. Been passing them out in the towns along the way. The large envelope goes to your Faneuil Hall."

"What news have you got, lad?" a man's voice asked as several patrons from the inn surrounded him and Dan. "What did the congress decide?"

The rider lifted the flap of the pouch in Dan's grip and drew out a circular, giving one to the nearest man.

Almost instantly the headline was read aloud: "Decisions of the First Continental Congress." The group moved toward the man, intent on poring over the remainder of the paper.

Dan secured the bag again and straightened as he moved to Esther and Jasper Lyons. "Good seeing you again, Mr. Lyons," he said, shaking the white-haired man's hand. Then with a smile, he hugged the man's dear wife.

"God be with you," she said, tugging his face down for a kiss. She handed him his summer coat and the bag he'd packed and set by the door.

Dan nodded. "And also with you." He swung up into the saddle of the horse Chip had led from the barn and waved to everyone as he rode off.

"Godspeed," several called after him.

As he neared the college, Dan spied students streaming out of the doors of Nassau Hall, black robes flying as they ran toward the coaching inn. Doctor Witherspoon and two other professors brought up the rear. Veering toward the stout Scottish gentleman, Dan removed a flier from his pouch and passed it to him without stopping. "I'm off. Take care."

"Fare thee well, Daniel," he said with a wave of his large hand. "Greet all my *brothers* in Boston."

The settlement of Paulus Hook was a more than welcome sight that evening as Dan neared the Hudson River and, just beyond, the wharves and buildings of New York Harbor. Passing broadsides to waiting hands in the villages all along the route to New York had made the day pass swiftly. His only stops had been to change horses.

Considering the seriousness of his mission, Dan sincerely hoped the ferry would be docked on this side of the river for the express riders. He'd heard it said that the owner deliberately made late morning runs so that stage passengers traveling south would miss their connection with the early stage wagons, thereby providing the local tavern with overnight customers.

Dan guided his mount through the shantytown, where boatmen and transients lived a meager existence, then started down the steep incline toward the dock. A feeling of relief washed over him at the sight of the craft.

The weary plodding of the horse on the slats of the wooden dock reminded Dan how tired he was, and the sight of a lad dozing atop a stack of bales only made it worse. He dismounted. "You there. Lad."

"Dan!" came a shout from behind.

Turning, Dan spotted Yancy's bright head as the sailor charged down the hill. "I thought 'twas you, mate!"

"I wondered when I'd set eyes again on that sunburned mug of yours," Dan said with a grin, grabbing the seaman's hand warmly.

Yancy yanked him into a bear hug. "Been hangin' out on this side of the river makin' sure they keep the ferry ready."

"That him?" someone called from the top of the bluff.

Yancy nodded and beckoned up to the men peering at them, and several bolted down to them.

"Where's your horse?" Dan asked, taking a flier out of the pouch.

"Saddled an' waitin' on the other side." He gave a shrill

whistle. "Time to get crackin'," he called out as a man emerged from the ferry shack, squinting his eyes in their direction.

"But what about the news? What'd they decide?" The wiry operator rubbed his jowls with one hand.

Glancing at the three men from the shanties, Dan gave one of them the broadside he was holding. "Tack this up on the ferry shack for all to read."

"Hear that, Clem?" Yancy yelled to the ferryman. "Curly's bringin' it to ye, so get those horses of yours workin'. There's a pouch here that's in a big hurry."

Dan felt himself beginning to relax after they'd boarded and the craft began its slow crossing. The setting sun turned the wide expanse of water to a bright ribbon of gold and orange.

"Well, mate, what did the representatives agree on?" Yancy asked.

The lad who'd been napping when Dan arrived also came near, his fair, freckled face alive with curiosity.

Dan looked from one to the other. "Actually, they made several decisions—and I can definitely see the fiery influence of Sam and John Adams on them."

"They're gonna be whoppers, then," Yancy said jubilantly.

"First of all, they've denounced English law as unconstitutional."

The sailor whacked his open palm with his fist. "Now, that I like!"

"And they deny that Parliament has any legislative authority over the Colonies. So," Dan added, his tone rife with meaning, "they're advising the people of Massachusetts to arm themselves and set up their own militia."

Yancy let the information sink in for a moment before commenting. "All the colonies agreed to this?"

Dan shrugged a shoulder. "All that were there. For some reason, the delegates from Georgia never arrived. But that's not all. The congress voted to stop all trade with England. A total boycott. They also asked John Jay, of New York, to draft an address to the people of Great Britain and send it to the London papers explaining our reasons for the action. John Dickinson has agreed to pen a petition to the king. And if the wrongs being done to our people have not been redressed by next May, the delegates plan to meet again at that time."

Yancy's golden brows drew together above the bridge of his nose. "Ye don't think King George or Lord North and the rest of the bigwigs are gonna sit still for any of this, do ye?"

"No, I don't. And neither does anyone else," Dan said evenly. "But it doesn't matter. What does matter is that all the colonies are forging together, burning as one flame in thought and deed, casting aside all their petty differences. Americans. With one Lord, and one King . . . Jesus."

A wistful half-smile drew up one side of the sailor's mouth. "Reminds me of a sermon Felicia's father gave from the book of Judges about a time when Israel had no king but the Almighty. The Lord raised up judges to speak his will to the people. When God was their king and when they followed his word, he always delivered them from those who would plunder them. Sometimes quite miraculously." As if suddenly aware of his enthusiastic oration, Yancy's face reddened to a shade akin to that of the sunset. "Guess I'm becomin' a wild-eyed enthusiast like my father-in-law!"

Dan chuckled and patted his friend's shoulder. "I wouldn't have it any other way. And speaking of family, once I've caught a few hours of sleep, I'll be heading north for my parents' farm. I'd like you to wait for me there. I won't be more than a day behind. That'll give you a chance to see Emily and Robert, too. They left for Rhode Island over a week ago. While we're there, you and I have got to figure some way of getting our wives out of Boston before Britain has a chance to act against the Continental Congress."

"Amen to that."

Dusk added its watercolor glory to the rolling pastureland of Haynes Farm, tinting everything a fragile peach. Dan let his gaze drink in the acres of whitewashed fences and the growing number of robust pacers prancing or grazing in the pastures. Father's enterprise had done extremely well. No doubt Ben was as good at passing the word along the post roads about the excellent horseflesh available in Pawtucket as he himself had been.

As he drew nearer, the sight of the two-story white house crowning the rise tugged at his heart, evoking bittersweet memories of his growing-up years when he and Ben had to vie for attention against four sisters. Even as he thought of those days long past, one sister ran out of the door and down the porch steps, her skirts flying. He wondered if Emily would forever appear so young and slight.

"Dan's home!" he heard her call over her shoulder.

The door opened again, and Mother and Father emerged and came down the steps to meet him.

Drawing up to the rose arbor, Dan dismounted and slid Flame's reins through the hitching ring, along with the leads from the two horses he'd picked up at relay stations along the way.

"We're glad you arrived safely, Son," Father said, beaming at him as Dan embraced his teary-eyed mother for the first time in two years. Then he hugged the older man. Dan closed his eyes against the pain of how swiftly his parents were aging. Their smiles carried all the same joy and love, but there was so much silver in their hair, and their bodies felt fragile in his arms.

"What about me?" Emily asked, cutting off his morbid musings. He swallowed and released his father, then opened his arms again to his youngest sister, who wasted not a second spilling into them.

"Glad you're here, Emmy, instead of down at the neighbors' as you so wisely planned," Dan said teasingly.

She giggled and raised her clear green eyes.

"Where's your daughter?"

"Upstairs asleep already. She was worn out after running and playing outside most of the day."

"Oh." He eased her gently away. "Well, get that lazy husband of yours out here, then, so he can help me put up these horses."

"He, um, isn't here." Emily fidgeted with the outer edge of her apron. Rob wasn't there? Dan was surprised. But perhaps they felt it would be safer to keep him out of sight in case of a sudden visit by the military; still, that seemed unlikely with all the troops called back to Boston.

"We'll talk inside, Son." His father put an arm around Dan's shoulders and guided him toward the house.

The strange expression on his father's face and the added peculiar looks exchanged by Mother and Emily began to wear on Dan. He felt rising apprehension. Something was amiss; he was certain of it.

"Let's go to the kitchen," Emily said as they all mounted the steps and went inside. "Dan looks hungry."

Until a minute ago he had been famished, but now his appetite had disappeared. Nevertheless he allowed himself to be tugged along.

The scent of roast beef still lingered in the cozy kitchen as Dan sank gratefully to a bench at the long worktable and swept his eyes up the rows of copper pans and skillets suspended on hooks on one of the walls. Emily sat on one side of him and Father on the other. He met Mother's gaze.

Flushing, she immediately turned and crossed to the hearth, then removed the water kettle, filling it with a dipper from a bucket at the sideboard. "Mistress Simpson—you remember her, don't you, Dan?" she began, her voice a little too casual. "Her daughter lives across from Long Lane Church."

"Yes." Dan's insides began to knot. The young woman and her husband lived just around the corner from him and Susannah in Boston. What dire news was about to be dumped in his lap?

"Well, dear," his mother said, continuing to fuss elaborately with the tea preparation, "her daughter wrote saying that that awful Lieutenant Fontaine returned from Salem and went on a bit of a rampage."

"What?" Dan lurched to his feet, almost upsetting the table.

His father grabbed his hand. "Sit down, Son. Susannah came to no harm."

"That's right," Mother said. "The letter was quite clear on that point."

Not altogether consoled, Dan reluctantly lowered himself down again. He looked pointedly at his mother, silently prompting her to go on.

She averted her eyes. "Apparently the lieutenant did have his men strip your house of all its belongings. Everything but the clothes Susannah and the children had on their backs, in fact."

Rage began to build inside Dan, gathering intensity as he envisioned the vile-spirited officer desecrating things Susannah loved. His teeth on edge, he seethed. It was long past time to rid America of Alex Fontaine and his subordinates once and for all.

Emily laid a comforting hand on his arm. "The minute Yancy heard what happened, he couldn't get out of here fast enough. And after all he's done for us, Rob could do no less than go with him."

"When was that?"

"This afternoon." She smiled thinly.

"Where has my wife gone? Where is she now?" Dan asked, struggling to remain calm.

"I would imagine," his mother said, setting a cup of tea before him, "she's still in the house."

"All your friends and neighbors brought things to her," Father added.

Dan massaged the bridge of his nose between his thumb and index finger to alleviate the throbbing in his head. "And when exactly did all of this take place?"

"Maybe a month ago," his father replied. "Perhaps a little more."

"It couldn't be too much longer. I haven't been gone much longer than that."

Mother brought the rest of the cups to the table and served them to Father and Emily, then seated herself.

Dan turned to his father, unable to believe he wouldn't have gone to Boston to check on Susannah the moment he had learned of Fontaine's action. After all, the whole family had to have known that both he and Ben were away as part of the relay.

"Son," the older man began, as if reading his mind, "we had no knowledge of any of this until just today. As a matter of fact, Yancy arrived here while your mother was visiting with Mistress Simpson."

Drawing a long, slow breath, Dan shook his head, his worry mounting by the second. "Then there's no telling what has since happened. I have to go." He rose to his feet.

"Now, darling," Mother pleaded in her consoling tone. "You must have faith."

"Surely," Emily piped in, "you've been praying for Susannah's safety every night, just as we all have."

"And every day," he injected under his breath.

"Well, then, trust God."

Listening to his baby sister's advice, Dan suddenly felt much younger than she . . . at least spiritually. He used to be the one mouthing wise sentiments and comforting truths.

His father rose and moved to his side, wrapping an arm around him. "You look exhausted, Son. Stay the night. Get a fresh start first thing in the morning."

He met the longing in his father's eyes, then saw it reflected in his mother's face. It had been forever since he'd been here and spent any time at all with them. And he was tired, that was true enough. But with Susannah and the children in peril, how could he not go?

An understanding smile curved Emily's expressive mouth. "At least visit with Mama and Papa while I fix you a plate, will you do that? And while you eat, I'll go tell Elijah to saddle you a fresh horse."

"Thanks, Emmy," he breathed. "There's no way on earth I'd be able to sleep anyway, not until I know my wife and babies are safe." He glanced at his mother, recalling their last bitter parting when she had accused him of caring more for Susannah than he did for his family. Did she still feel that way? But instead of anger, what radiated from her once-regal demeanor was loving acceptance. There seemed none of her old rigid intolerance or haughty mien. Sitting down at the table once again, he picked up the cup at his place and took a welcome sip of the rich brew. Even though the tea had grown tepid, it was soothing and refreshing. "Emmy, as soon as you're finished dishing up that plate, ask Elijah to put a lead and halter on a second horse, also. I'll switch off between the two."

Ben's shoulder ached as he rolled over on the hard floor of his darkened room in the boardinghouse. As tired as Yancy and Rob had been when they came in near midnight, he had given them his bed. He knew Yancy had been up more than twenty-four hours, and with every inn for miles around filled to the brim with teamsters since the port blockade, the least Ben could do was be hospitable.

The curtain of night was already giving way to dawn's first

rays off to the east. Thank heaven, he mused. It had been one long night.

Beside Ben on the floor, Ted groaned and shifted position.

Ben chuckled to himself. Surprisingly, his brother-in-law had shown up mere hours before Yancy and Rob, relating that Colonel Allen and Landlord Fay had both asked him to come to the seacoast. Now that General Gage had pulled all his troops within the protection of Boston, they wanted Ted to check out the types of fortifications Gage was preparing and, hopefully, find out if the general showed any concern about Fort Ticonderoga. And, of course, they wanted him to return with news of the congress in Philadelphia.

Slowly exhaling, Ben cupped his hands behind his head and stared up at the ceiling. Ted might be here in body, he mused, but his heart had stayed behind in Green Mountain country. The poor sot couldn't seem to utter one sentence without Jane's name popping up. But then, at least Ted was handling his separation from his wife calmly . . . which was more than could be said of Yancy. When the seaman had arrived last night, they came very near to tying him down to keep him from racing off and doing something rash. It was touch and go until finally Sean Burns came over and confirmed that Sue and Felicia were fine.

Ben's wayward thoughts shifted to Abigail. He would never be able to erase from his memory the disappointment on her face the last time he'd seen her. And in the interminable weeks since then, he hadn't been able to go back to explain— as if that would even help. Oh well, perhaps things happened for the best. But glancing at Ted and the others, he knew that at least they all had someone at home who loved them and pined for their return. He tightened his lips bitterly against the envy eating at him.

Determined to shake off his melancholy before it consumed him, Ben quietly got up and dressed, then combed his hair, tying a neat queue with a strip of leather. A horse's echoing clomps outside indicated that the morning traffic had begun. By now the coaching inn down the street should have some coffee made.

He stepped over Ted and reached for the door.

Just beyond it he could hear someone coming up the stairs. *At this hour?* Panic stole through him. Surely nothing had happened to Susannah in Boston.

"What is it?" Ted muttered, half asleep.

Ben held his breath and waited. Just as he was beginning to hope that the intruder would knock on some other door, a sharp, muffled rapping sounded.

Yancy and Rob each roused and propped up on an elbow, looking groggy and unfocused.

"Well, at least it can't be the authorities," Ted quipped. "Whoever it is is too quiet."

"Open it!" Yancy growled, grabbing his clothes. Beside him Rob did the same.

Ben reached for the latch as a second, louder knock sounded.

"It's about time!" Dan hissed when the door finally cracked. He shoved his way in. Seeing Ted, his face went white. He seized his brother-in-law's shoulder. "Has something happened to Susannah?"

"No, no." Ted raked a hand through his tousled hair and shook his head. "I'm on a mission for the Green Mountain Boys. As far as I know, Sue is fine—as of noon yesterday, anyway."

"Oh. Sorry." Dan relaxed his grip and jammed his hands into his pockets, shifting his stance.

"I'm amazed you've caught up so soon," Yancy remarked.

"I was picking up my family's horses along the way, so I had extras I could use."

"Well, I'm glad you're here. No matter what it takes, we must get the lasses out of Boston. Now."

Seeing that his brother was in absolute agreement, Ben felt elation course through him.

"Not without a plan," Ted injected. "Gage and the admiral have increased patrols along the bay and shoreline fourfold.

We may have to create a diversion of some sort to get past them." He sighed ominously. "But that will be easy, I fear, compared to sneaking out two babes who might cry out at any given moment."

"How about if we spirit the kids off to a neighbor ahead of time?" Ben suggested. "They could easily be brought out of Boston later with other families."

Dan frowned. "I can't do that. As Ted said, babies can be noisy. What if one of the guards happened to see where they were taken? Fontaine could use them as bait."

"Don't toss the idea out so quick, mate," Yancy said. "It just might—"

Rob moved forward a step and spoke calmly but forcefully. "I may be presumptuous in sayin' this, but we canna leave out the one who knows the situation even better than we."

"Aye!" Yancy turned to Ted. "What do you think we should do?"

Ben rolled his eyes. "He means the cobbler in Boston. We must contact him and—"

"Have ye all gone daft?" Rob asked incredulously. "I'm speakin' of God. We need to ask the Lord fer wisdom."

His statement silenced everyone.

"Surely you don't expect God to speak directly to you, here and now," Ben sputtered. "Or is there perhaps a burning bush somewhere in the room that I missed?" But his logic didn't penetrate their thick heads. Ben watched in speechless wonder as they all dropped to their knees.

Dan looked up and reached out to him. "Come, join us, little brother. Trust God with us."

Ben's first reaction was to balk. But the plea in Dan's voice and expression tore at his heart. *Oh, well,* he decided finally. *A little prayer couldn't hurt.* He took Dan's hand and knelt, meeting welcoming smiles all around.

Ted took Ben's other hand, closing the circle, and they bowed their heads.

"Our dear Father in heaven," Dan began, "you know why we've come. We're so thankful for all your blessings and the miracles you've bestowed upon us these past several years, all the times you've intervened to save each of us fugitives. And most of all—as I'm sure my brothers will heartily agree—we thank you for the pouring out of your love. Especially that most precious of all love which you've given us . . . our loving Christian wives."

"Amen," the others murmured.

As they did, Ben felt a tingling sensation pass from Dan's and Ted's hands and course through his body with warm vitality.

The Holy Spirit was here in the room with them. Here. Now.

Ben suddenly felt more than a little guilty for all his past doubt. Shame and humility assaulted him for questioning the Lord's power. He'd been nothing but a fool.

As though from a distance, he heard Dan continue in prayer.

"And now, Father, we beseech you again. For as your word says, where two or three are gathered in your name, you are in our midst. We need your wisdom now, Lord. Show us how to rescue Susannah and Felicia and my dear babies. All of us strongly feel the time to act has come. I pray most fervently that this urging is from you and that you will—"

Footsteps approached the door, and a light tapping sounded.

Ben rose, thinking how wonderful it would be if the cobbler had come, or the wheelwright, with the perfect plan. God's perfect plan.

The others got up also, that same hope-filled wonder in their eyes, and went with him as he opened the door.

Susannah and Felicia stood there, each with a sleeping babe in her arms.

Spying Dan, Susannah gave a cry and rushed to him.

Felicia thrust Miles at Ben and dashed to Yancy.

Ben gaped at the joyful reunions. Tears smarted in his eyes as he watched Susannah pull Ted into her and Dan's embrace.

With a wistful grin, Rob moved over to Ben and slipped an arm around his shoulders as they witnessed the amazing fulfillment of God's answer to their prayer.

"How on earth did ye manage to escape?" Yancy asked at last.

"Yes," Dan added, his expression turning hard. "What happened that was so horrible you were forced to flee with the babies into the dark of night?"

Susannah's light laugh bubbled out. "Oh, it was nothing like that. Not at all. We left an hour before dawn to avoid having to wait hours to get through the checkpoint at the Neck."

"Are you saying," Ted asked in disbelief, "that Alex actually allowed you to go?"

Susannah and Felicia glanced at one another in amusement. "One of the sentries delivered a note from Alex yesterday," Susannah explained. "A brief but most welcome note. It said he was returning to England before Christmas to celebrate with his family the birth of the Prince of Peace and he thought I might appreciate the opportunity to do the same."

"He said that?" Ted asked, his voice high with shock. "Those exact words?" When Susannah nodded, he looked toward the window. "Do you know when he's leaving?"

"Actually, he's already left. Private Williams was instructed not to deliver the message until after the ship had sailed."

"And that's not all," Felicia threw in. "The soldiers brought back all the furniture and the rest of our belongings, plus several pounds sterling to pay for any damage."

"Alex has repented?" Ted said with wonder, shaking his head. "But we did pray here for a miracle. Even while we were down on our knees, the Lord had already answered."

"Yes," Susannah said. "Felicia and I have been praying most fervently for him for some time ourselves. After his last assault, he never bothered us again. The guards at our gate told me the lieutenant rarely left headquarters. It had to be the Lord working through our prayers, I'm sure."

Ted gave his sister's hand a squeeze. "Soon as I've a chance,

I shall post a letter to him. Before all of this trouble he and I were fast friends. I should very much like to count him as one again."

"I know precisely how you feel," Susannah said, her face free of worry for the first time in ages as she softly stroked baby Julia's bonneted head. "I shall even miss the lads who guarded us. You should have seen how wonderfully they all gathered to help us restore the house and then pack to leave. Just before they left, Corporal Edwards said that not only would they be missing us, but also the treats we'd bake for them. He said we kept them all from missing their homes quite so much."

Dan pulled Susannah against his side. "They couldn't have missed theirs half as much as I missed you, my love." He kissed her cheek, then smiled. "And we wouldn't want to disappoint Alex, would we? After all, he shouldn't be the only one going home to spend Christmas with his loved ones."

Ben looked at the cluster of happy faces in the room, each one rapt with joy. He was glad for them . . . truly he was. But he couldn't ignore the deep sadness that filled his own heart, weighing him down and stealing his joy. *Yes,* he thought, *the rest will be with all their loved ones in Rhode Island this year. All except me.*

42

In the woods around Millers Falls, autumn's chill had tinted the leaves with brilliant hues. As a brisk wind swept through the trees, stirring the heavy boughs and dancing through the ferns, Ben hunkered down into the collar of his doeskin coat. How wonderful it would feel to be warming himself before a blazing fire. . . .

With apprehension he approached the Preston Farm. What kind of reception would he find when he showed up? No doubt Ma and Bertha would fall all over him, as always, seeing to his comfort, making sure he was fed. But Abigail was the real concern. Would she be at all glad to see him? Or would she leave the room and go upstairs until he left, not giving him so much as a chance to speak?

He dismounted and secured Rebel to the hitching ring, trying to force his thoughts to the presents he'd brought with him. They were for everyone this time, and he had taken great care in choosing something he felt each would like. But just to be on the safe side, he turned a gaze heavenward and whispered a prayer for courage. He would have been far less nervous in the face of an entire company of lobsterbacks than he was right now. Fearing the possibility of Abigail's final rejection, Ben's newfound trust in the Lord wavered.

Drawing a steadying breath, he removed the burlap sack of gifts tied to the pommel and went up the porch steps to the door. His hand poised in midair for several seconds before he called himself a dunce and knocked. He held his breath and waited.

Heavy footsteps sounded from the other side. Ben rolled his eyes, preparing himself for Bertha's usual exuberance.

But when the door swung wide, a total stranger stood there—a stocking-footed man, tall and brawny as a lumberjack, with curly brown hair and immense features—and with towheaded Corbin laughing and giggling atop his shoulders. A perplexed expression clouded the fellow's blue eyes. "What might I do for ya?" The words rumbled from his low voice like thunder.

"My Ben!" the tot squealed.

"You a peddler?" the stranger boomed, eyeing the sack Ben held in his hands.

"No. No," Ben started to say.

Ma Preston came up behind him and caught sight of Ben. Her face brightened immediately, and she stepped to the doorway. "Well, I'll be! If it isn't Ben Haynes. Where ya been, boy? Ain't seen ya in a coon's age."

"Around," he hedged. "I've been kept pretty busy." He watched from the corner of his eye as the hulking clodhopper bounced Corbin playfully on his high perch . . . Corbin, the little boy for whom Ben had begun to have possessive feelings.

"Well, come on in!" Ma hollered. "I want ya to meet my new son." She gestured with unconcealed pride toward the stranger. "Wesley Nelson. Wes, this is Ben Haynes, the postrider ya heared us talk about."

It was all Ben could do to clamp his gaping mouth shut as his hopes crumbled to ashes.

"Aw, I can see you're disappointed," Ma said kindly. "But fact is, with that handsome face of yours, you'll find somebody else. Right soon, too. See if ya don't." She gave a nod as if that made it so.

Ben struggled to regain his composure while shifting the burlap bag to one hand and extending his other. It was dwarfed instantly by Nelson's huge calloused one. "You're a very fortunate man, Mr. Nelson."

"And don't I know it!"

Ben would have given anything to wipe that knowing grin off the lout's face. But reason prevailed. The best thing for him to do now would be to make the swiftest exit in all of recorded history . . . which seemed highly unlikely, since he still gripped the bag of presents in his clammy fist. Switching his attention to Ma, he started backing toward the door. "Er, I just stopped by to see if my friend returned your horses in satisfactory condition."

"Why, sure," she said with a bob of her head. "Don't seem no worse for the wear, neither. Did they get ya to Boston in time?"

"Yes, in plenty of time. That's why I wanted to, er . . . here." He held out the sack to the older woman. "Would you be kind enough to pass these out for me? I'd best be on my way."

An incredulous frown wrinkled Ma's forehead beneath the straggly hairs under her mobcap as she planted her knuckles on her broad hips. "I ain't never seen a body in such an all-fired hurry all the time. What in the world kind of way is that to live?"

Ben felt his neck catching fire under the collar of his shirt. The sack still in his grip, he sank down to his knees and rummaged through it. He handed Ma a small wrapped box. "This is for you, Ma. In thanks for the use of the horses. And this one," he said, finding another and holding it high enough so Corbin could reach it from his roost, "is for you."

The tot squealed. His little hands snatched the gift and began tearing the paper off in reckless abandon. Chunks of wrap fluttered down in front of Wesley Nelson's face.

Ben tried not to recall how in his futile imaginings he'd begun to think of Corbin as his own little boy. In fact, to spare himself the pain of watching the tot's mounting excitement, he offered the bag of remaining gifts to Ma.

She folded her arms over her bosom and shifted her stance in flat refusal. "Don't you think the gals'd like to see ya?"

Just the thought of facing Abigail now—now that he'd been stupid enough to turn her away from himself and toward another man—was hard for Ben to accept. "Please. I really must be going."

Before the last word was out of his mouth, he heard Bertha's familiar step coming from the kitchen, and she entered the room.

When she spied him, the biggest grin Ben had ever seen splayed across her face. "Why, howdy, Ben! Thought I heard a strange voice."

He cringed as she rushed toward him. He was in no mood to be mauled at this particular moment. But nothing was left for him to do but brace himself for the assault.

Bertha cuffed him playfully on the shoulder.

"The dear boy brought presents again," Ma said. "For ever'-body."

"Oh, not for *everybody*," the girl boomed, grabbing Wesley's arm and tugging him next to her as she leaned into Ben's face. "Bet there's not one for this big strappin' husband of mine, is there?"

Ben gaped. But as reality sank in, a vast weight lifted from his spirit. It took a moment for Bertha's words to penetrate the thick fog shrouding his brain. For one split second, Ben could have grabbed the farm girl and plastered a huge kiss right on her mouth. But the inclination evaporated just as swiftly as it had come.

"Isn't he just the burliest, handsomest man you ever seen?" Bertha gushed, oblivious to Ben's profound relief. "He's a big strong boatman right off the Connecticut River. Oh, I knowed ya was sweet on me and all, Ben, but this was one fish that was too big a catch to throw back. I just knowed you'd under-stand." She smiled coyly into her husband's eyes.

"Sure," Ben muttered, still trying to regain his composure. "Of course. You make the perfect couple, in fact. I couldn't be happier." He bent to remove a package from the bag. "Here, I thought you might like this."

Bertie grinned and started shredding the wrapping while her big strapping husband peered over her shoulder, looking somewhat miffed.

The man probably could wrestle a bear and live to tell the tale, Ben decided. He remained on the alert for any sudden aggression, but instead he felt a gentle tugging on his coattail.

Cassandra stood shyly behind him, smiling around the finger she had in her mouth.

Ben stooped down to her level and took out the larger of two remaining presents. "Here, Cassie. I brought you something."

She knelt and began tearing strips of the wrapping paper so awkwardly that Ben joined in to help unveil the plush lamb.

"Hmph," Wes Nelson mumbled. "The kid's so bashful I'm surprised she even went to ya. Won't come within ten feet of me, always skulkin' in the doorway like she does."

Ma and Bertha snorted.

Ben turned his smile from Cassie up to him. "Well, she and I are old friends. Aren't we, sweetheart?" He ruffled her blonde curls.

"A kitty!" she cried, hugging the soft toy to herself.

Her joyful expression, so like her mother's, erased some of Ben's fears. Maybe Abigail would wear that same expression when she saw him . . . maybe. He cleared his throat and stood. "I have one gift left. Where's Abigail?"

"Diggin' potatoes in the garden," Ma said.

"I take you," Cassandra said, sliding her tiny fingers into Ben's hand.

"Yep," Ma remarked with a half-smile as the child tugged him out of the room. "Got yourself one fine little guide right there."

Ben followed Cassandra out the back door and into the garden, where he saw Abigail among the spreading clumps and coarse green leaves of the potato patch. She had a heavy knitted shawl tied about her and appeared to have half the mud of the plot coating the hem of her brown work skirt as she gave a spade a stomp with her booted foot.

Ben couldn't believe such a fragile angel had to tend the vegetable garden while Bertha's husband was inside, basking idly in newly wedded bliss. He was glad Abigail was turned away from him, for it gave him time to get his anger under control. And her plight made him all the more determined to rescue her from this life of drudgery.

"Mama."

Abigail looked up, her eyes widening as she caught sight of Ben. She took a step backward, one dirty work glove flying up in a hopeless attempt to tuck some damp strands of hair inside her floppy sunbonnet. Dismayed, she yanked the gloves off and shoved them into her apron pocket, then tried again. "I—I must look a sight," she said, flushing in embarrassment as she darted a glance toward the house.

"You're right about that," Ben said as a smile broke forth. A more incredibly beautiful sight he'd never seen.

"Look, Mama," Cassie said in her high little voice. She held up the lamb. "A new kitty."

Abigail still looked as if she wanted to bolt and run. But instead, she stooped down by her daughter and cooed over the treasure.

Watching the pair of golden-haired beauties with their heads together—one of whom seemed grateful to hide hers within the seclusion of her bonnet brim—Ben wondered fleetingly if this were Abigail's latest method of rejecting his presence.

He shoved a hand into his pocket and sighed. Then his fingers closed around the present he'd bought her, and it gave him the jolt of courage he needed. He squatted down with them and held it out to her. "I have something for you, too."

Abigail sprang to her feet. "But I'm so—so . . ." She made another attempt to tuck wayward tendrils within the sanctity of her bonnet, then brushed futilely at the smudges on her work apron. "Please don't look at me. I need to go inside and change. I—"

Ben smiled gently and put a hand on her arm. "Please, don't go. What's a little dirt? After all, you've been working hard out here. And—" his tone softened—"nothing can ever hide your beauty, Abigail." He offered the gift once more.

"Take it. Please. If one of us should feel ashamed in the presence of the other, it should be me, after the stupid things I said to you the last time I was here. I was wrong. Please give me a chance to redeem myself."

"Open it, Mama." Cassie tugged at Abigail's skirt.

"Yes. Please," Ben whispered, drawing her gaze back to his.

She stared for a moment, then took a deep breath and let it out as she undid the wrapping. An expression of sheer delight played over her smudged face as she lifted the bottle of French perfume up to the light.

Ben finally relaxed when he saw the change in her demeanor. Perhaps she'd listen after all to what he'd come here to say.

"What is it?" Cassie asked.

Abigail smiled. "Something that smells very, very pretty, sweetheart." She gazed through her lashes at Ben. "Thank you. It's . . . lovely." After pulling out the cork stopper, she passed it under her nose and inhaled, then did the same for Cassandra.

The tot's eyes grew in surprise, and she smiled. "It's like flowers. Lots and lots of flowers."

"That's right," Ben said. "And if this had been spring, they would have all been real. I'd have brought every single one I laid my eyes on to you and your beautiful mama. I love you both very much."

Abigail's lips trembled as her eyes misted over.

"I've been a fool, Abigail," Ben said softly, moving nearer. "I've spent the last several years of my life trying to prove I knew better than anyone—even God—what had to be done to bring freedom and happiness to the Colonies. I was willing to make whatever sacrifice it called for. Even us . . . you and me. But when the light dawned and I saw how unbelievably dumb I was in the face of God's infinite wisdom, I realized that he is the one who sets us truly free. The Lord wants the best for those who belong to him, and he gives us far more than we can ever dream of."

"I dream, too," Cassandra piped in. "I dreamed I had a kitty once. And see? You brought me one."

Dragging his gaze from Abigail's, Ben smiled indulgently at the shining-eyed tot. He didn't have the heart to tell her it was a lamb.

Abigail bent and kissed her. "And isn't it the prettiest kitty ever? We must thank Jesus for it when we say our bedtime prayers tonight. And most of all—" she swept a glance back to Ben—"we'll thank him for the one who brought it."

His heart caught at the depth of love now visible in her eyes and face. Surely it wouldn't have been there if she hadn't forgiven him. "For the first time in years," he went on, his own voice matching the huskiness in Abigail's, "my family is all going to be together to celebrate the Savior's birth. I'd like very much for you to be there, too." He took Abigail's hands in his, swallowing down the last of his fear. "As my wife, if you'll have me. . . . And daughter, of course." He slanted a lopsided grin at Cassandra.

The little girl peered up at her mother with great anticipation.

So did Ben. He could scarcely draw a breath as his pulse raced.

Abigail searched his face for what seemed like an eternity before she finally spoke. "Would you like that, Cassie?" The question had been asked of her daughter, but her eyes remained fixed on Ben's.

"Yes!" the child cried, jumping up and down, her lamb crushed under her arm. "Yes! Yes! Yes!"

A slow smile softened Abigail's lips. "Well, so would I. Very, very much."

A deep sense of peace wrapped around Ben. In one fluid motion, he scooped Cassandra up and drew Abigail into his embrace. He couldn't have stopped grinning if his life had depended on it. "Me, too," he said. "Me, too." Bending his head slightly, his breath and Abigail's intermingled for a sweet second. Then their lips met at last in a kiss that promised forever.

Dear Reader,

We highly regard your interest in our trilogy, and we would be pleased to receive your comments and to answer any questions you might have.

Sally Laity & Dianna Crawford
P.O. Box 80176
Bakersfield, CA 93380

P.S. Your self-addressed, stamped return envelope would be appreciated.

Also by Sally Laity and Dianna Crawford

FREEDOM'S HOLY LIGHT
#1 The Gathering Dawn   0-8423-1303-6
#2 The Kindled Flame   0-8423-1336-2

More Captivating Historical Fiction from Tyndale House Publishers

THE APPOMATTOX SAGA
Gilbert Morris
Intriguing, realistic stories capture the emotional and spiritual strife of the tragic Civil War era.
#1 A Covenant of Love   0-8423-5497-2
#2 Gate of His Enemies   0-8423-1069-X
#3 Where Honor Dwells   0-8423-6799-3
#4 Land of the Shadow   0-8423-5742-4
#5 Out of the Whirlwind   0-8423-1658-2

MARK OF THE LION
Francine Rivers
A Jewish Christian slave girl clings to her faith amid the forces of decadent first-century Rome.
#1 A Voice in the Wind   0-8423-7750-6
#2 An Echo in the Darkness   0-8423-1307-9

THE SECRET OF THE ROSE
Michael Phillips
Experience the plight and steadfast faith of a noble Prussian family during World War II and its aftermath.
#1 The Eleventh Hour   0-8423-3933-7
#2 A Rose Remembered   0-8423-5929-X
#3 Escape to Freedom   0-8423-5942-7

THE THEYN CHRONICLES
Angela Elwell Hunt
The culture, people, and spiritual life of medieval England come alive in this rich, historical saga.
#1 Afton of Margate Castle   0-8423-1222-6
#2 The Troubadour's Quest   0-8423-1287-0
#3 Ingram of the Irish   0-8423-1623-X